Blumedal

PRAISE FOR

Last Summer at the Golden Hotel

"Two families agonize over whether to sell their once-successful Catskills resort. *Last Summer at the Golden Hotel* promises snark, sass, and sunshine-filled fun."
—Bustle

"Friedland brings two families full circle over the fate of a storied hotel they've owned together for three generations. . . . Old tensions and new romances arise as they decide if the nostalgia and storied legacy of the hotel can save it, or if they're having their last summer at the Golden. . . . Episodes of intergenerational disconnect contrasted with unshakable family bonds make *Last Summer at the Golden Hotel* a great choice for fans of *Schitt's Creek* and feel-good family dramedies."
—Shelf Awareness

"You will laugh out loud at the antics of two delightfully dysfunctional families as they fight, share secrets, and fall in love in the once-prosperous Catskills hotel that they own. Once again, Friedland brilliantly wields her rapier wit—if Dorothy Parker and Joan Rivers wrote a book, this would be it!"
—Fiona Davis, *New York Times* bestselling author of *The Lions of Fifth Avenue*

"In *Last Summer at the Golden Hotel*, Elyssa Friedland creates a broad cast of characters who are at once touching and hilarious. Their fears, their secrets, and their dreams come together in a moving story that balances nostalgia for the past and hope for the future. A perfect book for a family book c̶l̶ ̶ "
—Jill Santopolo, *New Yor*

"Long known for her humor and wit, Elyssa Friedland has penned a charmer of a novel in *Last Summer at the Golden Hotel*, a story about two families who own a resort in the Catskills, which was a crown jewel in its heyday but is now in decline. Fans of *The Marvelous Mrs. Maisel* and *Dirty Dancing* will revel in the nostalgia of a bygone era and the richness of this intergenerational tale, which manages to be smart, funny, honest, and poignant all at the same time."

—Pam Jenoff, *New York Times* bestselling author of
The Woman with the Blue Star

"Chock-full of charm and wit, Elyssa Friedland's *Last Summer at the Golden Hotel* is the only family drama you need this year! Set in a ramshackle Catskills hotel and featuring a vibrant cast of characters, it's a laugh-out-loud funny novel with a heart of gold."

—Karma Brown, international bestselling author of
Recipe for a Perfect Wife

"Prepare to laugh. Take a trip to the Catskills with *Last Summer at the Golden Hotel* and bask in the hilarity and chaos that make Elyssa Friedland the queen of the family drama."

—Jane L. Rosen, author of *Eliza Starts a Rumor*

"Written with Friedland's signature wit and sharp dialogue, *Last Summer at the Golden Hotel* is an incisive novel that touches on family legacies, nostalgia, and multigenerational dynamics. Readers not content with armchair immersion will want to book their Catskills getaway immediately."   —*Booklist*

"The vanished history of the Catskills is evoked with love and plenty of schmaltz. A high-spirited party of a book. BYOB: bring your own borscht."   —*Kirkus Reviews*

"Friedland brings laughs and nuance to the family foibles and demonstrates a wide range in her convincing narration from the many points of view. Breezy and charming, this is great fun."

—*Publishers Weekly*

"When Annette Feldman decides to celebrate her seventieth birthday with a family cruise, drama—and hilarity—ensue."

—*People*

"Family reunions can rock the boat. This one does it on a cruise ship. When the Feldmans hit the high seas for their matriarch's seventieth, a lot of drama and laughs come out in tight quarters. Think *This Is Where I Leave You* meets *The Family Stone*."

—theSkimm

"*The Floating Feldmans* is a hilarious romp on the sea that is perfect for your poolside reading this summer! I read this book with a wide grin, and I know that you will too! Highly recommend!"

—Catherine McKenzie, bestselling author of *I'll Never Tell* and *Spin*

"Friedland uses multiple perspectives, witty dialogue, and complex characters that are incredibly relatable to deliver a funny, astute look at the family dynamic and the relationships shared within. Whether on a cruise or taking a staycation, contemporary readers will want to have *The Floating Feldmans* on deck."   —*Booklist*

"*The Floating Feldmans* is a fast, funny, surprisingly heartwarming ride on the high seas."   —Shelf Awareness

"Friedland creates vivid characters with distinct voices, from the outwardly critical matriarch to the insecure teenager. . . . A fun look at family drama on the open seas."   —*Kirkus Reviews*

"*The Floating Feldmans* is a story about an estranged family's wild vacation. This book is so dramatic that it might actually make your fam feel normal . . . even if you're losing your mind on day five of your own trip."   —*Cosmopolitan*

"Long a master of insightful books about modern life and relationships, Friedland turns her formidable talents to the family cruise. Uproariously funny, yet heartfelt and true, *The Floating Feldmans* will have each reader seeing her own family fun and foibles in the choppy waters, laughing and crying at the same time to the very last wonderful page."

—Pam Jenoff, *New York Times* bestselling author of *The Lost Girls of Paris*

"An intelligent, insightful, touching novel about the secrets we keep and the family that loves us anyway."

—Abbi Waxman, author of *The Bookish Life of Nina Hill*

"Elyssa Friedland's premise is perfect. Take three generations of an estranged family, put them on a boat—a forced cruise to celebrate the matriarch's seventieth birthday—and let the dysfunction fly. A pleasure to read."   —Laurie Gelman, author of *Class Mom*

"Such a smart, honest look at the modern American family. Elyssa Friedland has written a book that feels both up-to-the-minute contemporary and, somehow, absolutely timeless."

—Matthew Norman, author of *We're All Damaged* and
Domestic Violets

"All aboard! *The Floating Feldmans* is for everyone who's ever thought their family is absolutely crazy . . . but loves them anyway. Sibling rivalries and skeletons in the closet all come to a head in this fun, quirky family saga." —Georgia Clark, author of *The Bucket List*

"*The Floating Feldmans* was a blast: funny, moving, and immensely readable. Friedland's all-you-can-eat buffet of quirky characters walks right off the page and into your heart."

—Jonathan Evison, author of *This is Your Life, Harriet Chance!*

"Take a big, dysfunctional family, reunite them for the first time in ten years on a Caribbean cruise ship they can't escape, and add endless buffets, blindfolded pie-eating contests, and impromptu conga lines on the sundeck. What could possibly go wrong? Both cruising fans and skeptics alike will get a laugh out of this story of a family trying to stay afloat." —*National Geographic*

"Friedland's well-executed and smartly structured novel features chapters from each character's point of view. The simple but clever premise lets the author explore the complicated tensions of family relationships in a compressed and directed way . . . there is dry humor and a certain sweetness as well." —*Library Journal*

PRAISE FOR

The Intermission

"The snappy dialogue makes this an effortless page-turner, almost a movie treatment more than a novel . . . intelligent commercial fiction." —*The Wall Street Journal*

"*The Intermission* is a thoughtful look at the complexities of marriage, delivering deep truths about how we share a life with another person. It will have you wondering: How well do I really know my spouse?"   —PopSugar

"A multifaceted look at the difficulties and rewards of marriage."
                                                                —*Kirkus Reviews*

"Entertaining marriage saga. . . . Friedland insightfully dissects motives, lies, and love in this engrossing deconstruction of a bad marriage."   —*Publishers Weekly*

"Expertly paced and eerily realistic, this novel will make readers think twice about the line between deception and mystery in any relationship."   —*Booklist*

Titles by Elyssa Friedland

–⁖–

The Most Likely Club

ELYSSA FRIEDLAND

Berkley
New York

BERKLEY
An imprint of Penguin Random House LLC
penguinrandomhouse.com

Copyright © 2022 by Elyssa Friedland
Readers Guide copyright © 2022 by Elyssa Friedland
Excerpt from *The Floating Feldmans* copyright © 2019 by Elyssa Friedland
Penguin Random House supports copyright. Copyright fuels creativity, encourages
diverse voices, promotes free speech, and creates a vibrant culture. Thank you for buying
an authorized edition of this book and for complying with copyright laws by not reproducing,
scanning, or distributing any part of it in any form without permission. You are supporting
writers and allowing Penguin Random House to continue to publish books for every reader.

BERKLEY and the BERKLEY & B colophon are registered trademarks of
Penguin Random House LLC.

Library of Congress Cataloging-in-Publication Data

Names: Friedland, Elyssa, author.
Title: The most likely club / Elyssa Friedland.
Description: First Edition. | New York: Berkley, 2022.
Identifiers: LCCN 2022014352 (print) | LCCN 2022014353 (ebook) | ISBN
9780593199749 (trade paperback) | ISBN 9780593199756 (ebook)
Subjects: LCGFT: Novels.
Classification: LCC PS3606.R55522 M67 2022 (print) | LCC PS3606.R55522
(ebook) | DDC 813/.6—dc23
LC record available at https://lccn.loc.gov/2022014352
LC ebook record available at https://lccn.loc.gov/2022014353

First Edition: September 2022

Printed in the United States of America
1st Printing

Title page art: Floral graduation frame © Amanita Silvicora / Shutterstock
Book design by Alison Cnockaert

For my friends, the ones who text back quickly

"Happiness comes from being who you actually are instead of who you think you are supposed to be."

—*Shonda Rhimes*

Prologue

—:—

THE SMART-BUT-SOCIAL TABLE in the lunchroom was in the back corner, underneath a row of wall-mounted pennants boasting victories in swimming, wrestling, and football, and kitty-corner from the hot-and-popular table, which was next to the cafeteria line. This ensured the jocks, and those lucky enough to orbit them, got first dibs on the sloppy joes and hash browns. Scattered in between were the artsy types, the nerds, the Phish-heads, the goths, and the milquetoasts who defied classification.

Melissa Levin, Suki Hammer, Priya Chowdhury, and Tara Taylor had taken over the smart-but-social table during their sophomore year, inheriting it from students who'd graduated the year before. Bellport Academy, the tiny private school in their posh hamlet in Connecticut, had the usual Anytown, USA, teenage groupings. If the social cliques were any more stratified, it would be a pyramid scheme. Melissa, Suki, Priya, and Tara had been best friends since the eighth grade—a convenient time to fortify a social circle, or square, as in their case. They had agreed that upon entering high school they wouldn't attempt to penetrate the popular crowd, but they wouldn't fall in with the geeks, either. They'd occupy the precious space of honor roll students who still get invited to parties.

Their plan worked. The four of them stuck together, earning high marks—Priya always on top—and carrying enough social currency that the jocks and cheerleaders knew their names and the nerds knew better than to ask them to study. And now they were seniors. Graduation was only a month away. Today was the day they'd been dreading, anticipating, imagining, and stressing over all at once.

It was yearbook day.

Yearbook day meant finding out if all their efforts had paid off. Having the right clothes (a fake Kate Spade could pass muster if the stitching was fine enough), devoting time to eight-minute abs (and buns!), leading the extracurriculars, maintaining GPAs above 3.5. College admissions season had already come and gone, arguably the more important barometer of success in high school. But the four friends were more anxious about the yearbook superlatives than whether the college envelopes in their mailboxes were thick or thin.

There were fifty superlatives each year and approximately two hundred graduating seniors. The entire class voted. Some results were obvious. Kim Konner would get Most Popular. She was a blond Jennifer Love Hewitt, tits on a stick with girl-next-door approachability. Lulu Anderson would clinch Most Fashionable; her collection of baby doll dresses was ripe for a *Seventeen* magazine spread. Charlie Rice would get Most Athletic, and Byron Cox would get Most Likely to Win the Lottery (and lose the ticket). Suki, Priya, Melissa, and Tara had agonized over what they'd get, silently fearing how it would affect their dynamic if they didn't each clinch something.

Melissa didn't say it to her friends, but she couldn't imagine getting skipped over. She'd made her mark. Student body president. Editor in chief of the newspaper. Honor roll every term. Now she was headed to Georgetown, where she planned to study government and feminist studies. She figured with a track record like hers—not a single lost election for a leadership position—she might have a knack for politics in the real world. Most Likely to Be President had to be hers.

Suki was also feeling confident. She wasn't Melissa, with a list of extracurriculars that required an addendum on her college application. But she was well known around the school. For starters, she was half-Japanese. And in a lily-white school community with a disproportionate amount of Mayflower lineage, Suki's heritage made it so every student, freshman through senior, knew her story. Her mother was Japanese, a former model in Tokyo aged into reluctant housewifery, and her father a white entrepreneur with a run of bad luck (or poor business acumen). He seemed determined to declare Chapter 11 eleven times. A solid student, Suki switched to Japanese when she wanted attention—and what high school girl didn't—and was rumored to have dated a college boy for the past year. She floated the rumor, but only Melissa, Tara, and Priya knew it. Suki was likely to get a superlative, but even she didn't have much of a hunch as to what it would be. Hopefully nothing dreadfully on the nose, like Most Exotic.

Then came Priya. Overworked, cautious, and brilliant Priya Chowdhury. Another student of color, but somehow it didn't ring the bells that Suki's roots did. Maybe her lack of mystique stemmed from her father being the preeminent pediatrician in town. In middle school, the boys used to joke about Dr. Chowdhury grabbing their junk when he examined them. Priya brushed it off as best she could. It helped that her nose was always in a book, and her gaze firmly planted on her future path. First stop Harvard (already accepted), then Harvard Medical School, then a fellowship in orthopedics—she'd always loved the intricacies of the human body. She would study the skeletons strung as Halloween decorations around the neighborhood while the others stuffed Blow Pops into plastic pumpkins.

Finally, there was Tara, who had (Michelin) stars in her eyes after an appearance in middle school on the *Today* show propelled her to local stardom. She made a duck à l'orange for Al Roker that made him weep on air. She'd learned to make eggs with shaved truffles and deep-fried Jerusalem artichokes at age five; for her eighth birthday she requested a rondeau. Her palate was supernatural—at least double the normal amount of taste buds resided on her tongue. She could detect the presence of nutmeg with her eyes closed and demanded her parents plant an herb garden so she could have fresh thyme and rosemary. She showed off the burn scars on her fingers like Girl Scout badges. There was little doubt she'd open a restaurant one day.

Of their foursome, Tara was also the most fearless. With the same bravado she used to yield chef's knives, she snuck into the guidance counselor's office to see where everyone was applying for college. She filched copies of the winter math final off the fax machine in the teachers' lounge and painted red lipstick on the school mascot. Nothing ever landed her in serious trouble— Tara's parents were hefty donors. With her moment on national television, and her family's last name gracing the athletic center, there was little chance Tara would be overlooked in the yearbook.

"I am wigging out," Melissa said. She was nervously eating fry after fry. "I saw the boxes dropped off this morning. What's taking so long?"

"Take a chill pill," Tara said. "It's out of our hands now."

"Oh my God, he's here!" Melissa said, jumping out of her seat so quickly her orange tray upturned. She pointed to where David Grossman, the yearbook editor, was walking into the cafeteria, pushing a hand truck piled high with books. As though he were tossing hundred-dollar bills in the air, all the seniors in the cafeteria charged at him. At least they weren't the only ones obsessing.

"He's coming straight here," Melissa gasped, her overly tweezed eyebrows twitching. She was white as a sheet. None of them wanted to be around if she got something beneath her, like Most Likely to Teach at Bellport. *Can you imagine never leaving this town?* There were even grumblings that this year there might be superlative burns. Kim Konner swore there was a Most Likely to Pull a Tonya Harding, and Eddy Falcon suggested Most Likely to Speed in a White Bronco. They doubted Mr. Mackay, the yearbook advisor, would let those slide. But a more veiled insult, something the students would understand but would escape the faculty's attention, was a possibility they were all dreading.

"Just like I told him to," Tara said, grinning. She popped a fry into her mouth and visibly enjoyed watching her friends' anticipation. "God, these are overcooked. I don't know why Chef Mick won't try peanut oil like I told him to. The food at this school is like one step below a Hot Pocket." She dropped the half-eaten fry onto her plastic tray and fixed her eyes on David.

"I told Grossman he could squeeze my right boob if he brought the yearbooks here first."

"Tara!" Priya clapped a hand to her mouth.

"We'll see if I actually follow through. I bet he'll be satisfied with a look."

That was likely. David Grossman's raging acne hadn't quit since the ninth grade. There was little chance he'd seen a live breast.

"Why the right one?" Suki asked, clearly amused.

"Saving the left one to find out who the prom king and queen are going to be."

Melissa threw a Mike and Ike at Tara, though she was clearly grateful for the first peek.

"Oh, look, there's Josh," Priya said. "Right behind David."

Josh Levine was Melissa's boyfriend of the past two years. Their last names made an unfortunate combination—Levin-Levine—but it's not like she planned to marry him. They were an under-the-radar couple—a good thing because the rumor mill at Bellport could be vicious. Josh had an Adam's apple the size of a plum and teeth that couldn't be coaxed into submission despite years of braces, but he was sweet and dependable and put up with Melissa's exhausting schedule of extracurriculars. She just wished he would stop wearing carpenter jeans every single day. And making her mixtapes filled with Fiona Apple songs.

"Did Josh get new glasses?" Suki asked, cocking her head in his direction. She was remarkably observant. If any of them got new paper for their Filofaxes, Suki was the first to notice.

"Yes. I know, they're awful." Melissa shrugged. "He needs bifocals because of his astigmatism." His inability to wear contacts meant he could never wear the sexy Oakleys worn by the cooler guys at school. "I wonder if he got anything in the yearbook." Josh teetered on the edge of the defy-classification group, something Melissa tried to spin into a positive. Everyone knew the jocks were jerks. The skateboarders were always high. The theater guys were too emo. Maybe she was the Rachel to Josh's Ross. Her haircut was even similar to Jennifer Aniston's and Josh prized his childhood collection of plastic dinosaur figures.

"Hot off the presses, ladies," David said when he reached their table. Four hands grabbed at the top box on the pile, ripping into the packing tape.

"Got one," Suki announced, the first to pry a book free. She flipped ferociously until she reached the superlatives double spread.

"Most Likely to Cure Cancer . . . Priya Chowdhury!" Suki announced. "Very nice, my friend."

Priya burned with pride. Her parents would like that. They would probably frame it next to her older sister's valedictorian plaque on the mantel.

Melissa cheered when she found hers.

"Most Likely to Win the White House," she said, the giddiness making her bounce up and down on her heels. She could practically kiss David, blistering pimples and all.

"Nice job, babe," Josh said, throwing a wiry arm around her, his gaze still searching the spread for his name.

"Suki Hammer . . . Most Likely to Join the Forbes 400." Suki read her own aloud as her mind raced to make sense of it. She had turned the school bake sale profitable by swapping basic chocolate chip cookies for gourmet éclairs and apple tarts wrapped in paper-thin phyllo dough—she'd forced Tara to stay up all night baking. The triple profits came in handy when the student council was able to book the hottest ska band for homecoming that fall. Suki also got the student newspaper to source advertising from local businesses. And there was her Garbage Pail Kids side business dating back to elementary school. Yeah, her superlative fit. More importantly, she approved.

"And Tara Taylor gets Most Likely to Open a Michelin-Starred Restaurant," David Grossman said.

"The tire place?" Josh looked to Melissa for explanation.

Melissa looked at the floor. She wasn't about to admit she was confused, too.

"Yes. But they also award stars to the finest restaurants in the world," Suki explained in a voice that radiated maturity.

"I'll take it," Tara said, fastening the top button of her flannel shirt as David looked at her chest with laser beams.

"We did good, kids," Melissa said once David had moved on to another table and Josh had kissed her goodbye, clearly downtrodden about his absence on the pages.

"Think any of these things will actually come true?" Priya asked. Her dimples were out, loud and proud. It was obvious how badly she wanted to fulfill her destiny.

"Duhhhh," Suki said. The four of them clinked their diet Arizona iced teas together. "We're going to light the world on fire."

1

—:—

SEPTEMBER 2022

Melissa

"MOM, THERE'S A fire in the kitchen," Cameron, Melissa's teenage daughter, called at the top of her lungs.

In her bedroom, Melissa quickly shut her laptop. She was messaging with a promising guy she'd matched with on one of the apps her daughter insisted she download. She'd let Cameron set up her profile, but she didn't need her know-it-all, attitude-plus teenager getting involved with the correspondence. Besides, what she'd written to CTguy77 wasn't anything too ambitious or quirky. Would luv to meet up wasn't weird, even if she did regret writing "luv" to this man, who claimed to be an English professor—though nothing was for certain behind the curtain of Internet profiles. L-o-v-e would have been the better choice for a forty-three-year-old divorcée with a daughter nine months away from graduating high school. But it was too late. Melissa had quickly hit send when Cameron started shrieking about fire, and now her missive was in the ether, soon to crash-land in CTguy77's inbox.

Melissa ambled down the stairs, not exactly in a rush. Cameron was prone to hyperbole and drama, a trait that emerged hard-core during puberty, a hellacious two-year period that coincided with her parents' divorce. Who had Melissa wronged in a past life to have deserved dealing with a divorce and a hormonally imbalanced daughter simultaneously?

Melissa paused on the second-to-last step to study the crack in the bottom stair, and then felt her eyes wander to the peeling wallpaper. Their house, once the best on the block, was showing its age. Not unlike her. Getting the place shaped up would mean calling her ex, Josh. She'd rather live with the imperfections than fight with him to send over a carpenter. It pained her that her once blue-ribbon house was now flanked by two new builds, with stylish aluminum roofs and crushed pebble driveways that made her asphalt one look like a parking lot. But not enough to bargain with the man who shared her bed for fifteen years.

"Holy shit, Cam," Melissa yelped when she finally reached the kitchen. This time her daughter had not been exaggerating. Bluish flames were shooting in the air and a cloud of smoke was quickly overtaking the room. "What the hell happened? Get the fire extinguisher."

A tray of charred brownies sat on the counter, the tinfoil edges in flames. Melissa went to tamp them down with dish towels while her daughter moved to the pantry.

Cameron returned with the fire extinguisher and handed it to her mother, as if she were supposed to know how to use it. It was at times like these she wished she had a man at home. Not when she was alone in her bed, nobody to chat with in the moments before sleep descended. Not even when she had to third/fifth/seventh wheel it at a dinner. She missed Josh the most when there was a spider to kill, a tall object to reach, or in this instance, a literal fire to put out. The metaphorical fires had always been on her shoulders. Josh was kind of a dud when it came to dealing with emotional issues, especially where their daughter was concerned.

"Forget it," Melissa said, resting the fire extinguisher on the floor. "I think it's dying down."

Cameron had ripped off her sweatshirt, an overpriced Aviator Nation hoodie she'd begged Melissa to get her, doused it with water from the tap, and used it to put out the last of the flames. The ruined sweatshirt was now soaking in their kitchen sink, at least $100 down an actual drain.

"Good Lord. That was a scare. Why are you baking, anyway?" Melissa asked, hoping she didn't sound judgmental. She assumed her daughter's recent sugar binges were stress-related. Cam was in the midst of college applications, and she and her best friend, Hannah, yapped about "reaches" and "safeties" constantly. Melissa couldn't afford to hire a $300-per-hour SAT tutor for Cam. Instead, her daughter watched YouTube videos that defined words like "garrulous" and "inchoate" while inducing spontaneous narcolepsy.

Homecoming also loomed. Cam was surely anxious about who would ask her, or if she'd be asked at all. Though her daughter was a senior at Bellport Academy, walking the very same halls her mother once did as a teenager, high school felt like a lifetime ago. The hours of sitting in the library with Tara, Suki, and Priya, obsessing over whether they would get invited to this or that party, worrying that a poor performance on an exam would knock them off honor roll, counting the calories in their SnackWell's, were now only scattered memories. Four years seen through a single prism.

Melissa wished she could tell Cameron how utterly insignificant anything that happened in high school was in the grand scheme of life. To reassure her that one day she would barely be able to recall the details of the fights that made her hysterical, and, on the flip side, the achievements that brought on euphoria. But it was only partly true, and Melissa hated to lie to her daughter. The scars of finding a tampon taped to her locker—after she'd, in a regrettable phase where she attempted to sound British, said "bloody ridiculous" in class—were permanent. Some of Melissa's present-day insecurity could be traced to the indignity of not being asked to the freshman dance or the sophomore Halloween party. High school might turn into a blur, but that didn't make it less of a bitch.

For the time being, she decided it was best to say nothing at all.

"The brownies were for the senior class bake sale," Cameron explained. "It's tomorrow. We're using the money to get this insane DJ for the prom. If we also do a bunch of car washes in the spring, we'll get there."

The Bellport Bake Sale. Thankfully it didn't fall under the PTA umbrella or Melissa would be elbows-deep in dough alongside Cam. It was during Melissa's junior year that the annual fund-raiser went from a misshapen-cookies-in-disposable-tins affair to desserts worthy of bougie bakery prices. Suki had the brainstorm—she wanted to bring some ska band to perform at homecoming. Tara did the baking, and suddenly there were lemon squares with raspberry centers, éclairs filled with key lime curd, and an extra thousand bucks in the student council coffers.

"It sucks they burned. I was making mint chocolate ganache with a toffee crunch. Got the recipe off TikTok." Cam splintered off a piece of charred brownie from the pan and dropped it in her mouth. Crumbs sprinkled the floor and Cam made no move to pick them up. Melissa held her tongue.

She lacked the will to argue. After she and Josh split, her arguments with Cam took on a darker tone. Cameron had a place to run when she got pissed; calling her father to pick her up was a favorite move. And still that was preferable to *Kelly would never say that to me.* Kelly was Josh's new wife and only twelve years older than Cam. And while Cameron was supposed to hate her stepmother, if any of the Lifetime movies Melissa watched were accurate, she didn't.

"All right, don't worry about it. Bridget's Bakery has nice linzer tortes. We can ugly them up so they look homemade." Melissa reached for a wad of paper towels and crouched on the ground to collect the crumbs. She heard something snap in her back. When she bent over or reached for anything these days, her body responded with orchestral cracks and pops. Middle age, apparently, came with a soundtrack. And choreography. Her discs bulged this way and that, moving like the CDs in the beloved five-disc changer from her youth.

"I love you, Mom. You're the best!" Cameron said, wrapping her mother in a rare hug. Melissa's flesh goose bumped. She so rarely had physical affection. Not from men. Not from her daughter. Not even from friends, who were few and far between. After the divorce, many of the women in her orbit vowed to stick by her. Her closest ally in the mom world, Stacey, had sworn she was eager for company on date nights. "If I have to hear about Zach's golf score one more time," she moaned, sipping Cloudy Bay on ice, Bellport drink of choice for uptight mothers looking to dull the insipid pains of high-stakes parenting. But after one trip to a Mexican restaurant followed by a movie, Stacey never asked Melissa to join them for date night again.

The same went for the others. Her coworkers at the radio station where she was a marketing manager talked about girls' nights that never happened. There were book clubs that got canceled, even after Melissa devoted countless hours to reading whatever novel topped the *New York Times* bestseller list and was considered required reading in upscale suburbia.

"Should we go now?" Melissa asked, looking at her watch. It was 5:30 p.m. She could race over to the bakery with Cameron and make it back in time to start dinner, then start on the work she'd brought home with her. She was one of two marketing managers at the local radio station and her counterpart, Annie, was on maternity leave, which meant Melissa had to pick up the slack. She refused to resent Annie for being away from work for three months—girl code—though she was certainly staring at the calendar waiting for the weeks to wind down. If only the work was a bit more interesting, maybe she wouldn't mind the second helping of it.

Certainly she didn't aspire to this job when she was younger. Her career aspirations came in this order: princess, firefighter (her inability to operate a fire extinguisher as an adult proved she'd sidestepped a disastrous choice), then politics. Melissa dreamed of going to law school. But somewhere along the way she got derailed. That "somewhere" was actually a "someone" and she was in the same room as her now, still hacking away at the edible edges of a brownie. When Cam was born, Josh's contracting business hadn't taken off yet. He kept getting screwed by subcontractors and material delays that cost money he didn't have. Money they needed to buy diapers, which Cam seemed to shit through at an alarming rate. Melissa took a bookkeeping job, which led to a position at a travel agency that she enjoyed until the Internet ruined it with one-click airfare and hotel. After a few unmemorable stints at other jobs, she wound up in her present position.

"Cam?" When Melissa looked up again, her daughter was halfway to the front door. "Wait for me. I need to get my shoes on."

"It's cool, Mom. I'll just go myself. I'm meeting up with Hannah after. Her mom is hosting some cocktail thing and she'll pay us if we help out."

What cocktail thing? Melissa didn't recall any Paperless Post from Stacey. Melissa shook it off. Did she really want to be in high heels making small talk with the Bellport ladies, likely asked to give a donation to some charity at the end of the night? No, not when she could drink wine in peace and exchange flirty banter with CTguy77 on the FortyPlusLove app.

The front door slammed before Melissa could tack on marching orders: *No texting behind the wheel. Drive slowly. Don't park in an empty lot.* Hopefully they were imprinted on Cam's brain by now, even if she eye-rolled or unleashed a guttural "uch" every time Melissa dared to express concern for her.

Cam's departure meant she was spared making dinner. Often Melissa felt her life was an endless Ferris wheel of meal prep. First came the menu planning, then the grocery shopping, then the unpacking of the groceries, then the chopping and sautéing and roasting (fine, microwaving), then serving, then the eating, which took all of six minutes, then cleanup. When the last dish was loaded in the dishwasher, it was time to prepare for the next meal.

Tonight the reprieve filled Melissa with more sadness than glee. She vacillated often about the empty nest she would inhabit next fall. So many mother-daughter skirmishes avoided—their house flooring might as well have been made of eggshells when Cam was home. But it also meant no one with whom to discuss celebrity gossip, seek fashion advice, and wait for on the couch in the evenings. The house would be quiet, just the sounds of her wrinkles deepening to keep her company.

She had family nearby. Her sister, Karen, lived only fifteen minutes away, but she'd been unbearable since she started planning her eldest's bar mitzvah. The party was shaping up to be a combination of a White House state dinner and the Met Gala. Melissa could see her mother for lunch more often. But why subject herself to an hour of *Pink isn't flattering on redheads, you know* and *Shirley Spielman's daughter got remarried only six months after* her *divorce* just for a free meal and some companionship?

Melissa sat down at the kitchen desk and toggled to her email. There was a message from Cameron's guidance counselor. Cameron wasn't the student Melissa had been, so if Ms. Lafferty was reaching out, it wasn't to alert her that Cameron had won one of the numerous prizes that Melissa had collected back in the day. These trophies and plaques collected dust in the attic, along with Josh's old tools and the proofs from their wedding. She earned awards in categories whose relevance to her current life were about as useful as fluency in Swahili. And yet. She wouldn't have minded if Cameron scooped up the occasional prize.

She opened Ms. Lafferty's email and was relieved that it was just a reminder about an upcoming college meeting sent to all senior class parents. She jotted down the date in her calendar and looked back up to find a new email from Dr. Giffords, the school principal.

Dear Melissa,

Back to school already! It feels like summer just
ended. We are so proud of Camryn and all she has
accomplished at Bellport!"

At this, Melissa blanched. The principal couldn't even spell
her daughter's name properly.

As I'm sure you noted from the Save the Date sent in
the spring, your 25th reunion is around the corner.
We are looking for volunteers from the Class of 1997
to help make this weekend back on campus special.
Of course, you were the first person to come to mind.
Your track record as the longest-serving PTA
president speaks volumes about your energy and
organizational skills.

Please let me know if you can find the time in your
busy schedule to chair the reunion weekend. I can't
imagine anyone doing a better job.

Yours,
HG

Melissa blushed though she was alone. Flattery was her
Achilles' heel. It was one of the reasons she'd remained in the
thankless job of PTA president for the past eight years, chasing
down parents who didn't contribute to the teacher gifts (the
nerve of people who ignored Venmo requests!) and never signed

up for safety patrol slots. She loved the accolades at the end of the year, the moment when the student government president handed her a bouquet of roses at graduation in gratitude for her service. If Cameron could only experience the joy of this sort of recognition, she would be motivated to be more of a leader in school. But it was a chicken-and-egg scenario. She wouldn't reap the rewards unless she threw her hat in the ring. Which reminded Melissa, there was leftover chicken in the freezer, or she could make herself eggs for dinner.

Of course, she hadn't forgotten about the reunion. It would be like forgetting a scheduled colonoscopy—the prep would be just as bad. A part of her would have preferred a tube with a camera up her ass to facing her classmates en masse.

None of her friends had committed to going. When the save the date went out, they had texted about it, focusing more on disbelief that they had gotten so old. Melissa could hardly claim inconvenience; she lived just ten minutes from campus. But going meant seeing Josh, and all their classmates realizing that Josh had replaced her with a newer model. Melissa preferred to think of Kelly as a second wife rather than a new wife, because it implied there would be a third.

Dr. Giffords's offer shifted her perspective. Melissa was more likely to attend if she held the reins. She dashed off an acceptance to Giffords before she could overthink it and withheld correcting him on the spelling of her daughter's name.

She palpated the soft roll spilling over the waistband of her jeans and sucked in air. She'd love to lose a few pounds before the reunion. Maybe she and Cameron could diet together. Or was that the worst idea she'd had since . . . since . . . No, she didn't want to think about that right now. There had been enough self-flagellating for the day. She wanted to talk to Suki, Tara, and Priya and get them on board.

Melissa eyed a photograph of the four of them in Napa Valley tacked to the corkboard behind her desk. The Napa picture was five years old and slightly faded from exposure to the kitchen's south-facing window. Her high school friends had not disappointed in rallying around her after the divorce. It was Tara's idea that they do a girls' trip in lieu of attending their twentieth reunion. Tara had her own extremely valid reasons for not wanting to step foot on the Bellport campus after a heinous debacle at their fifteenth, and Josh had just dropped the bomb on Melissa that Kelly was pregnant. The 2.0 Levins would be attending the reunion: Josh, Kelly, and the little swell on Kelly's normally washboard abs that would turn into Madison, Cam's half sister.

Suki flew them to the Auberge du Soleil resort for a long weekend of drinking, spa, and fine dining. She picked up the tab for every last item, from their room service Diet Cokes to the gratuities on their massages. Tara's new business was in a fledgling stage and Priya was swamped as per usual, but the four of them managed the impossible feat of spending three uninterrupted days together, drunk on wine and sunshine. There was talk of making it an annual trip, and it did happen the following year, that time Suki bringing them all to a charming village in Colorado for skiing and marvelous après cocktails. But the trips had fallen by the wayside, as Suki's star burned brighter and her commitments grew in tandem. The rest of them were silently relieved. The efforts involved in getting away made the trips feel almost pointless—at least a 3:1 ratio of planning days to actual vacation days.

Unpinning the photo, Melissa brought it closer and studied Priya's face. When she smiled—all too rarely—it overtook her. Priya was the most pensive of their foursome. Of their group, her life had unfolded most predictably. Harvard undergraduate followed by Harvard Medical School, marriage to a fellow doctor, and then the juggle of her medical practice and three children, which she seemed to handle better than most working moms. Priya joked about being a walking stereotype, but maybe it actually wasn't funny to her. Something always seemed missing. Even when Priya's wide smile broke out, her eyes lacked a corresponding twinkle. Melissa figured it was probably something as simple as a much-needed nap.

Melissa chose her as the first target. Priya lived in Woodbridge, only forty-five minutes from Bellport, and she had no reason to dread a reunion with her classmates. After three rings, she answered. From the background noise, it was clear she was still at the hospital, well past dinnertime.

"You sound busy," Melissa said when Priya finally said hello after dispatching instructions to a fleet of nurses.

"Always," Priya said. "What's up?"

"Well, I've been asked to chair the twenty-fifth reunion," Melissa said. While moments earlier she felt proud, saying it out loud made her feel childish. She was still the kid who needed to be in charge of everything.

Priya laughed, without a trace of meanness.

"Well, of course you have," she said.

"Dr. Chowdhury, you need to sign some discharge papers before you leave," came a female voice in the background, and Melissa was holding again. This time there was elevator jazz music to keep her company. It was easy to picture Priya at the hospital, calm and composed while gurneys flew by and the intercom blasted a cacophony of alarms and pages. Priya would have her long dark hair tied into a simple knot. She kept her cool always, dating back to when the mean kids in middle school called her Clam Chowdhury. When Tara's shoulder popped out of place during their ski weekend, Priya said nothing, placed both hands on the dislocated bones, and reset it. She did not seek glory. Melissa wondered what that would feel like.

"Sorry, I'm back," Priya said. "So what's the plan for this reunion? I put the date in my calendar ages ago, but I don't know if I'll be able to make it."

"P, I need you there. I can't face Josh and the bimbo without my girls around me."

Priya sighed. Melissa could hear her gears cranking, thinking who could watch the kids, how many patients she'd have to reschedule.

"Isn't Kelly a yoga teacher?" was how she broke the silence.

Melissa bristled. Bimbo—yoga teacher. Tomato-tomahto. "Whatever."

"She might not be such a bimbo. I recommend yoga to my patients. I'm just saying that because I know it annoys you how much time Kelly spends with Cameron. She might not be that bad of an influence. If nothing else, Cameron should have good posture."

"She doesn't," Melissa said sharply. Her daughter struck a Neanderthal pose, her head permanently rounded forward because of cell phone addiction. "Well, please try to be there if you can. Even if you only drive in for one night. But, of course, I hope you spend the whole weekend. You can stay with me."

"I have to talk to Dev," Priya said predictably. Dev was her husband, an orthopedic surgeon with an ego that outsized any of the body parts he worked on. Melissa liked him well enough. They both obsessed over true crime podcasts and the *New York Times* Spelling Bee. And now Wordle.

"I understand. I'll follow up," Melissa said, trying to sound breezy when really her heart was pounding.

"I know you will," Priya said, and they both giggled. Melissa was a dog with a bone when she set her mind to something.

"Love you," Melissa said. "Ask Dev if he's listening to *The Murderer Next—*"

"Wait—" Priya interrupted. "Is Suki going?"

"I don't know yet," Melissa said. "But you know I'm gonna try."

She hung up the phone and repinned the photo to the corkboard, next to one of Cameron's elementary school drawings that she couldn't bear to take down. It was a family portrait, Melissa, Josh, and Cameron depicted as colorful stick figures. Cam had drawn her parents side by side and put herself to the left, next to Josh. It was unusual—Cam's kindergarten teacher had remarked on it. "She must really love seeing you two together," Mrs. Pritchard had said, beaming at Melissa and Josh during conferences. That was back before Josh's transformation, when he still had thick glasses and wore loose polos over his beer belly. When his pre-plugs hairline zigzagged with peaks and valleys.

Fortunately, tonight it was easy not to dwell on Josh because her head was swirling with ideas for the reunion. A luau for welcome cocktails on Friday night with tasteful ice breakers. A "back to class" Saturday morning session where alumni could visit with their former teachers, many of whom were still on faculty. They could even take subject quizzes to see how much they remembered.

Saturday night would be a formal dinner in the gymnasium; she could probably recycle some of the homecoming decorations to save money. Because of course Dr. Giffords would give her some dreadful budget to work with. But what should she do for the farewell brunch on Sunday? She googled ideas. Many of them had to do with playing "Where are they now?" games. She jotted notes down on the personalized pad, labeled MELISSA'S MISSION, she kept next to her laptop, and read it over. The schedule wasn't quite right yet, but she would think of something. She always did.

Reaching again for her phone, she thought of how best to approach her next victim. It would be hardest to convince Tara to return to campus. Melissa tapped out a straightforward text and crossed her fingers and toes.

> T . . . I miss you. Our 25th reunion is coming up and I've been asked to chair the weekend. I cannot fathom doing this without you by my side. And I think you facing everyone would prove that everything that was said about you was a total lie. Your absence would speak louder than your presence. Lmk. XOXO

The three dots of a reply flashed on her screen.

> Hm. Tempting, but no. Miss U2. X

Melissa flinched. She hadn't even gotten her to consider it. What could bend Tara's mind?

Suki is coming.

Melissa had never typed so quickly; her thumbs moved like Cam's tap-dancing on her phone.

Tara's three dots returned, disappeared, and then came again.

Really? Maybe I can make it.

Melissa smiled to herself. It was a harmless lie. Besides, maybe she'd convince Suki. It wasn't like getting to Bellport from Palo Alto was difficult when she could fly in and out on her private jet. Suki globe-trotted more easily than Melissa handled carpool.

A new email flashed on her laptop. She felt a thrill, hoping it might be from one of the vendors she'd already messaged about nineties props. Melissa could practically smell the CK One fragrance in the air.

The message was from CTguy77, the man from the dating app. Maybe if things went well between them, she could bring him as her date.

Melissa opened it, her pulse quickening.

Dear Melissa,

I'd really like to meet up soon. Might you be free for dinner this Saturday night? I can come to Bellport

and we can eat at one of the places on the water. Let
me know if that's convenient for you.

Fondly, Mike

Oh, she liked Professor Mike. This was not one to fuck up.
Melissa could already picture trapping Josh in an intellectual
conversation with him. Mike would talk about iambic pentam-
eter and Josh would mistakenly think it was a tool sold at Home
Depot.

She was about to respond when she noticed there was an
attachment to the email. It was titled "Hard to wait."

She clicked it open and gasped. There was a close-up of Professor Mike's erect penis, flanked by two hairy balls.

2

-:-

Tara

"WHO YA TEXTING?" Rachel asked, bumping Tara in the back with the spiky head of an immersion blender.

Tara clenched her jaw. Rachel always did that to her, asked whom she was texting, especially if she caught Tara smiling. In the background, fifteen third graders stood in line to wash their hands, wearing ill-fitting paper toques and triple-knotted aprons that would be a bitch to undo. Today's class included making fruit salad. The kids had long awaited the moment they could use the "big boy and big girl" knives. Tara had triple-checked that the first aid kit was well stocked before class.

Tara slipped the phone back into her jeans pocket, screen-side down. "Just Melissa. She wants me to go to our twenty-fifth high school reunion. She's chairing it, naturally."

"Why naturally?" Rachel asked.

Tara suppressed a groan. It was exhausting having to catch Rachel up on her life before they met, especially because Tara was so much older. Her middle-aged life didn't lend itself to summary. How could she even begin to explain Melissa? What cultural reference did Tara and Rachel share that could sum her up? Tara thought but came up empty. She still shuddered thinking Rachel had never seen *Troop Beverly Hills*. The woman had never laid eyes on a phonebook, let alone prank-called every plumber in the book.

"Melissa's always in charge of everything. She's very—"

"Miss Rachel?" A towheaded girl with a gigantic booger dangling from her nose approached. Saved by snot.

"Yes, Mika?" Michaela Jones was the biggest of their PITAs, Pains in the Ass, second only to her mother, Lorinda Blythe-Jones, who they called BJ because it was funny and she was obnoxious. Mika was her fifth child, and fifth one to take classes at Tara's school, Kitchen Kiddos. BJ was the kind of woman who kept having children to prove she could afford to raise a large family in New York City, and to keep her handsome hedge fund husband from roving too far.

Mika bit down hard on her bottom lip and cued up a tear to roll down her cheek. She had tremendous physicality and would totally crush it on *MasterChef Junior*.

"Aidan spilled Bolognese sauce on my leg and foot during clean-hands check." She lifted her moccasin to show them. "It was hot."

"Does it hurt?" Rachel asked. She was better at coddling the kids than Tara, which is why Rachel led the classes, while Tara stayed mostly back of house, balancing the books and fielding calls from parents like Lorinda, who needed a tranquilizer if her child didn't get first turn with the electric mixer.

Mika shook her head side to side, an exaggerated "no."

"It doesn't but he made this black line on my shoe. And Mommy said these shoes cost three hundred dollars." Mika slipped off her moccasin and handed it to Rachel to examine the scuff mark. Tara saw the inside label. Bonpoint. When she first started Kitchen Kiddos, she would have assumed Mika was exaggerating. But over the years, as more and more children left behind cardigans, hats, and other layers, from stores like Ralph Lauren and Christian Dior, Tara grew curious. She strolled over to Madison Avenue to check out the mini merchandise. She recognized the cashmere cardigans her students wore in the wintertime. They cost as much as Tara paid her teachers a week, and often the parents wouldn't even call to see if they turned up in the lost and found. Tara really ought to start a secondhand business selling the forgotten items. The thought appealed to her momentarily: sitting behind a register all day with a good book tucked on her lap instead of helping kids make watermelon balls. She was never meant to be a cooking teacher, especially one who instructed chefs still struggling to tie their own shoes.

"Tell Mommy to use a Magic Eraser pen and it'll come right out. Actually, tell Mommy to tell someone who works in your house to do that." Rachel patted Mika on the shoulder and nudged her back to her spot at the counter where her name was written in macaroni elbows—a craft project that had taken Tara hours and necessitated googling, with two of her fingers stuck together, how to remove Krazy Glue.

"Thanks, Miss Rachel. You're a good hooker."

"Excuse me?"

Mika looked agitated at having to repeat herself.

"I said . . . you're a good cooker."

Ah.

The child tottered off.

"I do not have your patience," Tara said.

"I like children," Rachel said, with a shrug that said, *Sue me.* "And I think I'd look damn cute with a basketball on my belly." Rachel buried her fists inside her striped T-shirt and pushed it outward.

"Looks like you have twin aliens in there. Can we talk about this at home?" Tara asked, yawning on cue. "We still have to get through the tween class."

"Fine," Rachel said, swinging her hips breezily, like a curtain in the wind, as she grabbed a stack of clean aprons. Tara found the weightless way her girlfriend moved irresistible. She'd plucked her for employment at Kitchen Kiddos from the diner near Tara's apartment, where Rachel was waitressing. She admired the way Rachel handled a rambunctious group of frat bros who demanded endless coffee refills while staring at her tits. Rachel would have the fortitude to put up with the brattier kids in her program if she could keep those guys in line. "And can we also discuss your reunion? I want to go and meet the fabulous Suki Hammer." Rachel fanned herself dramatically with a spatula. Tara threw a pencil at her, which Rachel swiftly caught and tucked behind her ear.

Hearing Suki's name on Rachel's tongue was strange. Tara was pretty sure she didn't like it.

"I don't even know if she's coming," Tara said.

"Fine. All right, guys, time to tackle petit fours. *Again.*" Rachel's voice, placid but bearing the slightest edge, called out as she went back to the kitchen.

Three injured thumbs and a lemon curd fight later, class was over. A tray of misshapen petit fours sat cooling as a mix of parents and babysitters trickled in to collect their oversugared darlings. Rachel hastily packaged the treats, subduing fights over whose pastry was whose, while Tara handed out flyers for the winter break intersession.

"You owe me a call," came a familiar voice. Tara looked up to see the friendly face of Marina Delgado, her favorite Kitchen Kiddos parent. She was an architect at a high-profile firm that specialized in museum design, and since she was almost always late to pick up her son, Luis, it meant Tara had time to hear about her projects while she cleaned up the kitchen. Today Marina was shockingly punctual, though still frazzled, carrying a tote bag overflowing with jumbo blueprints in one hand and clutching an iced coffee and a cell phone in the other.

"Mommy, try my peddy fort," Luis was saying to Marina, and Tara cringed as his mother took a large bite of his mangled creation. She had witnessed with 100 percent certainty Luis pick his nose, admire his retrieval, and put his sullied index finger directly back into the mixture.

"I know, I know," Tara said to Marina. She had told Marina in one of her weaker moments, after a particularly exhausting doubleheader involving the fire department, a crème brûlée torch, and a high-maintenance mother demanding to see the ingredient list for every recipe, that Kitchen Kiddos wasn't necessarily her life's goal. Marina followed up with a text about an opportunity elsewhere, and Tara had yet to pursue it.

"Mom, did you bring my Pokémon cards?" Luis tugged at Marina's bag and the blueprints spilled out, landing in a puddle left behind by a juice box.

"Oh my goodness, let me help you." Tara dashed to get paper towels as Rachel speedily appeared with a mop. "Those weren't important, were they?" She made eyes with Marina after noting the stamps across the page reading **WHITNEY MUSEUM EXPANSION—FINAL VERSION**.

"It's okay. Watching the ink shed just gave me a great idea for an indoor waterfall." Luis's mom was so genuine—the kind of woman who openly spoke about her perimenopausal vagina while earmuffing her kid. "I gotta get these plans under a blow-dryer stat. But call me, Tara. I have an opportunity that could be great for you." Marina nuzzled her son's hair lovingly. "I owe you for tolerating this one for two hours every week."

"I love Luis," Tara said.

Marina covered Luis's ears. "That's kind of you. Now call me back."

AN HOUR AFTER the last of the icing was scraped off the counters and the mise en place for the next day's omelet class was organized, Tara and Rachel were back in their Greenwich Village apartment, nearly catatonic. It was still weird for Tara to think of her home for the past decade as a shared residence. Rachel commandeered an entire half of the medicine cabinet with her herbal supplements on move-in day; she was clearly acclimating more easily.

Bernie was waiting for them behind the front door in anticipation of the treats Rachel and Tara brought for him. Their rescue terrier mix was the recipient of the squishies and shaker toys and worn-out blankies left behind by their younger students.

"Hi, Bern," Tara said, nuzzling him. For her dog, she had

infinite patience, even when he puked on the carpet and took bites of the foam filling from their sofa. "Today we have for you . . ." She reached into her tote bag, which had the Kitchen Kiddos logo, a broccoli head resting on an ice cream cone. "A pizza squishy!" She had actually seen Mason's nanny drop the toy by mistake and could have torn after her, but she knew Bernie would love gnashing this particular find.

"Where are we ordering in from?" Rachel asked.

They were the shoemaker's children when it came to food. Rachel wasn't a naturally talented cook. She was an asset to Kitchen Kiddos more for her way with kids and staggering genius when it came to retooling popular songs into class anthems. Her "Sgt. (Red) Pepper's Lonely Hearts Club Band" and "Strawberry Fields Forever" remixes were pure genius. Tara once loved the frenetic pace of a kitchen, the sound of timers dinging and smells erupting. But she had no interest in putting in the effort for just the two of them, and half-assing a meal wasn't in her DNA.

"Thai. We need something cheap."

"I'll order from Bangkok Gardens." Rachel opened Uber Eats on her phone and one-clicked their regular order. "Can we get back to your reunion? I wish I could have gone to mine but—"

Rachel was from a rural town in the Midwest and her parents were deeply religious. There was so much talk of praying the gay away that eventually they prayed Rachel away.

Tara rolled her eyes. "Of course you'd want to. You're still a kid. The twenty-fifth is a whole different animal. It's like VH1 *Behind the Music*, edited by the mean kids. Wait, you have no idea what that show is. You probably don't know what VH1 is. Anyway, people expect accomplishments by this age."

"Which you have," Rachel said, smacking Tara on the knee. "Kitchen Kiddos is really impressive."

"Debatable. Just trust me on this. Anyway, my fifteenth was a horror show. Like you know those nightmares where you're back in school and forgot to study for exams or realize you're standing in the hallway naked? Multiply that times a million."

"Tell me." Rachel crisscrossed her legs on the couch. She looked like she was settling in for a Bravo marathon.

Tara felt beads of sweat cresting on the back of her neck and wound her hair into a bun. Wine would help this go more smoothly. She reached for the open bottle of cabernet on their bar cart and poured herself a generous glass. When she settled onto the sofa, Bernie jumped on and began his nightly thrashing of their pillows.

"You know who Ricky DiMateo is, right?"

Rachel unfolded one of Tara's legs and began massaging her toes. It wasn't until her joints were pressed on that Tara realized how much tension she was holding on to.

"Of course. He's got that reality show, *Ricky's Kitchen*. He curses and they have to bleep him a lot. It's a pretty good show."

"Well, he's not a good guy. I knew him before he was on television. When he had a forty-seater in Los Angeles. It was a seafood place called Ricardo. I worked as his sous for a time."

"Wow. I can't believe I didn't know that about you."

Tara shrugged.

"I was there for about a year. And he assaulted me." When it first happened, Tara didn't use the word "assault," even in her own head. She soft-pedaled it, using phrases like "he made me uncomfortable" and "he crossed boundaries." After the others came forward, she stopped sugarcoating what was nothing short of a violation.

Rachel's eyes were saucers.

"He seems like a lovable guy on TV. I mean, like, a lovable asshole. He even has that spinoff with the kids. What happened between you guys?"

"One night he asked me to stay late to go over the receipts. He knew I had aspirations of opening my own restaurant. Ricky told me he'd consider partnering with me. That I had talent. He said he wanted me to see the other side of the business, not just the food. I was honored. And the timing couldn't have been better. It was basically going to be a partnership with Ricky or nothing. My parents were ending the gravy train. They assumed I was flitting around L.A., flipping burgers by day and partying by night."

"My dad said I had one more month to make a go of cheffing and then they were pulling the plug on my spending account. I was desperate to have my own restaurant. And Ricky believed in me. He kept promising me he'd promote me to chef de cuisine. One night, we were alone past closing. I don't even know where everyone else went, but he must have shooed them off. Ricky insisted we finish off a bottle of some thousand-dollar burgundy one of the two-tops didn't finish. And then when that was empty, he opened another. My eyes were so bleary. I was nearly sleeping and pinching my thighs to stay awake."

"And then?"

"And then he kissed me. I was literally in the middle of asking a question about the health department—probably slurring my words—and his tongue was in my mouth. I pulled back immediately. I mean, I had no interest in this man. And he was married with kids. He gave me this totally sick smile—I had never noticed how gross his teeth were before. He had these wolf fangs. Now he has cheesy veneers since he got on TV. He grabbed my breast and squeezed. Said something like, 'I have wanted to do this for so long. I know you have, too.'"

"I think I read something about this," Rachel said. "He got in trouble with some women. Like a long time ago."

Bernie made his way onto Tara's lap and yawned. Many times, he was the only male she liked. Probably because he was neutered.

"Yeah. He got into trouble, which lasted all of five minutes. Right after his TV deal was announced, a waitress who worked in one of his Las Vegas restaurants came forward to say he made advances on her. When she wouldn't play along, he fired her."

Rachel pounded her fist on the cocktail table. "Yes! I remember now. Some woman was on the morning shows talking about this."

Tara nodded, pressing her top teeth into her lower lip.

"Correct. Maria McManus." It was important to Tara that she be called by her name, not "some woman" or "that girl" or "just a waitress."

"Ricky made mincemeat of her in two seconds, no pun intended. On the weekends she worked as an exotic dancer at one of the clubs and that was all it took to discredit her. But other women started to come forward, too. It felt like a domino effect. Eventually, we would knock him down. Or so we thought."

"Back up. What happened that night in the restaurant with you two after he kissed you?"

The doorbell rang. Tara sprang up to retrieve their food delivery, grateful for the diversion, though she no longer had an appetite. She took her time unpacking the cartons and chop-sticks, filling glasses with water. Back on the couch with steam-ing noodles fogging the view, she continued.

"I grabbed my purse and bolted for the door. 'Where do you think you're going?' he asked me, still smiling.

"I said I was going home. That I would see him tomorrow when we were both sober." Tara remembered knowing that she shouldn't be driving home drunk, but willing to chance it to get away. At that point she still thought she'd be at work the next morning in time to start lunch preparations. She figured he would apologize. "He told me that if I left, he wouldn't back me in any restaurant. And that my job at Ricardo was finished. Stu-pidly, I said something like, 'What about my talent?' And he—"

Rachel handed her a tissue. It wasn't until she took the white square in her hand that she realized she was crying.

She took a deep breath and continued, balling the tissue tightly in her first.

"He said, 'What about my dick?' and unzipped his pants. He pulled out his penis. I ran outside. Stupidly, I waited for a week to hear from him, thinking he would call to apologize, say he was drunk or something and that the restaurant needed me. But nothing. I never heard from him again."

"Why have you never told me this before?" Rachel asked.

"Because it doesn't have a happy ending," Tara said, wrap-ping her fingers around Bernie's collar. "I was so disgusted by the whole thing that I booked a flight back east. I figured I had no chance of landing in a good kitchen in L.A. because Ricky was so well connected. Who was I going to list as a reference if not him? My parents were happy to have me home. I worked for my dad while I figured out next steps. I got the idea for Kitchen

Kiddos after seeing an advertisement for a class in Bellport called Theater Tykes that cost twelve hundred dollars per semester. I wasn't living my dream, but I focused on the business and barely thought about Ricky. And then Maria McManus happened. Soon after there was an anonymous email account that welcomed submissions from anyone Ricky had mistreated. The day after I emailed, I was on TV telling Katie Couric my story."

Tara twirled her chopsticks into the shrimp pad thai and let a begging Bernie slurp a noodle dangling off the end. She would *Lady and the Tramp* spaghetti with her dog any day. What more did they need than Bernie? Why was Rachel so fixated on a baby?

"For about twenty-four hours, I felt like a hero. It also happened to be the day of my fifteenth reunion. I went straight there from 30 Rockefeller Center. Many of my classmates had seen the interview and practically gave me a standing ovation. Suki was there and I swear I got more attention than she did. Which, if you knew how much she was revered, you would realize is a really big deal."

"And then what happened? How does this relate to us not going to your twenty-fifth?"

Tara looked at Rachel's innocent face and felt a pang of guilt. Even if Tara decided to go to appease Melissa, she wouldn't be bringing Rachel. "Also, I googled you the minute we met and I didn't see any *Today* show video."

"Ricky had it wiped from the Internet. That's a thing, apparently. Anyway, by the next morning, everything had changed. Ricky was on the warpath. His people put up a website discrediting anyone who had come forward against him. Those creeps photoshopped pictures of our heads onto porn star bodies and made it seem like we were all call girls. They found pictures of me—real ones—on dates with women and said that I'm just a man-hater and that's why I was doing this. It was like the pendulum swung so quickly I could barely keep up. In the court of public opinion, Ricky became the victim. It was like . . . how sad for men that their reputations can be tarnished by the whims of unstable women? By the Saturday-night dinner, I was a reunion pariah. Except for my close friends, of course, who knew about the Ricky thing the morning after it happened. Oh—and the kicker—is that my date ditched me. I had been dating this guy for about a month and I decided to bring him. A real estate lawyer. My father was ecstatic. He heard on the news that I'm an angry lesbian and literally drove back to Manhattan that day."

"Jesus," Rachel said. "That is so fucking unfair. And you don't hate men. You're bisexual, as you always like to remind me. So I have to be jealous of every woman *and man* around you."

"Stop it," Tara said, but she kind of liked it when Rachel became territorial. It would have been cloying in her younger years, but at the cusp of middle age, Tara appreciated that she could keep anyone on their toes.

"Well, now you have to go to this reunion. Everything's changed. #MeToo. Harvey Weinstein's in jail. Cosby served time—though not enough, obviously. Matt Lauer got canceled."

For each name Rachel mentioned, Tara thought about the countless predators who went unpunished.

"C'mon. I want to meet your friends and see where you grew up. Bellport sounds way more exciting than Falls River."

"Maybe." What she didn't add was that she would consider it only if Suki went. How did that woman still have such a firm grip on her?

"Yes! Let's book a bed-and-breakfast. We can talk about the ba—"

"You get one chance to harass me per night." She cupped Rachel's chin.

Rachel threw a mangled throw pillow in Tara's face. Wine splashed everywhere and five minutes later they were resolving their differences in bed.

3

-·:·-

Priya

THE LINE AT Whole Foods was so long that Priya, at the tail end, was pressed up against the freezer wall in the back. Bored and chilly, she started to group the footwear of the other customers ahead of her in line. About half were in some form of sneaker. A quarter of the ladies were in heels; Priya hurt for those women. At least she was in her work clogs. There were maybe a handful of men's dress shoes, probably bachelors buying prepared foods to nuke in the microwave. She laughed out loud imagining Dev in the supermarket, befuddled by the dairy aisle and texting her about which milk to get, then even more flummoxed by the vast cereal selection.

Was that her husband now, texting? She looked down at her dinging phone, which had buzzed at least six times since she'd been in the store.

When will you be home? I'm STARVING. Firstborn Asha was always hungry, incredibly picky, and impossible to please.

I can't find my soccer uniform, her baby, Vid, wrote, and then inexplicably followed it up with the poop emoji, which for the longest time Priya thought was a Hershey's Kiss. Until Asha clued her in, she had been responding **yum.**

I need help w my science project, her middle child, Bela, wrote. **U said u would be home already.**

The rest of the messages were work-related. The on-call needed input on a case stat and her favorite nurse, Carmen, texted to say that Priya had forgotten her sunglasses. Surely, she had another pair at home, but in the chaos that every morning brought, kids flailing in all directions, and Priya hastily searching for cash to give her kids lunch money, there was zero chance she'd find them. Which meant driving to work squinting the whole way, which she despised. At least her job at Yale New Haven Hospital was only a fifteen-minute drive from her home in Woodbridge.

Proximity to work was one of the reasons she and Dev chose Woodbridge, but she would have gladly commuted an extra half hour to live in her house. She loved their Georgian-style abode like another child, taking pride and pleasure in its stately features and verdant flat lawn. And, unlike the kids, the house never talked back. It was made of red brick and had big dormer windows framed by black shutters. Every time she walked through the glossy painted front door with its brass knocker, she felt like she was stepping into a fairy tale. It was so much more to her liking than the house she grew up in, which her parents had painted a jarring saffron color, because it was considered the most auspicious in their culture. She wondered if her children knew how lucky they were, that she sent them to school with cafeteria money instead of fragrant Tupperware filled with mysterious leftovers the other kids said looked like cow dung. She and Dev agreed their children should embrace their culture, but both prioritized fitting in over celebrating Ganesh Chaturthi. It felt like yesterday that Priya was scraping dal dhokli from a Tupperware into the toilet in the girls' room. She could hear Kim Konner's voice through the stall, saying "What is that smell?" while her lackeys hypothesized about what might be the cause.

"Dr. Chowdhury," came a familiar voice from behind her. She had inched up a bit in the line and was now only twenty minutes from getting out of the store. Priya turned around to face her boss, matching her in scrubs.

"Dr. Hiroshi," she said, flustered. She always got that way when she ran into people from work outside of the hospital. Like she wanted them to see her in only a professional capacity, not pushing a wagon filled with overpriced, precut cantaloupe and frozen waffles so thoroughly coated in preservatives that their expiration date was three years in the future.

"Have you given any more thought to what we discussed last week?" Hiroshi asked, leaning in, his eyes soft and curious. Priya was fond of her boss. He was a newly minted CEO when she arrived at Yale New Haven. He took the time to get to know the doctors on staff and assure them that feeling totally unprepared was par for the course, something Priya appreciated when she was still confusing the tibia and the fibula. Later, when her scrubs had milk stains and she needed to use a handheld breast pump in ridiculous places (more than once behind a vending machine), Hiroshi added a lactation room to every floor. She did not miss that breast pump. It whooshed eerily and sounded like it was repeating a mantra: *You make milk, you make milk, you make milk.* The day Priya shipped it to her sister was a happy one.

"I have," she said slowly. "I need more time, though. I know you need an answer soon."

He looked in her cart as if, based on the contents, he were trying to assess how much free time she had.

"What's Dev say?"

She stiffened, tightening her grip on the grocery wagon. She hadn't mentioned the opportunity Hiroshi had offered her to her husband yet and she certainly wouldn't want his first hearing of it to come from their shared boss. Maybe she'd do it tonight. But, no, tonight was no good. She had to make dinner, create a solar system using only recyclables, and find a soccer uniform that probably hadn't been washed since its last use.

"I haven't had a chance to tell him yet." Before Dr. Hiroshi could speculate as to why that was, she added, "The kids have been all-consuming lately." When she brought up her childcare duties at the hospital, it was the equivalent of telling her male boss she needed to change her tampon. Not everyone afforded her that same courtesy as Dr. Hiroshi. The chief compliance officer threw a hissy fit when Priya rescheduled a meeting to attend Asha's school play. In retrospect, Asha's pitiful performance as tree number six in the climate-change musical made Priya wonder if the CCO wasn't just looking out for her. Fortunately, theater excepted, her eldest excelled in all other school subjects.

"Ah, yes." Dr. Hiroshi opened a container and pincered a green bean. They had made their way to the midpoint of the line.

"Want?" He held the container in front of her.

"I'm all right, thanks."

She liked that Hiroshi was a guy for whom eating green beans with his bare hands in line at Whole Foods was totally normal. He made popcorn in the staff lounge every day, which he walked around in brightly colored socks with funky designs like avocados or dumbbells. Trained as a cardiologist but now fully devoted to administrative duties, he was brilliant, though you'd never know it from his low-key demeanor. She wouldn't mind working more closely with him. The opportunity he'd offered thrilled her. But how could she add one more thing to her plate? It already resembled the never-ending stack at IHOP.

"Please give the position some serious thought. You'd be a tremendous asset to the leadership team." It looked like he was about to pat her on the shoulder but stopped short. He was in his late sixties, that generation that didn't quite know what was appropriate anymore and found most interactions with the opposite sex befuddling. He took back his hand and instead went for another green bean, smiling at her sheepishly as a seed slipped out and landed in the pocket of his scrubs.

"I promise I will," she said. "Look—the express line just opened up. You can get out of here way sooner." She gestured to where customers were already swarming.

"A working mother always knows the shortcuts," Dr. Hiroshi said, and gave her an approving nod before heading off.

"MOM!" ASHA SHOUTED. "You are so late. I texted you six times. You promised you'd—"

"How about, 'Can I help you with the groceries?'" Priya said, jiggling her daughter's bun. "Or, 'I started dinner without you!'"

"Bela was melting crayons in the pots. I couldn't use the kitchen." Asha was riffling through the grocery bags spread out on the foyer carpet, a Moroccan antique collected on Priya's honeymoon with Dev. Within a week of having their new dog,

Wiggles, their treasured rug was destroyed. "Where are the chips? I texted you this morning that we were out of the fat-free barbecue Air Pops."

"Oh, shoot. I forgot to get them." Priya watched her daughter's face fall. She felt guilty for a half second before deciding that Asha could have texted her a reminder if the chips were that important. Since when had she ever asked her children to do something only once?

Priya stepped into the kitchen, fearing the worst. Half-melted crayons were spreading their pigment across her countertops.

"Bela!"

Her daughter, whose back was to Priya at the kitchen sink, spun around.

"What? I thought this was a good idea. We can use the melted wax to color the planets. And don't worry about our pots. Crayola wouldn't make anything toxic." Nonplussed, Bela took a wooden spoon from the utensil cylinder and gave the contents of the ten-gallon soup pot on the stove an aggressive stir.

Priya stared at her middle child, speechless. On the one hand, she wanted to applaud her for taking initiative with the science fair project. On the other hand, she was determined to research boarding schools.

"Okay. But there is fluorescent green wax dripping on our floors and I expect you to clean it up." Priya took a deep inhale through her nostrils and let the air out slowly through pursed lips, just like the Calm app she used exactly once instructed. "Where's Vid?" As she asked, she peeked into the den, hoping to find her fifth grader doing his homework at the built-in desk. He had promised to get his work done before dinner, in a public place where someone could keep an eye on him. It was one of the many unfulfilled promises made by the three children in exchange for getting the dog.

"The Vid Kid is playing video games in the basement."

Priya sighed. It did feel like she and Dev had sentenced their child to a gaming addiction by calling him Vidya. She'd wanted to call him George—*The King's Speech* was her favorite movie—but both sets of grandparents would have had heart attacks if they didn't pick traditional Indian names.

Shockingly, an hour later, all three children were fed, the striated pot was soaking in the sink in soapy hot water, and Vid's uniform had been unearthed from under a pile of stuffed animals. The kids and Priya were on the couch watching some game show with Jane Lynch that Priya couldn't follow when Dev came through the front door.

The three children bounded up to hug him. What the hell? When she came home, all she had faced were demands, complaints, and a science project gone wrong.

"Dad, my stomach felt weird all day. I feel like I'm getting a virus or something." Vid took his father's hand and placed it on his forehead.

"Actually, that reminds me, I have this weird bumpy thing on the back of my leg. I need you to check if it's a tick." Asha pulled up the leg of her sweatpants.

"Guys, I'm also a doctor," Priya called out from the couch. She was still in her scrubs, but whenever she was around her family, the uniform felt more like it belonged to a janitor.

"Your mom's right, kiddos. I'm not the only MD around here." Dev blew Priya a kiss. He was in a dress shirt and dark slacks, and had his white coat folded in the crook of his arm.

Damn, he was handsome. He could still take her breath away, even after twenty years of marriage. When he wasn't operating, Dev worked in tailored clothing more suited to a corporate office tower than an antiseptic hospital. His persona matched what Dr. Hiroshi was seeking for the CMO job so much more so than Priya's, who often had a coffee stain on her scrubs and sleeping sand crusted in the corners of her eyes. She didn't understand why Hiroshi hadn't approached Dev about the open position. He reeked of management.

Dev poured himself a scotch and joined Priya on the couch. The children followed. Bela curled into the crook of his arm. Priya felt herself prick with guilt. Why did she ever resent this man, who was a loyal husband and devoted father, and who didn't disappear into his home office at night to watch porn and text his friends about sports? Was it because her kids treated him as an authority figure and her a lady-in-waiting? Maybe. But did she really want to diagnose imaginary stomach bugs or yank off ticks with tweezers? She saw enough disgusting things at work to last a lifetime. Let the kids go to Dev for medical issues. Lord knows they came to her for everything else.

"We know," Asha said in a singsong voice. "Mom is coming into school for career day soon."

"I am?" Priya wished she could have said that as a declarative statement, but if she had agreed to participate in the program, she must have been in a deep trance.

"Remember the Women at Work assembly at school? For Women's History Month." Asha rolled her eyes dismissively, her expression a gigantic *duh*. "If you bail, Ms. Alverton might hold it against me. I'm averaging an A-plus now."

"Why is there a Women's History Month and not a Men's History Month?" Vid asked, surprisingly engaged in the family conversation.

Dev nuzzled the top of his boy's head. "Because women, like your mom, are amazing."

"Because the patriarchy is alive and well and in order to assuage their guilt about it, men throw women a bone by giving them one-twelfth of the calendar year to celebrate their achievements." Priya's hands fluttered to her mouth. It had been a long day.

"Damn, Mom! Sing it," Bela said, doing a mock applause.

"You okay, honey?" Dev asked, looking at Priya with a puzzled expression.

"Just dandy," she said, fixing her gaze ahead at the television, where a commercial for *Wife Swap* was playing. How about *Life Swap*?

"Anyway, you have to make a poster and also they want a video of you at work," Asha said.

"And when is my homework due?"

"October eighteenth," Asha said.

"You just said it was for Women's History Month, honey." Priya lowered the volume on the TV. "That's in March, I'm pretty sure."

"Yeah, but March is busy with the musical and boys' basketball championships, so they just moved the women's stuff to wherever it would fit."

Well, if that wasn't on brand, Priya didn't know what was.

"October twenty-first is the weekend of my soccer tournament. You need to drive me to Hartford." Now Vid was whining.

"And when are you going to take me to look for a dress?" Bela chimed in. "Homecoming is three weeks after that."

October 21st was also the weekend of the Bellport reunion. If one weekend could have this many obligations, there was *no* way she could take on more responsibilities at the hospital. The calendar gymnastics alone would resemble an Olympic sport. Priya felt surprisingly relieved. The decision about the chief medical officer position was being made for her. And she could spare Dev's feelings altogether.

"Hey, Pri," Dev said. "What's for dinner? I barely had time for lunch today. Operated all day. Six-hour lumbar spinal fusion." Dev lifted his arms and, good Lord, was he flexing his biceps?

"Dev, we're going to have to figure something out for that weekend." Priya swiveled to address the man who often felt like a fourth child. "I'm not available."

Four faces turned to her in wonder. She might not be able to take the chief medical officer job, but there was something she could do.

"I'm going to my twenty-fifth high school reunion." With that, she got up from the couch and went to warm up leftovers.

BELLPORT ACADEMY
HOME OF THE JAGUARS

WELCOME BACK, CLASS OF 1997!

WHEN: October 21–23, 2022

WHERE: BELLPORT ACADEMY

WHY: IT WILL BE A BLAST

The Deets:

Friday night welcome reception—Gymnasium,
    6 p.m.—Attire—Dress like it's 1997 (grunge, baby!)

Saturday morning—"Back to School"—visit classrooms
    and tour facilities, say hi to your favorite teachers.
    Best part . . . no homework!

Saturday evening—Reminisce under the Stars—
    8 p.m.—Festive Attire

Sunday brunch—Farewell! Until the 30th!

RSVP: MelissaLevinLevine@gmail.com
Reunion Chair

4

-·:·-

Melissa

AFTER SHE CLICKED post, Melissa made the mistake of rereading the invitation she had just put on Facebook. *Deets*?!? And grunge attire? What was she thinking? She hadn't looked good in dark lipstick and oversize flannel even when she was younger. Her red hair and freckles made her look perpetually cute, and cute and grunge did not mix. Of her close friends, only Tara had been able to pull off Courtney Love. Priya's parents never let her dress in camo and fishnets and Suki was too sophisticated to fall victim to trends. She wore more timeless fashions paired with accessories her mother scored on steep discount from her modeling connections. Maybe she ought to riffle through her closet and start pulling reunion outfits, but no, it was too early in the day to agonize over wardrobe.

Melissa was stationed at her kitchen desk, the space she affectionately called central command. Cam knew not to muddle through her papers or so much as lift a ballpoint pen from her Georgetown mug. This was a tiny space all Melissa's own, normally the place she felt like her best self. But this morning, staring at the computer screen and regretting her word choice, she felt angsty. She made herself a cup of tea, mulling her endless to-do list. Cobbling together a weekend she would be proud to have her name attached to was not going to be easy with so little time and a budget even paltrier than her worst fears. She vowed not to kick in her own money no matter how tempting the decorations at Michaels were.

She lifted the class list provided by Giffords, the papers wrinkled and full of her handwritten notes. The school did not have up-to-date contact information for a sizable chunk of her classmates and Melissa debated paying Cameron fifty bucks to source them, but in the end she opted to dig them up herself. It was best to go into the reunion weekend armed with the maximum background on the attendees. Today was as good as any to jump down the rabbit hole of googling her classmates.

The names denoted with an asterisk represented fellow parents at Bellport, more families than she had realized. It brought Melissa comfort to know others hadn't strayed from home, either. Eighteen-year-old Melissa never expected to live three blocks away from her childhood home, but that Melissa also never expected she would marry Josh, have an only child, and be divorced before she turned forty. She hated coming across the double asterisk next to Josh's name where in parenthesis it said Cameron (senior); Madison (kindergarten).

She posted a follow-up to the Facebook invitation with a call for email addresses and within a few hours she had over fifty replies. Most were friendly, sharing contact information along with messages of, Can't wait! or Man, we're old!

Suzanne Valentine, a sweet, artsy girl with a voice that landed her starring roles in all the school shows, wrote: Very excited to come. I'm going to bring the whole family. Hope you and Josh are doing great! Melissa and Josh were among the three pairs of high school sweethearts to get married, and the only to get divorced thus far. Clearly their split wasn't common knowledge. Well, Suzanne would know soon enough.

Eventually bleary-eyed from copying over the addresses to an Excel spreadsheet, Melissa was about to call it quits when another direct message chimed. It was from Kim Konner, now Kim Fields. Hi Melissa! Can't wait for the weekend. Brad and I will be there. Might even bring the kiddos. Xo, KK.

Melissa felt her stomach flutter. Kim Konner wouldn't have so much as waved to her back in the day, and now she was hugging and kissing her, alphabetically speaking. Melissa felt renewed joy about her reunion job, even if it was a ton of work. People responded to power. Her PTA presidency even came with a designated parking space in the lot.

"Who's that?" Melissa startled at her daughter's voice. On Melissa's computer screen were pictures of Kim, images she'd studied many times in the past, but which filled her with satisfaction every time.

Kim and her husband, Bradley, lived in Bronxville, an affluent suburb in Westchester with windy roads and perfect Tudor specimens mostly hidden behind thick foliage, at least according to Melissa's Google Earth search. Bradley owned a sports agency and Kim was the stay-at-home mother to three children, each so attractive they looked reverse-engineered. Keeping tabs on the Fields family, rereading their wedding announcement in the *New York Times* and studying their vacation photos on Instagram, calmed Melissa. They weren't friends in real life, but Melissa had access to her day-to-day life in a way she never did back in high school. God bless the Internet. Most of the time.

"Nobody," Melissa said, snapping her laptop shut. "Just some girl I went to high school with. I'm contacting everyone about the reunion."

"Oh," Cameron said, unimpressed. "Can you make waffles?"

Melissa eyed the clock. It was nearly 9 a.m. As a senior, Cameron didn't have to go in until after first period homeroom so long as she logged in her assignments from the night before. As much as Melissa felt premature pangs of longing thinking of Cameron moving out next fall, she felt equally irritated by her presence when she wanted the house to herself.

"Waffles? You sure, honey?"

"Yeah. I'd make them but I want to review my French flash cards. Quiz today."

Melissa went to the fridge to gather the ingredients. Cam was on the precipice of chubbiness. Melissa knew from personal experience how much easier it was to get through high school with a lithe frame. Melissa could chart her social highs and lows as they inversely correlated to the number on the scale. It wasn't fair. It wasn't the way the world should work. Inner beauty was what mattered. And maybe things were changing, slowly. More companies were using plus-size models to represent real shapes and sizes. Fat-shamers were rightfully shamed. And still the sea parted for a woman with a great body. A body like Kim Konner's had been, and by the looks of Facebook, still was. And like

Kelly's, the woman who replaced her in Josh's bed, metaphorically speaking. Melissa had kept the house and the furniture. Thinking of these women reminded Melissa of the gadget she'd ordered from Amazon. She pulled it from the cupboard.

"What's that?" Cam asked as Melissa rinsed blueberries.

"A food scale," she answered matter-of-factly, drying the blueberries with a paper towel carefully and placing them one by one on the scale until she reached eighty grams. It was futile to hide her diet from Cam; they lived on top of each other. Melissa's rationale was that Cam wasn't going to get an eating disorder from her—that was far more likely to come from TikTok or a Kardashian. Considering that Cam discovered Melissa crying in the bathtub with an empty bottle of wine floating in the water after Josh moved out, this was only moderately dysfunctional by comparison.

"You know that's crazy, right?" Cam said, eyeing the scale.

Melissa shrugged. Perhaps she'd underestimated the minefield this would become. "I won't go overboard with it. I'd just like to lose some weight before my reunion. Not much." Thirteen pounds, six ounces, but there was no need to be vocal about it. Melissa was certain she would get there if she stuck to the Busy-Mom-Diet, a plan she found online. It involved drinking four cups of green tea a day and consuming no more than twelve hundred calories, six hundred of which had to be from fresh produce. Hence the food scale.

"Kelly says yoga is all she needs to stay in shape," Cam said, as though she were trying to aggravate her mother on purpose. She probably was. Teenagers were the devil's spawn.

"Kelly is also thirty. Her metabolism runs like NASCAR. Tell her to call me when she tops forty. Actually, don't."

"I'll just eat breakfast at school," Cam said, zipping her backpack.

Melissa silently groaned as she contemplated the rock and hard place that was mothering. If she encouraged her daughter to diet, she'd be condemned as overly critical. If she did nothing, Cam might keep tipping into consuming an unhealthy amount of junk food. You could put on five pounds in three days, but it took three weeks to take them off. Maybe Josh could deal with this. Cameron never seemed to find fault in what her father said or did, and while Melissa knew she should be grateful her daughter wasn't bitter about the divorce, Cam's loyalty to her father stung.

"Oookay," Melissa said, holding up the eggs she'd already cracked for the waffles. "By the way, we need to talk about college applications. I want to read your personal statement."

"Uh-huh. I'm busy today. This weekend. And I'll eat the waffles for dinner," Cam said. "Love you, Mom." A moment later the front door slammed shut.

And just hearing "Love you" was enough to piece Melissa's morning back together.

MELISSA WAS HORNY.

Two weeks had passed since she posted the reunion invitation to Facebook and her head was spinning. Everybody had questions. What was the dress code? Could she recommend local accommodations? Would there be vegan options? What was she, a travel agent? And while September was typically a slow month at the radio station, with her counterpart out and Melissa subsisting on twelve almonds and a half grapefruit for lunch, even approving purchase orders and rubber-stamping boiler-plate contracts was proving excruciating.

The smart move would be for her to stay at the office late to avoid the distraction of Cam buzzing around at home. Her daughter was in the habit of walking around with her arm outstretched, FaceTiming compulsively. Often Melissa was captured in less-than-flattering positions in the camera frame—with a green cucumber mask on, a tattered robe coming undone, or cursing at some burned chicken. Sometimes all three at once.

"Still here?"

Melissa looked up to find Raymond, the evening custodian, plodding past her cubicle with his supply cart. He had headphones on and was bopping along to something peppy.

"Yep," she said, dragging it out with an eye roll. "I'm going to get out of here, though." She reached for her coat. Earlier in the day she'd felt a stirring down below and there was no good reason she should ignore it. Which meant a text message to Ken.

Kenny Alpert was Melissa's fuck buddy. She met him on a dating app about a year ago. He was a nerdy accountant from Westin, a twenty-minute drive from Bellport, divorced and with a passion for his presidential bobblehead collection. He had two dogs, matching schnauzers that nipped at Melissa's ankles and sniffed her crotch when she went to his house, and three grown children he said were only in touch when they needed money. Melissa and Kenny went on three mediocre dates before they slept together. The three Don Julios on the rocks helped her to overlook his comb-over and terrible sense of style. To her surprise, he was fantastic in bed, notwithstanding the nodding head of Richard Nixon keeping watch from a shelf. Kenny was nothing like Josh, who, after four thrusts and a grunt, was finito.

Kenny was a pleaser. He spent more time in her nether regions in one night than Josh had in fifteen years of marriage. Not to mention he had the cock of a Thoroughbred. Never judge a penis by the pants covering it.

Still, they lacked chemistry out of the sheets. The moment they went vertical, all passion evaporated. Melissa was honest with Kenny that she didn't see a future for them after they slept together the first time. Kenny didn't ask for an explanation. It was obvious she wasn't the first woman to bring him this news.

"But . . ." she added, looking over at him in bed, studying his limp-but-still-sizable penis flopped to the side, its work done for the night, "I'd be open to continuing the physical part of our relationship."

"Yes," he all but yelped. "Me too."

It turned out that if you offered a man sex with zero expectation that he take you to dinner, it was not a hard bargain to strike.

Meet at your place in 30?

Kenny responded **yes** before she zipped the phone back in her purse. She could picture him scrambling now—gathering yesterday's tighty-whities from the floor and fiddling with his Sonos system, looking for the corny jazz station he always played when she came over. Funny that he still bothered, knowing she was a sure thing.

A half hour later, she was parked in front of Kenny's ranch. His Acura was parked neatly in the driveway. Its vanity plate, I ADD 4U, made her cringe like always. She left her car in the street illegally. It shouldn't be a problem. She was unlikely to be there for more than an hour. Cam would be expecting her, so she'd be expedient about her visit.

"You look amazing," Kenny said when he opened the door. She doubted this was true. One of the pleasures of this arrangement was that she didn't so much as have to wipe the lipstick off her teeth for Kenny to compliment her.

"Thanks," she said, moving into the house and resting her bag on the black leather sofa in the open living room. "Can I have something to drink?"

"Of course," Kenny said. "I have white, red, and beer."

"White wine would be great, please," she said, recognizing that each glass was eighty calories and would cut into her dinner allotment, but she was on edge and it was a trade-off she was willing to make. He returned with a bottle that had a neon price sticker attached. $8.99. She lowered her expectations.

In the distance she heard the schnauzers pawing at the door of the den. Last time one of them had chewed up her new pumps and she was grateful Kenny had put the dogs away. The music playing was different, too. She had made an offhand comment about not loving jazz and apparently Kenny took note.

Melissa sipped her wine, which wasn't half-bad, quickly and self-consciously. She wished he would join her, but suggesting that felt like it was pushing the boundaries of their situation. They weren't on a date. This was checking a pleasure box. And the clock was ticking. Cameron had already texted her twice about dinner (was she not old enough to make scrambled eggs?) and Suzi Felcher, vice president of the PTA, was anxiously awaiting the spreadsheet of last year's Fall Festival expenses.

"Shall we?" she said when the last of the Chardonnay was down her throat.

Kenny's bedroom was off the living room. He had a low platform bed that tested Melissa's back every time, satin sheets that tried about ten times too hard, and a vaguely pornographic poster of a woman that she avoided looking at when she was on the bottom. At her request, he had relocated the bobbleheads to the den, so at least there were no more White House inhabitants casting judgment on her.

"You seem tense," he said as he unbuttoned her blouse with one hand and slipped two fingers inside her with the other. He had moves she doubted were commonplace among accountants. There was a joke to be made about using digits well, but she couldn't quite think of it.

"I'm fine," she said, trying to summon the urge she felt earlier that had brought her to Kenny's house. Why couldn't she get in the zone?

She wondered if it was the reunion. It was occupying more than its fair share of her mental load. None of her friends had officially confirmed. Suki hadn't even called her back. Melissa couldn't face Josh and the rest of her classmates without her support system, and it was too late to turn back the clock and tell Dr. Giffords she was out.

"If you say so," Kenny said, removing his fingers and pushing inside her. Luckily this time she succumbed to the pleasure. Time stopped and Melissa felt her extremities come alive as a thin layer of sweat slicked her bare skin. They rolled around, taking turns on top, until they both came with forceful grunts.

"It was good to see you," Melissa said as she zipped up her skirt. The waistband was definitely looser.

"So good," Kenny responded, propped on his side like a centerfold in *Accountants on Call.* "By the way, I think you might consider moving some of your 401(k) into a Roth IRA. Give me a call at the office to discuss."

Melissa's first dalliance with Kenny was back in the spring, right before April 15th. She had had it with TurboTax and, in a moment of poor judgment, asked Kenny to be her accountant. His rates were fair, and after he'd seen her naked, it wasn't a huge leap for him to see her finances.

She nodded and looked at her watch. Their whole exchange—wine, sex, and a little tax advice—had lasted twenty minutes. She lingered a moment after her blouse was tucked in and her heels were back on. The reunion ticked through her brain. Should she ask him? She could make sure nobody saw his license plate by saving a "special" spot for him near the deliveries entrance in back.

"You got everything?" Kenny asked. "Don't forget your purse."

Ouch. He might as well have used a catapult to get her out. Forget the reunion.

"Take care now," Kenny said, flipping on his back and folding his hands under his head. Emptiness filled her, where moments earlier she was inflated with distraction.

"You too," she said, and skittered out of the room.

When she was behind the wheel of her car, Melissa bit her lip to stop the quiver. A tear bulged behind her left eyelid; she wanted it to be allergies. She didn't have feelings for Kenny. *She told him* she didn't want a relationship. Why should his nonchalance unravel her? She looked at his vanity plate once again before driving off. Kenny was not worth getting upset about. At least she didn't have a parking ticket. This encounter wasn't worth writing a $35 check to municipal court.

She flipped the satellite radio to the nineties channel, aptly playing "Wake Me Up When September Ends." The Green Day song couldn't have captured her mood better.

"Cam," Melissa called out when she walked through the front door. She wondered if she looked like sex. She took a second to smooth the coitus from her skirt.

There was no response.

Melissa flopped onto the couch with her phone, which had just dinged. A part of her expected to find a text from Kenny asking when he would see her again. But it was a message from Josh, responding to her third reminder to pay the deposit for the senior class trip to Washington, D.C., planned for the spring. She saw **LEVINE HOMEBUILDERS** signs all over town and Kelly lived in designer loungewear plastered with labels. There was no reason he should be dawdling. **On it**, he wrote, and she relaxed. She was about to respond *thank you* when she saw he was still typing. **Really cool you're chairing the reunion . . . I know it will be great.**

Blurgh. Why did she get a thrill in her stomach just because Josh said something nice to her? She didn't want him back. But she still wanted him to want her back. Human nature was a beast.

Melissa decided to give Suki another try. She thumbed through her contacts until she got to *Suki: Assistant 1*. When Assistant 1's line went straight to voice mail, Melissa tried Assistant 2. She pictured these two women as Thing 1 and Thing 2 from Dr. Seuss, blue-haired and in red jumpsuits, taking naps in rotation as they tended to Suki's every need. Cam used to love those guys. "Can we get a Thing 2, Mommy?" she used to ask, which Melissa thought was her way of asking for a sibling. Maybe Melissa ought to be impressed Suki didn't have three or even four assistants. MakeApp traded on the New York Stock

Exchange, had five thousand employees and offices in every major city.

"Suki Hammer's line, this is Tracy."

Tracy. Which meant Assistant 1 was Stacy. She remembered
that Suki's assistants' names rhymed, but she had been so sure
earlier their names were Hannah and Anna.

"Hi there, it's Melissa Levin-Levine calling for Suki. I left a
message the other day with Assis—Stacy."

There was a brief pause.

"Yes, I have that in my notes. Can I tell Ms. Hammer what
this is regarding?"

The chyron running in Melissa's mind read: *I used to be one
of her best friends and I just want to fucking catch up with her.*

"Sure. It's about our high school reunion. It's the weekend of
October twenty-first and, well, I'm the chair and I would love
for her to come."

"October twenty-first, you said? Let me just check her calendar." Another pause. "Let's see. She's meant to be in Las Vegas
presenting at the Billboard Music Awards, and then she needs to
be in New York City for the Glamour Magazine Powerful Wom-
en's dinner on the twenty-first. We have Asia penciled in the
following week. And then I imagine she'll need us to schedule
some time with her children in between and—"

Melissa interrupted. "Can you just tell her that I called?" She
hung up before Stacy/Tracy could say another word.

The front door creaked open, and Melissa heard Cam tread
inside and drop her backpack.

"Who were you on the phone with?" Cam called out. "You
sounded pissed."

"I was trying to reach Suki," she said, bracing herself.

Predictably, Cam came charging.

"OMG. You have to let me talk to her next time. Do you have any idea how many people use MakeApp? It's, like, getting more popular than TikTok, I swear."

MakeApp, Suki's billion-dollar idea, was an application where a user could upload a photo of any celebrity, from a magazine or a screen, and the app automatically applied their makeup look to the user's profile picture. From there it was one click to order the products along with a link to video instructions on how to apply them.

"I believe you, honey. But we didn't connect today. How was school?"

Cam bit down on her bottom lip and Melissa snapped instantly into mama bear mode. Most of her daughter's issues at school were of the garden variety, but occasionally something more sinister was afoot. It was up to Melissa to have her antenna finely tuned enough to parse the difference.

"It was fine. The usual." But Cam was fiddling with the string of her hoodie. Melissa needed to tread lightly. Cam clammed up if she sensed a firing squad.

"Ready for dinner?" Melissa asked, her voice lilting. She hated that food was becoming a source of weirdness between them.

"Nope. I ended up eating with Dad and Kelly. Madison tried squash soup for the first time. She's the pickiest eater so this was a really big deal." Cameron flopped down next to Melissa on the couch.

"She asked me to tell Auntie Mel and show you pictures," Cam said, without a trace of discomfort at the fact that her half sister gave Melissa the nickname Auntie Mel. Everyone just ate it up, oohing and aahing over how cute it was. It *was* cute. And Madison was adorable. So Melissa tolerated her lispy voice saying, "Hi,

Auntie Mel," whenever they ran into each other. It wasn't like she wanted to explain their actual relationship to the five-year-old.

Melissa studied the pictures, ignoring Madison because she was focused on whether those were new countertops in Josh's kitchen. It looked like he'd replaced the speckled gray Silestone with a thick-veined white and gray marble, while her kitchen cabinets were chipped and falling off the hinges. Cam pulled the phone back as soon as a text message appeared on-screen. Heaven forbid her mother should see a single piece of communication she received. Melissa rose to make herself a salad.

"Holy shitballs. Isn't that Priya's daughter?" Cam was suddenly next to her at the kitchen counter, holding her phone under Melissa's nose.

Melissa squinted to focus on the curvaceous teenager in a string bikini posed provocatively in front of a mirror. Melissa recognized Asha, Priya's eldest, in the Instagram post. Melissa knew her friend would die if she saw this. Asha and Cam were about the same age. Melissa had access to all of Cam's social accounts and surreptitiously monitored them. She could imagine that Priya was asleep at the wheel when it came to stuff like that, buried at work and oblivious to any dangers her daughter might get up to, considering her own virtuous adolescence.

Should she tell Pri? It was like those hypotheticals her friends used to play when they went for Moms Night Out. *Would you tell me if you saw my husband out with another woman? What if you saw my kid doing drugs?*

"Oy. That's Asha. Don't you go posting things like that." She watched Cam make a *duh* eye roll, as if she weren't one ill-fated crush away from sending a naked photo to a boy. "Anything else going on? A lot of homework?"

"This is a little awkward, but I need to tell you something," Cam said.

Aha! A mother's instinct never failed.

"I saw Kelly's email open on the laptop in Dad's kitchen. You know her friend Liza, with the twins who play lacrosse? Anyway, Liza basically told Kelly in the email that she's planning to run against you for PTA president. Said you're 'overcommitted' and that it's not fair that you've been in charge for so many years. She called it a dictatorship."

"Did she now?" Melissa asked, her jaw going slack. Seriously? Now she was the Fidel Castro of Bellport? She'd barely given the election any thought. It was the week after the reunion and she didn't expect to have to do anything beyond put her name on the ballot.

"Yeah. I felt bad telling you but . . ."

Melissa patted her daughter's knee. "Never feel bad telling me stuff. We need to be honest with each other."

"Cool," Cam said, her load visibly lightened. She bounded upstairs and Melissa knew she wouldn't see her until morning. She hadn't expected Cam's apprehension to have anything to do with her. Melissa took a moment to appreciate her daughter thinking about someone besides her herself. It was a teenage miracle and deserved appropriate recognition.

Melissa started on her salad. She took a heavy-duty steak knife and sliced even tomato wedges on a cutting board, falling into a rhythm.

Good luck, Liza Jones, with your late yearbook dues and a car that looks like it hasn't been washed in a year. May the best woman win.

5

Tara

"ARE YOU SERIOUS?" Tara said, shifting her laptop so Rachel could see it. In the process she knocked over her half-full coffee mug, milky brown liquid skidding across the table and onto the floor. "Cooking fucking Cuties."

"It's going to be okay," Rachel said, bending over to read the fine print as Tara went for paper towels. "Their location is far worse than ours. They're in that basement of the smelly church where the elevator is always out of service."

Tara stared hard at Rachel. "How would you know anything about Our Lady of Grace? You're not Catholic. Aren't you—weren't you—Baptist?"

"I . . . I . . ." Rachel looked down at her fingernails, painted purple with avocados on them. She invested heavily in nail art, de rigueur for millennials.

"You knew about this and didn't tell me," Tara said. "That is really not okay. I could have sent out our winter semester registration forms earlier or spoken to the parents."

Tara was seething. Rachel had obviously known that a rival company was opening in the same neighborhood and yet she had to stumble upon the news when a banner ad flashed on her computer screen.

"It doesn't matter. Kitchen Kiddos is an established business. People aren't going to just drop off their kid at some new place no one's ever heard of. I bet they're going to use peanuts in a recipe the first week and get picketed by parents."

It was a seductive thought, but Tara highly doubted it. Everyone knew not to bring peanuts around children these days. A lesser-known allergen, though . . . maybe sesame?

"Whatever," Tara said. She was pacing the room, her breath coming in shallow bursts. She was carrying her laptop, studying the Cooking Cuties website. "Did you see they are listing the farms where they are getting their produce from? They are using one hundred percent nongenetically modified ingredients. We are finished. Pack your shit, we're moving to Jersey."

Rachel raised an eyebrow. Tara knew she was being overly dramatic. Her parents sent her enough money each month to sustain what they considered a safe and appropriate lifestyle in New York City. Doorman building in a nice neighborhood, no subway after dark, groceries from Whole Foods. But taking money from her parents came with strings attached and the dependency was hitting Tara harder with the reunion looming. If her business flailed, her attachment to her parents' purse strings would only deepen.

Last week, beat down by Melissa's persistence (daily texts!), Tara promised she'd go to the reunion. Now she wanted to renege. Why bother returning to Bellport? To brag about her mediocre after-school program that mainly serviced parents who didn't want their kids home until 5 p.m., soon to be outshined by a competitor? Even if she inflated the success of Kitchen Kiddos, because everyone was likely to pad their accomplishments by at least 20 percent, it would elicit the same old question: *And do you have children of your own?* She'd respond *No* as flatly as possible, and then an awkward silence would dangle while the other person waited in vain for Tara to add, *Hopefully soon.*

"We're going to be fine. I promise," Rachel said. "I have a lot of ideas for the summer camp. And I was thinking for fall we could try indigenous cuisine classes for the teens. It would look good on their college applications. Let's make a list of ideas later. I'm going out for a jog."

Rachel pulled off her top and reached into the laundry basket for a sports bra. She was about to slip it overhead when Tara stopped her.

"Wait."

Tara pulled her into their bedroom, positioning them in front of the full-length mirror attached to the closet door. She pulled off her Kitchen Kiddos sweatshirt and unhooked her bra, a front-clasped granny underwire.

"Now?" Rachel bit her lip seductively. "I guess I can put off my run."

Tara shook her head. Rachel was entirely misreading the spontaneous stripping. She studied the reflection of their four breasts lined up. Rachel's were like helium balloons at a children's birthday party, ready to take flight. Tara's were shaped like sandbags that could double as paperweights.

"Unbelievable. We're ten years apart and . . . and . . . and . . . this." She gestured wildly at their reflected images.

"Will you stop?" Rachel said, wriggling away and securing her buoyant breasts with a jog bra. "You look amazing. And, by the way, if we have a kid, my tits will fall way worse than yours. We can sag together. Now cheer up and stop worrying about your boobs or Cooking Cuties."

"Whatever. By the time you're back from your run, there will probably be a Flambéing Five-Year-Olds or Chopping Children or Baking Babies opening up shop."

Rachel threw a balled-up pair of athletic socks at her. "Seriously? Those all sound like places where people eat children."

"I have more. Taco Toddlers. Small Bites."

"I'm leaving," Rachel said with an exasperated head shake, slipping in her AirPods to drive the point home that she was done with the conversation. And Tara hadn't even asked her if she preferred Hoboken or Jersey City.

Alone, Tara let out a guttural groan. Was she being a grinch? Her mother had commented on Tara's moodiness. After their last phone call, Susan sent her overpriced yoga pants with a note that said: *A brisk walk can really lift the spirits!*

An idea occurred to Tara now.

She snapped a selfie of herself topless, her breasts flopping to the sides like opposing magnets. She sent it to her mother with the message: I know one thing that could give my spirits a "lift." She and her mom could go in together for the procedure. Susan Taylor did not believe in keeping one's original parts. Even her secondary parts needed tune-ups.

Tara knew better than to believe lifting her breasts an inch would be enough to change her mindset. Maybe Rachel was contributing to her malaise. Tara felt like the perpetual party pooper next to her endlessly optimistic girlfriend, who still had energy and a wide-eyed curiosity about New York City. Barely thirty, Rachel wanted to go to speakeasies and see drag queen shows in Williamsburg. Tara turned into a pumpkin at 9 p.m. and was happy to watch HGTV. Rachel was also the nearest scapegoat. The Zoloft Tara started taking after leaving California a decade ago wasn't helping; how could Rachel be expected to outperform an SSRI? Perhaps no woman could make her happy. Every one of them she dated failed in a major way. They weren't Suki. If only she would come to the reunion, it would give Tara something to look forward to, at least in the short term.

But Suki wouldn't commit. Even Melissa had backed off claiming she was coming. MakeApp was making a brick-and-mortar play and there were flagships opening all over the world, which demanded Suki be there to cut the ribbons.

Tara wondered what it would feel like to attend the reunion if she were as successful as Suki. Would she relish her classmates fawning over her, with stories of visiting her bistro in San Francisco or her trattoria in Chicago? Or would she deem the whole concept of a reunion beneath her? It was hard to say. And because she wasn't a superstar, it was irrelevant.

Tara pulled up her most recent text exchange with Suki.

I hope you can make it! We all miss you! Tara wrote.

Me 2 u, Suki wrote. Just "u." *You, you, you.*

Tara could ask Suki for business advice. Certainly others had attempted to copycat MakeApp's success, and there was a reason Suki's was a household name and nobody talked about Celeb-Blush or StarPowder.

Tara's phone dinged. She hoped it was Suki reading her

mind, but it was just her pharmacy notifying her that the latest addition to her pharmaceutical cocktail—Ambien—was ready for delivery.

Bernie came into the room and settled at her feet.

"You'll always love me, right, Bern?" Tara said, bending to nuzzle his golden fur.

The assorted blankets on the bed, a mix of cotton, sateen, and a fuzzy mohair throw, teased her. She imagined how it would feel to slip underneath them, Bernie at her side. Her therapist said she should be out as much as possible in the daylight, as though if enough vitamin D seeped in, there would be no room for sadness. And she would get outside. But first she had to check something.

Tara woke her laptop and typed in the URL for Ricky's latest prime-time cooking show, *Blazing Burners*. She'd searched the site so many times that it autofilled after pressing only the B. The latest news was that Ricky was launching a podcast called *The Lazy Chef*. That would bring him to two shows, a full product line, five restaurants, and now a podcast. He had emerged from the scandal unscathed—hell, better than before. The world ate up Ricky's version of events: "I'm not a perfect man . . ." "I have strayed in my marriage, but I love my wife of forty years very much . . ." "I did not do these things that are being said about me."

She snapped the laptop shut. She had to focus on the here and now. Which meant checking out Cooking Cuties in the flesh.

Thirty minutes later, she was in the basement of Our Lady of Grace. Though she wasn't religious, Tara crossed herself when she passed the chapel. She nearly collided with a tall, gangly man wearing a T-shirt that said LETTUCE TURN UP THE BEET.

He was carrying a wooden crate filled with oversize, beefsteak tomatoes that Ina Garten might have birthed herself.

"Are you here for pickup?" he asked. "Caregivers are expected to wait in the lobby."

"Um, no," she stammered. "I think I dropped something earlier. Just looking around."

He shrugged and moved past her.

Unfriendly staff, she noted.

Alone again, Tara inched forward to peer through the glass pane into the classroom. The children were on step stools and seemed to be actively engaged in spreading mashed avocado on heart-shaped slices of toasted bread. Her knees buckled. Avocado toast was a universal crowd pleaser. These folks weren't messing around. She pulled out her phone to snap a photo for Rachel.

The door swung inward and Tara nearly fell into the classroom.

"Matilda, hold your pee-pee. Hold your pee-pee, my love. Remember what Mama said. You can have any toy you want at the store if you don't have an accident today."

Tara chuckled to herself, making sympathetic eyes at the woman exiting the classroom. She looked vaguely familiar. Could she be a Kitchen Kiddos customer already sleeping with the enemy? Her first Benedict Arnold. But the kid, Matilda, wasn't familiar, and Tara knew all the students' faces like the back of her hand. She also had their allergies memorized as well as their preferred spots at the counter and their unique deficiencies when it came to measuring ingredients.

"Sorry, do you happen to know where the bathroom is?" the woman said, holding the toddler precariously under her bum. "This is our first class here."

"Um, I'm sorry, I don't. I've never been here before," Tara stammered. Where did she know this woman from?

"Okay, I've got to find it, excuse—" But as the woman moved to pass Tara, a stream of liquid trickled down the little girl's legs and puddled on the grimy floor.

"Oh my God, did she splash you?" The mother was plainly horrified. Indeed, a small amount of urine had ricocheted from the floor onto Tara's pants. "You have to let me pay for dry cleaning. Wait, hang on a second." She lowered her child to the ground as her eyes twinkled with recognition. "Are you Tara Taylor?"

So, they did know each other. It clicked for Tara a beat later. "Lauren Wilson. Volleyball player. Bellport class of 1997. How the hell are you?"

"Good, I mean—hang on a second." Lauren tried to maintain normal eye contact with Tara as she crouched on the floor and fished through a purse the size of a carry-on suitcase until she found sanitizing wipes. When she'd finished mopping the floor, she continued.

"I'm okay. Matilda is my fourth. She was a bit of a"—she covered the little girl's ears—"surprise."

Tara nodded her understanding.

"Do you have kids that take classes here?"

"No, I . . ." What should she say? She was not a liar. "I actually own a competing business called Kitchen Kiddos. I guess you could say I was doing a little reconnaissance."

Lauren nodded with a smile. She had a poppy seed in between her front teeth. Tara edged back and subtly gave her a once-over. Lauren's yoga pants were a faded black and covered in fuzzy pills. There was a milk stain on her shirt and her copper hair had a half inch of gray roots. It was hard to find any trace of the competitive athlete she had once been, tall and muscular and an animal on the court.

"I'd say the bathrooms are too far from the classroom, but this is really Matilda's issue. Anyway, we will definitely check out Kitchen Kiddos. I have to say, Tara, you look amazing."

Tara flushed with appreciation.

"We would love to have Matilda," Tara said. "And her siblings." And cousins and friends and anyone else who could keep the business afloat.

"Now that I think about it, I think Matilda's whisk had a dried booger on it."

"We are booger-free," Tara said. "The cooking tools, at least. The noses are a different story. Take this." She produced a business card and placed it in Lauren's palm.

"Are you going to the reunion?" Lauren asked. "I'm so excited. My mom is watching the kids. I cannot wait for forty-eight hours of no one calling me Mom. Actually, my eldest is a nasty tween and calls me Lauren. But you get the idea."

"I'm not sure that—" Tara started when Matilda interjected.

"Mommy, remember when you had diarrhea and you said we had to leave you alone and that we could use the iPad as much as we wanted? But then you never really let us? Can we do that tonight?"

Lauren looked as though she wanted the earth to swallow her up whole.

"Honey, we don't talk about bathroom stuff outside with other people, remember?" Lauren looked back at Tara, her cheeks redder than the Elmos on Matilda's underpants. "I'm so sorry, Tara. She's normally so . . . actually, she's always like this. Diarrhea of the mouth. And, yes, pun intended."

"No worries. As you can imagine, I've seen and heard it all at work."

Lauren laughed appreciatively.

With the earnest way Lauren asked about the reunion, it was clear that she was not aware of what happened to Tara at the fifteenth. Or forgot. Which meant perhaps it hadn't been as big a deal as Tara thought.

"I am going," Tara said. She ought to do this for Melissa. Priya would show, too; she always did the right thing. And Suki? That shouldn't affect her decision. What happened between them was a lifetime ago. There was even the distinct possibility that Suki didn't remember. They had both been drunk. Tara could imagine Suki telling Graham, her husband, about the time she kissed a girl. *Who,* Graham would say? *I can't even remember,* Suki would respond.

Tara patted Matilda on the head, said goodbye to Lauren, and walked back home with purpose. She was strategizing outfits, imagining the conversations she would have with her peers: *Oh, I run a business in the city . . . Thanks, I just exercise and avoid the sun . . . Why, thank you, you look the same, too . . .*

"Good day, Ms. Taylor?" one of the older doormen who worked in her building asked as he started the revolving door.

"Yes, I guess it is," she said.

"Think that's you," the doorman said, eyeing the ringing cell phone in her hand.

Her father's number was on the screen. Dear Lord, let him not have seen the picture she texted her mom.

"Hey, Dad, what's up?"

"Tara, I need to make sure you have no intention of attending your reunion."

6

— :· —

Priya

LIKE A MIGRAINE, the weekend of the reunion arrived without warning.

The volume of things Priya still had to get done in order to leave her family for a measly two nights was staggering. At least three times she considered canceling, only because from a purely mathematical perspective, there was very little way to justify this much preparation and angst for a weekend that was far more likely to be awkward than pleasant. But she couldn't let Melissa down, and the thought of peeling away from her house *alone* on Friday afternoon was so delicious it propelled her forward. That and the six cups of coffee she'd had.

But, as was typical, it was one step forward and two steps back. Instead of being at work early to catch up on paperwork before rounds, she was at her mother-in-law's house, delivering groceries in a severe windstorm. Dev's mother, Jeet, was a spry seventy-two-year-old perfectly capable of driving herself to

Bombay Market in Fairfield to stock her own pantry. But she insisted that Priya do it for her every two weeks, claiming that driving made her hips stiff, never mind that she did a belly dancing class at the senior center three times a week. Priya was sure it was just another way for Jeet to insert her influence into her marriage, to remind Priya that even though she had a career, family should always come first.

"You look tired," Jeet said as they unpacked jars of tamarind paste and bags of roti. Priya lifted the heavy sacks of rice and emptied them into glass canisters. "You have bags under your eyes. Also, you look pale."

An hour of pushing past Indian grannies fighting over the basmati delivery could do that to a person, is what Priya wanted to say. Jeet pulled two brown maple leaves from Priya's hair.

"I am tired," Priya said instead. "Dev snores." It thrilled her to criticize her husband to his mother, even in the most attenuated form. She could never say to Jeet that he wasn't a perfect father or an incredible doctor. But having a deviated septum, that she could accuse him of.

"Probably because you are serving him too much dairy. It clogs the sinuses. I'll make him a turmeric drink that will bring down inflammation." Jeet pointed to a high shelf in the pantry where the blender was stored, indicating for Priya to get it down. For a tiny, elfin woman, she spoke with the authority of a war general. "Go to the couch. Actually, bring some Darjeeling tea to Ba. It will take me just thirty minutes to brew something for Dev."

"Ma, I can't wait here for a half hour. I have to get to the hospital." She was already running late, notwithstanding the grocery detour. Bela had forgotten to ask her to proofread an essay until that morning as they were scrambling into the car, Vid had misplaced his math binder, and Asha had come downstairs carrying bedsheets covered in Wiggles's vomit.

Just two months earlier, they'd expanded their overwhelmed, overcommitted, barely functioning household with a rescue cocker spaniel. The school psychologist suggested to Priya and Dev that a family pet might help Vid learn responsibility and distract him from video games. Priya could wring the guy's neck. *License in social work, my ass.* Wiggles turned out to be more work than colicky triplets. He didn't sleep through the night, pissed everywhere, and according to the vet, probably needed a hip replacement. And Vid did nothing to care for Wiggles other than scratch his belly, which he did while playing video games. Dev was no help, either. "Surgery," he would say the moment Priya looked at him around a walk time. It wasn't clear if that meant he had to leave to perform a surgery at that moment or whether the fact that he performed surgeries exempted him from puppy duty.

Priya couldn't really blame her husband for his entitlement. With his mother, it was impressive he could wipe his own ass.

"Ah, yes, Dr. Agrawal. Very busy always," Jeet said, frowning slightly.

Priya blew raspberries with her lips. She was just about done.

"It's Dr. Chowdhury. Remember? I use my maiden name professionally."

Jeet pursed her lips. "Of course, how could I forget? You are an independent woman."

You just did forget, lady. But, no matter, Priya just needed to get out the door and into the car.

"I'm sorry but I really can't stay. Bye, Ma. Always nice seeing you. Tell Ba I said hello." Priya gestured to where Dev's father was sitting on the back porch, staring at the fall foliage. Though he had advanced dementia, Jeet refused to put him in a home, not trusting anyone to care for him but herself and an aide she watched over vigorously. Jeet supervised as the aide massaged lotion into Papa's cracked heels, often bending down herself to show that it should be done in counterclockwise, concentric circles. She ought to cut her mother-in-law more slack.

"Fix your hair before work," Jeet said, reaching up to smooth strays that had escaped Priya's bun. "It's a mess."

Maybe Priya would cut her slack starting tomorrow.

AT THE OFFICE an hour later, Priya felt calmer. She liked sitting at her desk, swiveling gently in her ergonomic chair while reviewing patient files and toggling over to her guilty pleasure, the *Daily Mail* website. She was obsessed with the royal family. *RIP Princess Diana*, she thought with a disheartened head shake. *The Meghan-Kate squabbles are a disgrace to your legacy.*

Clicking through photos of Fergie's newest granddaughter on a walk at Windsor Castle, Priya found her thoughts returning to the reunion. In less than twenty-four hours, Priya would be back on campus, encountering the ghosts of her youth. Melissa had organized a spectacular program, and on Saturday the class of 1997 would have a chance to return to the classrooms and see their old teachers—many of whom were still there—and learn about the curriculum's evolution and the integration of the latest technology. From visiting her own children's school, a fancy private school in Woodbridge where half the children had parents on the Yale faculty, Priya already knew that chalkboards, hall passes, and paper attendance slips were a thing of the past. But it would be different to see it at Bellport, the building where she had logged hundreds of hours in classrooms, in the labs, and in the library.

Would she have the guts to enter the chemistry lab? Priya wondered this as she chewed on a pen cap, a nasty habit that returned when she was on edge. Would a magnetic force bring her there against her will? To the third row of lab counters where she would lie down on the cold floor and imagine she was back where she was twenty-five years ago. The recollection made her shudder, her body flush with goose bumps and the sense that molten lava was flowing through her veins.

"Dr. Chowdhury, your eleven o'clock is in Room Three," Nurse Robbins said, poking her head into Priya's office. She snapped back to her present responsibilities, a welcome reprieve from the hurricane of her thoughts.

After a follow-up with one of her whinier patients, a retired schoolteacher who complained about every muscle and joint in her body but refused to take her meds or stop playing tennis, Priya headed to the cafeteria for a cup of black coffee. It was her seventh of the day, but who was counting? Returning patients were easier, but they lacked the challenge new cases presented, firing up her neurons to solve a puzzle. The human body was like a jigsaw puzzle to her; only with her regular patients, she'd already put it together.

She fist-bumped her favorite cashier—Vid taught her that move; it had the effect of endearing her to anyone under the age of thirty—and sat at a table by herself to enjoy the caffeine and quiet. The cafeteria, normally a dizzying swirl of white coats and mint scrubs and anxious visitors who took an eternity to make their selections, was quiet before the lunch rush. Again her thoughts traveled to the weekend ahead. Was this where she thought she'd be twenty-five years after graduation? On paper, absolutely. She was a doctor, a wife, and a mother. She'd checked the three boxes she'd drawn for herself, on schedule and in the right order. So why did she feel uneasy? Was it that while she had succeeded by objective metrics, she had not defied anyone's expectations? That was for sure. The hardworking child-of-immigrants doctor, married to another doctor. It had never bothered her before, but the reunion was forcing a whole lot of "taking stock."

Maybe it was just the logistics of being away and she was confusing apprehension with dread. The family schedule she tacked to the refrigerator was color-coded and organized down to the hour, and still she knew it would elicit confused calls. And heaven knows what would happen to Wiggles. What a fool she had been to believe her children would take care of a puppy. Their faces had been so earnest, eyes pleading and shiny, that she believed they would pause YouTube to feed him. The whole notion that she'd have a child-free weekend was laughable. Just because they weren't physically there didn't mean they weren't *with* her.

"I heard Dr. Chowdhury is up for chief medical officer," came a male voice from behind her. The voice sounded young, likely belonging to a resident.

"Yep. She's Hiroshi's first choice. I saw the list on his desk when I was in there for a meeting. That guy is so old-school. I don't think he can use a computer. He literally had a handwritten list on his desk that said, 'Choices for chief medical officer,' and Chowdhury was number one." A different male voice, also youthful, filled Priya's now-burning ears.

"She's fine. I did rotation with her a while back. Sucked at explaining things. And her cell phone buzzed like ten times while she was leading grand rounds. But we know why she's top of the list, obviously." Priya recognized the third voice, female, immediately. It belonged to Dr. Cutler, a dermatology resident who had been particularly annoying as she followed Priya down the hallway during rounds, asking pointless questions just to suck up.

"Double diversity, baby," came the first voice again, who Priya now recognized as that of Dr. Miller, a frat-boy surgery intern who had a reputation with the nurses as a dirty-dick lothario.

"Yep," Dr. Cutler said. "Female and brown. She's a shoo-in, all right. A two-for-one pick."

Priya wanted to turn around and say something incredibly biting, but instead she felt her body folding like a fan and a hot tear roll down her cheek. She didn't move from her spot until she heard them get up from their table. Her coffee had turned bitter and cold and she tossed it into the trash, not caring that the backsplash hit the tiled white walls.

LATER THAT NIGHT, back home and her spirit depleted, Priya washed her face, removed her contacts, and rubbed in three layers of face cream by rote. She climbed into bed next to Dev, who was reading a medical journal with his tortoiseshell readers on. He looked ridiculously good in glasses, but she could see he was as exhausted as she was. She tried to remember how hard he worked, sometimes rising at 4 a.m. to prep for surgeries lasting upwards of six hours, when she silently cursed him for not helping more around the house. He sliced patients open almost every day, faced their insides while they were induced into a powerless sleep by drips in the arm, and faced the pressure that one wrong nick or cut a millimeter too deep could paralyze somebody. These were pressures she did not face in her job.

With the residents gossiping about her promotion offer, there was no way Priya could put off telling Dev. She should have officially declined the job weeks ago when she made up her mind, stopping the chatter before it mushroomed into hospital fodder, but she kept finding a different excuse every time she went to turn down Hiroshi. Now, though she was about to pull the plug, she still had to tell Dev lest he hear about the offer from someone else.

She had her weekend bag packed, resting on an armchair, but she tried to avoid looking at it. Priya felt guilty enough leaving. Especially on the heels of what she was about to say. But first, logistics. Amateurs talk tactics, mothers logistics.

"I'm sure you saw the schedule I put on the fridge," she said, hoping to summon Dev's attention before he drifted off to sleep. "And obviously just call me with any questions." *As if he would hesitate.*

Dev put down his journal and looked at her with a smile.

"Don't worry. Just go and enjoy yourself."

"Thank you." She fiddled with the strap of her nightgown.

"There's something else I wanted to talk about." Priya sat up in bed and he instinctively placed a hand on the inside of her wrist. He liked to feel her pulse, not in a clinical way, but as a means of connection. She shivered under his touch. When was the last time they had sex? Maybe it had been a month. It wasn't for lack of desire, at least not on her part. It was that by the end of the day the effort to brush her teeth sometimes felt like too much work. She and Dev ought to go away for their anniversary in the spring. Jeet could watch the children. Wiggles could be boarded for a few nights. There were a lot of things that ought to be done, but after the musts were taken care of, the oughts were all too easy to set aside for a later date.

"What's up?" ᴠ slipped off his reading glasses and Priya preciate how soulful his brown eyes looked, was tired.

She gathered a fistful of blanket and used it to dry her clammy hands.

"Dr. Hiroshi offered me the chief of medicine post." She didn't add that this had occurred a month earlier.

"Wow," Dev said. He looked genuinely surprised, and she was relieved this was the first he was hearing of it. "Of course he'd want you."

Of course he'd want you? What was that supposed to mean? That she was a superb doctor with fewer complaints on her record than most others with her experience? That she was beloved by the nurses and clerical staff and the residents actually found her approachable? That she was organized, dependable, and had the kind of egoless personality that would gel with management? All those things were possibilities, and accurate when Priya took the time to give herself the credit she deserved, but what if Dev meant something else entirely? What if he meant the same thing that had been said about her in the cafeteria?

She was hesitant to pry. If she suggested that Dev wasn't

happy for her, it would come off as petty. And without evidence. There were dozens of Indian girls whose mothers had offered them up on silver platters to Dev. Girls far more beautiful than Priya, with aspirations only to make a lovely home for Dev that might even include his parents living with them. But he'd chosen her, asking her for coffee during their first year of medical school, the two of them bent over a cadaver reeking of formaldehyde.

"Well, what do you think?" Priya asked, feeling like there wasn't just one elephant in the room, but a whole stampede of them. Dev's hand was no longer on her wrist. And her pulse, that beat Dev liked to feel, was now racing.

"I think it's madness to even consider taking the job. All you do is complain that you're exhausted and overwhelmed and don't have two minutes to yourself. How could you possibly consider adding to your burden when you're already spread so thin?" Dev almost sounded angry that she hadn't already told Hiroshi a flat-out no on the spot. And was that really how he heard her? As a whiny harpy? She did complain a lot, but if she didn't, would anyone even realize how hard she was working? Women did volumes of silent work, and the only way to earn any recognition for it was to be loud about it. She carried a mental load the weight of a ten-car pileup.

"Yeah, you're right," she said, softly but curtly, and climbed out of bed. She had so many feelings coursing through her body that the only thing she knew for certain was that this wasn't the moment to react. She was angry at herself, at Dev, at the patriarchy, at the residents, even at Hiroshi. "I forgot to pack a sweater for the weekend," she mumbled, stepping into their shared closet. Priya leaned into the wall of her neatly lined doctor's coats, each one embroidered with her name in red thread on the pocket, and cried silently into the sleeves.

Her tears having run dry, she reached for her cell phone, charging on the built-in dresser. She scrolled to Hiroshi's contact information.

> Thank you so much for this incredible
> opportunity. I am so flattered by the
> trust you have shown in me.

Priya took a deep breath and sat another minute in silence. Dev's snoring trickled through the closet door.

> Unfortunately, I will not be able to
> accept.

To: Melissa, Pri, Tara

Girls! I'm so bummed but there is no way I can make the reunion. Work is CRAZY (but good!)!! I want a million live updates and you better FaceTime me. Miss you SOOOO f-ing much.

xoxo S

CC: Assistant 1

7

-:-

Melissa

SUKI'S EMAIL WAS hardly a surprise.

Melissa tried not to let it dampen her spirits when it arrived the Friday afternoon of reunion weekend. The last-minute notice begged the question of whether Suki had actually been trying to come or if she was just putting off letting them down. Fortunately, Melissa was far too busy trying to tie the waxy laces of her Doc Martens to dwell.

In happier news, Melissa had reached her goal weight, even dipping a few pounds below the number she'd set as a target back in September. It turned out grapefruit, black coffee, and blueberries was a highly effective diet, if you didn't mind raging heartburn and poops that came out as liquefied bombs.

Cameron had begged to do her makeup and Melissa wearily submitted to her daughter's artistry. She nervously tried to sit still as Cam powdered, lined, and swiped her face. When Cam placed a mirror in Melissa's hand, she gasped. Her daughter had transformed her into a redheaded Liz Phair. The look was more becoming than she would have imagined, the thick black stripe on her eyelid bringing out the green in her eyes and the dark purple stain on her lips making them appear fuller.

"You're good at this," Melissa exclaimed, wondering briefly why Cam didn't bother to put on makeup if she had this talent.

"I got all the products from MakeApp. I uploaded a picture of you and some nineties models and, voilà, I got a whole kit of makeup and directions. Christy Turlington was really pretty. Have you heard of her?"

Had she heard of her? Melissa spent the four years of high school striving for Kate Moss's weight, Christy Turlington's cheekbones, and Claudia Schiffer's glow.

"Oh, I used your credit card. I hope you don't mind." Cam leaned closer to line Melissa's lips with a darker purple pencil.

Why should Melissa mind? She was already in credit card debt, paying a ridiculously high APR each month to keep her credit score respectable.

"It's fine," Melissa said. She felt too good about her appearance to get angry. "But next time ask me in advance. Suki will send us the products for free."

"You. Are. Joking." Cam's jaw went slack. "You're just telling me this now?"

Melissa nodded, taking a sip of her coffee daintily so as not to smudge the lipstick. "Why do you care? You don't wear makeup."

Cam took a step back. "I do. I just keep it natural-looking. That's what Kelly says looks best on me."

Melissa frowned. Kelly was also supposed to help Cam get

in shape with yoga, but there hadn't been much progress on that front. Now she was giving her makeup advice that only worked if you had naturally tawny skin, bright eyes, and well-defined features. Cam was beautiful, but in certain lights and when she didn't get enough sun, she could resemble Josh's mother, a Hungarian balabosta who brought the boys to her yard with tasty goulash more than her looks.

"Voting for senior superlatives in the yearbook started," Cam said, apropos of nothing. She fiddled with the loose knob of Melissa's vanity table.

"Oh, that'll be interesting," Melissa said neutrally, though she was sure her daughter was as nervous as she'd once been.

Melissa worried Cam could be overlooked. If she'd made her mark on Bellport Academy, Melissa didn't know how. There was the Environmental Club that Cam founded last spring. So maybe Most Likely to Join Greenpeace? Though the club had gathered only once to clean a local park and disbanded after someone claimed they spotted a needle in the grass.

"What was your superlative when you graduated?" Cam asked.

Melissa tensed, though Cam's question was more of an afterthought. She was already glued to her phone, gyrating as she tried to copy a dance better suited to a stripper pole. Cam's entire generation lacked self-consciousness. It sounded like a good thing, but it often wasn't.

"Oh, who can remember?" Melissa finally said. "It was ages ago."

She looked at her watch. Her friends would be arriving any minute. Go time.

. . . .

MELISSA COULDN'T CONTROL the big goofy grin on her face when she saw her friends step out of Priya's car. They had both come through big-time on their costumes. Tara, who a month earlier needed coaxing and a dash of fabrication to attend, was dressed as Uma Thurman's character in *Pulp Fiction*, black cropped pants, crisp white button-down, and the pièce de résistance, a pin-straight black wig with a fringe of bangs.

Priya was wearing a replica of the yellow and black checked suit that Alicia Silverstone had worn in the movie *Clueless*, down to the white kneesocks and patent leather Mary Janes.

"Girls," she squealed, rushing outside to envelop them in hugs. "You guys are amazing."

Priya laughed, bringing her saucer-like dimples to the surface. "It was actually fun to do this. I watched *Clueless* with Bela and she admitted that nineties movies were actually not that bad. We got halfway through *Misery* before her friend texted about something called a "sneaker drop" and she went poof. But she and Asha did a great job putting this outfit together for me. You can get anything on eBay."

Melissa turned to Tara. Something was different about her, aside from the getup.

"Did you get your tits done?" The words flew from Melissa's mouth before she could claw them back.

"Oh my goodness, I've been wanting to ask that since I picked you up from the train," Priya said. Two sets of eyes trained themselves on Tara's rack.

"Can we have this conversation inside, please?" Tara pleaded.

"I did," Tara said once they were standing in Melissa's foyer.

"But it wasn't meant to be obvious. Just needed a little pick-me-up. I was going to do just a lift, but the doctor convinced me to get an implant at the same time."

"They are subtle," Melissa said, moving in for a squeeze. They were firm, like summer peaches. Produce-wise, her own were week-old bananas. She had only one kid, but, man, had Cam sucked the living daylights out of her chest. "But obviously we were going to notice. I mean, you and I have been having sleepovers together since we were twelve. Priya changed your tampon for a week when you broke your arm. I'd say we're better acquainted with your body than most. They look great. Rachel like 'em?"

"Sure does. I'll be sure to tell Dr. Mann you approve of his handiwork. You ready for tonight, Mel?" Tara could only be referring to Melissa having to spend the evening in the presence of Josh and Kelly; she could hardly be doubting her competence at pulling off an event. "For what it's worth, you look fantastic."

Melissa twirled. Now it was her turn to show off. "I did a little pre-reunion dieting. The makeover is courtesy of Suki's app; Cam did it. I was at school all day setting up and I've already instructed the bartender to give me heavy pours all night."

"Right there with you," Tara said.

"I assume Kelly will arrive in a onesie and carrying a rattle, seeing as she was *born* in the nineties."

"Melissa," Priya said, her tone didactic. She could be a bit holier-than-thou sometimes, with her refusal to disparage Kelly. Melissa felt a sudden urge to call Cam downstairs to show Priya the skimpy images of Asha.

"You've had a real glow-up, Mel," Tara said, defusing the tension. She elbowed Melissa playfully in the ribs. It was unfamiliar having a visible collarbone and protruding ribs; she felt a bit like a skeleton in an anatomy textbook.

"And you had a blowup," Melissa said, pointing at her friend's enhancements. They all burst out laughing.

"Let's have a drink," Melissa said, linking arms with her friends and moving them into the den, where she had a bottle of tequila and a plate of limes waiting. Their chain fell short, the missing link an iconic, spunky billionaire probably crossing the Atlantic in her private jet at the moment, her high school memories feeling every bit as far away as the thirty thousand feet she was from the ground.

As if reading her mind, Tara said, "I wonder what Suki would have done with the theme. She escaped most of the nineties trends, except for when she got obsessed with Drew Barrymore and wore daisies in her hair."

"I remember Mac Miller was allergic and kept sneezing during history, but Suki wouldn't take them out," Melissa said.

"She would have done something fabulous, I'm sure," Priya said, surprising Melissa when she seized the bottle of Patrón and poured herself three fingers' worth. Melissa joined her, but with a gentler first pour. She squeezed lime into the drink but skipped salting the rim. There was no sense in bloating just before the festivities kicked off.

"Tar, you never told us why your dad didn't want you to go to the reunion." Melissa suddenly remembered a cryptic text from Tara saying she wasn't *allowed* to go to the reunion, followed up by a message the next morning that reversed course.

Tara knocked back her first sip. "My dad had gotten a call from Dr. Giffords out of nowhere. He said they're taking his name down from the athletics center."

Melissa's eyes widened. The George and Susan Taylor Athletics Center was a focal point on campus. George Taylor, who played football for Bellport Academy in the sixties, had donated a hefty sum to build it when they were freshmen. The garbage shed in the back was a known place to smoke up, and over the years the stench of marijuana had inured itself to the walls of the entire facility. Kids called it Taylor, never the athletics center, and getting high outside at 4:20 p.m. was called Tayloring. It was hard to imagine it going by any other name.

"Really?" Priya said. "They're tearing it down?" She used to complain that the athletic facilities were nicer than the science labs.

"Apparently some guy from *our* class donated twenty-five million dollars to rebuild it. It's getting ripped down and, Pri, you'll be happy to know, in its place will be a state-of-the-art science and technology center, with a greenhouse, an organic farm, and a university-standard research lab."

"Giffords must be psyched. Though I can't imagine he was happy about calling your father." Melissa couldn't believe she didn't know about this. Normally her ear was so close to the ground that if a teacher was going out on maternity leave or a kid got suspended for vaping, Melissa knew before Cameron.

Tara shrugged. "I guess it's hard to turn down twenty-five million dollars. Even my dad backed down after a day. His lawyer looked over the original gift documents and there was really nothing to be done."

"Who could it be?" Priya asked as both she and Tara turned to Melissa.

But Melissa honestly had no clue. And she thought she had done such a thorough job researching the class of 1997.

Emily Poster, who swore she made out with Matt Damon at the club Limelight, had expensive clothes and a nice-house-in-the-suburbs kind of money, thanks to a chain of organic yogurt shops she founded. But certainly not big, fat, bold-letter-name-on-building money. Richard Gable had donated a few hundred thousand dollars five years ago to refurbish the auditorium, but rumor had it his ex-wife got the lion's share of his money after their divorce. There were others in their class with lofty private equity and tech jobs, names that were googleable for this and that, but still no one stood out as capable of such an extraordinary gift. Except for—but no. It couldn't be.

"They'll announce the donor's name tomorrow at the class dinner. I'm just assuming it's a man," Tara said.

"It's always a man," Melissa said, and the statement thudded among them like a lead balloon.

"What if it's Suki?" Priya said. Their heads cocked to the side in tandem as they contemplated what was the most likely explanation, the one Melissa had just considered but dismissed. "But, then again, wouldn't she have come to the reunion?"

"They might announce her name as the benefactor and have one of her minions make a speech on her behalf." Melissa could imagine the scene. Either Assistant 1 or 2 smashing a shovel into the ground while a jumbotron blasted Suki's face from Dubai or Hong Kong or Geneva.

"Guess we'll have to wait for tomorrow," Melissa said, still stinging from being out of the loop but unwilling to let it ruin her night. "Ya know, Cam asked me the other day what my high school superlative was."

"Do you have our yearbook here?" Tara asked. "After my mom turned my room into a Peloton studio, I haven't been able to find any of my old things. Weirdly, I wanted to find my troll dolls."

"I do." After Cam's probe, Melissa had stealthily moved the yearbook from its spot on the bookshelves in the den to the drawer of her night table. "I'll go grab it."

She returned with the book and put it on the coffee table. The three of them hunched over it, the crowns of their heads touching. They had done this once before, bent over the yearbook, albeit with a fourth head.

"I feel like we're studying," Priya said.

"Of course you would," Melissa said, but her tone was all wrong. She meant only that Priya was naturally studious and seeing her slender neck curved over a book reminded Melissa of their library days.

"Look at Suki," Tara squealed, pointing out their friend dressed in a furry cat costume. *Cats* was the spring musical their junior year. The theater nerds had lobbied for *Rent*, but the PTA quickly nixed the idea. A musical about AIDS, sex, and drugs was too much of a stretch for the argyle sweater sets calling the shots. "I remember this. She wanted to play Mimi but ended up playing Macavity."

"Flip to the superlatives," Priya said. "Maybe we can figure out who the donor is. Though I don't recall Most Likely to Donate Mega Bucks as a category."

"Even if it were, it's not like the superlatives were such great predictors." Melissa hoped she didn't sound as bitter out loud as she did in her head.

"Most Likely to Open a Michelin-Starred Restaurant," Tara read her own aloud. She was wearing an apron in the photo, working the annual bake sale. "More like most likely to be sexually assaulted by a misogynistic chef and have her reputation destroyed."

"Mine's not much better," Melissa said. "Most Likely to Win the White House? I am president, but of the PTA." She guffawed, staring at the picture of her wearing a VOTE MEL OR GO TO HELL pin. How in the world had that gotten past the faculty advisors? "Pri, yours is close. Most Likely to Cure Cancer."

"I'm not an oncologist. I'm a physiatrist, the ugly stepsibling of the orthopedist. I deal with morons who get into motorcycle accidents and old ladies who pull muscles in water aerobics."

"At least you're a doctor." Tara and Melissa said variations of the same thing at once.

Melissa sensed the yearbook bringing a heaviness to their gathering, their unreached potential like a rain cloud forming overhead. This downward spiral simply wouldn't do. She needed levity now. Her smile when she walked into the gymnasium tonight had to be thousand-watt.

"Look at Suki, though. She did it for real." Melissa emphatically tapped the spot where it said *Suki Hammer: Most Likely to Join the Forbes 400*.

Melissa slapped a hand down on the table. "It's not too late for us. It can't be! What if we did a challenge for ourselves— something we work on together? We try to fulfill our superlatives. We keep each other accountable. Support each other, give advice. Remind each other of our worth and potential."

"You're going to be president next fall? It's not even an election year." Tara gave Melissa an incredulous head shake.

"No. But I'm going to do something in politics. Do you know that I have been planning a takedown of some lacrosse mom who wants to run against me for the PTA? I've had the job for eight years. Who the hell cares if someone else wants it? Let her have it. It's decided—I'm going to do something way more exciting."

"And I—" Priya started to stay, and then bit down on her lip like it was going to run away from her face.

"Yes?" Tara and Melissa said in unison. Was Tara as desperate as she was to find out that Priya's life wasn't superlative spectacular?

"I was offered a huge promotion at the hospital but turned it down because there was no way I could handle the kids and any more responsibility at work. Dev says all I do is complain." She took a large gulp of her drink.

"Wow," Melissa said. She wasn't quite sure how to react. Dev surely could help more. He spent at least an hour a day on the damn Spelling Bee. Just that morning he texted Melissa to see if she'd cracked the pangram. And he certainly listened to his share of podcasts. The man needed to multitask. Put in AirPods and grab a load of laundry. It wasn't rocket science.

"Me next. A competitor business opened a few blocks from Kitchen Kiddos and they're using all this non-GMO, free-range, artisanal, locally sourced crap that the parents are going to eat up." Tara said. "I'm pretty sure there's not much demand for a washed-up middle-aged chef that hasn't worked in a real kitchen in years, so if it's a Michelin I'm after, I'm better off buying a tire."

"Enough," Melissa said. "We are doing this." She lifted a lime and squeezed a healthy drop onto a plate. "Lemons into lemonade, people."

"That's a lime," Tara said. "Not to get all professional chef on you or anything, but . . ."

"Limeade. Whatever." Melissa's voice broke a little. "Guys, I need this. Please. We really can change things. Together."

"You know what? I'm in," Priya said, slamming her highball on the table. It was hard to take her seriously dressed as Cher Horowitz, but her voice was strong and determined. If anything, she was more Elle Woods announcing that she was applying to Harvard Law School. "I'm going to call my boss and tell him that I want the job after all."

"Fuck it, I'm in, too," Tara said, pushing up the sleeves of her white shirt. "Back to *making* ratatouille instead of just watching it on Disney."

"Great!" Melissa was ecstatic. She eyed her watch with renewed verve.

"Guys, I think we better go. Bottoms up." The three of them lifted their glasses and clinked. It was the sound of hope. "To becoming our Most Likely selves."

A SHORT CAR ride later, Melissa was standing in the center of the gym admiring her handiwork. She had sent Priya and Tara to the lobby to ensure the name tags were alphabetized after the question of how to arrange hyphenated last names sent a hostess from the catering company into a tizzy.

"I don't remember any Carly Tucker. Who is that?" Tara called out through the double doors to the gymnasium. Bellport graduates had white name tags with blue borders, their guests had red borders.

"Charlie Tucker, that kid whose parents owned the travel agency. He's now a she," Melissa explained, looking up from the clipboard where the evening's playlist was printed. "Get back to work, T." She shooed her friend out the door.

Melissa eyed the DJ in his booth. Per her request, he was dressed like Joey Fatone from NSYNC, down to the shredded jeans vest and frosted tips. She tapped the face of her watch to indicate showtime was approaching, and he flashed her a thumbs-up.

Melissa had worked very hard on the playlist. The number one song in 1997, which Melissa and her friends would belt out off-key riding around town in Tara's Mazda Miata, was Elton John's "Candle in the Wind." But that was way too dramatic and depressing and would certainly send Priya into a tailspin. She made them hold a vigil at the town playground the summer Princess Diana passed away. Priya's royal obsession hardly dovetailed with her bookwormy brain, but maybe that was the case for all of them. They weren't one thing. They were complex fucking humans.

Instead of Elton, the DJ would fire up "Believe," as in "Do you believe in life after love" by Cher, when Melissa gave him the signal. The song reminded her of Josh, but the tempo was up-beat, and ultimately all songs were either about being in love or getting dumped, and there weren't many choices that would both hit the nostalgia note and get people dancing. The "Macarena" was being saved for later in the evening once everyone was lubricated and ready to jump into a line dance.

Everything looked to be in place. The decorations, balloons, and small floral arrangements in the school's colors were arranged tastefully on highboys. The registration tables, where thankfully Priya and Tara were up to the Zs, were being manned by current Bellport seniors volunteering to check people in. Melissa was particularly proud of the name tags. Besides having first and last names printed in a large font—after all, they were of reading glasses age now—she had included senior portraits.

In her yearbook photo, Melissa's hair was in braids that hugged her scalp and she wore a black lace choker around her neck. Her face was so much fuller then, thanks to the bags of Cool Ranch Doritos she would share with Josh. "Were we really this ugly?" Tara asked, fastening her name tag to her button-down. Her breasts were so buoyant that the tag sat perpendicular to her chest. In her yearbook photo, Tara wore nearly black lipstick and a dog collar with spikes. Her brush with goth coincided with the senior portraits. Her parents took away her Nokia 8210 for a month when they realized.

"You were never ugly," Melissa said. She turned to Priya. "You either." But Priya wasn't listening. She was staring at her phone with an exasperated expression.

"Poop bags are in the garage."

Priya looked at them. "Sorry, voice dictation texting." She was the most unchanged from her senior picture. Her parents had never let her have a grunge phase beyond flannel shirts, so long as they were tucked in, and she still dressed conservatively today, wearing her hair in the same shoulder-length, no-nonsense ponytail that had been her go-to since forever.

"Should we call Suki?" Tara asked. "This shindig isn't starting for another ten minutes."

Melissa felt fresh irritation at her friend's absence. She didn't need the rejection of Suki's voice mail or to listen to hollow rambling about how much she wished she could be there.

"No time," she said. "I have to make sure the coatroom has

enough hangers." Melissa marched off in the opposite direction and ducked into the girls' bathroom. In the smudged mirror above the sinks, she gave herself a once-over. The bathrooms had not been touched in decades, and Melissa was sure this was the very same mirror where she stood back to check her l.e.i. jeans and baby tee ensemble, reapply her MAC Stone lipstick, and pull two strands of hair to hang in front of her face like seams on a pantleg. She remembered the dozens of times she dried her nails at the clanky radiator after painting them with Hard Candy polish.

Her makeup was intact, despite the sweat she'd worked up hauling boxes of customized napkins and dragging folding chairs from the storage room. If she was feeling more charitable toward Suki, she would have texted to compliment the quality of her products. Though she couldn't see her full outfit reflected—teenage Melissa and friends used to jump up and down to see their full selves—she was still feeling confident. The Doc Martens she found online gave her a nice lift, her black dress fit like a glove, and Cam had applied a faux rose tattoo to her arm that was subtle enough to raise the question of whether it was real or temporary.

A brief flash of panic hit suddenly. What if nobody else came in costume? The anxiety hit her bladder, and she ducked inside a stall to pee.

Melissa's nail snagged on her fishnet as she hiked up her dress, but luckily the rip was on theme. She sat down on the toilet and heaved a gigantic sigh. The inner walls of the stall were covered in scribbles, which Melissa scanned as she nervously peed twice. *Amy Bollo is a dyke. Scott Templeton has one nut. Ricky Roth is a cocksucker.* Melissa cringed at the cruelty of high schoolers. She was surprised this type of graffiti still existed when kids could easily, and stealthily, be assholes over Snapchat.

Melissa touched the inside of the stall lightly and felt the layers of paint caked on. Decades of insults underneath coats of mint green shellac. When she stood up to wipe, her eye caught a thread of text that made her sink back down. *Cameron Levine is a loser.* It was hardly the worst of the insults, but the message infuriated Melissa. Thank goodness she had decided to bring a Sharpie in case they needed to create extra name tags. She dug it out from her purse and drew thick, angry lines to cover up the message.

ABOUT AN HOUR into the event, a lost hoop earring in the style of a nineties J.Lo sent Mariel Winter into a tizzy, forcing the DJ to cut the music so that a few hundred middle-aged, moderately drunk attendees could get on their hands and knees to look for it. Mariel was famous in high school for claiming her older brother was in the Waco cult; now she would be famous for sending half the crowd to physical therapy.

The earring turned up in Mariel's own wineglass fairly quickly, raising some eyebrows about whether it was genuinely lost to begin with. Other than that, the first event of the reunion weekend was flowing seamlessly. Melissa's fears were for naught; the Bellport class of 1997 brought it when it came to the costumes. Around the room there were two Monica Lewinskys in blue, one with a partner dressed as Bill, a number of Rachels, Phoebes, and the other Monica, three Kurt Cobains, and an Andre Agassi balancing a drink on his racket. Amanda Major, now a top gallerist in Miami, fashioned an outfit out of Delia's catalogs. Kim Konner and her groupies were dressed as the Spice Girls, managing to be a clique even in costume. Melissa didn't mind their exclusivity, because they could have just as easily thumbed their noses at the idea of dressing up. Naturally, Kim was Posh. Carrie Sackler, Kim's most faithful follower, was Baby Spice. She had her hair in butterfly clips and was carrying a rattle.

"I just saw Ginger Spice puking outside," Priya said, approaching Melissa with an appletini in hand. "Which is ironic because ginger is good for nausea. And why is Ethan Anderson dressed in bell-bottoms?"

"He's Matthew McConaughey from *Dazed and Confused*. Which, yes, is a seventies movie but apparently came out in the nineties."

Turnout was solid. Almost every name tag was snagged from the registration table, and the inclusion of the senior portraits made for the perfect icebreaker. Melissa had to admit the pictures were not only funny, they were useful. Many of her peers were unrecognizable. The men, for the most part, had bigger bellies and sparser hair. The captain of the football team, once a hulking swell of pure muscle, was now as wide as he was tall. Rob Parker, Bellport champion debater who went on to work in Obama's speech-writing office, formerly cute in a nerdy way, now looked like he hadn't seen sunlight in a decade. Lawrence Bott, who everyone suspected was gay in high school, was flashing pictures of a girlfriend "in Canada" on his iPhone.

The women were a mixed bag. Some trended down into saggier versions of their teenage selves. But others had swanned themselves completely. Louisa Paulson, a math geek who was the type of girl people always referred to as mousy, had cashed in on Wall Street and clearly channeled her earnings toward self-improvement. She flounced into the reunion with a head of blond highlights, a figure crafted by a precise combination of SoulCycle and Pilates, and high heels that read as expensive even from across the room. Kim Konner was proving that, for a lucky few, once a beauty meant always a beauty. She looked like a more sophisticated, polished version of her high school self, even dressed as Posh Spice in a leather mini dress and strappy heels that crisscrossed her legs to the knee.

"Uh-oh, Melissa, three o'clock," Tara said, approaching Melissa and Priya at the bar. Melissa's ex sauntered into the gymnasium. He was Josh 2.0, new and improved flavor, sleeker design, and more user-friendly. In a narrow button-down that hugged his muscles and slim jeans resting on trendy neon sneakers, which admittedly he was pulling off, Josh was sure to cause their peers to do a double take. And, Jesus Christ, had he spray-tanned? He was glowing like a firefly.

"What the—" Tara started to say, gesturing to Kelly, but Melissa had already figured it out.

"She's Julia Roberts. From *Pretty Woman*. My husband's new wife came to the reunion dressed as a whore."

"Technically she's done whoring when she wears the red dress," Priya said.

"Cliché much? Pound the Propecia, get a new wardrobe, and complete the look with a new wife," Tara said, wagging a finger in Josh's direction.

"So true. I'm sorry, Mel. You deserve better." Priya rested a hand on Melissa's back.

Melissa nodded but said nothing. Even her best friends

didn't know the truth. That she'd brought this situation on herself. She'd encouraged Josh to lose weight. She'd found the hair transplant doctor. She'd suffered through him taking out his Invisalign at every meal until his teeth looked like a line of Chiclets.

Josh's makeover was spawned by Melissa's feeling a sudden itch, her loins finally waking up after a long nap. Cam was eleven. She no longer needed constant watching over and more and more she spent nights out at sleepovers. Melissa, for once, didn't feel like she had MOM painted across her forehead. She suggested to Josh they "experiment." What she meant was that they watch porn or go to a strip club on Josh's birthday, maybe a little role play. But it was a Pandora's box. Each new thing they tried raised the stakes for what they both wanted. As Josh got more and more handsome, his body morphing into that of a high school quarterback, his teeth straight and gleaming, Melissa felt her grip on him loosening.

"We should do a threesome," she said one night when they were on the couch watching TV. It had been three weeks since they'd had sex and she had been waiting for him to pounce, but it was crickets in the bedroom.

That got his attention.

"With who?" he asked, suddenly ignoring the action show he'd been engrossed in moments earlier.

"My yoga teacher. She's adorable. Super young. And up for anything." Melissa had shown a picture of Josh to Kelly after vinyasa class one day and she'd said, "I'd do him." It didn't sound purely hypothetical, either. Kelly was a free spirit. She wouldn't be hard to convince.

Fast-forward to three months of ménage à trois-ing once a

week. At first Josh seemed worried about Melissa's feelings, making sure she was included, that he never had both his hands on Kelly. But as time wore on, Melissa would find that for large stretches of the lovemaking, she was left in the cold, staring up at the ceiling listening to Josh and Kelly moaning. She felt like broccoli on a plate of steak and french fries, only there because it made everyone feel better about the meal, but ultimately scraped into the trash.

"Let me get this over with," Melissa said, sucking in her stomach and quickly coating her lips with an extra layer of gloss. She pulled her friends in Josh's direction and drew strength from The Plan. Soon enough, she'd be a politician. A real one. And Kelly would still be adjusting people's behinds during downward dog.

"THIS WAS TOTALLY awesome," Tara said to Melissa. They were the last two guests; only staff remained resetting the room for the next day's festivities. Priya had driven back to Melissa's house a half hour earlier, calling it a night after receiving a frantic call about Wiggles eating a full tube of toothpaste, contents and packaging.

They were standing by the trophy case in the school lobby, Tara with her black leather jacket in the crook of her arm. She was stifling a yawn, the kind that came at the end of a good night. "I ordered an Uber. Want me to drop you? Not sure how much you had to drink. The Long Island iced teas were a nice touch, but they were way stronger than the ones we used to make at my house."

Melissa hadn't touched one. They had to be at least six hundred calories. She'd stuck to tequila, neat.

"No, but thanks. I'm going to stick around to help clean up."

"Okay. Love you." Tara kissed her on the cheek and Melissa squeezed her elbow gently.

"Thank you so much for coming."

"I'm really glad I did, actually. Nobody mentioned Ricky and it was worth coming just to see Zoe Wintshell in those pearls. I think her husband had two argyle sweaters wrapped around his neck."

Zoe Wintshell was terrifyingly goth in high school. She had a tongue ring shaped like a screw that she would play with in class. If you looked at her the wrong way, she would remove it and pretend to jab you. Her earlobes had holes stretched to the size of a quarter and her hair was striped like a skunk's. But she showed up to the reunion dressed like a Stepford wife. At first there was chatter that it was a costume. Was she supposed to be Reese Witherspoon in *Election*? But somebody's dive into her Facebook quickly circulated confirmation that she owned a mommy-and-me clothing store in Charleston, South Carolina, and was vice president of the local Junior League.

"Ha. I'm still processing that the chess club came dressed as the Backstreet Boys. Simon Cohen looked surprisingly good. Kee-Won Park, though. I don't ever want to see his jeans under his ass again," Melissa said.

"Totally. Anyway, don't stay too late. You must be wiped. I'll see you in the morning."

Melissa motioned for Tara to skedaddle. She *was* exhausted and dying to remove her clunky Doc Martens, which felt like ankle weights by this point in the night. The last thing she wanted to do was break down highboy tables and stack folding chairs, but it was not in her nature to leave the work to others. Besides, she had another reason for hanging behind.

Be right back, she motioned to the catering captain.

Melissa turned down the hallway toward the girls' bathroom. All night what she'd seen written about Cam bugged her. She worried she hadn't entirely obscured the message with the Sharpie. And what about the other stalls? She needed to inspect those as well.

Melissa pushed open the door to the bathroom.

"Oh my God," she said, the marker in her hand dropping to the floor.

In the right-most stall, the door open, Carrie Sackler was on her knees giving Kim Konner's husband a blow job.

"Shit," Carrie and Kim's husband said in unison, scrambling to collect themselves.

"Oh my God," Melissa repeated after she stumbled outside the bathroom.

"You okay, Melissa?"

Dr. Giffords appeared next to her. His tie was undone and his bloodshot eyes made it plain that he'd visited the bar a number of times throughout the evening.

"I'm good," she squeaked out.

"You did a great job," he said. "I knew you were the right person for the job. The only person, in fact. I should have asked you months earlier." Giffords was slurring, but the alcohol was acting as a truth serum. She could probably find out who the donor was, but she was too rattled by the scene she had just stumbled upon.

"About that," Melissa said, feeling like she was on national TV, about to hand over the Miss America crown from her head. "I'm not going to run for PTA president this year. Let lacrosse mom whatever-her-name-is have it."

"Really?" Giffords was clearly taken aback. "What's next for Melissa Levin-Levine?"

What was next? Not the White House, but something worth her brains, energy, and gumption.

"I'm going to be mayor. Of this town."

8

-;-

Tara

TARA FLEXED HER feet in bed, replaying the events of the night before. She had to hand it to Melissa. Her friend had put together a wonderful evening. The costumes and name tags had pierced the inherent awkwardness and the DJ's playlist was spot on. Janet Jackson's "Together Again" was still buzzing in her head, making her smile as she caught the double meaning. She didn't know why she had panicked about attending. Nobody so much as gave her a second glance, other than to compliment how striking she looked with dark hair or to jokingly ask her to do the twist. Ricky DiMateo was long forgotten, or at least her peers were too focused on themselves to dwell on what happened ten years earlier. It helped that word spread about the twenty-five mil donation, and speculation about who the donor was carried the buzz all night.

She popped out of her childhood bed, wedged in the corner of her old room behind a Peloton and a Pilates reformer, and made her way downstairs for breakfast. Melissa had offered Tara the guest room in her home, but Tara knew her parents would be insulted if she didn't stay with them. This was yet another downside of being on the dole. She had little margin to piss them off.

"Morning, darling. How was last night?" Susan Taylor was posed at the kitchen table, thumbing through a *Vogue*. Susan was the mother who unironically wore silk robes and slippers with tiny heels at home. The click-clacking around the house was useful in high school, giving Tara ample warning to flush a joint down the toilet before her mother barged in. Tara looked down at her own faded T-shirt and plaid pajamas pants and frowned.

"It was nice," Tara said, studying the spacecraft-like coffee-maker her parents must have installed recently. She missed the bodega coffee in the city, dark and aromatic, extra delicious drunk from a paper cup.

"What did everyone wear?" Susan asked. She removed her reading glasses and studied Tara's chest. "They look good, by the way."

Susan had always been more friend than parent. She loved the high school gossip, thrived on knowing who was popular and who was dating whom. Susan would have preferred a daughter more interested in perfecting cartwheels than a duck pâté en croûte, but when cooking proved Tara's passion, Susan bought Le Creuset pots and flew over a young cooking teacher from Paris to live with them for a summer. Little did Susan know that the gorgeous and sexy Chef Michel put more than Roquefort in Tara's mouth.

Tara fidgeted with her pajama top. "Thanks. Melissa did an amazing job. The decorations were beautiful, and the food was actually good." Tara knew these were not the details that interested Susan, but she wasn't feeling particularly indulgent.

"Hi, pumpkin," her father said, entering the room in golf attire. George liked to hit the links before eight on Saturdays. "You have fun last night? Still can't believe that bastard Giffords is tearing down my building."

Tara blanched at his wording. Her father seemed to miss the point of philanthropy. He viewed the athletics center as an extension of his own brand, not unlike the way he viewed his children. Both of Tara's brothers worked for him at his mortgage securities firm. Tara's chef aspirations appealed more to George than Susan initially—having a foothold in hospitality, secret numbers to score hard-to-get reservations, could work to his advantage. But when her success wasn't immediate, George lost interest in what he came to call her "hobby."

"Well, I'm glad you got over it enough to let me go to the reunion." Tara regretted saying "let me go," as though she were a teenager granted a curfew extension. She took her first sip of coffee. Good God, it was glorious. She would never look at her bodega coffee the same.

"How's the business going?" George asked as he poured himself a large glass of the freshly squeezed orange juice their uniformed housekeeper prepared for him every morning. "You haven't sent me the financials in a while."

"It's great," Tara lied. "We're super busy. Might even open up a downtown location."

"With what capital?" George asked, though she could see he enjoyed knowing that an expansion meant her coming to him hat in hand.

Tara ignored the question. Her back was to him as she poked through the refrigerator.

"Was Suki there?" Susan asked. She was fascinated by Tara's childhood friend, whose face often graced the pages of the fashion magazines Susan treated as holy scripture.

"No. She's in Dubai. Or Malaysia. I can't remember what she told us." It was obvious who "us" was. Melissa, Tara, Suki, and Priya had been a squad since freshman year, and since Tara's house was by far the nicest, it had been the default hangout. They lived on the Long Island Sound—you could see clear to the water from almost every room. The home could be a metaphor for Tara's parents. The house was sizable—a reasonable real estate agent could round up to ten thousand square feet—but it showed its size from side to side with relatively little depth.

Susan nodded, clearly let down, and produced an emery board from the pocket of her robe. The grinding made Tara jumpy.

"If she needs investing advice, tell her to call me." Tara's father was warming up his golf swing by taking drives through the air. "I'd be happy to get that book of business."

"Uh-huh," Tara mumbled, with zero intention of pimping out her father.

It went unspoken that the Taylors were disappointed that Tara wasn't the standout success among her high school friends. Susan often remarked that she was the prettiest, which implied a natural progression to achievement. "Men like an all-American look," she'd comment, dinging Suki and Priya. "Everyone respects a thin figure," she'd add, which eliminated high school Melissa, who tended to roundness.

Though they said the right things, Tara doubted how much

her parents sympathized with her about what happened with Ricky. Susan had been working for George, who was married to someone else, when they got together. After a few glasses of champagne, Susan would tell anyone listening that George squeezed her butt while she was standing at the copy machine one night and the rest was history.

A welcome call from Rachel saved Tara. Tara ducked back into her room to answer. Her parents didn't know she was dating a woman, and certainly not that said woman lived with her. After testing the waters by introducing them to a girlfriend a decade earlier, her dad said: "I hope this is a phase." Her mother offered her a Vicodin. After that, as far as her parents were concerned, Tara mentioned only men.

"Hi, Rach," she said, infusing her voice with warmth. She knew Rachel was put out not to be included in the weekend.

"Hi, babe. I want to hear all about last night. But I have a bit of bad news first. Our winter registration was due last night and we're down like twenty-five percent. It has to be Cooking Cuties. I don't know how we're going to make rent next month."

Tara dropped onto the bed. It was fitting that she was receiving this news in her childhood home. Her father would need to cover them, or they would lose their lease and their employees.

"Shit. We'll talk about it once I'm back. I miss you." She didn't really mean it. Tara was overwhelmed with so many other feelings at the moment that she lacked the bandwidth to miss anybody.

"Miss you, too," Rachel said.

"How's Bernie?"

"Thrilled with the cashmere cardigan I brought home from yesterday's toddler class. We really ought to resell this stuff instead of letting our dog make confetti out of it." Tara pictured Bernie ripping the expensive sweater to shreds with his sharp teeth and laughed. Hopefully it belonged to Jolie, the most obnoxious student in the threes program.

"Thatta boy," she said. "Kiss him for me. I gotta go. We'll talk about registration when I'm back."

Tara went to the bureau and studied her reflection. She had dark circles under her eyes. A swipe of a tissue confirmed it was exhaustion, not residue mascara. Maybe the encroachment of Cooking Cuties was a sign that she ought to change direction. She replayed the clink of glasses last night as her friends toasted their grand plans for fulfillment. Perhaps opening a restaurant wasn't just a pipe dream, the wishful thinking of three wistful and inebriated friends staring down their teenage superlatives in a yearbook. She could do this. She should do this. Why not?

Tara emerged from her bedroom and flew down the stairs. She had an hour before she had to be back at Bellport.

"Who wants an omelet?" she called out, her fingers itching to test out her parents' top-of-the-line equipment.

TARA COULDN'T BELIEVE the beanbag was still there. The blue denim was faded and it had lost its shape—it was now more dimpled and deflated than round—but it sat in almost exactly the same spot she remembered: far-left corner, backstage of the auditorium, in between the wall-hung ladders and painted slabs of scenery. She plopped down on it.

Tara closed her eyes and took a deep breath. It was hard to believe how many years had passed since she'd been kissed on this beanbag. And that the person who kissed her was Suki. Suki, who was dressed like a ginger tabby, drunk on cheap vodka someone had brought to the cast party, and giggling nonstop. She and Tara were the last two left. Suki was supposed to drive them home, but she needed to sober up first. Tara was at the cast party only because Suki had convinced her to join the crew, despite her utter lack of painting talent or facility with lighting design. Though she was busy with SAT practice (and nailing a mille-feuille to enter into a local competition), Tara acquiesced. She was powerless against Suki.

"You were awesome," Tara said to Suki that night. They were splayed on their backs, sharing the beanbag, looking up at the complicated stage lights as if they formed a constellation. Suki had rolled onto her side to face Tara. Maybe it was the effect of the brown-bag vodka flooding her bloodstream, but Tara could feel Suki's heart racing as much as her own.

"Why, thank you. I liked seeing you backstage." Suki patted Tara's leg a few times and then let her hand rest on her thigh. There was a rip in the knee of Tara's Pepe jeans and she could feel the warmth of Suki's fingertips on her skin. By now Tara's face was burning hot. She hadn't even realized how much she wanted Suki until that moment. Yes, she always said yes to Suki, whether it was to study together, go to the mall, or watch her at rehearsal, but all of that she had attributed to her friend's undeniable charisma. This was something else entirely.

While she tried to figure out what was happening, a light pressure indented her closed lips. Suki's mouth was on hers, her lips melting on Tara's own like wax poured into a mold. Suki's hand fluttered to Tara's ribs, where it settled. Her insides were screaming, *Move your hand up, move your hand up!* But the hand stayed in place, rising and falling with the frantic rhythm of Tara's breathing.

Just as soon as it started, it was over. Two lighting crew members stumbled backstage, clearly intoxicated and reeking of clove cigarettes. They didn't seem to notice anything out of the ordinary and Tara and Suki quickly detached from each other like the pages of a book snapped open.

"Sorry, looking for our backpacks," one of them said, collapsing into a fit of giggles. The two freshmen, whose names Tara didn't know, stomped around the room clumsily while Suki rose from the beanbag.

"Let's head to the cast party," she said to Tara, producing a lipstick from her pocket and replenishing the color that she'd transferred to Tara's mouth. Leaning in to whisper, she added: "Sorry about that. Guess the theater makes me horny."

There was nothing to be sorry for, Tara thought then and again now.

"Nobody painted scenery like you did," came a voice out of nowhere, startling Tara out of the memory. The curtain skittered open. It was still a heavy red velvet with an elaborate gold rope pulley system that screeched, desperately in need of WD-40.

"Evan! You scared me." Tara was glad he hadn't caught her ten minutes earlier, wearing the Ursula wig from *The Little Mermaid* and then furiously scratching phantom head lice.

Her high school ex-boyfriend of two years smiled back at her from stage left. His hands rested casually in the pockets of his slim khakis. They met each other halfway across the stage and hugged. She detected the scent of apple shampoo and spicy

aftershave. Evan had always been well-groomed, his metrosexu-
alism a welcome change from the rest of the boy-animals at
school covering their sweat with Axe.

"Sorry about scaring you. I saw you slip in here and I wanted
to say hi."

This was an interesting development. She was nearly certain
he hadn't been at the event last night. She'd sorted the name tags
and his hadn't been on the table.

"That's nice," she said, tucking a lock of her hair behind her
ear. Was Evan Cooper making her jittery?

"I just drove up from D.C. this morning. I had to be in court
all day yesterday. But I heard it was a lot of fun."

"You know Melissa. Everything she's in charge of is always
perfect," Tara said.

"I remember you as the perfect one," Evan said without
breaking eye contact.

What was going on? He was downright flirting with her. She
was certain he was married. Tara distinctly remembered meeting his wife at the fifteenth, a petite, button-nosed brunette in a
white shift dress, pushing a double stroller, and thinking that
Evan certainly didn't have a type. Tara knew she ought to walk
away now. But nobody had ever called her perfect before. Just a
month ago she was in a plastic surgeon's office having her imperfections outlined with a Sharpie.

"That's generous," she said, followed by a gigantic sneeze.
"Whoops. The dust is terrible back here."

"Let's go for a walk then," Evan said, looking at his phone
quickly. She tried to eyeball his home screen. It was often the
clearest window into a person. At work, she always preferred
the parents who had candid family shots on their phones in-

stead of the staged, airbrushed pictures where everyone was in a white T-shirt and jeans fake-running on a beach. And anyone with a picture of their dog on their home screen was automatically solid. "Unless you have somewhere you need to be. I already went into some of the classrooms. Mrs. Rosario remembered giving me detention for using my Game Boy in class."

"I remember that!" Tara was uniquely skilled at Tetris. She would play on his Game Boy under the desk during Spanish. Evan was a master of *The Legend of Zelda*. She dated him partially because he got to the Bested Ganon achievement.

She glanced at the wall clock. Tara had nowhere else to be. Visiting with her former teachers held no appeal. If anything, she was ashamed to see them. Her father had certainly used his influence on more than one occasion to get her barely earned Bs cranked up to A minuses. She recalled a particularly nasty comment from her calculus teacher. *How exactly does your daughter plan to be a chef if she can't handle simple fractions?* George Taylor was more excited that he'd ratcheted up Tara's grade despite her lack of acumen than outraged by the teacher's rudeness.

"Sure. I just promised Melissa I'd help her set up for the banquet tonight around three." She pulled her jacket from the costume rack and flung it over her shoulders.

"I'll have you back by two thirty," Evan said, and extended an arm for her to loop through his. They meandered around the campus for about fifteen minutes chatting about nonsense ("Do you remember when Principal Giffords's wife chewed him out over the loudspeaker?" "What was the name of the cafeteria lady with the hairy knuckles?" "Why did Scott Safron tell everyone his dad invented Beanie Babies?") before Tara couldn't stand it anymore.

"How's your wife?"

Evan stopped walking. His placid face appeared prepared for the question. "I think she's very happy. With her new husband, that is. We divorced a few years ago."

Oh. Tara liked hearing that. She tried to push thoughts of Rachel out of her head. Her therapist said compartmentalizing was a good thing, though she probably wasn't referring to adultery.

"I'm sorry to hear that," she said, noticing that she was making an effort to purr her words. She discreetly reapplied lipstick and pulled back her shoulders. Dr. Mann hadn't turned her into Dolly Parton. He'd simply reconfigured her breasts to their 1997 version. What better place to showcase them than on the Bellport campus, where they made their debut? She got to sloppy second with Evan Cooper in Melissa's basement after they watched Doug and Carol finally kiss on *ER*. It occurred to Tara suddenly that there was a chance of someone seeing her undressed this weekend. Her scars had yet to fade.

"It's all right. Sometimes things work out for a reason." Evan gave her a suggestive smile. Once lanky and prone to pimples that he religiously treated with Clearasil, now he was filled out and had a healthy glow peeking out from behind a stubbly beard. Narrow pants cinched by an embroidered belt hit his suede driving loafers at the perfect spot and a crisp shirt in a flattering pale blue matched his eyes. Despite his better-than-average grooming, the Evan she remembered tended to oversize Izod shirts and cargo pants.

"So, what kind of law do you practice? I remember seeing on Facebook that you went to Duke." Tara didn't mind Evan knowing she kept tabs on him. She wanted him to be flattered.

They had reached the tent where the night's festivities would be held. Already the tables were set, clothed in the school colors, with scattered votives that had yet to be lit serving as paperweights. Each table had a name associated with a high school memory—the senior play, the homecoming theme, the destination of the senior trip, the band that played at prom. Tara paused to consider if Melissa would have pushed herself to these limits if Josh hadn't been in attendance. Why did any of them feel they had something to prove? Wasn't the perk of getting into one's forties supposed to be leaving the insecurity behind? Some Instagram post on an inspirational feed she followed had promised that. Maybe that was true only for men. Most of her feed was populated with ads for antiaging creams.

"Corporate law and some lobbying work. It's been good to me." Evan pointed to the tables. "Want to sit down? I see some beers in the cooler I can snag for us."

"Sure." Tara was happy to rest her feet. Back in high school she traversed campus in tennis shoes, but for the reunion she'd chosen three-inch wedges. When Evan returned with the sweating bottles and handed her one, she noticed a gold Rolex on his wrist. "That's wonderful you're doing so well." She waited a beat. "Have you heard about the big donation?"

Evan's eyes twinkled. "I certainly have. Guess we'll find out who the mystery man is soon enough." He lightly grazed her knee with his fingertips as he went to shoo away a fly.

Was he implying it was him? It certainly seemed that way. She had no idea if a lawyer could earn that much money. But if he was also a lobbyist, and billion-dollar industries relied on him, well . . . it was possible.

"Tara, you really look amazing. Being back on campus with you . . . I don't know. It just feels great." He inched his chair closer to hers. She could feel his warm breath in her ear. Tara made a note to put their chairs back into place when they left, before Melissa had a conniption. "I have to ask you something."

"Yes?" Tara felt the beer's effects already after only two sips. She was light-headed, dizzy with hormones. It was almost the way she'd felt when Suki's mouth was on hers. That kiss was still the sweetest feeling she could recall, though she didn't know if it was enhanced by hindsight or if it had really been that wonderful at the time. Evan had been her first of everything else.

"What was it like being a call girl? Sorry, I mean escort. Maybe you prefer that term." Evan was now inches from her. His breath smelled like the beer wasn't the first alcohol he'd consumed that day.

"Excuse me?"

"I'm not judging, Tara. To be honest, I think it's kinda hot. And those porn pics. I enjoyed those. Not very nice of Ricky DiMateo to go releasing them, but I guess you gotta be prepared for stuff like that in your line of work."

Tara stood so quickly her chair fell backward. Fortunately, she had the wherewithal to dump the remainder of her beer onto his lap once she regained her footing.

"Stay the fuck away from me for the rest of the weekend."

She fled the tent, the sound of her heart beating in her ears like a steel drum. She never should have come to this reunion. Never.

9

-:-

Priya

PRIYA STOOD IN the cafeteria line behind Melissa, unsure how to hold her tray properly. She was hardly a stranger to cafeteria-style dining. At the hospital it was how she took her meals daily. She was expert in knowing which foods the line cooks could do well (oatmeal, steamed veggies) and knew what to avoid (salmon at all costs; anything vaguely ethnic). But standing in the cafeteria line at Bellport, she might as well have been sixteen again, worried that she would say or do the wrong thing.

"This was a cute idea," Priya said to Melissa in spite of herself. Melissa had pulled out all the stops for Back to School day. Besides offering a traditional school lunch from 1997, sloppy joes and grilled cheese sandwiches on white bread, she'd managed to unearth copies of their textbooks (word problems so painfully outdated it was comical . . . *If Julie has two dimes and four nickels, and a pay phone call costs* . . . not to mention the total lack of diversity . . . *If there are three pizza pies each cut into eighths, how many slices of pizza do the twelve blond, white kids get?*). She also found old art projects boxed in the school's deep storage. These were spread on large tables in the gymnasium, and everyone seemed to be loving digging though the sketches and papier-mâché to find their work.

Not that Priya was able to enjoy any of it. She learned of the details only from Melissa and the chatter around her in the lunchroom. Priya had spent her morning back at Melissa's house, on the phone with Bela, who was freaking out about an upcoming AP exam and wouldn't let her mother off the phone until they ran through her chemistry notes flawlessly. While she was talking Bela off a ledge and quizzing her on chemical reactions, Asha grabbed the phone to complain that the dog had thrown up in her bed and Vid texted her at least half a dozen times asking her to approve purchases of gems for some game on his iPad. Dev was unfusing someone's spine at the moment—an emergency weekend surgery—so Priya couldn't exactly ask him to pitch in.

Why couldn't she tell them all to (politely) go fuck themselves? People said that to their family members sometimes, didn't they? She wanted to hate Dev for not letting her have this weekend to herself, but it was hard to summon that much rancor toward him when he texted her at 6 a.m. to say he was sorry he couldn't be more helpful.

"Should we take our old spot?" Melissa asked, gesturing to the corner table where they had taken every meal since sophomore year.

Priya nodded, looking dubiously at the gray chopped meat spilling from the bun on her plate. Her arms had steadied. At least the rattle of her fork against the tray ceased. She'd successfully avoided eye contact with Mark Seaver, the tennis player she'd made out with freshman year, presently seated at a table by the wall of windows with his family. Sunlight bounced off his blond wife and towheaded children as they posed agreeably for a family selfie. What horse tranquilizer had those kids taken to stand so still for pictures? She wondered if Mark still moved his tongue in and out like a lizard when he kissed.

"No other choice, anyway." Melissa was correct. The other cliques had colonized their old domains. The jocks and cheerleaders were at the central table, the artsy folks were near the fire exit, the chess nerds were by the bathroom—actually playing chess on a travel board—and every other group had returned to their designated areas. How could so much and so little change in twenty-five years? There had to be an anthropological study to be done here.

"I saw Tara walking around with Evan Cooper this morning," Melissa said once they had settled at the table.

"I never liked him," Priya said, putting down her sloppy joe and pulling two Kind bars and a banana from her bag. "Mel, what are you doing?"

Her friend was picking out the raisins from a bran muffin and lining them up. The only other food on her plate was a translucent slice of cantaloupe.

"You're smart," Melissa said, forking the melon and dangling it under Priya's nose. "Do you think this is more or less than fifty grams?"

Priya *was* smart—enough to recognize the signs of an eating disorder when she saw one. In her practice, she saw young girls who whittled themselves down to such a hollow weight their bones snapped like twigs.

"I think you need to eat. You are seriously way too thin. What about Cameron?" They had just encountered Melissa's daughter a few moments earlier. She was handing out schedules outside the cafeteria along with several other volunteers. All appeared equally annoyed to be on reunion duty.

"What *about* Cameron? You think she's fat?" Melissa didn't even sound mad, more curious. As if a doctor's opinion on the matter was very important.

"No, of course not," Priya said. Cameron wasn't thin the way some girls in high school looked like spaghetti. Make that angel hair. But Priya could see just from eyeballing Cam that her BMI was within normal range. She had the type of frame that could only be lithe through starvation, which was apparently Melissa's current MO. "I meant that high school girls are under a lot of pressure. And having a stick-thin mother isn't so easy. I don't think counting calories around her is a great idea. You've said in the past that Cam can be insecure."

Melissa harrumphed.

"Your children aren't perfect, either."

Priya blanched. Melissa didn't sound merely retaliatory. There was an assuredness in her voice that made Priya uneasy.

But what could she know? Their families lived forty-five minutes apart and the kids attended different schools. Asha and Cam were a year apart, but they'd met only once a few years ago at a barbecue for Dev's birthday. They had little interest in each other, which disappointed both Priya and Melissa. They were admittedly different kids. Asha was a dean's list student who had memorized the acceptance rate at each Ivy League school. Cameron, by Melissa's own admission, was an average student lacking direction. It made Priya question if she would be friends with Melissa if they met first as teenagers and hadn't spent years trading Barbies and playing epic Monopoly games when they were younger. Melissa needed her name up in lights. She ran every extracurricular, even the science club, for which Priya would have been infinitely more qualified. To be fair, Priya hadn't put her name forward, but Melissa didn't know carbon dating from speed dating. At forty-three, she still couldn't approximate a gram.

"I know that. Vid's teachers want to seat belt him to his chair." Priya offered this as an example of her family's shortcomings, hoping it might get Melissa talking. She did not mention that the school administration was pressuring her and Dev to put him on ADHD medication.

"Well, that's just boys," Melissa said dismissively, the implication being . . . *That's not what I was referring to.*

Priya felt the urge to call Dev for reassurance. She wished he weren't in surgery, but the spine was a doozy. He'd be tied up for at least six hours.

"Tonight we'll find out who the donor is," Melissa said, obviously keen to shift topics. She speared her cantaloupe, brought it to her lips, took a gerbil-size bite, and replaced her fork. "Giffords told me he's announcing it at the banquet. I'm back to wondering if it's Suki."

"I miss her," Priya said. "Honestly, I was really hoping she'd change her mind last minute and come. I just don't know how she balances it all." She pictured the medical scale in her office and layered each of Suki's components on it: the supersize job, the adoring husband with a successful career of his own, the impeccably dressed children—twins, one boy and one girl—it was like Suki played MASH in real life and landed on all the good ones. And she always looked amazing. The bag matched the shoes which matched the nail polish which matched the belt buckle. And when they didn't match, it was intentionally so, because mixing metals was in fashion or red nails were the thing to pair with a natural lip. And Suki had a quick sense of humor with the perfect level of edge, just like her wardrobe. Priya looked down at her outfit, a pair of jeans her girls would scoff at and a pilled sweater from Talbot's at least a decade old. She was used to hiding under a white lab coat during the week. On weekends, she wore leisure wear sets ordered from places that targeted her with ads online. The algorithm for exhausted working mothers was remarkable; the sidebar on her laptop knew her better than anyone. "Suki is just one of those people who seems to have thirty hours a day while the rest of us are stuck with twenty-four."

Melissa nodded. The tension between them had eased. "I know. She's superwoman. She can be our inspiration for the pact. Hey, let's bus our trays and get out— Hang on, Tara is coming in. She looks upset."

Priya swiveled around. Tara was scanning the room, her standing posture crumpled like a paper fan. From across the room, her nose looked bright red. Melissa waved her over. They watched as she hobbled over to them, wearing only one wedge shoe, the other in her hand.

"What happened?" Priya handed Tara a tissue from her bag.

"Thank you," Tara murmured, blowing her nose loudly.

Priya carried Kleenex, Wet Ones, Band-Aids, Benadryl, and Advil at all times. Mary Fucking Poppins, MD. Her right shoulder was permanently sloped downward from the weight of the supplies. Dev left the house with only a cell phone he slipped into his back pocket.

Tara flopped onto the bench, her loose shoe thudding to the floor. "I'm leaving. Evan Cooper just asked me what it was like being a call girl. He believes all that shit Ricky said about me. Probably everyone but you guys does. I felt like everyone was being so nice and normal, like maybe they forgot. Now I realize they were just being polite and laughing behind my back. I'm heading to the train station now. Just wanted to find you guys first to say goodbye. I'm sorry, Melissa, but I just can't."

Priya felt something big well up inside her, a monster trying to burst out of her vocal cords. She threw an arm around Tara and pulled her close.

"No, you are staying and you are going to enjoy yourself. Forget Evan and anyone else that believes everything they read. You're letting them win when you deserve to win. Not Ricky. Not these losers." She gestured to the crowd in the cafeteria with a sweep of her hand.

Priya never spoke this forcefully. Not to Dev, her children, her parents, not even to the insurance companies that gave her patients a hard time. But she had had enough. "And take these." She pulled a pair of rubber flip-flops from the bottom of her bag. "Bela made me carry these for her the last time she got a pedicure."

"Thank you. I ran away from Evan and tripped over the wires taped to the ground for tonight's stupid broadcast. Sorry, Melissa."

"We need the wiring for the A/V guys who—" Melissa started to say, but Priya shot her a look.

"If I stay, I'm not going back to my parents' house. I had to hide talking to Rachel from them. I'm like seven years away from menopause, for God's sake, and I'm sleeping in a twin bed!" Tara started to cry again. Priya and Melissa instinctively blocked her from view, the way they used to form circles around one another when one of them needed to change in public.

"You won't," Melissa said. "You're staying with us tonight. Priya has the guest room, but you can take the downstairs. It's huge. Cam is at Josh's anyway. We have the place to ourselves. Forget everyone else. Let's just focus on being together."

"Exactly," Priya said, forcing her extra Kind bar into Tara's hand. "Remember last night? The pact. This is going to be our year."

Tara gave the subtlest of nods. She would stay.

Priya snuck a look at her watch.

"I just want to visit Mrs. Dega before she leaves," Priya fibbed as she got to her feet. She had no interest in visiting the art teacher, who fancied herself a Bohemian and nearly threatened Priya's perfect GPA because of a subpar gouache Matisse.

There was someplace else she wanted to be. Down the hall from the art room, second door on the right from the stairwell.

THE CHEMISTRY LAB was empty when Priya entered. She'd counted on her classmates getting their touring and teacher visits out of the way in the morning so that when she made her way to her old spot in the third row and touched the Bunsen burner, an upgraded model, she would be alone. She knew her chemistry teacher wouldn't be there to greet his former students. Gavin Walter was long gone from Bellport Academy. Long gone from teaching AP chemistry. She didn't know where he was, though she had thought about seeking him out online. But Priya barely used Facebook and didn't trust social media. She imagined Gavin would be alerted if she looked him up. If J. Jill knew to send her ads for discounted sweaters five minutes after she noticed a hole in the one she was wearing, then surely Facebook users could figure out who was stalking them.

The classroom, even without the burble of beakers and test tubes, still managed to ignite Priya's senses. She felt baking soda and vinegar stirring inside her, one pipette of acid away from combusting. In her mind's eye she saw the yin-yang patch on her JanSport; she could hear Heather Mott detailing last night's episode of *Friends*—"and then Emily told Ross she would only come to New York if he agreed not to see Rachel again"—until Zachary Marks shouted that he had taped it and not to spoil it.

Priya had been the uncontested science star at Bellport Academy. Dr. Giffords mentioned in passing yesterday that still nobody had surpassed her. She doubted he meant it; he probably just wanted her to come back to campus for Career Day, especially once the new STEM facility was complete. She excelled in biology and physics, but her absolute favorite subject was chemistry. Her friends had posters of Leonardo DiCaprio and Jared Leto over their beds; she had the periodic table of elements. When Dr. Giffords entered the school into the statewide science fair, he asked Priya to captain the team effort. She wasn't naturally charismatic, and only two other students signed up. They were just doing it for their college applications and didn't make it past the first meeting. That left Priya alone. But not for long.

Her chemistry teacher, Mr. Walter, was new to Bellport. He was fresh out of college, from which he'd graduated at age twenty, and personified nerd cute. Plastic-framed glasses, shaggy hair, and a uniform of jeans and button-downs paired with Nike Air Maxes made him irresistible to most of the girls in school. They gossiped about him in the locker room, joking about stroking his test tube. Gavin had an energy that Priya didn't detect in any of her other teachers, most of them middle-aged and jaded, bored of the school politics and sick of the entitled parents nagging them. Gavin, as he insisted his students call him, was totally different. When Dr. Giffords mentioned that Gavin had volunteered to be the faculty advisor for the science fair, Priya wondered if it had something to do with her. She often stayed back after class to ask about homework. Even when the students trickled in for next period, Gavin never shifted his focus away from her. One time he showed her a cartoon of a man and a woman in a lab. The woman asks the man, *Is that barium-sodium squared in your pocket, or are you just happy to see me?* Priya had burst out laughing. *BaNa²*. Mr. Walter was pleased. "Not everyone would get it, Priya," he said.

Together they worked on the school's entry, a seasonal flu vaccine made entirely from compost. The smell was unbearable at first, and Gavin held Priya's nose as she scraped specimens onto the microscope tray. The gesture was silly and lovely and soon they were taking turns pinching each other's noses until they both became immune to the smell. If executed properly, the project was certain to place in the competition. She and Gavin would meet after school to work. It was after a month of working together that they kissed. It was only three years that separated them, but in reality it might as well have been a century. Her parents would kill her, or at the very least lock her in the basement for the rest of her life. They would definitely kill Gavin. If it didn't end his life, their relationship would certainly end Gavin's career. He wanted to teach at the university level, and fooling around with Priya would make that impossible if he were found out. His entire future rested on his ability to resist her. She loved having that power, though it made her guilty at the same time. This was nothing like the tennis boy from freshman year, with his reptilian kisses. The same way potassium explodes when mixed with water, their connection felt inevitable at the cellular level.

Priya told no one, though every time she hung out with the girls and listened to them blather on about high school boys, she felt her secret on the verge of spilling out. For a month, she and Gavin only kissed. Their lips touching and their tongues mingling felt like a natural extension of their friendship. Priya tried to think of it as chemistry itself: What is the reaction when Gavin's slightly alkaline saliva mixed with her slightly acidic mouth? Pure and total bliss. One night in November, on the eve of the project's deadline, they worked extra late. Priya was exhausted. She had spent the past two nights putting the finishing touches on her early-decision application to Harvard. She wondered if Gavin noticed that her eyes were watering and how hard she was trying to suppress yawns.

For the first time since they'd been together, there was no daylight pouring into the large windows of the chemistry lab, only the trickle of stars and moonlight. When they'd finished for the evening, they kissed, like usual. But this time felt different. The kissing felt like prologue. Gavin reached into her jeans and she felt exhilaration like never before; her insides were erupting—she wondered if whatever was flowing inside her would burble over and spill out. She unbuttoned his shirt with tingling fingers and kissed the downy hair on his chest. Gavin separated from her, grabbing his barn jacket from his chair and laying it on the floor. Together they lay on it, both of them panting in expectation of what was to come. He eased his way into her gently. It hurt at first—she knew from Tara's first time with Evan Cooper that it would—but with the pain was also pleasure. When it was over, Priya had no doubts about what she'd done. For once, everything felt right and calm and certain.

A week later, her world turned upside down.

She came to class early to find Gavin hastily emptying his desk drawers into the messenger bag he wore to work every day.

"Priya," he whispered. "They know. Giffords. The school board."

She nearly fainted. Her future unspooled like a carpet of doom. Her meticulously typed application to Harvard might as well be kindling.

He squeezed her elbow, his thumb pressing softly into her flesh. "They don't know it's you. There was a camera in the classroom but all they know is that it was a student with dark hair. They saw a backpack and that's it. It's going to be fine. You're going to be fine."

All these years later, Priya still couldn't believe that her life had gone on as planned but that Gavin's may have been ruined. He was right. The school didn't know it was her. And they didn't find out because another student came forward and took the blame. A fellow senior girl admitted to sleeping with Mr. Walter that night. She also had dark hair and a JanSport.

Priya collected herself now and snapped a photo of the classroom, which though it had been modernized, was still very much recognizable. She sent the picture to Suki with the words **Thank you.**

Her future had been given the ultimate lifeline that day. She would not squander another opportunity. If nothing else, she owed it to her friends. Suki, who'd saved her so long ago, and Melissa and Tara, who'd vowed to change their lives last night, using one another as scaffolding.

She dialed a familiar number. Hiroshi answered on the first ring.

"Hi. Sorry to bother you on a weekend, but I wanted to let you know that if the CMO position is still open, I'd like to take it."

10

-:-

Melissa

MELISSA WAS ABSOLUTELY never going to speak to Alexa or Siri again. Both of those bitches told her that the forecast was clear for the whole day. Liars. Rain was pelting the grass and the perimeter of the tent was quickly turning into a brown Slip 'N Slide. Nobody was talking about the incredible decorations she'd procured or the theme tables. All anyone from the class of 1997 could focus on was staying dry. If Melissa heard one more comment about a wasted hair appointment or a muddy shoe, she would really lose it.

The dress she had planned to wear, a one-shoulder sheath in microfiber, was too exposed for the elements, so instead she had to resort to a Diane von Furstenberg wrap dress. She tied it snugly to showcase her narrow waist, the belt circling her twice, but the pattern screamed *tablecloth*. Meanwhile Kelly floated into the party as though she'd arrived in a different weather pattern. She had wavy hair that looked nice when worn natural and her white jumpsuit was wrinkle-free, draping her figure like a fitted sheet. Josh looked equally coiffed in a felt blazer and dark slacks. She recognized a worried expression on his face as he stared down at his phone. Melissa knew her ex's every facial move. This type of familiarity was possible only if you grew up with your partner, and it gave Melissa a sliver of pleasure that she would know Josh better than Kelly ever would. She wondered what was troubling her ex, if it was that the Patriots were down or that his business was in trouble. His child support came a week late for the second month in a row. He blamed it on his new assistant, but Melissa wasn't so sure. She didn't want to think about the financial consequences to her if Josh was in trouble. Right now, Melissa just wanted the rain to stop.

There was an audible buzz in the tent as her peers zipped around in search of seats, kissing and hugging and making chitchat. Above the din, the same question echoed: "Who is it?" Melissa was back to thinking the donor couldn't be Suki. There was no good reason she would choose Bellport as her main philanthropy. She spoke far more highly of her time at Boston University, where she fell in with a chic, sophisticated crowd.

Their friend group had *survived* high school, but not dominated it. Yes, there were some remarkable highs along the way. Priya winning the state science fair. Her annual election to student government. But mostly they were dodging heartbreak, avoiding ridicule, covering up zits, and hoping to make it through the day intact. Girls like Kim Konner, presently holding court next to the sushi table, glided through high school in a rainbow of J.Crew cashmere on a parade float. Melissa, Suki, Tara, and Priya trekked. Though would she have traded Kim's ironclad grip on popularity for the closeness she had with her girls? Not for a second; certainly not after what she'd seen *go down* in the bathroom stall with Kim's husband last night.

From across the tent, Dr. Giffords signaled for Melissa to join him on the dais. She passed Evan Cooper chugging a beer and shot him an icy glare. Priya and Tara were seated at the best table in the house, at place settings designated by tented pieces of paper that said RESERVED. Melissa stopped off to drop her purse at her seat.

"You got this," Priya said, squeezing her hand. Melissa felt sorry for what she'd said earlier about Priya's children not being perfect. She had no intention of divulging Asha's provocative pictures, so why make her friend worry for nothing? Cam hadn't said anything since. It was probably a onetime folly.

"Anyone hear from Suki?" Tara asked. "I keep expecting a helicopter to land on the football field."

"Nope. I really don't think it's her," Melissa said. She was newly irked Giffords hadn't told her who the donor was. Surely after so many years of working closely together, she deserved some professional courtesy. She did another sweep of the room. Nobody stood out as a possibility, but then again, what did someone who had $25 million of disposable income look like? Melissa could think of only Suki, her sole exposure to that level of riches.

"Let me have that." Melissa motioned for Priya to pass her the champagne at her place. If there was ever a moment that warranted three grams of sugar, it was now. Not to mention the reunion was almost over. She could go back to carbs and cream sauces and put the food scale on a high shelf. She knew she should. Her current lifestyle wasn't healthy and Priya was right about Cam. She was setting a terrible example for her daughter, who would soon be away in college, where Melissa couldn't even keep an eye on her. The trouble was she liked being thin more than she should and took a surprising comfort in taking up less mass in the world. She wondered how easy it would be for her to sink her teeth into a buttery croissant come Monday. The barista at Starbucks probably thought she was dead. It had been at least six weeks since she'd stopped in for her morning muffin.

"Take a bite," Priya said, sticking a seeded roll under her nose. "You're going to be wasted if you don't eat something."

Melissa took a nibble. She chewed slowly to avoid a poppy seed intrusion, and to savor the forgotten joy that was bread. Melissa told herself she would find a middle ground when it came to food. She wouldn't devour a pint of ice cream because she was bored or let sweets fill the void left by a bad Match.com date. But she wouldn't count her blueberries anymore.

She took another swig of champagne and walked toward the platform steps. This was the moment she'd imagined so many times during the planning. Even if nobody noticed that the party favors were miniature lockers filled with nineties candy (Bubble Tape and Astro Pop), they would remember a magical weekend and her as the mastermind.

"Would you take this? Thanks." Melissa handed off her flute to a waiter in a white shirt and black slacks. Last thing she needed was to seem like an alkie in front of her peers.

"I'm not a—" the man started to say, but Melissa was already onstage next to Dr. Giffords. Inexplicably, Kim Konner and her two sidekicks, as well as a few of the jocks, were also on the dais. Giffords hadn't clued her in on this part of the playbook, either. The group of them were loudly reminiscing about an epic homecoming game against Westin while Melissa stood awkwardly to the side. It was like the popular crowd couldn't move past their glory days, even with their mortgages and bad marriages and health scares, the hallmarks of middle age. Or maybe *because* of all those things. She thumbed her printed speech until she got a paper cut.

"Shall we get started?" Giffords said, tapping the microphone three times. A hush descended as guests filed to their tables. Melissa took an end seat on the dais, the only one left, as though suddenly they were playing musical chairs. She felt exposed with nobody flanking her left side. The bow on her wrap dress bulged like a third boob.

"Welcome back, class of 1997! I can't tell you how much it means to me to see you all on campus. As most of you know, your freshman year was my first year as principal here at Bellport."

Some cheers and hoots rippled through the tent. "Go Dr. G!" Bobby Lopez, class clown then, class moron now (he wore the same Hawaiian-printed shirt last night and today) shouted.

"This school has always been a wonderful institution, with a dedicated faculty, talented students, and that unmatched Jaguar spirit." Unmatched indeed. There were at least ten actual Jaguars in the parking lot at any given moment at Bellport.

It occurred to Melissa she ought to have hired someone to dress up in the mascot costume to greet guests and take photos. Oh well. She would do it for the parent volunteer luncheon in the spring. No, actually, she wouldn't. The Plan had officially kicked off. She was no longer going to be PTA president.

"Rumors spread like wildfire around this place, and it seems most of you know by now that one of your esteemed classmates has made an unprecedented gift to our school. We will be taking down the Taylor Athletics Center this fall and, in its place, building a state-of-the-art STEM facility that will be on the order of major universities. But before I have the pleasure of revealing who our benefactor is—and I know you're all curious—we have another surprise in store."

Melissa's stomach twisted in knots. What surprise could Giffords be referring to? She had created a precise run of show with his assistant just yesterday. The evening was beginning to slip through her fingers.

"A group of your classmates, sitting up here on the dais—well, not Melissa, but the others—alerted me a few days ago that they had something special to share with you this evening. And it dovetails quite nicely with our other announcement of the evening, as you'll see. So, without further ado, I'd like to call up Kim Konner to tell you more."

Kim rose, her mega smile amplified into a million-watt from the spotlight trailing her. If she only knew what Carrie and her husband had been up to last night, that smile would go upside down pretty quickly. Both Carrie and Kim's husband had pleaded with Melissa not to say anything, blaming the booze. "I won't," Melissa said. Meddling in that mess was beyond unappealing. "But you should be ashamed of yourselves."

"Hi, everyone," Kim said, motioning for her friends to join her at the podium.

"You look hot, Kim!" Bobby called out, and instead of turning red or waving him off, Kim took the opportunity to twirl.

"This weekend has been so much fun. It's such a blast to be back together on campus and reunite with our friends." She wrapped her arms around Carrie and the other woman onstage, a cheerleader named Poppy, who required three nose jobs due to successive falls from pyramids. She was diagnosed with vertigo senior year. "So, we have some pretty cool news to share. Last night, Joey remembered that we buried a time capsule under the watershed next to Taylor. When we heard the building was going to be knocked down, we knew we had to dig it up."

"Yeah, boy," came a round of cries from the swim team, of which Joey Lazar was a part.

Dr. Giffords produced a cardboard cylinder from behind the dais, which he passed to Kim with the fanfare of an Olympic baton. The crowd was oohing and aahing.

Melissa was fit to be tied. She crossed and uncrossed her legs so many times it had the effect of making her bow come undone. This evening was turning into the Kim show.

Kim uncorked the capsule and squealed.

"Without further ado, I give you a walk down memory lane. Welcome back to the nineties, people!" She tossed the cap into the crowd and people dived for it like a fly ball.

"I don't even remember what's in here," Kim said, which just seemed to build the suspense. She motioned for Jordan Bilson, Bellport's kicker, to pull out the first item.

"Oh my God, the *Titanic* soundtrack CD," a woman seated at a front table called out. Melissa didn't recognize her. Even the dates and spouses were getting in on the action.

"A.J., you do the honors next," Kim said. The lacrosse team captain, still lean and tall and looking sharp in a dark suit with no tie, retrieved a coiled roll of paper. He yanked off the rubber band and unspooled a poster.

"Nice!" He held up a movie poster for *Armageddon*. Melissa remembered seeing the movie with Josh in the theater. They had run into a bunch of their classmates at the concession stand. She cringed at the memory of Josh pulling two bags of Smartfood from her LeSportsac bag. "We always bring popcorn from home because the movie prices are ridiculous," he said, offering a bag to Danny Feldstone, a kid in Melissa's world history class whose family had a mansion with three hundred feet of waterfront on the sound that made the Taylor home look like a dollhouse. The Josh of today would never. She'd cultivated his swagger. Now Kelly was reaping the benefits of her labor.

The next items extracted from the capsule were a panda Beanie Baby, a worn copy of *The Da Vinci Code*, a Motorola StarTAC, an empty bottle of Elizabeth Arden Sunflowers perfume, a Gap flannel shirt, a Dave Matthews CD, and a Koosh ball. Each one received more cheers from the peanut gallery than the last and Melissa felt like she was watching someone else's family reunion.

"There's something else at the bottom," Joey, the swimmer who had remembered about the capsule, said, his hand in the tube. He was first cousins with Josh, but the relation did nothing to enhance the latter's social capital.

The crowd gasped as Joey extracted a purple lace bra.

"Kim, it's your—" Poppy started to say as Gifford seized the mike.

"That was, um, wonderful," Dr. Giffords said, his cheeks blazing. Kim was hysterically laughing, her gang collapsing around her in fits. Her husband was hooting from his table.

"What fun to remember the nineties like that," Giffords continued. It took a few minutes for everyone to settle down and the principal looked at Melissa in desperation. *Now you want me*, she thought.

"Anyway, let's all quiet down because it's time for the big announcement. It is my tremendous pleasure to introduce our school's greatest benefactor. This man, one of your peers, made his fortune in pharmaceuticals, creating a medical device that has saved millions of lives and is used in hospitals and doctors' offices around the world."

So it *was* a man. But who? Who was Giffords describing? Nobody in her pre-reunion sleuthing matched that description.

"This member of the class of 1997 keeps a low profile and so when our development team identified him as a potential donor, I must admit I didn't even realize we had such a distinguished alumnus in our midst. Ladies and gentlemen, it is with the greatest pride and appreciation that I call to the stage your class-mate, the hero of Bellport Academy, the man who with this gift has shown more generosity to our school than all other gifts combined. Please welcome, everyone, Nathan Romonofsky."

The Koosh ball elicited more of a reaction. It seemed every-one was too stunned to react appropriately. Was everyone think-ing the same thing Melissa was—Who the hell was Nathan Romonofsky?

Melissa watched as a short, balding man mounted the stage and the cheering climbed to a more acceptable level. Melissa made eye contact with him and startled. Staring back at her was the man she'd handed a half-drunk glass of champagne to not ten minutes earlier, thinking he was a cater-waiter.

He gave her a knowing salute.

11

- ❖ -

Tara

THE MINUTE KIM seized the microphone, Tara knew Melissa was going to have a ministroke. To be fair, Tara would be pissed, too, if she'd put in that much work only to be sidelined by Miss Popularity.

After the time capsule, Nathan Romonofsky, whom Tara couldn't have picked out of a police lineup, gave a short and uninspiring spiel about wanting to give back to Bellport, and science saving the world, and believing the children are the future. Or some such. She was barely listening. She couldn't stop seething about Evan, who had the audacity to approach Tara as she entered the tent.

"I'm sorry I upset you before. I don't judge you for what you did to get ahead."

Tara resisted the urge to jab the end of her umbrella into his spleen.

"I am not, nor was I ever, a call girl. Or a porn star. Did you ever consider that Ricky DiMateo was lying? That he would say and do anything to protect his reputation?" She was close to yelling. A few people nearby had stopped their conversations to listen.

"Sheesh, I said it wasn't a big deal." Evan shook his head.

"Who is that?" Tara heard an unfamiliar voice behind her.

"Oh, that's Tara Taylor . . . One of . . . accused that chef . . . but disproved . . . can't believe she showed." Tara could gather only snippets. She whirled around to face Peter Egghart, someone Tara had actually considered a friend in high school. They were paired together during the square dancing unit in PE. After a semester that involved more foot stomping than do-si-doing, they chatted amiably in the halls and Tara once gave him her Spanish notes after Peter left his behind at an away soccer game.

Rage boiled inside her. She was about to set Peter straight, but when she opened her mouth, nothing came out. It was as if no matter how much anger she possessed, her body couldn't expel it. She wondered if this was what giving up felt like.

"I'm sorry," Peter mumbled when he caught her eye. She still couldn't address him. Her voice returned in earnest only when Kim's bra came out of the time capsule.

"Oh shit. Melissa's gonna blow."

Priya nodded in fright. They were equally terrified of their friend today.

"I had that same one from Victoria's Secret, by the way," Tara added. "Miracle bra."

When Melissa finally got to the podium to make her remarks, a speech she'd practiced for them a half-dozen times earlier in the day, most people were on their feet pushing to talk to Nathan. At least she was spared the certain embarrassment that would accompany her closing line. Melissa had been intent on saying, *Let's "scream" for the class of 1997*, and putting on the mask from the campy horror movie. Priya and Tara had not been able to dissuade her, but with no one listening to her, Melissa on her own decided to scrap the idea.

Now the three of them were back at Melissa's house, sitting at the kitchen table with a box of chocolate chip cookies Melissa had unearthed from behind a Costco bag of thirty-calorie popcorn. The popcorn had overturned and was sprinkled onto the kitchen floor like confetti. Priya went to clean it but Melissa barked at her to leave it.

Tara wanted to tell the girls about Evan's audacity, and Peter, and all the other misinformed schmucks, but waited her turn. This was Melissa's moment to wallow.

Priya went to make coffee for everyone. She seemed to drink six to eight cups a day. Despite the caffeine infusion, Priya yawned frequently (always with an apologetic "excuse me") and had dark circles under her eyes that Susan Taylor would not abide. Apparently, there wasn't enough coffee in the world to sustain doctoring full-time and raising three children. She pictured Marina, the architect mother from Kitchen Kiddos, who often had sleeping sand crusted in the corners of her eyes and drank diet Red Bulls like a college kid.

"The weekend has been perfect," Priya said over the sound of the percolating coffee. "I agree it wasn't nice that Kim hijacked the stage. And it was hard to hear your remarks after the gift announcement, but everyone knows you were the brains and the muscle behind the entire reunion."

"She showed off her bra. Her fucking purple lacy Victoria's Secret bra. How is that a symbol of our time?" Melissa popped two cookies into her mouth, continuing her rant as she chewed. "The nineties were about *Seinfeld*. *Clueless*. Grunge. Clinique. Juicy sweatsuits. Fucking fanny packs. Not Kim Konner's lingerie."

"That was not ideal," Tara relented. "I'm assuming she honestly forgot it was in there. But can we discuss the really insane moment of the night? Nathan Romonofsky? I swear to God, I have a memory like an elephant and I do not think that guy even went to our high school."

Priya returned with her mug. "He looked kind of familiar to me. I think he was in my study hall but I'm not sure. Are you saying you think this is some kind of hoax?"

Melissa jumped out of her chair. The humidity had all but electrocuted her natural curls, and when she unleashed her hair spontaneously from her updo, it flared around her face like a ring of fire.

"Yes! This has to be a trick of some kind. How is it possible that we can barely remember someone who became so wildly successful? Like wouldn't this Nathan at least have been in all the honors classes? Gotten a prize at graduation?" She reached for another cookie but replaced it. "I need more than carbs right now. I need a drink. A big one."

Tara's mind flashed to what was in her purse.

"I have something that might work better at the moment." She pulled out a dime bag of weed she'd purchased Friday morning from the kid on her corner. Damon, a seventeen-year-old Stuyvesant kid, sold product that never disappointed. The kid was a chemistry whiz, with an early admission to MIT in his pocket. Tara shuddered to think what the pot might be laced with.

"Marijuana?" Priya's mouth fell open.

"It's medicinal, Doc." Tara smiled and started rolling a fat joint on Melissa's kitchen table. Just the smell of the herb relaxed her. "I left my license at home."

"You're quite expert at that," Melissa said, and Tara felt a perverse sense of pride. She did roll a mean joint.

"I've had some practice. Besides, it's the same technique as filling a Moroccan cigar." She missed preparing that recipe; her tahini-and-mint dipping sauce was the perfect complement to the sautéed beef and onion rolled in phyllo dough.

Tara brought the joint to her lips and lit up. Sometimes a blunt was the only way to relax after a hellish day at work.

She passed the joint to Melissa.

"Slow down," Tara said, watching Melissa suck the living daylights out of it. "Do you even know what you're doing?"

Melissa reddened. "I may have smoked a few cigarettes to kill my appetite. It turns out grapefruit and coffee aren't that filling."

"Priya?" Tara asked tentatively. When they raided her father's well-stocked liquor cabinet, Priya would say things like, "The boiling point of alcohol is lower than water" and "Did you know all vodka is chemically the same and the rest is just marketing?" If she took more than a sip, Tara never saw.

"Why not?" Priya took the joint. She had long, elegant fingers but she never wore any jewelry or had a manicure. The first puff made her cough, but after another try, she succeeded.

They passed the joint around a few more times in meditative silence. The mood was mellower; Tara felt warmth for her friends displacing the anger that had seized her earlier. With the equanimity came a return to her earlier confidence. Screw Evan Cooper. Screw Cooking Cuties. She had a plan. *They* had a plan. She, Priya, and Melissa were going to make shit happen.

"We should call Suki," someone said, and then Tara realized it was her.

"Yes! Let's FaceTime her," Priya said, thudding her coffee mug on the wobbly kitchen table. "What time is it where she is?"

"Who cares? Let's just do it," Melissa said, already trying to connect.

Suki's face filled the screen in seconds. It looked like she was in a hotel lobby with lots of shiny marble and brass.

"Girls!" Suki looked overjoyed to see their faces, which they had squeezed together to fit into the camera frame. "I miss you all so much. Tell me everything. Who looks good? Who's bald? Did all the Jennys show?"

Suki's voice was honey on a sore throat. They all started speaking at once.

"Jenny T., yes."

"Jenny P., no. Jenny R, no."

"Jenny K., I think so."

"Evan Cooper is a jerk."

"Kim Konner showed everyone her bra."

"Ellen Rondell has an entirely new face and may or may not have been coked up the entire weekend."

"Rick Elton drove his Porsche around the parking lot like six times, pretending to be looking for a spot."

"Bill Beldon got disbarred for sleeping with his client."

"Paris Wheeler lied about having cancer."

"David Grossman still has acne."

"Carrie Sackler gave Kim's husband head in the bathroom," Melissa said, stopping all the chatter. "Sorry, I forgot to mention that last night."

"Wow. I missed a lot," Suki said, shooing away someone approaching with a clipboard.

"The biggest news is that Nathan Romonofsky donated twenty-five million dollars to the school."

"Who?"

"Exactly," Tara said.

"Hang on a sec, girls." The screen went black but they could still hear the conversation.

"Ms. Hammer, I need you to sign off on your speech for tomorrow's luncheon. And the president of Bloomingdale's Abu Dhabi wants a few words with you on the phone."

"I told you at least twenty times to leave a copy of the speech in my hotel room. Do not interrupt me when I'm on the phone. Another lesson I'm sick of repeating. As far as Bloomingdale's goes, you know the scheduling procedure." Suki was all but barking at this faceless woman. Tara, Melissa, and Priya exchanged glances.

"Sorry about that." Suki was back. "Nobody can follow protocol around here. So, tell me more."

"We wondered if the gift was from you, actually," Priya said. "Giffords will probably hit you up for double now."

"Right," Suki said distractedly. "Sounds like most people looked terrible. Except for you ladies. Tara, is that a new pair of breasts I see?"

Tara flushed. Suki always had a discerning eye.

"Yep," Melissa said. "I squeezed them and they feel like a memory foam mattress."

"That's very specific, Mel. Anyway, I miss you all— Wait, hang on again." This time Suki didn't put the phone down. "Can someone please bring me the numbers from our Sephora collaboration? I asked for it fifteen minutes ago." The group assembled around her quickly scattered.

"Can't get anyone to do anything right around here, you know?" But they didn't. Tara didn't command an army. She employed a plucky group of out-of-work actors moonlighting as children's cooking teachers, whom she constantly allowed to skip work for auditions. Melissa had one of those jobs where nobody was really sure what she did, though it was clear she didn't have a team of minions brewing her coffee. Maybe Priya could relate, though Tara couldn't really picture her barking orders at the hospital.

"Sorry, girls, but I gotta hop," Suki said, and blew them an enthusiastic kiss before disconnecting.

The effect of the pot had all but evaporated. Tara lit up another joint. She wondered if Melissa and Priya were thinking the same thing she was. Yes, their friend had made it, but at what cost? The voice they heard on FaceTime didn't sound particularly happy or satisfied. Suki could light the world on fire, but she couldn't add more hours to the day. She still had to juggle work, a husband, and children like any other mortal.

"I liked her new hairstyle," Melissa finally said, and they left Suki at that. "What did they say Nathan Romonofsky sold again? I think medical supplies for the heart. Priya, you must know him." Melissa sucked the joint deeply and passed it to Priya, who demurred in favor of more coffee.

"Um, no. Also, I'm not a cardiologist." But instead of saying "cardiologist," she said, "cardodologist" over and over, trying to correct herself, until the three of them collapsed in laughter.

"Who are you, Nathan Romonofsky?" Melissa said. She pulled

open a kitchen cabinet and it dangled on a broken hinge. "Buy me a new house, Nathan Romonofsky." It was the last thing Tara remembered any of them saying until morning.

THE NEXT MORNING, the three women gathered in Melissa's kitchen. Melissa looked hungover. Priya was biting her nails. And Tara was wondering where they all stood on The Plan. What she was sure of was that she was getting out of Bellport before the closing brunch.

"I have to get back to the city," she announced. Melissa was eating an icy scone she'd dug out of the freezer and barely looked up. Priya nodded. It was as if they were all in mutual agreement. Enough was enough. It was time to get back to real life. Whether it was to make dramatic changes or to return to the status quo, Tara wasn't sure. But she had a business to attend to and a campus she needed to escape.

"Let me drive you to the train," Melissa offered, but Tara waved her off.

"I'd rather see you eat that scone," Tara said, and pulled out her phone to call an Uber.

Two and a half hours later, she was back home with Rachel. Something on her face must have told Rachel not to ask too many questions about the weekend, because Rachel simply hugged her and took her coat when she walked through the door.

"What's our next move?" Tara asked once she had settled in, though it was more a question to herself. Rachel wasn't a partner in the business, not financially. She was an emotional partner, for sure, but not the person charged with fixing the bottom line.

Rachel did not sense the question was rhetorical. Or that it was far vaster than she could have imagined.

"I think we modernize our class offerings. We partner with private schools in the area to offer field trips. That would cover the dead zone during the day. We raise our prices because our classes should cost more than these kids' shoes. And, finally, we plant mouse droppings in the Cooking Cuties quiches and call it a day." Rachel had snuggled up next to Tara on the couch.

Tara only nodded and said, "Maybe," after a long beat. Then feeling bad, she added, "Those are some great ideas, Rach."

"Tara, I'm sensing you're on another planet. Do you want to save Kitchen Kiddos? BTDubs, we can totally hightail it out of New York and try again in Memphis or Austin or something. Nothing is keeping us here. We can head down south and master deep frying."

Tara didn't know what to say. She wasn't comfortable telling Rachel about her pact with Priya and Melissa. She would never understand The Plan, unless it had an Instagram hashtag challenge associated with it. And moving to a cheaper city with Rachel? It wasn't the craziest idea in the world, but somehow it was more natural for Rachel to fold into her life in New York than for the two of them to take a new step together. Tara truly didn't know if that meant she was long-term-relationship-phobic, or that Rachel just wasn't The One. How the hell did anyone ever figure that out?

"I'm okay. Sorry. Just tired from the weekend. But not that tired. You wanna . . . ?" She grazed Rachel's knee with her index finger.

"Maybe later," Rachel said. "I'm going to make a list of private schools within twenty blocks of us."

Instead of rejection, Tara felt relief. More than anything, she wanted to take a hot bath and burn some of Rachel's sage to purify the Evan Cooper air still lingering around her.

"Okay, if you need me, I'll be hiding in a bubble bath." Tara was practically whispering, and Rachel wasn't listening anyway.

12

Priya

"DR. CHOWDHURY?"

Priya looked up when she heard the gentle rap on her office door. She pulled off her reading glasses and motioned for the woman to enter. It was a civilian, sadly. Priya was in no mood for nonmedical talk.

"I'm Carol Lewis, one of the hospital's HR coordinators. I thought I'd just pop by to see when I could schedule your sensitivity training screening and your orientation with our workplace behavior team?"

Crap. The stupid training video. Not stupid in that Priya didn't believe in a respectful work environment. She'd been called sweetheart far too many times. Once, as a resident, a group of intoxicated frat guys needing a battery of stitches asked her to play naughty nurse. The attending had just laughed.

But she didn't have time to sit through a two-hour video and participate in a role-playing session where some hired hack told her he liked her legs and she had to playact reporting him to HR. She had ignored at least half a dozen emails with links to the same irritating scheduling websites her children's school used, where it was impossible to decipher which times were free or taken. Did the half-open eye mean available or not? Honestly, she would volunteer more if the instructions were clearer.

Since Priya joined the management ranks, her email volume had quadrupled. She got reports on the daily admissions and discharges, updates on every lawsuit involving the hospital (a surprising number of surgeons left things inside people; Dev's name was thankfully absent from that list), and heaps of administrative minutiae. Her coffee intake was moving in lockstep with her email, which meant that at night she couldn't fall asleep. It was a vicious cycle she was helpless to break.

"Yes, I'm sorry I haven't responded to the email."

When Carol raised an accusing eyebrow, Priya corrected herself. "Emails. I promise to get on this today." Priya slipped her glasses back on to indicate she needed to get back to work. Carol didn't budge. At least five long seconds passed and the darkening shadow cast by Carol's body didn't retreat.

"Can I help you with something else?"

Carol fiddled with the button of her blazer.

"The thing is, Dr. Hiroshi told me I'm not supposed to leave here until I get you signed up." Carol offered a genuine smile. "They serve very nice snacks at the training."

Priya sighed so forcefully the papers on her desk ruffled. "What are my options?" She really needed Carol gone so she could review patient charts and because her stomach was positively killing her.

Her digestive tract was not taking kindly to the promotion. Sometimes she had to practically crab-walk to the bathroom.

Carol rattled off three different dates as Priya checked her Google Calendar. It was color-coded by family member and had unique colors for combinations of the family (turquoise for Bela-and-Asha-only outings; lime green for Vid and Asha; yellow for hers and Dev's couple commitments). Her patients and work-related events were in navy. All together it looked like a giant Rubik's Cube—one of those 6x6 models that Vid was into for a moment in fifth grade—and just as difficult to solve.

The first date Carol offered clashed with the college fair. Asha needed her there; she turned green whenever Yale was mentioned, that's how badly she wanted it. The second was orientation for Vid's overnight camp. She could skip that and send Dev, but then Vid would never have the right clothes and equipment and she'd end up having to spend more time at FedEx overnighting him what he actually needed. The third date was her mammogram. Her tits would have to wait. She accepted the December date and sent Carol packing.

Priya fixed her gaze on the computer screen. How was it only nine thirty?

A text message dinged and Priya expected it to be her scheduler, Louise, an aspiring novelist, describing—with a surplus of adjectives and adverbs—the mutiny in the waiting room. But the message was from Melissa, to her and Tara, on their group chat. It was called The Mostly Likely Girls. They were hardly girls, but the name evoked a more hopeful and promising time in their lives. The contact photo was a unicorn. Melissa loved it, so Priya abstained from pointing out that they might not want to choose a mythical creature as the symbol for a woman achieving her goals.

Melissa had sent them an article from *Forbes*, a cover story about Suki. The headline, ALL EYES ON SUKI HAMMER, topped a glamour shot of their friend, her dark hair shimmering as she stood in the middle of the Golden Gate Bridge, literally stopping traffic.

If she can do it, so can we! Melissa wrote, and inserted the biceps emoji that Dev always used when he went to the gym, which made Priya hate him just a little bit each time he sent it.

When Priya thought about Suki's astronomical success, she dwelled on its rarity. A doting husband with a career of his own, a gargantuan business, two stunning children, three homes, and a magazine-ready face . . . How many people were going to have that? Even two of the above felt out of reach most days. Melissa clearly felt differently. She took every one of Suki's triumphs as inspiration for what she could accomplish. Priya wondered how Tara felt. She'd always worshipped Suki, but in a different way. And she didn't have children, so the amount she could get done in a given day was probably three times what Priya could.

She looks amazing! Great profile, Tara texted back, making Priya feel obliged to chime in. She didn't have time to read the article, which looked even longer than the report on the hospital's proposed renovation of the north wing that she was supposed to mark up. She wrote **agree!** and bolstered her one-word response with a series of thumbs-up emojis.

Excluding Suki from The Most Likely Girls chain made Priya uneasy. When had they ever triangulated in any meaningful way? They'd decided collectively she was too busy to receive their frequent updates, but Priya wondered if there wasn't also the element of embarrassment. Weren't they a bit old for pinky swears and girl pacts? If you were within striking distance of a Centrum Silver vitamin, what business did you have trying to do over your life?

Her cell phone dinged again. This time it *was* her assistant, warning that her third patient of the day had arrived and was flinging his *gargantuan* crutch around *menacingly* because his appointment had started fifteen minutes earlier. Priya swallowed another large gulp of coffee, cursing herself for watering it down with almond milk and ice. As she walked to the first examination room, she thought about the song Bela used to sing as a baby: *Head, shoulders, knees, and toes . . . knees and toes!* Priya's patient roster was hips, back, knees, and knees. Then an executive committee meeting followed by shoulders, back, back, and back. She tried to hum her schedule to the same tune, but instead added tone-deaf to her list of deficits.

A CAR PRIYA didn't recognize was in the driveway when she got home from work. There was no Hopkins School bumper sticker on the back windshield, which meant it was unlikely to be the parent of one of her children's friends whom she'd be expected to schmooze with. Small talk after a day at the hospital was a no-no.

During her short lunch break, Dr. Hiroshi had popped into her office to see how she was settling into the new position. She wondered if he noticed her yawning during the ex-comm meeting. What could she do but say it was all roses so far? It wasn't the first time she'd had to fake something, and it wouldn't be the last.

"All okay at home, by the way?" Hiroshi was halfway out of her office door when he'd turned back around.

Once again, Priya opted for fibbery. Her boss didn't need to know that Bela had developed an eye twitch that was probably anxiety-related. That dependable Asha was suddenly hanging out with a new friend who wore heavy eyeliner and smelled so strongly of perfume she had to be masking other scents. That Vid was in trouble at school because he copied another kid's homework assignment verbatim, including writing *Kyle* as his name. And his trial of ADHD medications was starting this week and she was a basket case.

"Business as usual," she responded with a smile, her cheek muscles working harder than normal to get the corners of her mouth up.

Hiroshi's face still crinkled with concern. She appreciated his regard for work-life balance, even if it didn't manifest itself in cutting back on her patient load or the stream of emails she was expected to read.

"Okay," he said, not sounding convinced. For the rest of the day she couldn't shake their exchange. And now there was a strange car in her driveway, which meant she would have to interact with somebody she wasn't related to, not that she was particularly keen to talk to her flesh and blood, either.

"I'm home," she said, pushing open the front door. There was a version of her life in which she entered her house to find her husband at the stove preparing their dinner, Vid quietly doing homework at the kitchen table, her daughters laughing together about something on TV, and their dog controlling his bladder while indoors. Unfortunately, that version existed only inside her head.

"Finally, you are home," came a voice from the kitchen.

Shit.

"Is that you, Ma?" Priya addressed her mother-in-law in what she hoped was as neutral a tone as possible, given her internal monologue. She found Jeet in the kitchen, retrieving a large tin from the oven, wearing an oven mitt Priya hadn't laid eyes on for at least a year. Which meant Jeet had gone through her drawers, an obvious violation of the daughter-in-law–mother-in-law code of conduct. "Where are the kids?"

"They are in the basement. I can't believe what a racket they make. I couldn't concentrate on the food with all their noise."

Priya wanted to believe her mother-in-law was expressing sympathy by talking about how disruptive the children could be, as in, *Kudos to you for working a whole day and coming home to this chaos.* But instead, she heard: *What is wrong with you as a mother that you have raised such an unruly brood?*

"Nice of you to come by," Priya said, eyeing what turned out to be dal and shaak simmering on the stove. "It smells delicious. Whose car is that out front?"

"It is my neighbor's car; ours is in the shop for at least a month after Papa's aide cracked it up. Meanwhile, this one drives terribly and I'm not sure I'm comfortable driving it home in the dark."

Was this when Priya was supposed to offer that Jeet spend the night? The idea of seeing Jeet's face before she eyed her coffee-maker the next morning terrified her.

"Anyway, Vid told me he'd been eating a lot of pizza lately so

I figured I ought to come over and make everyone a decent meal. These children will forget their roots if they eat only Kraft mac and cheese." Jeet did that thing some people were amazing at, which was to smile while saying something incredibly rude.

"You talk to Vid?"

"We text." Jeet put out a spoon for Priya to taste the dal, which was spiced to perfection. "I thought tonight was a good night to come because I know Dev is out having his relaxation evening."

If by "relaxation evening" you mean drinking scotch and losing money at poker with a bunch of the other male doctors, then sure. Priya nodded. "Quite right." She was in no mood to argue or do anything that would delay dinner. If Jeet was so eager to usurp Priya's role, maybe she could take a crack at Asha's calculus homework and help clean Vid's room. She started to set the table.

"We can't eat on those," Jeet said, looking at Priya as though she had had a lobotomy. "Paper plates may work for pizza, but not for my food."

"Kids, get up here and help set the table," Priya called out, and slumped into a chair. How much would she need to pay them to wash the dishes after? And could she make the deal without their grandmother noticing? She pondered this as the thunder of three sets of footsteps overtook the kitchen.

"HOW WAS POKER?"

Priya and Dev were in bed, the evening news playing in the background. Mercifully with one swift look at Dev, Priya had communicated how badly she didn't want Jeet to spend the night, and he'd arranged for an Uber to collect her and promised to drive the neighbor's car back tomorrow.

"I won a hundred bucks off Dr. Sherman. Also found out Holston's getting divorced."

"What else is new?" The plastics doc was on his fourth or fifth wife now. "Did you have a good day at work? I hoped to see you in the cafeteria. I heard Chef Louie attempted steak au poivre, but I ended up not having time."

Dev turned to face her.

"You're still happy you took on the new position? They're working you so hard." He rested a hand on her belly, and she felt a little tingle run south. They wouldn't have sex tonight. She was far too tired for that. But she appreciated the affection regardless, especially because Dev knew that when she put on the ratty Harvard Medical School T-shirt with the armpit hole, the shop was closed.

"Yes. I think so." She still didn't want to talk about it much at home. With the promotion, she and Dev now earned equally at the hospital. He was a full-time surgeon and she practiced nonsurgical medicine four days a week, but with the stipend from the management position, their salaries had leveled. They shared a bank account; surely Dev had noticed the swell from her meatier paychecks.

"I'm proud of you," he said. "You're not letting the politics spoil this for you."

She turned on her side, wriggling out from under his hand.

"What is that supposed to mean?" Their faces were inches from each other. Priya saw nose hairs that needed trimming and clogged pores. This close up, Dev wasn't as devastatingly handsome.

"You know. Promoting women. Diversity. Blah blah."

Dev flipped off their bedroom light. She flipped it back on.

"Is that what you think? I deserve this," she said firmly. She was happier than ever that she'd sidestepped the black nightie in her pajama drawer. For a millisecond, sated from Jeet's food and grateful that Dev had Ubered her away, Priya had thought about slipping it on.

"Of course you do." He flipped off the light again and this time she didn't object because her cell phone dinged.

It was a message from Tara on The Most Likely Girls chat.

> Guys, check out the latest Suki profile.
>
> The comments are getting NASTY.

MAKEUP QUEEN PAINTS THE WORLD RED

Suki Hammer's Empire Is Smashing Success

BY COURTNEY COLLINS

When Suki Hammer was six years old, she stole her mother's makeup and gave her dolls and stuffed animals makeovers. Her mother, a former model of Japanese heritage, was far more amused than angry.

"Let's just say I wasn't great at coloring inside the lines," Ms. Hammer said, laughing while retelling the story on the veranda of her seventeen-acre lush estate in Ojai Valley. "I nicked the bedspread with lipstick about a dozen times."

The older Mrs. Hammer made her help with the laundry and promise never to touch her products again without permission. But at bedtime, after tucking Suki in, her mother said, "You have a natural flair for makeup. Do mine next time I go out."

Suki never intended to be a cosmetics titan. She had other aspirations as a child and throughout her high school years, which included investment banking ("I watched *Wall Street* as a kid and wondered where the women were") or law school ("I was always a good little arguer"). But life had different plans for her and lightning struck when she was just thirty, a graduate of Columbia Business School and working at a boutique bank in Chicago.

MakeApp's founder and CEO, then a junior associate doing mergers and acquisitions, was getting ready for a client dinner in the bathroom of her office. She remembers trucking to work with a gigantic cosmetic bag that weighed a ton because she didn't have the time in the morning to organize her products and choose only what she needed for that evening. "The fluorescent lighting in there was just awful," Ms. Hammer recalled. A female coworker came into the bathroom and produced a similar-size monstrosity and commented how ridiculous it was that they were lugging huge bags around when all they needed was one lipstick, an eye shadow, and mascara.

"I went home that day and organized my own to-go makeup kits. One for a simple, neutral palette, one for a more glam look, and so on. It definitely helped when I needed to travel or was in a rush to get out the door. MakeApp was born in that bathroom, but it was still a few years before I realized it could be a real business."

Being her own boss was always important to Suki Hammer. She says her banking job was interesting and challenging, but she felt stifled having to take orders from the top down. Suki wanted to be the top dog, a fact evident even in her high school yearbook superlative: Most Likely to Join the Forbes 400. A friend from high school recalls that Suki was always fascinated by makeup and celebrity culture, so it came as no surprise to Kim Konner, her peer from the posh private school Bellport Academy in Bellport, Connecticut, that Suki went on to form a company that channeled her passions into profits.

"I remember Suki had pictures of celebrities she ripped out of *Seventeen* and *YM* taped to the inside of her locker," Ms. Konner said by telephone. "She had an eye for what looked good and what didn't work. Suki's success is no surprise. She knew her passion and ran with it."

Indeed, it was Suki's ability to combine a common dual interest of many women—cosmetics and celebrity culture—that made MakeApp a huge success from the outset. The app has twenty million active subscribers, who receive monthly subscription boxes for which they pay $75. Each box includes four different "looks" named for a different celebrity of the moment, including their favorite products and instructions on how to achieve their red carpet and casual looks. Ms. Hammer has said publicly many times that MakeApp is committed to featuring women of all different skin tones and backgrounds.

"As much as I loved my fashion mags growing up, I missed seeing faces that looked like mine. Let's just say the makeup department at my local mall didn't quite meet my needs."

Beyond the subscription box, MakeApp sells products from over one hundred cosmetics companies. Each product has a tip on how to use it to best effect. All multiproduct palettes come with a battery-operated light to help with application. And possibly the most innovative feature of MakeApp is its CelebSnap, adored by phone-crazed teenagers especially. Simply upload a photo from a magazine to MakeApp and the app will fill your cart with the products needed to copycat the look.

The question on everyone's mind is: Just how does Suki Hammer do it all, and look so good while doing it? I shadowed Suki for a day to see for myself. The "momtrepreneur"—as she likes to call herself—rises at 6 a.m. and takes a morning yoga class with a private trainer. After, she wakes up her children, Francesca and Lucas, and readies them for school. The family sits together for breakfast. Her husband, Graham Marks, a private equity investor and one of the first to seed capital into MakeApp, joins the family as he returns from a run. Francesca and Lucas, both adopted at birth by Suki and Graham, leave for school with a driver. "I would love to take them every day but I can't do everything," Suki says with a self-effacing smile that indicates that, actually, maybe she can. But she and Graham use their alone time after the children leave for school and before they part for work to have what they call a "morning date." It often lasts just ten minutes, but they catch each other up on what's going on in their hectic lives.

By nine, Suki is behind her glass desk at MakeApp's headquarters in Palo Alto. Her assistants—yes there are two of them—hand her an oat milk latte and a stack of articles for her to go through. Many are favorable press clippings, which summon an approving nod from Hammer. Then it's meetings, meetings, meetings for the rest of the day. By 6 p.m., when Suki is ready to get into a town car that will whisk her off to the Boys & Girls Clubs of San Francisco benefit—she is emceeing the event—I'm not sure how she's still standing in her four-inch stilettos. She did what she calls a "disco change" for the event, slipping into a lace and tulle gown that materialized somehow in her office, and selecting the "Gwyneth" box for her makeup artist to use, channeling Ms. Paltrow's understated elegance—the actress and Goop founder is a close friend of the entrepreneur.

At the benefit, Suki spoke to the room of a thousand about the value of hard work, believing in yourself, and being open to new ideas. These were common themes to be heard at a benefit like this one, but coming from Ms. Hammer, they rang fresh and genuine. The standing ovation made it clear the audience felt the same way.

Back home by 9 p.m., Suki was able to catch one of her twins, Lucas, still awake. In her gown, only heels removed, she read him a chapter of Harry Potter and tucked him into bed.

What does the future hold for this whirling dervish whose business just keeps expanding? When I ask her, she answers me with one word: sleep.

COMMENTS: 211

·*Omg I want to BE her. She is AMAZING.*

·*Obsessed with MakeApp. I gift the box to everyone.*

·*I #wannabesuki*

·*I #wannabesuki2*

·*I #wannabesuki3*

·*The MakeApp foundation gave me a rash. Anyone else?*

·*Suki Hammer is not who she pretends to be. I used to work for her and she's a huge B.*

·*I heard those kids don't even live with her. She rents them for photo ops.*

·*I bet she's a psycho #tigermom*

·*Child labor in China makes her products. She belongs in jail.*

LOAD MORE COMMENTS HERE.

13

-:-

Melissa

MELISSA DREW A deep breath and smoothed the fabric of her skirt before knocking on her boss's door. She quickly snapped a selfie for The Mostly Likely Girls, captioning it: *One step closer to Mayor Levin-Levine!*

It was exactly nine and Barry had just settled at his desk, newspaper in one hand and breakfast muffin in the other. Melissa's stomach rumbled at the sight of it—a crumbly, cinnamon swirly thing that would travel directly to her ass. She'd moved beyond ten-berry meals, but she still feared pastries.

She wasn't sure how her announcement would go over. Barry was the first person outside of The Most Likely Girls she was letting in on her plans, other than Principal Giffords, who seemed to think she was joking and called to check on her when she didn't show up to PTA elections. Assuming all went well with her boss, later that day she would tell Cameron, so long as her daughter wasn't in a particularly mercurial mood. She was far more afraid of her teenage daughter than Barry. Her boss was legally obligated to treat her with a certain level of respect; Cam had no such parameters.

"Come in," Barry called out. Melissa stepped into his messy office and took the seat opposite the desk after moving an enormous stack of accordion folders to the floor. Her fingertips itched to organize his papers and turn the books on his shelves so they faced spine out. Would it kill him to get a proper inbox and a pen holder? Her office supplies were arranged like a Mondrian masterpiece in a Lucite tray. Barry would surely be grateful, but she held herself back. If she was going to be seen as an authority figure—*a political leader*—she had best stay away from the Container Store.

Melissa smiled at Barry. What she was asking for was going to be tricky, and she repeated her mother's mantra: *You catch more bees with honey than with vinegar.*

"I just want to say how much I love working at WCTR," she began, eyeing the photograph of Barry's family behind him. It was covered in a thick layer of dust, but she could make out a pretty wife and three little girls dressed in Christmas plaids with matching bows. "I feel constantly challenged in this job and love thinking of ways to help WCTR's bottom line."

Barry leaned back in his chair and put his hands behind his head. He seemed more interested in digesting her compliments than his muffin. Up close, she saw it had a raspberry jam filling. She knew it would taste orgasmic.

"That's wonderful to hear. I must say you're doing an excellent job."

Jobs, Melissa wanted to correct him. Annie was still on maternity leave, but this wasn't the time to get technical.

"The reason I asked to meet with you is that I've decided to run for mayor of Bellport. I don't want you to worry that it will affect my performance at work. I'm more committed than ever." Another lie. "But politics have always interested me, and this is something I think I would be very good at. I believe I can help our town."

She wanted to retract her last sentence. She didn't even know if Barry lived in Bellport. Melissa was going to have to get to know her constituency better.

The smile on Barry's face had mellowed into a flat line.

"Mayor? Do you have any political experience?"

"Well, I have run the parent-teacher association at my daughter's school for the past eight years. And trust me, that is no picnic." She forced a laugh. One of many she'd have to fake after she formally put her name on the ballot.

"I'm sure you're right," Barry said. "My wife does a lot of that volunteer stuff. Thankless job, if you ask me."

"Well, yes, it can be at times. But I like to think I'm doing some good."

"You know, Melissa, as I think about it more, you running for office could present something of a problem." He rolled his desk chair away from her and bent down to retrieve something in his briefcase. Melissa pinched a tiny crumb off the muffin. "As the public radio station of Bellport, I'm not sure how it would appear if we had a political candidate on our payroll. I mean, obviously you're not the talent, but still." Now Barry was upright again, and he was frowning. Melissa didn't like the way he said she was "not the talent." How talented was Mary-Emily Watson, the octogenarian who droned on about gardening for sixty minutes during the lunch hour? Or Bob Whittaker, the "cultural" disc jockey who had yet to recommend a single movie that wasn't based on a Marvel comic?

"I wouldn't ask for anything in the way of favors from WCTR. No free airtime. No endorsements. Nothing of the sort. I plan to do my job, quietly and efficiently, like always."

"I don't know how you'll manage to get it all done, though."

"Well, the current mayor has a full-time job. He's a partner in a law firm." *Which is a lot harder than the mind-numbing, repetitive contractual work that I do.* Melissa assumed that went without saying.

"Good point," he said. She felt like a yo-yo getting yanked up and down.

"I'm a single mother with a full-time job. I multitask in my sleep."

"If you think you can manage, then I wish you luck, Melissa. I was unaware that Mayor Thompson was retiring, though. I should give him a call and take him out for a beer."

Melissa rose from her seat.

"He's not retiring," she said. "I'm running against him."

AFTER A FEW hours of work, on which, contrary to what she told Barry, she could barely concentrate, Melissa was ready for her next order of business. Her campaign was going to need funding. Thompson was an old-boy politician. He got his votes at the golf club, the gym, and the men-only cigar lounge in nearby Greenwich. Lord knows how many favors he did for votes. She was a nobody outside of Bellport Academy—and even there, probably half the parents didn't know her name. If she was going to present any meaningful challenge to the incumbent, she would need visibility. And visibility was expensive.

"Nathan Romonofsky, please," she said when the billionaire's direct phone line was answered by a woman with a charming British accent.

"Whom may I tell him is calling?"

"Melissa Levin-Levine. From Bellport Academy. We chatted at the reunion." She was sure they must have exchanged some words. Surely, she said thank you when she handed him her champagne glass.

Getting Nathan's private office number had not been easy. His company, HeartRx, had only a flimsy online presence with an email address that ricocheted an autoreply when she pinged it. But Melissa would not be deterred.

The next day, she asked Principal Giffords for Nathan's number. His refusal to share it came as no surprise, but she had an ace up her sleeve.

"You know, Principal Giffords, I met Liza Jones for coffee. I gave her all my files and I think she'll make an excellent PTA president." They were standing outside the front entrance to the school at dismissal time. Hundreds of students were pouring out of the building and a few dozen parents were milling about the parking lot.

"I think it's wonderful you stepped aside," Giffords said. "Let someone else have a turn. Rollins—that's senior parking only!" he called out to a letter-wearing athlete.

"Of course," she said. "And I think it's very good of you to protect Nathan Romonofsky's privacy. A busy man like him has many people vying for his time."

"That's exactly right, Melissa. I'm glad you understand my hands are tied." He was speaking to her like an elementary school student forced to stay in for recess, which made her next move all the more delicious.

"By the way, I was just wondering, I know last year's spring musical was canceled due to Covid. But I don't recall the thousand dollars the PTA gave your office for costumes and a cast party being returned. Would you know anything about that?" She lowered her sunglasses so she was looking directly into Giffords's eyes.

"I'll have my office look into that first thing," he said, shifting uncomfortably. "Stop by tomorrow and I'll have Nathan's number ready for you."

"Terrific," she said. Easy, peasy, lemon squeezy, just like Cam used to say when she was little.

And now Melissa was on hold, waiting for Nathan.

A cough and a throat gurgle told Melissa someone was on the line.

"Hello, this is Nathan."

"Hi, Nathan. This is Melissa Levin-Levine. We were on the dais together at the reunion last month." Her voice, lilting upward as she started to lose her nerve, was met with silence.

"Anyway, I just wanted to start off by thanking you for your incredible gift to the school. That was certainly unexpected." She hoped he took her meaning to be that the massive gift was the surprise, not that it came from him, though both were true.

"You're welcome," he said. He sounded like a robot. Melissa found herself counting his syllables. It made sense he created some artificial heart–type thing; he himself was battery-operated.

Melissa took a sip of water to cool her suddenly parched

throat. She needed to get used to asking for money, something she was terrible at. Every time the school holiday fund fell short, Melissa laid out hundreds of her own dollars rather than hound people. She struggled to ask Josh for money to cover some of the extras Cam wanted. Now was the time to man up. Unless she could get a lawn sign into at least a quarter of the front yards in Bellport, her campaign was doomed.

"I'm reaching out to you because I know how much you care about our community. I mean, your gift makes that obvious."

"It does? I mean, yes."

This guy was awkward as hell. She should have just gone to Suki. In fairness, she tried, but every time she and Suki set up a time to chat, one of her assistants would call to reschedule. Melissa was still puzzled over why Kim Konner was interviewed in the *Forbes* piece and not one of them. Could Suki be upset with them? With her?

"Of course. Anyway, I also care deeply about Bellport. And that's why I'm calling. I'm running for mayor. The same man, Bill Thompson, has held the job for more than twenty years. He's not done anything to improve our town, help local businesses, or improve the school district. He spends more time on the golf course than in the office."

"Interesting," Nathan said, followed by an interminable pause that brought pesky hives to Melissa's flesh. It was nothing Benadryl couldn't quash. She had come this far—practically blackmailing Giffords to get Nathan's number—and she wasn't going to give up.

"I was wondering if perhaps I could buy you a cup of coffee and tell you about my campaign. I mean, I know you don't need me to buy you the coffee. You should buy it for me. Ha!" What the hell was wrong with her? She could actually picture her foot in her mouth and was tempted to leave it there rather than risk saying anything else moronic.

"I would like that," Nathan said, finally with some inflection. "Why don't I come to you? Should we say in two weeks? I'd do it sooner but I'm due in Japan for a trade show and I leave tonight."

"Um, yes. Yes, that would be amazing." Her heart was beating a mile a minute. She had worked up the nerve to call Nathan, but she hadn't expected it to be this easy.

"Sure. I'll be in touch."

"Wow, thank you for trusting me and wanting to hear me out," she gushed.

"Of course. You want something done? Missy's the one."

Melissa nearly dropped the phone. She hadn't heard that since, well, 1994. It was her sophomore-year campaign slogan when she ran for student government.

"How did you—" she started to ask, but Nathan said, "I've got a meeting to get to," and the next thing she heard was a dial tone.

MELISSA SWUNG OPEN the door to her house and relished the momentary quiet. Cam would be home from Hannah's house any minute and Melissa, energized by her call with Nathan, was pumped to tell her about the mayoral run. Cam would cringe at the thought of her mother shaking hands at the supermarket and tacking posters to trees with her slogan (*Mayor Levin-Levine Would Be Divine* was the best she had come up with so far—and it didn't even rhyme unless her last name was mispronounced). Eventually Cam would come around. Some new Tik-

Tok would get posted or group chat drama would unfold and Melissa would recede back into her usual role in the Life of Cam: background-furniture-slash-ATM.

She walked into the kitchen and pulled open the refrigerator door, wondering for the umpteenth time what to make for dinner. If there was anything about her life that most resembled *Groundhog Day*, it was the nightly dinner decision. She preheated the oven to make a frozen cauliflower-crust pizza for the two of them and practically fell onto the sofa. The moment she felt her body start to relax, her cell phone dinged with a message from her sister.

> KAREN: Are you bringing a date to
> Jordan's BM or not? I'm in table seating
> hell and you're not helping.

> MELISSA: IDK yet. Can I pls have
> another week.

> KAREN: Fine. A date would be > for the
> table symmetry. Though I could put you
> with the widows and Jordan's math
> tutor. Actually, that might be better.
> Love u.

Her sister wasn't a bad person. She just grossly overestimated how much everyone else cared about the minutiae of her life. Melissa once consulted a nine-point checklist of what defined a narcissist. When Karen satisfied the first four on the list, Melissa stopped reading.

She was not thrilled about being put with the widows, who

were all at least thirty years older than she and talked exclusively about cruising, but who could she bring? Melissa hadn't touched the dating app since the hairy-penis photo. There was always I ADD 4U, but their last encounter was a letdown and Melissa would bet dollars to donuts Kenny was a terrible dancer.

Her thoughts returned to Nathan. She was still in disbelief that he remembered her campaign slogan while she could scarcely remember if they ever had a class together. Well, Nathan was having the last laugh. On display in the school lobby was a model of the megacomplex Nathan's dollars were funding: The Nathan Romonofsky Center for Science and Technology. He wouldn't go unnoticed again.

She initiated a group FaceTime with The Most Likely Girls and told her friends about the phone call. "He ended the call by quoting my campaign slogan."

"Weird." Tara was at work, scrubbing down a countertop. "'Go to Hell' or 'Missy's the one'?"

"'Missy's the one.'"

"Super weird," Priya seconded. She, too, was at work. Her glasses magnified the fine lines around her eyes, which appeared to have multiplied since the reunion. "I remember 'Save a Penny, Vote for Jenny'—but that's because the idea of Jenny being treasurer was absurd. She was in remedial math."

"Which Jenny?" Tara asked, tossing a soggy sponge into a slop sink.

"Jenny R. She won," Melissa said. It had been insufferable to work with her on the student council.

Melissa heard the front door swing open, trailed by the sound of sniffling.

"Guys, Cam's home. I gotta go."

Melissa rushed to greet her daughter, who was standing limply in the doorway, staring at her phone.

Cam thrust the screen in Melissa's face. Melissa squinted to make out the tiny text on Instagram. The profile page said @BellportBlabber. Melissa could feel the pit in her stomach already forming.

"Do you see it?" Cam took the phone back and zoomed in on the picture, magnifying the words: Cameron Levine, Most Likely to be a Contestant on The Biggest Loser.

"Who did this?" Melissa asked. She had plenty more dirt on Principal Giffords pocketing extra change here and there. She would use whatever leverage needed to make sure the punk behind this was expelled.

"Nobody knows," Cam said between sniffles. "Somehow a draft of the yearbook got around—a joke version, anyway." Cam was now lying facedown on the couch in their den. Melissa could barely hear her with her face muzzled by a pillow. She gently placed her open palm on Cam's back. Her daughter was normally resistant to touch but Melissa felt the need to connect.

"I will find out. I will speak to Dr. Giffords immediately and somebody will pay for this. I promise you that." Melissa was already back on her feet, going for her cell phone. Cam snapped upright.

"No, stop! I can't have my mommy getting involved. And mine wasn't even the meanest one. There were way worse."

Melissa dropped the phone. She wasn't committing to abiding by Cam's wishes and not following up with the principal—it went against every fiber in her being—but she didn't need to do anything rash. If she did speak to Giffords, she would do it without Cam knowing.

"I promise, this will be old news in a day or two. Nobody cares about the superlatives, real or fake."

"You do. You and your friends have that Most Likely Girls challenge! I heard you talking about it on the phone with Tara last week."

"Hang on a sec." Melissa climbed the stairs to her bedroom quickly and returned with her yearbook. "Sit with me a second."

Reluctantly, Cam obliged.

"Let me show you where my former classmates are today."

Melissa circled her finger over the spread and landed on Steven Mathers, Most Likely to Win an Olympic Gold Medal.

"This guy, amazing soccer player. Went on to play at UNC. Got so drunk at a toga party at his frat that he dropped a keg on his bare foot and lost three toes. Needless to say, no medal for him."

She scanned the pages for her next example.

"Ah yes, Marley Morgan. Most Likely to Write a Bestselling Novel. You know when you buy medicine and it has all those warnings like, if you take this, you could bleed internally and grow an extra hand? She writes those."

Melissa could see she was getting through to Cam. There was even the hint of a smile peeking from behind her pout.

"Who's that?" Cam pointed to Kim Konner and her superlative: Most Likely to Be on the Cover of *People*'s Most Beautiful.

"Oh, her. Yeah, she's still really pretty. But I've never seen her face on a magazine. And I—" Melissa broke off. Should she share the rest with Cam? If there was ever a time to push boundaries, it was now. "—saw her best friend blowing her husband in the bathroom at the reunion."

"Are you serious?" Cam's mouth fell open.

"As a heart attack," Melissa said. "The most successful person from our class—even more than Suki—is some guy we can barely remember. The point is, my love, you don't want to peak in high school. Then it's all downhill after that."

Cam rested her head on Melissa's shoulder. Their closeness made Melissa tingle.

"Got it. Be a loser in high school. Leave room to grow."

Melissa wrinkled her brow. It wasn't exactly what she was saying, but it was close.

The timer on the oven dinged.

"Pizza's ready," Melissa said. "It's cauliflower crust."

Melissa surprised herself by taking one slice, then another, then a third. The two of them were about to polish off the pie when Melissa dropped her crust.

"Grandma! We need to call Grandma Barbara. Right now." Before Cam could object or slink away, the line was ringing.

"Is everything okay?" Melissa's mom said as a greeting.

"Yes, why wouldn't it be?"

"Because you never call. I haven't heard from you in at least a week, so I assume something is wrong. Your sister calls me all the time."

"That's because Karen likes to hear herself speak and you're the only one who won't hang up on her. Anyway, there is something wrong, actually."

"I knew it. Is it Cam? What happened? I'll kill anyone who hurt her."

Melissa smiled. The phone was on speaker and she liked the idea of three generations of Levin women ready to kill for one another.

"Somebody in school wrote something nasty about her.

Which reminded me that you need to tell her the Louis Tanzer story."

"Who's Louis Tanzer?" Cam asked.

"Louis Tanzer was the hottest number at PS 129 in Bensonhurst," Barbara said. Melissa pictured her mother, hair in rollers for the evening, holding a mug of herbal tea. In the next room, her father would be watching *Jeopardy!* with the volume on too loud. There was something comforting about living close to them, knowing this scene was taking place within walking distance.

"Turn it down, Stan!" Barbara said, as if on cue.

"Like I was saying, every girl in Bensonhurst and as far as three subway stops away was in love with Louis. He was a terrific athlete. Not much going on upstairs, but looks he had. And, supposedly, he had a very big schlong."

"Grandma!"

"It's true, at least that's what Suzie Shapiro said. They got to third base. Anyway, everyone at school knew what a whiz at math I was. To this day, I'm sharp. The ladies I play canasta with can't add to a hundred and eighty to save their lives. But I can do it in my sleep."

"Mom, speed it up. Cam should hear the story before Final Jeopardy! comes on."

"You're very snarky, Melissa. I don't think that's a good quality in an elected official. Men don't like it, either. Anyway, one day, Louis comes over to me. Tells me he likes my sweater. I was wearing a pink twinset from Lord & Taylor that I got on a big sale. He asks me to study with him for the math final. I'm overjoyed. I had friends but I wasn't exactly Miss Popularity. And I didn't get my chest until after I had Karen. Well, Louis and I studied for a few hours. He flirted with me all night. And do you know what I agreed to by the end? He said he was allowed to take the final at home because of some farkakte football game. I agreed to take the final for him."

"That's so not like you, Gram," Cam said.

"Of course not. Not like the cheaters I play mah-jongg with. Needless to say, he never talked to me again once he turned in the final. I was miserable. I had convinced myself he really liked me. But he was back in Suzie Shapiro's pants the next day. Fast-forward six years. I met your grandfather at a wedding. He wasn't a heartthrob, but good enough."

"Mom, he's in the next room."

"Oh please, with his hearing? We got married quickly. Your grandpa Stanley made a nice living right away. He worked at a bank. We were the first of our friends to buy a house. It wasn't anything to write home about, but in those days, being a home-owner in your early twenties was a big deal. We were living there for about six months when I lost it on your father. There was bird crap all over the windows. I said, 'Stanley, get on a lad-der and clean the windows.' He refused. 'Call a window washer,' he said. I didn't have to be told twice. The next day, the van shows up. Now I happened to look really great because it was Minnie Markowitz's engagement party that night so I had my hair and makeup done. The window washer rings the bell. I open the door and who is on the other side of it? Louis Tanzer. Swear to God."

"You're kidding?" Cam was bouncing on the sofa.

"Cameron, don't interrupt me. Anyway, I don't think he rec-ognized me at this point, and of course, I had a different last name. I showed him what I wanted done and went back to watching *Days of Our Lives*. Suddenly, I heard a crash. I thought it was from the TV. You know on those soaps someone is always having an accident. But it wasn't. It was coming from upstairs. Louis Tanzer had fallen off the ladder while cleaning my bedroom window and landed smack in my azaleas. I ran outside to help him. He hit his head pretty bad. I guess the concussion brought back his memory—he looked at me and said—'Bobby Singer? From PS 129?' And do you know what I said?"

"That he was a jerk?" Cam volunteered.

"Nope. I said, 'You missed a spot' and pointed to the window he fell from. And then I went right back in the house and poured myself a huge glass of lemonade."

"Grandma, that story is crazy."

"Listen to me, Cameron. Whatever schmuck hurt you, forget about it. The cool kids become window washers. The nerds live in nice houses."

"But I'm not a math nerd or a cool kid."

"You don't know who the hell you are at seventeen. And you don't have to. But what happens now doesn't mean a thing later on. Remember Louis Tanzer next time you're upset."

"Got it. Louis Tanzer and his enormous schlong," Cam said. "An inspiring tale."

"Thanks, Mom," Melissa said, hanging up.

"What was Grandma saying about you being an elected official?"

"About that." Melissa looked at her daughter, whose spirit had indeed been buoyed by the Louis Tanzer story. "Your mom is running for town mayor."

Cameron's face fell. "For fuck's sake, can this day get any worse?"

Well, nobody said this would be easy.

14

-:.-

Tara

"C'MON, STEP ON it," Tara said, her head poking forward from the backseat.

"Miss, the light was turning red," her driver said.

"You could have made it."

Tara leaned back and groaned. Her job prospects and her Uber rating were plummeting simultaneously.

She was headed to a tiny street she'd never heard of on the Lower East Side. A quick Google search showed it was about two hundred yards long and featured two speakeasies and a drag queen piano bar. A far cry from the heels-and-highlights neighborhood of her day job.

Her stomach lurched as the car creeped forward in traffic. She hadn't been to a job interview since Ricardo. How many drinks had she had before she called her favorite Kitchen Kiddos mom, Marina, about the job opportunity with her cousin? At least three. Chased by a full joint.

She was motivated by the incessant ding of The Most Likely Girls text chain. Only three weeks had passed since they made their pact, and already Melissa was campaigning like Hillary Clinton on steroids and Priya was presenting at hospital board meetings. Tara was the only one dogged by inertia and fear. Yes, she ached to be back in a real kitchen, not the Fisher-Price version of her workplace, but she hated the idea of starting at the bottom again. Restaurant kitchens were brutal environments, tempers flaming stronger than the stovetops, and the rookies were put through the proverbial blender before given even a modicum of respect. And what if she had to face another predatory head chef, or restaurateur? She would risk losing faith in humanity entirely. Still, she owed it to The Most Likely Girls to find out.

Marina's offer seemed safe from Tara's worst fears. A brand-new kitchen started by her cousin Maya, who had never owned a restaurant before and needed Tara for more than just cooking. Tara could use the respite from Kitchen Kiddos. Just yesterday in a tween class, Zoey, the queen bee, squeezed strawberry jam onto a sweet kid named Laurel's pants and said it was her period bleeding through.

Maya and Tara spoke briefly about the new venture a few days earlier and arranged an in-person interview, unfortunately scheduled for the same time thousands of commuters were tunneling back to New Jersey. Tara reviewed what she knew as the car crawled. The restaurant was called TIK. The twenty-table space would open in approximately a month. Maya was desperately behind on her plans. This excited Tara. She had always wanted to stretch herself into restaurant management.

Except now she was going to be unforgivably late. Timing was everything when it came to service. To distract herself from the traffic, Tara snapped a selfie in the Uber holding up her résumé and sent it to the ML girls. The résumé was secured in a leather folder she'd picked up at Staples the day she spoke to Maya.

"What's that?" Rachel had asked, running her neon yellow nails over the résumé folder, which Tara had mistakenly left on the coffee table. "Nothing," Tara said, snatching it up. She would tell Rachel about the interview if, and only if, she got the job. There was enough humiliation in the failing of Kitchen Kiddos already. And she didn't want Rachel to panic prematurely about getting another job or blabbing to the other staff.

En route to interview for chef job!!! Tara texted the girls, inserting every related emoji she could find. Three whisks, four spatulas, and six refrigerators later, Tara glanced out the window to discover they had advanced only one block.

Cool! Tell us more! Melissa wrote back.

But Tara had little she could add with certainty. Maya hadn't given her more than two minutes on the call. All Marina had said was, "It's a fusion place. Maya is very hip. She's part Thai, part Australian, and totally spunky and gorgeous."

The Thai heritage had been useful information. And the fusion hint. TIK, Tara guessed, stood for Thai, Indian, and Korean. It was an interesting concept for sure, a promising flavor trifecta that hadn't been mashed up yet, as far as she knew. The only trouble was that she had little experience with any of those cuisines. Ricardo was a seafood restaurant where she practiced California-style cooking, roasted vegetables and legumes prepared with limited oil and muted spice. Avocado in every meal. She doubted the mushy green vegetable she fed daily to Angelino diners, and the source of the jagged scar on her thumb (only the mango was harder to peel), would make its way into many dishes at TIK.

Rachel was on a camping trip the weekend before the interview, away with her young friends who still found pleasure in sleeping on dirt and waking up in a sleeping bag soaked with dew. Tara enjoyed having the kitchen to herself to experiment. First, she hightailed it to a restaurant supplier in Queens to load up on the kitchen equipment she was lacking. With shame she pulled out the credit card still linked to her parents' account. She was really trying to cut down on her reliance on them. But there was no way she could afford a new cleaver, chopping block, wok, mortar and pestle, tawa, and belan on her own. It occurred to her she could have gotten a crash course from Priya's mother-in-law in Indian cooking. To hear Priya tell it, as much as she wanted to tell off Jeet, the minute the older woman stuck a homemade samosa in her mouth, she lost all resolve. That said, restaurant Indian and homecooked Indian food were distant cousins at most. Tara didn't think she'd had naan even once at Priya's growing up.

Passing through the aisles of the restaurant supplier, Tara felt electricity sizzling through her veins. She wanted to elbow the guy wielding an eight-inch paring Wüsthof to ask if he was going to use it for a tarte tatin. When her cart collided with another pushed by a young chef in a checkered uniform, she could practically smell the fresh sourdough that would be made with the bread maker inside.

After the supply store, she picked up spices from a hole-in-the-wall in Elmhurst recommended on a foodie blog. Towers of brightly colored pulverized spices dazzled her and she filled clear plastic bags with coriander, cumin, cloves, and cardamom. Halfway back to Manhattan, she realized she forgot to buy fresh cinnamon, which she would need to experiment with desserts. She wanted to tackle some recipes she found online. Kheer, an Indian rice pudding, as well as sujeonggwa, a cinnamon punch. The Uber turned around and Tara tried not to think about the increased fare. If the axiom that you had to spend money to make money was true, she was well on her way.

By the end of the weekend, her apartment smelled like what she imagined as an open market in Mumbai crossed with a kimchi cart, but Tara was satisfied she would be able to speak intelligently with Maya. She could even demonstrate a few dishes if the interview went well. There was so much food to sample, Tara felt guilty Rachel wasn't there to help consume it, though mostly she relished the weekend of quiet. It had been ages since she'd had the apartment to herself and she found herself enjoying the solitude more than she should. She deliberately slept on the diagonal in their king bed each night.

"This it?" Tara's Uber driver wound around to question her and she sized up the desolate street with hesitation. It didn't seem like the location for a new restaurant, but what did she know? The area was probably some up-and-coming neighborhood.

"This is it."

Her rubber clogs hit the sidewalk with purpose. Dress for the job you want, not the job you have . . . Didn't her father used to chide her brothers about that when they headed out of the house in sports jerseys?

It took a few minutes for Tara to find the building number— she was in a full sweat by the time she finally spotted it. It had the tiniest sign imaginable that read TIK. Above it was a sketch of a musical note. *Lord, let this not also be a piano bar*, she thought. She'd worked at one of those once—"Piano Man" got requested at least three times a night. She would chop vegetables to the beat, way too slowly for her boss's liking, and then the song would be stuck in her head the whole next day.

TIK's ground floor had one large window, which she quickly peeked through before pulling open the heavy black door. It hardly looked like the ideal footprint for a restaurant. The space was impossibly narrow, and Tara could already hear the servers grumbling about bumping into one another. Service would be like a game of *Frogger*.

She was greeted by a tall, thin man with a goatee, dressed all in black. He had a tattoo on his inner forearm that said TIK. Maybe he was the financial backer for the place? She prayed his ink was temporary. Didn't he realize that more than 50 percent of restaurants fail within the first year?

"Maya!" he called up a narrow staircase leading to a balcony where Tara imagined more tables would be set up. "She's here! The chef is here."

The chef is here. Tara clicked the heels of her clogs subtly. She didn't look like a candidate for the hostess position, or a bureaucrat from the health department making an impromptu inspection. She looked like a chef. Tattoo guy had known it without asking her name.

"I'm Matt," he said, extending his hand. She shook it, unable to control the goofy grin on her face. She felt ready. She felt alive. It was the first time she didn't swallow her antidepressant and think, *Please work, please work.* She was already dressed and caffeinated when her alarm clock went off.

"Tara," she said, placing her hand in his. "It's nice to meet you."

He took out his cell phone from the back pocket of his jeans and Tara was about to retreat when he pulled her close with one arm and extended the phone with the other.

"Say TIK," he said, and suddenly Tara was posing for a selfie.

"TIK," she said, but it came out like a question, which it was. What the hell was going on?

"You must be Tara," said a breathy voice, and Tara looked up to see a woman coming down the staircase, double-fisting iPhones and wearing a tank top with the same music note on the building's exterior. "I'm Maya."

"Woman" was a generous term. The person Tara was facing, with hot pink hair piled in a messy bun at the crown of her head and a dozen studs crawling up her ear, looked no more than eighteen. Tara cursed Marina. She might have mentioned that her cousin was fresh out of diapers.

"It's nice to—" Tara started to say, but Maya did the same thing Matt had just done. "Say TIK!" This time Tara complied more gracefully. She wondered if there was some sort of scrapbook planned to record the opening of the restaurant. Suki would approve; her office had a number of blown-up photos of MakeApp's corporate headquarters from the construction phase. There were puns to be made about foundation, and they were made indeed, but mostly the photos were there to remind employees about MakeApp's mission, the power of transformation. Tara remembered reading that in a *Wall Street Journal* article a good five years back. She hadn't liked the way the sketch artist had captured her friend, who looked cold in the black-and-white image. Suki's face was warm and friendly in real life. The puff pieces in the glossy magazines captured it more accurately.

"Let me show you around," Maya said, looping an arm through Tara's. That Tara was at least six inches taller than Maya just drove home how ridiculously old she felt in comparison to her potential new . . . boss? She felt like handing Maya a Kitchen Kiddos apron and sending her to the wash-up station.

"Great. I can't wait to see the kitchen," Tara said, meaning it. A real kitchen. Not one with step stools and posters with class rules taped to the walls. A place where food could be made without a ballad about salad or a rhyme about thyme.

"Glad you're not in heels," Maya said, looking at Tara's clogs. Maya was wearing high-top Converse sneakers in hot pink; the same shade as her hair. Yellow music notes were hand-painted on them. She didn't seem like a "Piano Man" kind of girl. Nor did she seem like a graduate of a culinary school. She looked like an extra from *School of Rock*. "The kitchen is on the fifth floor."

Fifth floor? Tara was dumbfounded, with an emphasis on the *dumb* part. Why would anyone choose to put the kitchen so high up? The food would be ice-cold by the time it reached the patrons. TIK seemed doomed to fail from the start. As if mixing Thai, Korean, and Indian wasn't risky enough.

She wouldn't accept the job if the restaurant didn't stand a chance, but she still needed to be polite for Marina's sake. She tried to find the silver lining. At least she had material to put into the Most Likely group chat about her earnest attempt to get a restaurant gig. It wasn't her fault Marina's cousin was quite possibly the worst restaurateur in history and had remedial spatial-planning skills. She climbed the stairs behind Maya, now more amused than irritated.

Maya paused on the second-floor landing. Her high-tops had been squeaking something awful on the metal stairs.

"You ready?"

"I can manage another four flights," Tara said.

"Not what I meant," Maya said. "I'm talking about the grand reveal. The second floor is the main attraction. Fifteen hundred square feet. Great light. It's literally perfect. You didn't think the ground floor was where the action would take place?"

"Of course not," Tara said. She couldn't have been more confused.

"Right. Ground floor is for props. And to sign the waivers. Speaking of, I like your folder." Maya gestured to Tara's leather-bound résumé. "We could put the waivers in something like that." To think Tara had spent an hour debating between Arial and Times New Roman for her résumé.

Waivers. Props. Tara was now wondering if she was here to audition for a porno. It would explain a lot about the nondescript building and the scant information provided thus far. Good grief, had Marina noticed her new chest and the desperation on her face and connected some very peculiar dots?

"This is it," Maya squealed, unlatching a red velvet rope and splitting a black curtain in two. She stepped into the room and Tara followed cautiously behind.

"Oh my God," Tara gasped, proud that she'd managed that instead of *What the fuck?* She had truly entered a fun house. The floor was black-and-white-checkered tile. There were booths with pink vinyl seats and a giant, revolving disco ball overhead. In neon lights above the booths were signs that said THE CHARLI and THE ADDISON. Tara flashed to the girls in her teen class who were always talking about someone named Addison. She had assumed Addison was a popular girl in their school they worshipped. And she had thought the Charli they gushed over was a boy.

"What do you think?" Maya said. She was filming Tara's reaction on one of her phones.

"It's . . . unique. It's very unique. Not very Asian, though."

Maya laughed. "Well, I'm not against an Asian booth. I mean, we could do something with BTS. They're huge on TikTok."

"TikTok?" Tara felt the ground beneath her start to shake and she took a seat. Above her shoulders, the words THE BELLA sizzled in their neon casing. She put her forehead directly on the table, willing the dizzy spell to pass.

"Are you okay?" Maya asked. "Do you want some water? Matt! Get our chef some water. And cut the damn disco ball."

Our chef . . . our chef . . . our chef. This *was* a restaurant. She was here to cook. It might look like a Nickelodeon set, and the kitchen might be an elevator ride from the customers, but there was still food to be prepared. Bellies to fill. Menus to create.

"I'm okay," Tara said. It was starting to make sense. She knew that music note symbol and why it had felt familiar when she saw it from the street. The teen class she taught at Kitchen Kiddos. The girls were always on that app. TIK. TikTok. She burst out laughing. She had spent four hours trying to crisp samosas to get a job at a restaurant that was nothing more than a backdrop for videos. "I just didn't realize what this place was exactly. It is a restaurant, right?"

"Of course. Check this out." Maya tapped the screen in the booth where Tara was sitting. A menu filled the black. "Everything is electronic. No waiters. You just tap your order. The phone mounts haven't shown up yet. Annoying, I know. We'll figure something out. Not gonna have any shaky videos on opening night."

Tara looked at the menu. Locally grown fried potatoes, aka french fries. Dairy-free milkshakes. Grass-fed burgers and organic chicken wings. It was a bougie McDonald's. One item nearly made her gag: hot Cheetos mozzarella sticks. Not hard to make, but utterly revolting.

"Check out the desserts," Maya said, and tapped the screen. A new heading appeared: *Mug Shot*. "It's a double meaning, obv. Like take your picture with one of our mug cakes."

"Uh-huh," Tara managed. The interview would be more comprehensible if it had been conducted in a mix of Indian, Thai, and Korean. She studied the desserts. Apple Pie *a la Mug*. *Mug-nificent* Brownie Cake.

"That's how I got my start, BTW." Maya pointed to the brownie, a layered, gooey death by chocolate arranged in a glass mug. "I made that on TikTok and it went viral. That's when I dropped out of cooking school. "I'm more of a visionary than a cook. Which is where you come in. Are you good with mugs?" Maya didn't wait for an answer. She pulled Tara over to a corner booth, smaller than the rest, with thick glass walls all the way up to the ceiling.

"That's our soundproof booth. For ASMR."

"What is that?" Curiosity was getting the best of her, though Tara knew she ought to bolt for the door.

"Autonomous sensory meridian response. It's huge on Tik-Tok. Let me show you."

Maya pulled up a video of a teenage girl dipping a deep-fried drumstick in ranch sauce and taking bites. The only sound in the video was that of her chewing and smacking her lips together. It had 1.2 million views.

"Isn't that soothing? We'll have to figure out some menu items that are good for ASMR. Maybe cloud bread."

"Sure," Tara said, because who cared anymore. And there

was nothing remotely soothing about listening to this chick chew on camera.

"Listen, Maya, I'm sorry if I've wasted your time. I need to be honest with you. This isn't really what I had in mind." She picked up her purse off the banquette to signal goodbye.

"Aunt Marina said you're amazing and that you have great energy with teenagers. And, honestly, I have a financial backer bankrolling this place and your starting salary would be—"

And Maya then said a number that was double what Tara netted from Kitchen Kiddos in a good year.

"What do you say? We have a sick PR firm repping TIK. The place is going to be bussin. Facts." Maya was beaming.

Tara was going to have to learn an entirely new vernacular to work here. *Facts*.

She shrugged her shoulders in physical assent. "I do make a mean eighth note sugar cookie."

Maya's eyes widened with pleasure. She looked even more childish when she smiled because of the space between her two front teeth.

"But I need a little time to think this over. Let me see the kitchen. I assume I don't have to do any TikTok dances while I cook?"

"That's actually an amazing idea," Maya said, but judging Tara's reaction, she quickly pulled back. "Course not. Listen, I'm really vibing with you. I think this could work out great. Let's go upstairs. I could use some help unpacking the microwave."

Microwave?

She'd already come this far. And that salary . . .

"Let's go."

. . . .

BACK IN HER neighborhood and still in disbelief, Tara wound her way into the park closest to her apartment and planted herself on a shady bench. She scrolled through her phone and saw six different versions of **well???** and **tell us!** from Priya and Melissa.

She muted the group chat. Tara wanted to talk to only Suki, who didn't bullshit and wasn't in on this ridiculous pact to actualize outlandish dreams from high school. Tara never chimed in when Melissa and Priya complained that Suki was out of touch with them, because it was different with her. Suki made time to text or FaceTime her from some fabulous location and to send her not-yet-released MakeApp products. Their friendship circle wasn't a neat pie chart divided exactly into fourths.

You cannot imagine what just happened to me, she texted Suki. The three dots of Suki's reply appeared, causing Tara's heart to flutter. She stared at her phone as the three dots disappeared and reappeared several times. Either Suki's phone was malfunctioning, or she was typing and erasing over and over. It wasn't like Suki to hem and haw.

Her phone rang. Even better. What Tara had just experienced at TIK deserved an oral retelling.

"Hi, Sukes," she said. "I have the craziest story to tell you."

"It's your father." Tara's shoulders slumped. Expecting Suki and getting George. Talk about a letdown. "Why didn't you tell me you were behind on your rent? Your landlord at Cooking Kids sent me a pretty terse email."

Her father could never get her business name right. "Because

I've got it, Dad. I'm sorry, but I can't really speak now." She looked up at the swings where three bored mothers were push- ing squealing toddlers in unison. "There's a line of parents out- side my door waiting to sign up for summer camp."

"Fine. But I don't want this messing up my credit score or my reputation," George said.

A call waiting beeped.

"I'll call you later, Dad," Tara said, and clicked through. "Sukes, I'm so happy to hear from you. How are you?"

"I'm all right," Suki said. Her voice sounded strained, as if squeezed through a colander. "Just wanted to say hi. I've been a shit friend recently. I feel bad about missing the reunion."

"We all understand. But we missed you." Tara was surprised. Suki wasn't prone to sentimentality or regret. Tara decided not to bring up the online trolls. Instead, she told Suki all about the interview at TIK, how she hadn't felt so out of touch in ages.

"I have an entire team dedicated to that nonsense. Did you know there are different 'sides' of TikTok?"

"Well, I am definitely on the wrong side. When did we get so old?" Tara sighed. She knew Suki understood the gravitational forces of middle age, the way they pulled everything—from your jowls to your spirits—down. If not from her own experience, then from watching her mother go from successful runway model to housewife in velour sweats.

"I don't know. I'll send you a package of our best antiaging serum. It actually works. Swear." Suki's voice was brightening. Tara was pleased to have that effect on her. "Listen, duty calls. I just wanted to tell you that I appreciate your friendship. And how you always have my back."

"Of course, Sukes. Always."

"Talk again soon?" Suki asked, her voice seesawing upward.

"Of course."

"Take the job, Tara," she added quickly before hanging up.

And, Tara, despite being fairly certain it was a bad idea, did.

15

Priya

THE LARGEST BOARDROOM at Yale New Haven Hospital was on a high floor of the main hospital wing and featured a stunning barreled oak table and butter-soft padded swivel chairs. If she were alone, Priya would put her head down on the table and take a really long nap.

The board was assembled for the November meeting on an unseasonably warm day. Sunlight streamed in through the large windows and Priya was tempted to put her sunglasses on, but as this was her first appearance before the board as the hospital's chief medical officer, she didn't want to look shady. There was already a coffee stain on her silk blouse she strategically tried to cover with her nametag.

Yale New Haven Hospital was in late-stage talks to merge with a smaller hospital in Bridgeport, which would expand access to health care to at least 100,000 more people in the state. A hospital merger was about as complicated a matter as possible, and Priya was energized in a way she hadn't been in years. She was prepared as hell for whatever questions the board would fire at her, but so far it was still Dr. Hiroshi at the podium, working through a slide presentation that was putting most of the room to sleep.

"I think we're going to take a short recess now," Dr. Hiroshi said. "There are pastries and coffee set up outside the boardroom. I've lost count of your yawns."

Polite laughter sounded through the room. Priya stood up, realizing that her butt had fallen asleep. At least one of her body parts was getting rest.

This was the part she had been dreading. While her eyes glazed over studying Hiroshi's Venn diagrams and revenue charts, it was preferable to glad-handing the fancy people whose names were sculpted in bronze and emblazoned above each wing of the hospital. She thought of Nathan Romonofsky, how different he was from this well-heeled set. In fact, surrounded by these powerhouses, whose net worths had so many zeroes Priya couldn't keep track, she was struck anew by the mystery of Nathan's gift. Each of these board members had a story that explained their philanthropy. Priya had been asked by Hiroshi to study their bios ahead of the meeting. One Wall Street superstar had been criticized by the media for not being charitable enough—a month later he donated enough money to rename the cardiac center. Another board member who earned a billion dollars from a tech IPO gave back to the hospital after it saved his mother's life. What was Nathan's story? Why had he chosen his high school as the recipient of his largesse over so many other worthy causes? Far more worthwhile ones, if Priya was being honest.

"Priya, let me introduce you around." Hiroshi was at her side.

"Sure," she said, grateful to have a wingman. Perhaps her boss sensed her apprehension, the way she was perusing the buffet to avoid mingling. Chitchat was never her forte. At the reunion, she fell back into her old habit of riding on Melissa's coattails. Priya wished she were there now. Melissa could make small talk with a doorknob.

"Make a plate first if you want," Hiroshi said. He snatched a gooey Danish for himself.

The food in the cafeteria was prison quality in comparison to this spread. Downstairs, the fruit cup, a whopping $8.00, was mostly melon with a few sliced strawberries to trick the unseasoned buyer. But for the board, there were heaping trays of buttery croissants, golden brown mini muffins, and ripe, glistening berries. The blueberries looked like they had been injected with steroids. Her belly rumbled but she didn't trust herself to balance utensils while shaking hands. She tended to klutziness, which was why surgery was never a viable option. That and the fact that she wasn't an egomaniac.

"Paul, how are you?" Hiroshi patted the back of a tall, broad-shouldered man in a bright orange golf shift and starched khakis.

"I'm great. Got in eighteen holes before the meeting. Love a fall golf day. You gotta get out there with me sometime soon." Khaki Pants set a curious gaze on Priya.

"You bet. Paul, I'd like you to meet Priya Chowdhury. She is our new chief medical officer. Paul is one of the top restructuring lawyers in the state."

"And I owe my golf swing to this place. Got a new shoulder two years ago. It's nice to meet you, Dr. Chowdhury." Paul extended his hand warmly and Priya took it. This wasn't so bad.

A little flattery. Some banter; hers clumsy but passable. Muffins that wouldn't chip a tooth. She planned to snag three on her way out to serve the kids for breakfast the next morning.

Hiroshi motioned for somebody else to join their huddle. A woman Priya hadn't noticed before, with red hair piled on top of her head in a messy bun and a camera dangling off her arm.

"Janet, will you grab the three of us?"

Before Priya could straighten her blouse, she was wedged between Hiroshi and Paul and mugging for the camera. Janet checked the screen and flashed a thumbs-up and suddenly both men released Priya from their clutches.

"Ahh, there's Nancy Prentiss Doyle. I'd love for you to meet her as well." Hiroshi guided Priya toward an elegant woman in a wool dress topped with three strands of pearls the size of eyeballs. He motioned for the photographer to follow.

"Nancy, aren't you looking marvelously tanned? I take it you and your husband enjoyed St. Barts?"

"The Caribbean is marvelous this time of year. Of course nothing like the Med in summer, which can't be beat."

The Med, the Med . . . Priya was fairly certain this bejeweled woman wasn't referring to Club Med, where Dev and Priya had taken the kids year after year until Asha revolted.

"Certainly not. There's a medical conference in Nice I'm trying to get myself invited to." Priya conjured the man eating green beans with his bare hands at Whole Foods and had a hard time connecting him to the person hobnobbing beside her. He was so much more facile at making conversation than she was. Could he actually be enjoying it? It seemed he was. She would clearly need to wear many hats in this new role. Unfortunately, hats didn't suit her.

"Nancy, this is Dr. Priya Chowdhury. Our new chief medical officer. We are so lucky to have her. Let's get a photo together, shall we?" And once again Priya was sandwiched between two people, saying "cheese," praying she didn't have lipstick on her teeth.

The fake smiling was tiring her out. She needed a moment alone to catch her breath. She had to pee. She wanted to try the steroid-infused berries. But Hiroshi was now guiding her in a different direction, aiming her around the room like a billiard ball. Why did the board care about her? Unless—

"Priya, one last person I'd love you to meet. Our newest board member, Abejino Naranjio." Hiroshi whisked her off to meet a dark-skinned man in a smart, navy suit.

Dev's voice in her ear crawled back.

You're not letting the politics spoil this for you . . .

Then the voices of the interns in the cafeteria.

A two-for-one pick . . .

She blinked back a tear and said, "Pleasure."

WHEN THE MEETING broke up, Priya dashed back to the medical wing to see a patient, a young mother with persistent pain in her hips. Priya ran through a full physical exam and wrote her a script for thrice-weekly physical therapy.

"You're joking," the woman said. "There is no way I can do PT that often. Can't you just give me meds?"

Priya felt her frustration. The patient was a school librarian with three-year-old twins at home. She probably didn't have time to use the bathroom.

"I'm sorry. At least go twice a week," she cautioned with a sympathetic smile.

Finally, behind her desk at the end of the day, Priya slipped off her pumps and massaged her arches. She hadn't worn anything besides rubber clogs or ballet flats to work in ages. The balls of her feet were on fire. She wondered if she could barter a blowjob for a foot rub tonight with Dev. It was probably easier to detour to the nail place on the way home and spend twenty bucks there.

She wanted to tell The Most Likely girls about what had happened today. She could predict their responses practically verbatim—*You're amazing, of course you deserve this promotion, yada yada*. Wasn't that what friends were for? To deliver standard-issue pick-me-ups and platitudes that somehow have an effect?

She pulled her phone from her purse and jolted when she saw six missed calls from an unfamiliar number.

The area code was 761. Wasn't that Vermont? Vid was at a weeklong outdoors program with his class in Stowe. She called back without even listening to the voice mails.

"This is Nurse Vicki," came the voice on the other end.

Priya's stomach seized. Six missed calls from the program's on-site nurse . . . that couldn't be good. She never should have let Vid go on this trip. The kid could barely be trusted to brush his teeth. And he had just started the ADHD meds. If she wasn't so busy at work, she wouldn't have let him. It was the temptation of having one less kid to manage that swayed her. And Melissa's assurance. "You're worried about sending him away for a week? We Jews send our kids to sleepaway camp for seven weeks every summer. It's good for them!"

Seven weeks without kids? Priya considered converting.

"Hi, it's Vid Agrawal's mother calling. Is everything okay?"

"Yes, Mrs. Agrawal, everything is fine. But your son hurt his leg. He fell off the ropes course and he's in quite a bit of pain. We've been trying to reach you for several hours. We need to know if you'll be picking him up or if you want him brought to the local hospital."

Oh no. Poor Vid. This wasn't what he needed. He didn't connect easily to his peers. With an injured leg, he wouldn't have the soccer team as a social outlet. Were those local hospitals any good? How would she find the time to drive four hours to get him?

"I, um, let me think about it for a moment. Do you think it's broken?"

"I'm not sure. A fracture at the very least. He took quite a tumble."

"Oh dear, I suppose I will come get him." Her brain scrambled all the things on her calendar, trying to figure out what could be moved and what could be rescheduled. Asha's driving test. Bela's SAT tutor. Grocery shopping for Jeet. "By the way, I apologize for not calling back sooner. I had my phone on silent."

Nurse Vicki chuckled. "I did wonder. Most parents pick up immediately when they see me calling."

A thought occurred to Priya.

"Well, did you try Vid's father?"

A brief pause.

"Well, no, I didn't want to disturb him at work. It's always the mothers who deal with these things anyway. I'm sure you agree, Mrs. Agrawal?"

"First of all, it's Dr. Chowdhury, not Mrs. Agrawal. And my

husband and I work at the same place. And we make the same amount of money. So the next time something goes wrong with one of your campers, you might think twice before making assumptions."

She ended the call there, stunned at her bravado, realizing too late she had forgotten to ask to speak to Vid. She reached into her handbag and retrieved the muffins she had filched earlier. Famished, she popped one into her mouth. She had a four-hour drive ahead of her and she needed reinforcements.

She went to find Dev on the surgery floor. The nurse might not have felt it incumbent to notify him of Vid's injury, but Priya certainly felt she ought to.

"Hi, Dr. Chowdhury," called out Ethan Baker. He was the only male nurse who worked in Dev's department, and he liked to joke with her about her hunky husband. Dev was irresistible in green scrubs, especially when he used his surgical mask to hold back his longish black hair. Ethan was gay, happily married, and shared Priya's obsession with the royals.

"He's in surgery for another twenty minutes at least," Ethan said, rolling over to her on a wheeled, backless stool. "But look what I got." He pulled out the latest issue of *Hello!* "You wanna? I think Princess Eugenie's baby looks like Winston Churchill."

"I wish. I have to get to Vermont tonight. Long story. I'm going to grab a leg brace from Dev's office."

Inside his cluttered office, Priya found a sticky note and scribbled the situation in messy doctor scrawl and affixed it to his monitor. She opened the closet when she heard a buzz and spotted his cell phone on the desk. Without thinking, she picked it up and read the text exchange on the screen. It was from someone in his phone labeled M. Who was M?

I'm always here if you need me, M had written, followed by a smiling emoji with hearts for eyes. **Call me when she's not around**.

The message vanished from the home screen and Priya realized she didn't know her husband's passcode. Who was M? And who was the "she" in "she's not around"?

Could *she* be she?

And M was . . . M was someone Priya was sure she was going to have a problem with.

She searched her brain for an honest explanation. M could be a salesgirl at a jewelry store helping Dev choose a gift. Hers and Dev's anniversary was coming up soon. She wasn't much of a jewelry wearer. Rings didn't work well under latex gloves. Necklaces just drew attention to the lack of makeup on her face. She said she was open to a bracelet.

She didn't want four hours alone on the open road to overthink this and imagine the worst. She tried Melissa's cell.

"Yes, I will drive with you to Vermont," Melissa said, and Priya could swear she heard the sound of an overnight bag being zipped open. "Cam is at Josh's. I could use your thoughts on my campaign strategy, anyway. I'll be at your house in under an hour."

Was that desperation Priya heard, seeping through the phone like the droplets of a contagious virus? She had expected a nighttime drive to pick up Vid would be a tougher sell. It made Priya think they ought to see each other more often.

Priya tried one last time to get into Dev's phone, using a combination of the children's birthdays. The screen said *Incorrect passcode. Please try again.*

At least it was polite.

· · · · · · · ·

PRIYA, MELISSA, AND Vid decided not to spend the night in Vermont. The nearest hospital was an hour away, and Priya preferred to have his leg examined by her favorite pediatric ortho in the morning. Vid was surprisingly energetic when they reached him, having helped himself to at least ten lollipops while he waited in the medical center. Priya had hoped to meet the nurse she spoke to earlier, but she had gone home for the night.

"She leaves at five p.m. every day because she has three little kids at home," the night nurse informed Priya. *Isn't that lovely for her*, Priya thought.

Priya piled Vid into the backseat after securing his leg in a removable brace. Melissa, despite the rush, had remembered to bring a blanket for him and a bag of healthy snacks.

"You're amazing for bringing these things."

"It was nothing. Always happy to help." Priya heard in Melissa's voice a dogged eagerness. She deserved to be mayor of Bellport. She deserved more than she'd gotten with Josh.

Melissa fiddled with the radio as Priya studied Waze. "Yes! '90s on 9."

"Barbie Girl" was on. It didn't take long for the two of them to start singing along.

"I think it's because I only have one child," Melissa said spontaneously, cutting into their chant of "*made of plastic . . . it's fantastic.*" She lowered the volume. "You have this super full life. Three kids, big job, husband. How are you supposed to remember the baby carrots?"

Priya found herself biting back tears. Everything Melissa was saying was correct. Why didn't she appreciate her life more? Why did she feel something was missing? She ought to kiss the ground every single day that she had three healthy children. So what if Vid had ADHD and Asha worshipped that new friend with the tongue ring? Priya ought to know better than most the importance of gratitude. How many times had she run scans because of back pain and had to refer the patients for biopsy?

"Barbie Girl" bled seamlessly into "You Oughta Know" and Priya turned up the dial. They belted out, "*Does he go down on you in a theater?*" as Vid opened one eye dubiously.

"Your mom was once cool," she said, flinging her head around briefly to look at him.

"Sure," he said, but he was smiling.

Melissa raised a playful eyebrow at her.

"Well, maybe not cool," Priya corrected herself. "But I was young."

Vid's eyes were already closed.

"Thanks for coming with me, M," Priya said. Her foot slammed the brake.

Melissa was an M.

Dev and Melissa were friendly. They liked to listen to the same podcasts, true crime serials that give Priya the willies. They did that word game online and compared notes. Priya had appreciated that Dev paid attention to Melissa. It spoke well of Dev's EQ, that he was sensitive to Melissa being alone. Now she wondered if she'd been played a fool.

"Yikes. What was that?" Melissa asked.

"Thought I saw a rabbit," Priya hastily covered.

"Well, I was happy to come along. Gave me a break from—"

"You know what?" Priya interrupted. "Do you mind if we ride in silence for a bit? I have a headache."

For the next hour, they listened to more of the same station, the disc jockeys bantering about forgotten nineties trends: baby tees and chain wallets and "talk to the hand." It was the soundtrack to their friendship, to the four years spent huddled together in survival mode at the Bellport Upper Campus. Melissa fell asleep about an hour outside of New Haven. Priya thought about reaching into her friend's purse and stealing a look at her cell phone. She could make an excuse if Melissa woke up and say she needed to use her Waze since hers wasn't working. But she decided against it. Melissa, sweet Melissa with the drool threading down her chin at that very moment, couldn't be M. Or the exchange with M wasn't anything inappropriate. Or she just really didn't want to find something out that she couldn't unknow.

Priya didn't have the bandwidth to handle any additional problems. Not with her injured son in the backseat, her pouty husband at home, her bitchy teen daughters, her new position at the hospital that demanded she have two brains and six extra limbs. She really just needed coffee. Only coffee wasn't quite doing it anymore.

"Are we there yet?" came Vid's voice groggily from the back. "My leg hurts."

"Almost, baby. Almost."

16

- ❧ -

Melissa

IT WAS A quiet morning at home, and Melissa was studying a photograph of her and her sister at Walt Disney World in a family album. She was trying to remember what she loved about her. On that trip, when they were twelve and ten, respectively, Karen hadn't cared that Melissa was scared of roller coasters. They spent half their time in line for Space Mountain. When Melissa finally braved it, Karen teased her for being a wuss in the first place.

All of this was typical older-sister behavior. And ancient history. When it counted, Karen was there for Melissa. She checked in daily while Melissa was going through the divorce. At least once a week there'd be a bottle of some expensive wine or a fancy skincare product at her doorstep. Karen was the only person who knew about the threesome with Kelly. She vowed to hate Josh forever, even though excommunicating him meant losing text message privileges with the man who built her McMansion and could get subcontractors over to fix problems quickly. She never forgot Cam's birthday, or to send her a Hanukkah present, or to include Melissa and Cam at every holiday meal.

She was just being so unbelievably annoying about this damn bar mitzvah. Karen had just called yet again to ask if Melissa was going to bring a date. She blamed it on the party planner. "Alicia needs to know. She's waiting to do the final table arrangements just for this. Her team is going crazy."

"Maybe Alicia is in the wrong business if she can't handle the presence or absence of an extra guest."

"It's not just the seat. It's the symmetry. The calligraphed place cards. Whether your table will be one of the round or square ones. Please, Mel, you don't know how stressful Jordan's BM is."

"Must you call it a BM? That's what Mom called our poops."

"Well, now that's what everyone calls a bar mitzvah. Anyway, I have a few different men I can introduce you to. Bruce plays tennis with a guy he thinks would be perfect for you. He's tall, athletic, has a great job . . ."

"Then he's a serial killer. He has at least a dozen bodies in his freezer. Nobody who is all those things you mentioned needs to be fixed up."

"You watch too much crime TV. Are you still skinny? Face-Time me."

"It's eight a.m. No."

"Okay, fine. But don't get any skinnier or I'll look like crap next to you in the photos."

It was too early in the morning for this. "I have to tell you about the party favors. Each kid is going home with a personalized—"

"Karen, I have to say something. About the bar—the BM."

"Yes?"

"Are you sure a big party is a good idea? Jordan is a really shy kid. I can't imagine he wants to get lifted in a chair in front of a few hundred people. Or make a speech. You could just do something small, with only family and maybe one or two of his close friends."

The party had been troubling Melissa since the glitzy, three-pound, metallic invitation had shown up in a FedEx box six weeks earlier. Her nephew had anxiety. It had taken him an entire month to be left at school alone in elementary school. To this day, he'd never had a sleepover. This wasn't a kid who wanted his name up in lights.

"He's so excited," Karen said flatly.

"He's so excited, or you're so excited? C'mon, Kar. We both know what this is about."

A small pause and then her sister's voice came through, fainter than before. "We do?"

"Nineteen ninety-one. Denise Shulman's bat mitzvah at the Golden Hotel. It was the same weekend as yours. Your party was scheduled for Sunday afternoon. You wanted a Saturday night but Mom and Dad said the place was too expensive to rent out for a night party. Along comes Denise Shulman, with her crimped blond hair and clear braces. Her parents invite the entire class to a weekend getaway at an amazing hotel with a roller skating rink and ski slopes and promise that the bus will be back in time for your party Sunday. Only half the kids didn't show because they were too tired."

"That Denise was such a little bitch, wasn't she?" Karen's voice sizzled. Melissa remembered her sister refused to go to school for a week after. "It doesn't matter, though. I've already spent so much money and time on this. I can't cancel."

"Just promise me you'll think about it. I love you."

She hung up before Karen could protest. Melissa doubted her sister would actually pull the plug. Which meant she had to figure out this date situation. She ought to just bring a friend. Maybe Priya. She had been a little chilly toward Melissa by the end of their road trip, though she was probably just tired. Cam's claws definitely came out if she got less than eight hours of sleep. Or when her blood sugar got low. And on days that ended in Y.

Maybe Tara. She'd get a kick out of watching the awkward, pimply teenagers playing Coke and Pepsi, if that was still a thing. But she was really busy at her new job and it was doubtful she'd be able to skip out on a Saturday night. Cameron was beyond impressed with Tara working at TIK; it was the first time Suki's stardom had ever dimmed. She was begging for reservations. Cam wanted to sit in the Bella booth so she could have something called the Inferno Experience. This was a classic exchange with her daughter, one that left Melissa entirely befuddled. She wasn't fluent in teenager, and the TikTok vernacular was like an offshoot dialect that might as well have been a lost language from an ancient civilization. Melissa promised she would take Cam into the city soon to try TIK and that Cam should choose a few friends to bring along. Melissa was not above using connections to increase Cam's social currency, especially after the @BellportBlabber fiasco.

Melissa had a big day ahead of her. It was her coffee with Nathan Romonofsky. They were going to meet at Paula's Diner, a dingy coffee shop that had been around since the dawn of time. There were many nicer places to meet in town, artsy coffee-houses with fair-trade beans and organic scones, charming luncheon spots with kale salads and exposed brick walls. Nathan had suggested Paula's and Melissa certainly wasn't going to argue with the man who she hoped would bankroll her campaign.

In advance of the meeting, Melissa asked her "intern" to do a deep dive on Nathan. Her air-quotes-essential-intern was Cam's best friend, Hannah, who belatedly realized she didn't have a single extracurricular to list on her college applications and therefore agreed to join Melissa's campaign. Cam begged Melissa "not to be weird" when she was around Hannah. A tendency to weirdness was not a known problem of hers, but Melissa made a solemn vow to be as unweird as possible. It was apparently weird to use the word "unweird," so that was that.

Hannah was proving her weight in gold. She'd stalked a crush for over a year, so her sleuthing skills were CIA level. She discovered that Nathan's mother lived in a nursing home in Bellport, which received funding from the town's coffers. His father was buried in the Jewish cemetery in town, which was on semi-public land. Melissa had a binder full of materials to show Nathan, tabbed, color-coded, and organized by issue. Her trip to Staples to buy the supplies had given her goose bumps. She missed her Trapper Keeper covered in Lisa Frank stickers more than she'd realized.

Now the question was what to wear. She wanted to look professional and polished. And pretty. Not because she was interested in Nathan. Simply because it was her experience that attractive women got more of what they wanted in life. And she wanted $50,000. That amount probably violated campaign finance law. Maybe she needed to form a PAC. Maybe she needed to not get ahead of herself.

Meeting with Nathan, she texted the group chat. **SOS.** She sent a picture of her open closet.

Tara, all you . . . I'm just grateful most things match white coats. Good luck! Priya's response assured her that everything was okay between them.

Blue short-sleeve fuzzy sweater with white collared shirt underneath. Black pants. Gotta go. Shooting a carrot bacon video. It's a thing, Tara wrote.

Melissa dressed as instructed and applied her makeup quickly but with extra care. She rimmed her eyes with dark gray pencil and used two colors of shadow, swiping the darker shade into the crease like the MakeApp tutorial said to do. She grabbed her binder, phone, purse, and sunglasses and headed out the door, but first stopped to appraise herself in the full-length mirror inside the coat closet. She could barely see a trace of the girl gunning for student council. The wrinkles in the corners of her eyes had their own tributaries and the brown sunspots on her upper chest were so numerous she appeared tan. But she felt good and stepped confidently into the crisp November air, crunching a rainbow of fallen leaves as she walked.

NATHAN WAS WAITING for her when she arrived. When she entered Paula's, the clangy bells on the doorpost making her jump, she spotted him at a corner table studying the menu. Nathan's face when he was concentrating had a pinched quality, like his features were being pulled into a binder clip.

"I'm sorry I'm late," she gushed, taking the seat opposite him. She was neither late nor sorry, and yet that's what spilled from her mouth.

"I'm early," he said. "I didn't know what you'd like to drink so I ordered coffee with cream, coffee with almond milk, and tea, herbal and caffeinated. They're on the way." He smiled sincerely. Was this how rich people operated? They just ordered everything that was available to them and didn't care what went to waste? Suki wasn't like that. She made her twins share desserts and only if they cleaned their plates could they order another. Maybe this was rich *man* behavior.

"Thank you so much for meeting me. I would have come to New York." She stared down at the four mugs that were placed in front of her. Paula, the waitress-owner, gave Melissa the stink eye. She had just dinged Paula's as a caterer for the school graduation brunch, and based on the way Paula was looking at her now, it was clear word had traveled.

"Ouch," she yelped, spitting out the scalding hot tea. She wondered if Paula nuked her drinks on purpose. "I'm so sorry," she said, dabbing with her napkin at a brown splash that landed on Nathan's shirt.

"I have three more of this exact shirt at home," Nathan said, laughing so that he had wrinkles around his eyes that matched hers. "I'm not exactly into fashion. I have someone who buys all my clothing for me."

"You mean a wife?" Hannah hadn't found evidence of a wife. But a girlfriend was a possibility.

"No, not a wife. My assistant. I hate stores. Dressing rooms. I don't like small spaces or crowds. I don't like a lot of fabrics. Or too many buttons. Not a huge fan of snaps, either."

"Maybe you should just walk around naked," Melissa said. She wasn't sure if she meant it earnestly or as a joke.

"I would but . . . splinters," Nathan said. He delivered it so deadpan it took a second for Melissa to catch on. "Anyway, it was my pleasure to come to Bellport. So, tell me about your plans. You know I still remember when you got better snacks in the vending machines. Those 3D Doritos and Gushers were a game changer."

Melissa's heart skipped a beat. It was like he was some sort of savant, spewing Bellport trivia.

"You've got some memory. I've always been interested in government. I thought I'd work on a campaign after graduation. Move to D.C., do the whole Capitol Hill thing. Life intervened and I ended up on a different path. But I'm ready for a change— something funny happened at the reunion."

"A person barely anybody remembers gave a huge donation?" Nathan volunteered, unsubtly popping a Lactaid pill. She, too, was lactose intolerant. What a thing to have in common. She noticed his watch, platinum with a lot of dials on the face. She knew it was a diving watch, though she suspected Nathan wasn't one for scuba with his clothing sensitivity. Josh had wanted a similar watch for his birthday. They started looking, but by the time his birthday came around, he was living with Kelly.

"Well, yes, that." She was sad he saw himself as forgettable. "I got inspired to recapture some of my . . . I guess you could call it moxie. I got caught up in the it's-never-too-late momentum, and before it had worn off, I had put my name on the ballot."

Nathan took a sip of his latte. Foam crested his upper lip. He didn't wipe it off, and after a few attempts at signaling him, she gave up.

"I think that's wonderful. Do you want to tell me about your platform? I met Mayor Thompson on one of my visits to the school. Smarmy guy. Kept trying to get me to play golf with him. I don't play golf."

This was appealing to Melissa. Golf was Josh's favorite pastime. He would disappear for hours on the weekends to play. Melissa bought him custom club covers with pictures of their family to make it known on the course he was a married man, especially because the driving glove obscured his wedding ring.

"I have a lot of ideas of how to improve the town, but my campaign is focused on three areas: environmental protection, infrastructure improvements, and incentives for small businesses. I really want to focus on—"

Her cell phone rang just as she was finding her groove. As a mother, she didn't have the luxury of ignoring the ring. Sure enough, it was Cam.

"It's my daughter, I'm sorry," she mouthed. She wished he would pull out his phone while she talked to her daughter, but he maintained his gaze, like a serial killer. Karen was right. She needed to cool it with the true crime.

"Hi, sweetie, what's up?"

"Everything's fine. Don't worry."

For all her moodiness and teenage angst, Cam cared enough to reassure her mother that everything was okay before launching into whatever noncrisis she was calling about.

"Aunt Karen texted me three times today. Literally during my physics test. She said you haven't gotten back to her about Jordan's bar mitzvah. Whether you're bringing a date. And she wanted me to ask you."

"Oh my God. Listen, Cam, we'll talk about this at home tonight, but if she texts again, tell her you're in school and that she is messing up your chances of going to Harvard."

"I'm not going to Harvard, Mom. *Hartford* is my reach school. Remember what Ms. Lafferty said at the college meeting?"

"Not the point. Just ignore Karen."

"Mom, Aunt Karen is kind of a . . . Karen."

"I know, honey. I gotta go. Campaign meeting." Melissa glanced back at Nathan, who was still fixated on her.

"I'm so sorry about that," she said, making it her third apology of the meeting. *Grow a pair, Melissa. You are allowed to answer a phone call. Men don't apologize this much.*

"No date for the bar mitzvah, huh?" Nathan said. "When is it?"

"You heard all that?"

"Your daughter has a loud voice." He stated it matter-of-factly, without judgment. There was something so refreshing about being in the company of a person with no artifice.

"My nephew is having his bar mitzvah. And my sister is very insistent on knowing whether I'm bringing a date. It's December fourteenth. I should just tell her no already."

"I remember Karen. Red hair. Redder than yours. She was a swimmer."

"That's right," Melissa exclaimed, though by this point she ought not to be surprised.

"I'm free," Nathan said.

"Excuse me?" She wasn't following. What was he offering? Free campaign advice? Free parking?

"I'm free on December fourteenth. If you want a date. No pressure. And I'll happily contribute the maximum to your campaign, whether you bring me or not."

Melissa was stunned.

"Wow. Okay, yes. I'd love you to come. My sister will be thrilled. Table symmetry."

"Wonderful. You'll tell me the details when it gets closer. I'll give you my private number so my assistant will just patch you through next time."

It was when Nathan said "patch" that Melissa remembered. He had terrible psoriasis in high school. Red, flaking scales crusted his arms and legs. They looked like continents with their jagged borders. Some upperclassmen nicknamed him "Patch" and taped a pirate hat to his locker. Now his skin was smooth, save for a few shaving cuts on his neck that had scabbed over.

"Nathan, can I ask you something?" Melissa lowered her voice. Paula was eyeing their table from behind the counter.

"I will wear a shirt with buttons to the party," he said, smiling. His teeth could use a whitening, but he wasn't her project to fix up. Her track record making over men was disastrous anyway.

"That's good. Karen will appreciate that. But that's not it. Why did you donate so much money to our school? I mean, it's not the neediest cause out there and—"

"And I wasn't exactly Mr. Popularity?"

She hesitated before saying, "Well, yeah."

"Want my therapist's answer, my stock answer, or the real one?"

Melissa moved so close to the edge of her seat she nearly slipped off. "All of them. Slowly and in detail."

"My stock answer is that as a health care and technology entrepreneur, I believe in investing in young minds and focusing on STEM in particular. I want to give back to the school that educated me and pay it forward with the next generation."

"Not buying it," Melissa said. "Next."

"My shrink would say I'm conflicted about my childhood. That it's my mother's fault. That I need to have my name on something to confirm my identity. Doc's a Freudian."

"Aren't they all?" Melissa said, though she hadn't been in treatment for years. She had wanted Josh to crawl back to her. Dr. Yamata wasn't able to make that happen, so Melissa didn't see the point in returning. It was an easy expense to cut. Highlights went a lot further toward increasing her happiness than forty-five minutes of talk-and-nod. "And the real reason?"

"The real reason is that I was a nobody in high school. And now I'm a somebody. A somebody with more money than the rest of our entire class combined. Yes, including Suki. I didn't seek out this opportunity. When Giffords first approached me, I said, 'No way.' But the more I thought about it, the more the idea appealed. This was a way for everyone to know how I turned out. Everyone who was rude to me. The jocks who made fun of me and stuffed me into lockers, when they noticed me at all. The girls who ignored me because I was short, had terrible skin, and wore bad clothes. I wanted to go back and show everyone that who you are in high school has no bearing on who you are later in life. I wanted to show off. I wanted to make sure no one would ever forget me again. What do you think of that?"

Melissa lifted one of the four drinks in front of her.

"I wish this was champagne. Because I would toast the hell out of you right now."

THE NEW YORK TIMES

November 27, 2022

ONLY SKIN DEEP: SUKI HAMMER'S PERFECT EMPIRE IS JUST A FACADE

Reports of Verbal Abuse, Unrealistic Expectations and Harassment Plague Beauty Business

BY LOUISE COLE

It was a Sunday morning in May and the sun was not yet up in the sky. Paige Andrews was fast asleep in her fifth-floor walkup in Bushwick, an affordable part of Brooklyn known for its young professional and artistic scene. Her phone rang six times but it was on silent, so she didn't answer. When she woke at 8 a.m. she noticed the missed calls from her boss's cell phone. Her heart skipped a beat.

"My first thought was that someone had died. I was in a total panic," Ms. Andrews said, speaking from a coffee shop near her home. "I called back immediately."

What she heard on the other end of the line wasn't what she expected at all. Her boss, Suki Hammer, the founder and CEO of MakeApp, harangued her for not answering the phone.

"She was in a total rage. She told me I was never to have my phone off again." Even when Andrews explained to her boss that because it was the middle of the night in California, where her boss is based, she therefore felt it was okay to turn her phone to silent, Ms. Hammer was not remotely mollified. "I felt so upset at myself after that. Being one of Ms. Hammer's assistants is a huge privilege. After that night I slept with my phone next to my pillow and set to the loudest volume."

It wasn't until a profile of Suki Hammer and Make-App appeared in Forbes magazine a month later that Ms. Andrews began to reflect again on what had occurred.

"I read through all the negative comments that started pouring in. And I realized I wasn't alone. Things over there are messed up. Ms. Hammer used to joke about my name, saying that because it was Paige she could page me anytime. I didn't like that."

The Forbes piece was overwhelmingly complimentary to Ms. Hammer, highlighting her meteoric rise to success, her ingenuity and her closeness with her family. But within 24 hours of the article going live, there were more than 500 negative comments posted. Some from former employees citing a toxic work culture. Others were from customers who claimed the MakeApp products caused their skin to flare up, in some cases requiring emergency care. A few cited more serious concerns about animal testing and one whistleblower claimed that MakeApp's cruelty-free labeling isn't accurate, going so far as to post what they claimed to be a true ingredient list. The most vicious of the comments went after Ms. Hammer's personal life.

"Her husband is gay," said one commenter, who did

not post their real name. "I've seen him out with men on dates."

"She's not a humanitarian like she claims," stated another comment.

Since the onslaught of the negative comments, Ms. Hammer has remained largely out of the public eye. She canceled several public appearances, including being a headline speaker at the TEDWomen conference and receiving an honorary degree from the Wharton School at the University of Pennsylvania, where she has spoken to undergraduates often about entrepreneurship. When called to comment on this article, her publicist released the following statement, which was then posted on Make-App's website.

"Suki Hammer and the entire MakeApp leadership team are reading through each comment thoughtfully. While some of the feedback is valuable, much of it is malicious slander and steps will be taken to litigate spurious claims about the safety of the MakeApp products as well as the unfair labor conditions at the company. Ms. Hammer kindly requests that people cease and desist from attacking her personal life, as she is the mother of two young children and these attacks are unfounded and hurtful. Ms. Hammer and her team want to extend their heartfelt appreciation to those who have spoken out in support of her and the company. Your kindness will not be forgotten."

Requests for further comment were denied.

The *Times* has launched its own investigation into

the employee practices at MakeApp. Early findings include the expectation of 18-hour workdays, a culture of yelling and unfounded firings. Several current employees who spoke on the condition of anonymity described Ms. Hammer as "a tyrant," "vicious" and "the devil's spawn."

There were those who quickly came to their boss's defense.

"I love working for Suki. I've been at the company for five years and feel privileged to call the headquarters my second home. Suki is an amazing and inspiring leader," said Mitchell Myers, a senior member of MakeApp's research and development team.

Many celebrities have also spoken out in defense of Ms. Hammer and her company, most notably the A-list film star Eva Sugar, who took to Instagram to defend the MakeApp CEO. It should be noted, however, that Ms. Sugar is under an ambassadorship contract with MakeApp that insiders value to be worth at least seven figures.

As MakeApp comes under more scrutiny, its stock continues to tumble. Shortly after the Forbes article was published, earnings per share fell by more than 20 percent. With so much uncertainty, including rumors of resignations from multiple members of the board of directors, all eyes will be on MakeApp in the coming weeks.

MR. MAKEAPP SEEN MOVING
OUT OF FAMILY HOME

*Will the king and queen of cosmetics
kiss and makeup?*

Private equity superhero Graham Marks, better known as the man married to MakeApp CEO Suki Hammer, was spotted with suitcases outside of the family's palatial Palo Alto estate. Neighbors reported seeing a moving truck outside the home days earlier. Marks, whose firm Spring Equities was one of MakeApp's first backers, was seen having drinks at the Four Seasons in downtown San Francisco with a mystery blonde. Sources are raising the possibility that the woman is a divorce attorney; others wonder if it's a new gal pal for Marks. With his wife's name and company being raked over the coals, the pressure may have been too much for Marks, 46, father of two.

THE MOST LIKELY GIRLS—GROUP CHAT

7:42 P.M. MELISSA: OMG, SUKI. WTF?

7:43 P.M. TARA: This is terrible.

7:43 P.M. PRIYA: We have to help her.

7:44 P.M. MELISSA: Agree. What can we do?

7:45 P.M. TARA: Dunno but we need to band together to help Suki ASAP.

17

—∴—

Tara

"WHERE ARE YOU going in such a rush?"

Rachel was standing in front of their shared dresser, a distressed-wood Elizabethan on curved legs that mainly served the purpose of stubbing Tara's toes. They'd picked the beast up on an antiquing excursion in the Hudson Valley. Tara had been bored the entire time. She wanted to try a farm-to-table restaurant in Rhinebeck with a Parisian chef supposedly making an incredible vichyssoise. But Rachel didn't want to leave the antiquing. They'd gone with a group of her friends, all impossibly eager, intent on posing with the furniture they planned to restore and coming up with clever Instagram captions.

"California. To see Suki. Can you move, please? I have underwear to pack."

"Who needs underwear?" Rachel pouted. She reached her index finger into the waistband of Tara's jeans and pulled her closer. Tara groaned. Why had she found the one woman who didn't succumb to lesbian bed death?

"I do. And socks, bras, and pajamas. So please move. My flight leaves in three hours and I can't find my driver's license or passport."

"And Melissa and Priya are going, too?" Rachel had stepped aside and was now being helpful, rolling Tara's socks into balls and placing underwear and bras into a monogrammed lingerie bag that was a gift from the girls on her fortieth birthday. Suki had sent something extra, an apron embroidered with Tara's name and a box of expensive truffles from Alba, Italy. Surely the gift was ordered by an assistant, but Tara treasured it regardless. The truffles she portioned out slowly, shaving thin wisps on her scrambled eggs until the only trace of them was the lingering aroma. The apron she used so often the stains had stains.

"Yes. But not for another few days." Melissa had a town hall debate. Priya had the hospital benefit, which, as an officer of the board, she was required to attend.

Tara was only a month into her new job at TIK, but she needed to get to Suki. She promised Maya to sell the trip on TikTok as a scouting location for TIK 2.0 and post at least four videos a day.

The restaurant had not had its official opening yet. So far the soft-opening guests were all friends of Maya and investors. The ambience was nothing like Ricardo, with its linen cloths and gleaming silverware, Riedel glasses filled to the two-thirds mark with expensive wines. TIK was loud, goofy, and full of laughter. Food was secondary. Maybe tertiary. Maybe irrelevant. As long as what she prepared lined up with the latest TikTok trend and looked good against a green screen, Maya was thrilled.

Tara hoped over time the gimmick of TikTok would wear off and the cuisine could take center stage, but for now she was grateful to be in a functional kitchen. There was an energy that couldn't be found anywhere else. All her senses were in overdrive. Her ears buzzed with the sound of sizzling pans, her nose tingled with spices, her fingers went from grabbing meat from the industrial freezer to burning oven handles, her eyes were delighted by the rainbow of colors of the fresh produce, and her taste buds were at their highest use. She might be the only person at TIK who cared whether the carrot bacon was crispy outside and tender inside, or that the ramen lasagna wasn't overcooked, but it didn't matter. Her goal was simple—have at least one customer enjoy their meal so much that they forgot to record a video.

"A lot of the parents are bummed we're shutting down, you know," Rachel said. She was pressing down on the top of the suitcase so Tara could zip it. They were in many ways a good pair. Rachel often knew instinctively what to do. She handed Tara her apartment keys on the way out the door and they alternated Bernie walks with nonverbal cues. And yet, Tara wanted more than someone whom she worked well with on the assembly line of life. She wanted a spark. Many would say that at her age it was the time to settle, that butterflies and sparks were a younger woman's game. She thought differently. She'd already come this far, why settle now? She really ought not to string Rachel along. Her mother called the thirties the "good" years. It made Tara feel like a thief.

"They'll live," Tara said. It came off brusquely. She would miss some of the parents and certainly some of the children. But all good things must come to an end. The same held for mediocre things. "Don't forget Bernie's pills," she added at the same time Rachel said, "I won't forget Bernie's pills," and handed Tara the jeans jacket she had mistakenly left on the bed.

Her stomach lurched. How was one ever supposed to know anything when each glimpse of clarity was just as quickly obfuscated?

TWO GIN AND tonics later, Tara was physically thirty thousand feet above Cincinnati, but her mind was in Suki's garage. It was fall of tenth grade, and her parents, Harold and Sakura, were in Japan for a convention.

Suki wasn't the type to throw parties in her parents' absence. She was more enigmatic than social, someone that the Bellport kids sought to understand rather than befriend. When her parents were gone, she was apt to invite over one friend at a time to do something naughty. Drink her father's expensive gin. Try on her mother's jewelry. On this particular day, she invited Tara, ostensibly to study for their precalculus test, but they both knew they'd get into some kind of trouble. Tara brought over a pack of cigarettes she'd found in her mother's purse. Tara wanted to watch Suki place the white cylinder between her bow lips. Suki would smoke like a French waitress on break, pouty and sensual.

"Screw math," Suki said predictably. She was sitting on the hood of her father's convertible. The windowless, cramped space added to the furtiveness of what they were doing. Smoking cigarettes, passing a bottle of whiskey back and forth.

"What else should we do?" Tara asked after they'd each smoked two full cigarettes. There was little chance Suki would suggest what Tara really wanted, but she wanted to find out.

Suki hopped off the car and plopped down next to where Tara

was sitting cross-legged, her textbook spread on her lap like a prop. It was June and the final was a week away. At Suki's suggestion, Tara would end up pilfering the exam from their teacher's desk a week later and they'd both get As. Jason Collins, the center forward on the Bellport basketball team, would make a nasty crack about Suki's grade, saying that since Asians were supposed to be good at math, what took her so long to finally ace an exam? Tara remembered Suki's response like it was yesterday: "Tall guys are supposed to have big dicks, so why don't you?"

"We could tell each other who we like? I'll go first. I like Brian Madigan." Suki had her face so close to Tara's that her breath landed on her cheeks in a wisp.

Brian was a senior on the soccer team with classic teen idol looks, but he was dull as the day is long. Tara knew she wasn't Suki's crush, but she had expected someone worthier of Suki's affection.

"Cool," Tara said, because she wasn't exactly going to tell Suki she was disappointed. It was hot in the garage. The talk of crushes was making her sweaty. "I don't have a specific—" She started to say that she didn't have a crush at the moment, but Suki cut her off.

"And I think Sarah Sturnhill is really gorgeous. If I went that way, I would be into her."

Tara's jaw dropped. Sarah Sturnhill was a stunning senior. She had legs out of a Coppertone commercial, sparkling turquoise eyes, and a smattering of golden freckles on her nose. It wasn't that she was surprised Suki thought Sarah was pretty. Everyone did; her boyfriend was the greeter at Abercrombie & Fitch. It was the randomness of Suki bringing up Sarah at all.

"I sort of wish I was gay sometimes," Suki went on. "Women

are just so much better than men in every way. Or even if I could be bi. Hook up with men and settle down with a woman. That would be nice. I heard on the news—some show my parents were watching—that there are people who think bisexuality isn't a thing. That bi people are just gay people who won't admit it. So dumb. I hate bigots and assholes. And dumb people."

Tara was now relieved they hadn't moved into the house. She didn't want to have this conversation in natural light, where her expression would betray her in countless ways.

"I mean who cares what anyone is anyway?" Suki was now on her feet, her back to Tara. She was digging through a cardboard box. "Found it!" She pulled out a photo album, releasing a cloud of dust bunnies. A few loose photographs spilled from the album.

Tara scooped it up. It was a faded modeling shot of Suki's mom. Sakura was in a bathing suit and sarong, laughing coquettishly on a beach. She was magnificent, similar-looking to Suki but with more dramatic features, the kind the camera lens found and magnified until they seemed almost supernatural.

"Love this," Tara said. "Your mom is cool." Her own mother was jealous of Sakura. "Find out what special Japanese cream she's using to look that good," she'd said.

"Yeah, but check this out." Suki reached into the center of the photo album binder and retrieved a small bag filled with what looked like oregano.

Spices were Tara's latest obsession. She'd perfected a tarragon chicken that her father had asked her to reproduce for a client dinner at their home. Of course she knew the bag held something else entirely. She'd never tried weed, and had little interest, but suddenly the idea of doing it with Suki was irresistible.

"Not for tonight," Suki said, dangling the bag under Tara's nose. "But soon."

Only later did Tara realize that Suki never asked her about her own crush. Not only that, she had brought up bisexuality out of nowhere and emphasized how lame it was to be judgmental. Two years later they kissed behind the curtain after the school play, and while Tara savored every second of Suki's touch and the warmth of her lips, she knew it was a friend doing another friend a favor. Scratching an itch. Satisfying a curiosity. And for that, Tara would always be grateful. And for her kindness in that garage two years earlier. And for always making Tara feel like the special one in the group.

Tara came out to Melissa and Priya as bisexual during college, but she never bothered telling Suki. She already knew. Of that Tara was certain.

She woke up from a long nap on the plane and the wheels were already on the ground in San Francisco. It was her turn to help Suki.

"YOU HAVE GOT to be kidding me," Tara said, dropping her bag onto the hardwood floor and spinning a full 360 degrees. Suki's driver had collected her from the airport and driven her to Lake Tahoe, where Suki was staying in the rich person's equivalent of a safe house. The mansion was a sprawling stone-and-wood edifice, with a pitched roof and the largest single panes of glass Tara had ever seen. You could see directly into the rooms from the outside, which would have made it an unlikely place to hide out, except for the fact that it was set back at least four hundred feet from the road and had a Quantico-style security booth at the curb.

"I know. It's nice. Elon reached out and offered me the place for as long as I need it."

Elon. As in Musk.

"When I had my public flogging, I went home and cried in my old room, which, as you know, my mom had turned into a Peloton studio. I literally had no place to sit but on a bike with a saddle digging into my vag."

Suki, a filled-to-the-brim glass of red wine in her hand, hugged Tara. She was put together but more low-key than usual, her thick hair worn in natural waves. She wore a neat cashmere sweatsuit in a soft heather gray and was barefoot, toenails painted a glossy burgundy that matched the wine. For the first time Tara could remember, Suki's face was bare. Her eyes were rimmed only in the redness that comes from crying.

"If you're going to be hated anyway, it's better to be rich than not." Suki took Tara's hand and pulled her toward a sumptuous-looking couch in a gargantuan living room. "Oprah offered me her ranch, too, but I'd already said yes to Elon."

Tara sank into the buttery fabric and extended her legs. Her coach seat on the six-hour ride had been cramped and it didn't help that she'd been squished into a middle seat in between a woman who didn't understand armrest etiquette and a man spewing guttural snores.

"Thank you for coming," Suki said. Her voice edged into teariness.

"Of course. I would have been here sooner but Maya needed to find a temp. Tell me what's going on. Did Graham really move out?"

Tara had hoped the tabloids were wrong, printing a photograph out of context to make it seem like something else. Tara didn't know Graham particularly well, but she had always liked him, as much as she could like a person who got what she wanted.

"He's holed up with the kids in our country house. They are homeschooling. He said it was to protect them. That he doesn't want them around the media and having to watch me go through this. My mom flew out and is taking care of them while he's working."

Suki took another gulp of wine, which left a cherry red stain around her lips. Noncombusting Suki would create a new lipstick line to match if she caught a glance of herself in the mirror and would partner with a vineyard for some fabulous and lucrative collaboration. Imploding Suki just looked like a crazy person who needed a wipe.

"Sakura to the rescue," Tara said. She tapped a remote on the coffee table she thought would turn on music—the atmosphere needed something besides their collective stress—but instead it sent metal bars descending on the windows.

"What the hell? There's a G-clef on this button," Tara said, shaking her head.

"This house is crazy. Meanwhile, I haven't heard from Graham since I got here."

Tara didn't know how to respond. But she did have an idea of something she could do.

"Can I see the kitchen?"

"Which one? The butler's kitchen? The family kitchen? Or the catering kitchen?"

All of them, please. And let me open up every single cabinet and pantry.

"Whichever one Elon and his kid with the alphabet name use. I guess that would be the family kitchen?"

"Right this way. I am starving. I don't think I've eaten a bite since I saw a blog post where one of my former assistants, Mandy, called me the C-word."

"Classy?"

"Rhymes with 'bunt.'"

"Ouch. I thought your assistant was named Randy."

Suki made a petulant face. "I had Mandy and Randy. But not at the same time!"

They moved into the kitchen, gleaming with top-of-the-line appliances, four oversize refrigerators, and a hanging rack of Le Creuset pots above a marble countertop sparkling with exquisite veining. Tara couldn't help laughing at the comparison to the shoebox at TIK, where the appliances were about as sophisticated as her old Easy-Bake Oven.

"What do you feel like?" Tara said, her head buried in the closest refrigerator. There were plums in deep purple sitting in paper cartons. A pie was definitely in order sometime this week.

"Anything that will cause amnesia. Are there foods that do that? Like oysters are supposed to make you feel romantic. What can I eat that will make me forget the past two weeks?" Suki was sitting at the counter, her chin resting on her hand.

Tara pulled chicken breasts and coconut cream out of the refrigerator, her mind developing a menu as Suki rambled.

"Any mushrooms in there? Oh, but the regular kind doesn't make you hallucinate," Suki said. "Remember we used to think green M&M's made you horny?"

Tara nodded. She was chopping scallions, the rhythm of the slice, slice, slice like a beloved melody returned to her.

"Who started that rumor? Like the M&M company or some teenage boy? Also, remember the rumor that Screech was dead from *Saved by the Bell*? That was weird." Suki was deep into her third glass of wine and had started to slur. "He really is dead. Now, though. Before it was just a rumor."

Tara put the knife down, filled a tall glass with water, and set it before Suki. "Why are we discussing urban legends of the 1990s instead of discussing you and MakeApp? Seriously, Sukes, what happened?"

"What happened is that the world sees women in power differently than men." She was speaking emphatically, but her eyes were wandering all over the room. "Did I make some mistakes? Yes. Was I tough on my employees? I guess, but I think I treated them fairly. When I first started, I hired a vice president for sales and marketing from Revlon. I was so green in this field and I needed someone with more experience and connections. You might remember him—Daniel Hopkins."

Tara knew the name. In the beginning, she read every single article about Suki's budding business.

"I would notice in meetings that when I gave orders, there were these little glances around the room. Even something innocuous like my saying the workday ends at six p.m. and I expect people to stay until then. There'd be snickers, like, Who is this tough bitch? But Daniel would say something restrictive about the vacation policy and nobody would raise an eyebrow. Tara, it was so fucking obvious."

Tara wasn't remotely surprised. There was a reason almost all the top chefs were male. It wasn't a talent issue. It was that marshaling a kitchen staff was a lot easier when the head chef was naturally viewed as a leader, not someone "on her period" if she barked that the duck skin wasn't crisp enough or the pans weren't adequately hot before the oil went in.

"For a while I just let Daniel deliver the bad news. When I had to cut back on the health care plan, I made him write the memo. When it wasn't practical to have free snacks in the company kitchen, I had Daniel post the note. I wanted to be the nice one. I wanted to be liked. I know, I know. It's so classically female to be a pleaser."

Tara nodded in solidarity as she rinsed the chicken under the faucet. She agreed with everything Suki was saying and wondered why her friend had never mentioned any of this before. They were together on two girls' trips, the four of them, spilling secrets while drunk on Napa's finest, and Suki didn't so much as give up a single chink in her armor. Melissa talked about Josh's crooked penis, that it used to poke her the wrong way. Priya complained about Jeet and how annoying it was to work in the same hospital as Dev, saying marriages should be 12/6, not 24/7. Tara opened up plenty, about relying on her parents for money and rehashing Ricky DiMateo. But Suki never went beyond garden-variety grievances. She said Graham insisted on keeping their bedroom thermostat at a frigid sixty-six degrees, that one of the twins was getting in trouble in preschool for not sharing blocks. Why did she keep her real problems from them?

"That smells amazing." Suki joined Tara at the stovetop and dipped a manicured pinky into the simmering cream sauce. Like always, Tara felt special in Suki's orbit, like Suki was a planet and Tara one of her rings.

"Thank you. Now go sit back down and tell me the rest. I want to know why anyone would dare call you the C-word."

"One day I was in the company break room, where I honestly never go because, you know, but I was looking for Stella, my assistant at the time."

"Let me guess. Your other assistant was named Bella?" Tara lifted her wooden spoon and popped a sautéed pepper into Suki's mouth.

"Very funny. I think the other one was named Maria. Or maybe Marla. No, wait, it was Tiffany." Suki bit her bottom lip. "Fine, I'm not a perfect boss. But, anyway. I went into the break room and I overheard some of the people who work in R and D talking about me. Basically they had sent me a proposal which I had marked up, something to do with our new organic line, and it was total shit. I used a red marker, because it's easy to read, not because I'm Satan. They were really pissed off about my comments. Said I was being super harsh, expecting too much, and hadn't I ever heard of something called a shit sandwich?"

"Sounds like something on the TIK menu," Tara said. She pulled open a cabinet and took out two dinner plates.

"Apparently a shit sandwich is when you criticize someone but you layer it in between compliments. Honestly, it seems like a waste of time. I don't want to treat my employees like elementary school students."

"Oh my God," Tara said, dropping the tongs she was using to turn the chicken. "I just realized that's what Ms. Abrams did. Remember our history teacher who flipped out on Kim Konner for not knowing what was happening in Rwanda? Anyway, that's what she did with my papers. She'd be like . . . excellent introduction . . . the supporting arguments are poorly developed . . . but great use of secondary sources."

"Well, I guess that's why we liked her. And because she had

a very cool choker collection. So, I listened to them bash me for doing the exact same things Daniel was doing. They said I was demanding and had unreasonable expectations because I emailed them on a holiday. They called me cranky and said Graham was probably cheating on me, that's why I was such a bitch at work. Nobody cared anymore about everything I did for women of color, celebrating their beauty and making it easier for them to shop for products that worked with their complexions. They just wanted to have the day off on Arbor Day. Arbor Day! Tara, I flipped out after that."

"Uh-oh," Tara said. She had assembled their dinner plates by this point. A bed of seasoned spinach for both of them, with two thin chicken cutlets arranged on top of each other with a drizzle of red pepper coulis zigzagging across. Fortunately she remembered to shoot a quick video for TIK's feed.

"Yeah. And I hated Daniel, which was wrong. It wasn't his fault the world respects a man more than a woman. Instead of backing off and coddling everyone, I doubled down. I figured the only way I was going to command their respect was to act one hundred percent confident and to be exacting in my standards. I suppose I took it too far. Who knows? It's not like there's some secret female CEO club where we can all exchange tips. I don't have Sheryl Sandberg on speed dial, despite what the papers say. I've only met her once. And what the hell does 'lean in' even mean? If I was going to have a motto, it would be 'stand tall.'" Suki's face gleamed with pleasure as she chewed her first bite. "Jesus, this is delicious."

"Glad you like it. Yeah, I can see how a slogan encouraging bad posture isn't that useful for a female executive. I wish you had come to the reunion, Sukes. Melissa, Priya, and I got super high after the first night—yes, even Priya—and we just kind of admitted that none of us is where we thought we'd be at this point in our lives. We even pulled out the yearbook and looked at our superlatives. It was cathartic."

"I'm going to need seconds of this," Suki said, nearly halfway through her first cutlet, pausing only to take sips of the wine she'd recaptured when Tara's back was turned. "I wish I could have come."

"You were in Dubai?" Tara was back on her feet, checking the freezer for dessert possibilities. There was a TikTok trend involving frozen blueberries and melted marshmallows that wasn't half-bad.

"I wasn't in Dubai. I was hiding, in a Courtyard Marriott in Sacramento where no one would expect me, along with my war team. I didn't know when the story would break. I've known this was coming for a while. And I didn't want it to break while I was at the reunion, away from Graham and the kids. Plus Giffords was hounding me for a donation and I couldn't exactly be generous, given my legal fees and possibly a very expensive divorce."

"I wish I could have been there to help you sooner. Priya and Melissa, too." Tara handed Suki another glass of water.

"I appreciate that. Honestly, I didn't tell you guys because I was embarrassed. I loved being the superstar in the group, knowing you guys were impressed by me and my perfect family." Here she air-quoted "perfect." "Not to mention that telling you guys would make it real. You wouldn't be thinking like my publicist or my CFO, all damage control and mitigation strategies. You guys would make it about feelings, and want to know how I really was inside, and I just wasn't ready for that. Did you wonder why Kim Konner was quoted in the *Forbes* article and not one of you guys?"

"A bit," Tara admitted. In reality, she was crushed. Melissa had harped on it as well.

"I just didn't want you guys near this thing, especially if it meant reporters calling when the bad stuff broke."

"You know, Suki, there's a reason I took the job at TIK besides your encouragement."

"What's that?"

"The three of us made a pact at the reunion to make our senior superlatives come true."

"What? Melissa is going to be president of the United States? If Hillary couldn't do it, not sure there's much hope for our girl. Priya probably could cure cancer, but I don't think that's her area. You, though, I get. Cheffing definitely gets you closer to that Michelin star."

"We realized at the reunion that we needed to go after what we want. We are The Most Likely Girls, The Make It Happen Women, The Don't Fuck with Us Femmes. Call it what you want, but you're one of us. The poster child, really. We have a group chat, though about seventy-five percent of the texts are from Melissa. She's running for Bellport mayor, by the way, not president. And Priya isn't trying to cure cancer, but she did accept a major role at the hospital that has left Dev kind of in the dust. And I'm making pizza rolls for kids that all want to be influencers when they grow up."

"Don't underestimate the purchasing power of the social media–obsessed." Suki took the cell phone from Tara's hands and began scrolling through the Most Likely texts. Tara's stomach knotted. She hoped they hadn't said anything unkind about Suki.

"Vid broke his leg and the nurse didn't call Dev once?

"Melissa went to put her name on the ballot for mayor and the clerk asked if she was joking?

"You thought TIK was a fusion restaurant and spent an entire weekend perfecting naan?"

As Suki read aloud their texts, Tara couldn't help but laugh. Stoned, determined, and down on their luck, the three of them had hatched a plucky plan to make their age-old dreams an old-age reality. They held Suki up as their role model. They believed she had managed the impossible, the elusive *having it all*. They had been dead wrong. With the reality of Suki's life exposed, Tara had a lot to process. They all did. Was being a successful, happy, fulfilled woman nothing but a pipe dream? That you were a ball-busting professional with no personal life or the idyllic stay-at-home mother with an Ivy League degree collecting dust on the wall? Or maybe you have the adorable kids and the enviable career, but your spouse hates you for it? There seemed no way to win. There should have been a course in high school on reasonable expectations. Instead, they were memorizing SAT words and figuring out what parabolas were, useless knowledge taking up precious space in their brains.

"So now what? Your poster child is in hiding, her career may be finished. What happens to The Most Likely Girls?" Suki seemed to be sobering up.

"I . . . I don't know. But your career is not finished. Nobody expected the plan to be easy and for us not to face setbacks," Tara said. "In fact, it's better that we don't strive for perfection. Because, clearly, it doesn't exist. And we are going to help you out of this mess. We have your back."

Tara's phone beeped with a notification from Maya's TikTok

account. She opened it, oddly missing her bizarre, *Jetsons*-like workplace. As much as she wanted to judge the self-absorbed customers who twirled their spaghetti to the beat of "Beggin'," it was kind of adorable. And fun. Tara hadn't had fun in a long time. She tried to remember the last time she'd laughed out loud and couldn't.

She opened the app and saw Maya, dressed in an oversize T-shirt that said SWING, SNAP, ROCK. She was using a filter that made her skin look neon green. Amazing news, guys. Ricky DiMateo is going to host opening night and guest chef!!! And he'll put clips on his TV show. OMFG!!!!

Tara's hand started to shake. She passed the phone to Suki, who watched in horror.

Obviously, Tara couldn't face Ricky. She would have to call in sick. Or maybe quit her job altogether. She wasn't sure she could be associated with a place that kowtowed to Ricky Di-Mateo. Maya would have been in diapers when Tara was assaulted. If she looked up articles, she'd find only a story or two about an up-and-coming chef on the brink of stardom harassed by the bitter women he'd passed over.

"No chance I'll be there," Tara said, stating the obvious.

Suki was thumbing through her own cell phone now, looking like she was on a mission. "I need to make a call." With that, she slid off the stool and placed a hand on Tara's knee gently. "Maybe this will work out in your favor."

"Huh?" What the hell was Suki smoking? But all Tara got in return from her friend was a good-night hug before she disappeared up a grand staircase.

Tara stared down the dirty dishes and pots spread out around Elon Musk's kitchen. She was going to go out on a limb and assume that his hideaway came with a full staff. It was probably just a matter of finding the proper button on the wall panel to summon them. Tomorrow's problem. Tara stood, wobbly in the knees, and collected her bag from the living room. She unzipped the front pocket in search of her Ambien and found a folded square of notebook paper.

Already miss you! Rachel had scrawled.

Tara's clarity returned with a sudden sharpness. She needed to end things. Tara could not in good faith pickpocket Rachel's thirties as she passed through the decade like an absentminded tourist.

Her phone beeped as she was making her way down an endless hallway in search of a guest room.

The Most Likely Girls

What's the latest?—Melissa

How does she seem?—Priya

Tara looked down at her phone, unsure how to respond, before settling on her answer.

About as lost as the rest of us.

The girls replied with a chorus of **hug her for us** and **send our love**.

I'll update you guys in the morning. And then, uncharacteristically summoning a dose of Melissa's Pollyanna spirit, she added: **Long live The Most Likely Girls.**

18

−:−

Priya

"WHOA, MOM. YOU look hot." Bela nudged Asha, who was sitting next to her on the couch in the den, Wiggles nestled in her lap. All her children loved the dog when he didn't need a walk or to be fed.

Priya shimmied around to show off her dress. It was a floral chiffon, winter white with deep blue and purple flowers and a jeweled belt cinching the waist. She wore a three-inch stiletto heel that was so painful she'd actually used the goniometer in her office to confirm that the heel wouldn't give her plantar fasciitis. But when she caught a glimpse of herself in the full-length mirror and noted the way the heels realigned her posture, she knew she'd suffer through.

"Come closer," Asha said. "I want to see the shoes."

Priya gathered the skirt of her gown and teetered into the den to show off her heels.

254 • ELYSSA FRIEDLAND

"You're blocking the TV," her daughters whined in unison, craning their necks to see past her silhouette.

No matter. Her girls' praise wasn't the only she'd received that day, and the earlier was far more meaningful. Hiroshi had caught her in the break room and told her how grateful he was that she'd accepted the position. "The reason that it was still available weeks after you turned it down is because I honestly couldn't think of anyone more qualified. You're an all-star, Dr. Chowdhury."

She moved into the kitchen, where she heard Dev rattling around the cutlery drawer.

"Well, look at you," he said, looking at her admiringly from head to toe. "Scrubbed out, I see."

"You don't want no scrub," she said, moving closer to him. She wanted to kiss him but knew not to get too close. He had been complaining of a sore throat, and this morning he said the pressure behind his eyes was excruciating. Priya couldn't risk getting sick. She had far too much to do at work the next few days, especially in light of her trip out west to see Suki. The likelihood that she would actually board the plane felt slim, but she liked clinging to the hope that she could offload her patients to the other docs and get ahead (technically, catch up) on her management duties so she could get away. She owed Suki so much. Her entire life, actually.

"Huh?" he asked, looking at her quizzically. She would have liked to see him in a tux tonight, to enter the party holding hands. Maybe turn some heads, even if they were mostly angled at Dev.

"TLC. 'No Scrubs.' You don't remember that song? We used to sing it in the cadaver lab." She hummed it and began to sway in time. What was this dress doing to her? She was reminded of tagging along with a colleague a few years ago to a Zumba class. Priya lasted all of two numbers before the teacher had them moving their arms and feet one way while sending the hips off in the opposite direction, and Priya bolted for the door.

The teacher had caught up with her afterward in the locker room.

"You might prefer Zumba Gold," she said, unselfconsciously peeling off her unitard. "It's the same moves, but a little gentler. It's designed for more mature women."

It *was* awfully immature to voluntarily gyrate to "Bamboleo," Priya agreed. It took her a moment to realize "mature" was code for "old."

"Can't say that I do," Dev said. "But you look great. I'm sorry I can't go with you." Dev was still rummaging through the drawer, moving around the silverware with no regard for the divider system put in place by the overpriced home organizer Priya had hired a few years back, mistakenly believing that labels and cubbies would be a cure-all for the chaos.

"What are you looking for?"

"The ice cream scooper."

"Under the microwave. Second drawer. Fourth divider from the right." Her photographic memory had been a major boon in medical school. Now it was mostly useful to find lesser-used utensils, AirPods buried in couch cushions, and car keys.

"Great." Dev retrieved it and dug into the pint of open Ben & Jerry's melting on the counter. Her family members were fond of abandoning perishable items. Why wouldn't they be? They weren't the ones going to the supermarket for replacements.

"Dairy isn't great for sinuses, honey," she said. "I'm sorry I didn't have time to make you dinner. I guess you'll order in."

"It's fine," Dev said around a mouthful of Chunky Monkey. He eyed his latest toy, a brand-new Garmin running watch. How was it that he had time for six-mile runs on the weekend and she sometimes had to forgo basic personal hygiene?

"You better go, hon. There will be traffic."

Traffic was a plus. Schmoozy parties were her kryptonite.

"I'm leaving. Asha and Bela are both going out. Bela is sleeping at Kara's house and Asha at Lucy's. They have rides so don't worry about getting them there. And Vid is at robotics until eight. Jack's mom will drive him home. I'm just gonna run up to Vid's room to get his math stuff organized. If you're not in bed when he gets back, can you make sure he studies a little? He has a test tomorrow."

Dev gave her a thumbs-up that wasn't particularly reassuring. She dreaded mounting the stairs again in her heels, but removing them was an even greater feat. The leather straps crisscrossed her ankles twice and necessitated working a strap through a minuscule metal buckle.

Vid's room was a disaster, as per usual. She hopscotched over sweaty jerseys, weaved between crumpled pairs of underwear, and nearly wiped out thanks to a tangle of wires. How many electronics could one child have? She counted a gaming computer, school laptop, iPhone, headphones, and PS5. There were at least twenty wires spiderwebbing across the carpet. The kid, leg brace be damned, needed to clean up this mess immediately. The room was unsanitary and unsafe. If he tripped over the wires, he'd end up with another injury, and she had no time for that.

She poked her head into his bathroom. The smell of mildewed towels combined with dried urine lining the toilet made her gag. So Vid had great aim with neither the soccer ball nor his penis. Her eye caught the amber pill bottle next to the sink, striped with pastel warning labels. She picked it up and studied the small font. VYVANSE. VIDYA AGRAWAL. 30MG. TAKE ONCE A DAY.

Vid was two weeks into his meds. The dog, the organizational coach, the color-coding his binders, the whiteboard schedule on his wall, hadn't been enough. He was still a ship lost at sea, and the only directional compass left to try was a stimulant. When Priya was in middle school, the kids that had to go to the nurse to take Ritalin were considered the bad seeds. Things were different now. Half the students in Vid's class were on something. Still, Priya couldn't shake the feeling that giving Vid pills was a personal failure. And yet. He was responding well to them. He remembered to remove his brace when he showered. He hadn't forgotten to turn in a single homework assignment. And he just looked more energized, the perpetual glaze over his eyes evaporated.

Priya palmed the bottle, curling her fingers around the plastic. She weighed at least forty pounds more than her wiry son. This was a low dose they were meant to ramp up eventually. She had paperwork to do after she got home from the benefit. These pills were incredibly safe, otherwise they would never be given to children. She unscrewed the cap and pincered an orange capsule. Before she could reconsider, she placed the waxy pill on her tongue and cupped a handful of water from the sink to get it down. Wiping a dribble of water from her chin carefully so as not to disturb her makeup, she stared at her reflection. She felt better already. She had hope.

"Now I'm really going," she called out to Dev when she was at the front door.

"Let me see you one more time," he said. He was at the

kitchen table with a James Patterson novel in one hand, a mug of tea in the other. Dev wolf-whistled. When they were first dating, she'd loved that he could do that. She partially married him because he could always hail them a cab when they were residents at Columbia, in Washington Heights, where taxis were sparse and preferred to cruise farther downtown rather than pick up brown people. "I want a picture of this."

He pulled his cell phone from his pocket and she tried to casually glance at the code he entered. 720688. It was a meaningless string of numbers to her. After he'd snapped the photo, she said, "Dev, I know you're not feeling well, but can you please grab my purse upstairs? I want to use the navy one with a strap. I know I'll misplace this clutch. I'd get it myself, but you have no idea how hard it is to climb the stairs in these shoes."

When she heard Dev reach the wooden landing of the second floor, she reached for his cell phone and punched in the digits. Her hand shook as she scrolled through the texts until she found the last exchange with M.

> DEV: She's going out tonight.

> M: Great. I'll come over after she leaves.

> DEV: Fantastic.

> M: You poor thing. She's never home
> anymore.

It was exactly what she'd feared. Why had she given him the benefit of the doubt the first time around? *Idiot, idiot, idiot!*

"I think I got the right one," Dev called, and she heard him padding down the carpeted stairs. She quickly but quietly put the phone back on the table.

"That's the one," Priya said, mustering all her strength to contort her face into normalcy. She took the bag from his hands and fumbled to place her lipstick and cell phone in it.

"Have a great time," Dev said as she turned to leave.

"Fuck you," she whispered in return.

"WHAT DID YOU say?" Priya was struggling to hear the person seated to her right at the benefit, a former hospital board member and CEO of one of the largest roofing manufacturers in the world. He was one of the evening's honorees and Priya read in his bio that his company was a major supplier to Habitat for Humanity. She wanted to ask him about that, to the extent she could focus on anything besides her lying, cheating husband, but the man wanted only to ask her how he could manage his sciatica. And to discuss roofing shingles. He was very passionate about asphalt over slate.

Then an extremely coiffed lady to Priya's left started talking to her, her face merely an inch away. She had definitely consumed an onion bagel at some point that day.

"As I was saying, the pain starts in my groin, radiates to my rear end, and then goes into my hip. Here," she said, taking Priya's hand and placing it on the trouble spot. "That's where it's the sharpest."

"Advil," Priya said. "Try Advil and ice. If it doesn't get better in two weeks, call my office for an appointment." Two weeks. It seemed like a lifetime from now. She could be separated from

Dev by then. She was certain in two weeks her life would look nothing like it did when she woke up that morning. Fucking M. Fucking Dev.

"Dr. Chowdhury, excuse me." She felt a gentle tap on the shoulder and Priya turned to see a woman dressed all in black, an earpiece with a wire dangling over her shoulder. "They need you on the dais for the award ceremony."

She rose slowly, feeling unsteady on her feet and not just because of the shoes. The room seemed at an angle, like all the plates and glasses were going to slide off the tables and come crashing to the ground any second. She looked up to center herself, but the bright chandelier crystals streaming from the ceiling made her dizzy. She reached for her water glass and took a large swig. *Get it together, Priya.*

"Right this way," the woman said, and Priya watched as she crossed her name off a list on a clipboard. The letters were jumping off the page. One letter in particular. She saw M, M, and M. Ms so large they looked like their legs would strangle her, that the sharp corners would stab her in the heart.

"Are you okay?" The woman was looking at her like she had three heads. Priya felt her heart beating a mile a minute. Thump, thump, thump, like a hammer banging a nail. She looked up at the dais. It was like a Benetton ad. Faces of every color. Half were women.

"Double diversity."

"Female and brown."

"A shoo-in."

"Dr. Chowdhury, what are you saying?" She didn't realize she'd been speaking out loud.

The woman had forced her into a seat and was pushing a

glass of water into her hand. The ice cubes clicked together and made a hissing sound that scared Priya.

"I have to go home. I have to leave right now."

THERE WAS NO shortage of doctors in-house to examine her and someone, maybe it was the chief of hematology, declared her capable of driving home. Priya collected herself enough to convince them that she'd eaten some bad shellfish earlier and just needed to drink some Pepto Bismol, and mercifully, she was spared the embarrassment of being piled into an ambulance.

As she expected, there was an unfamiliar car in the driveway when she arrived. Her heart rate had slowed, but at the sight of the blue Saab parked next to Dev's BMW, it skyrocketed again. She *knew* Dev was screwing a nurse from the hospital. They all drove Saabs. She peered in the window and gasped when she saw a baby car seat strapped in the backseat. Dev was involved with a young mother? How many homes did he wish to wreck at once? At least it wasn't Melissa's car. Unless she drove a loaner for subterfuge.

She struggled to fit the key in the front door lock, trying to be as quiet as possible. Priya was ready to catch Dev and his lover *in flagrante*. No more second chances; no more benefit of the doubt.

Stepping into the foyer, the first thing Priya noticed was the smell. Dal, she thought. And the sweet scent of freshly baked roti.

So Dev and M were sharing a romantic dinner before they got busy. Or maybe this was a postcoital feast. Or an interlude.

She stopped in her tracks when she heard Dev's voice.

"Looks amazing," he said. "I want all of it."

Uch, how cheesy could he be? Purposely being suggestive in the way he spoke about the food. *Gross.*

"And you should have everything you want, sweetheart."

Oh my God.

M.

Priya knew exactly who M was.

"So I just have to heat each container at three-fifty for twenty minutes?" Dev said.

"Exactly. Call me anytime you have questions."

Priya darkened the entrance to the kitchen and stood watching Jeet stir a pot while Dev sat drinking a beer at the counter.

Jeet was M. M was Ma.

Her husband was secretly texting his mommy. Jeet must have borrowed a neighbor's car again.

Holy hell. Priya didn't know whether to laugh about how wrong she had been or cry about how pathetic her husband was. So she screamed.

"Priya! Priya, calm down," Dev said when he noticed her. "What's wrong?"

"There's no need to get excited, my dear," Jeet said. "Are you hungry?"

"Stay out of this," Priya barked. She was still amped up from the pill and she liked it.

"Dev. Our bedroom. Now." Priya turned her back and went up the stairs. A moment later, Dev's footsteps followed.

"Listen, please, it's not what you think," Dev said. He was sitting on the edge of their bed while Priya paced the room. "I really did feel sick."

"Pop quiz, Dev," Priya said. Her voice was booming, but she didn't care a lick if Jeet overheard this.

"Huh?" Dev looked at her, confused and with pleading eyes.

"What is Vid's shoe size?"

He gave a blank stare.

"When are the kids due for their next dental checkups?"

He offered an embarrassed shrug.

"Name three of Bela's teachers. You know what, name one."

"Mrs. Halloway—no, no—that's not right. Is there a Mr. Rogers?"

"Like in a red cardigan? No, there is not. You have to step up and help out more around here. And that doesn't mean 'warming up the car' while I get everyone's things together. Or running out for bagels the minute Wiggles vomits. It means being a full and complete partner. If the children need something, I want them to be able to turn to us equally for help. And if you're going to have weekly poker nights, then I'm going to . . . Well, I'm going to . . ." Priya paused. She didn't actually know what she liked to do when she was by herself. "I'll figure something out."

"Priya, can we talk about this? You don't need to get so worked up."

"What I am is hungry. I left before dinner was served. Make me a plate of your mother's food and bring it up here. You can think about what I'm asking from you. And then send Jeet packing."

19

—·:·—

Melissa

THE SALESWOMAN RAPPED gently on the door of the dressing room where Melissa was supposed to be trying on an emerald green cocktail dress with beaded straps.

"Do you need help with the zipper? It can be tricky to do it by yourself."

Ha! As though Melissa hadn't already been managing by herself for six years since her divorce. She was a contortionist when it came to maneuvering zippers and fastening bracelets.

"I'm okay," she responded. She hadn't even removed the dress from its hanger. She was sitting on the bench in the dressing room, texting with Nathan. He was helping her prepare for the mayoral debate the following evening. She hadn't realized just how out of her depth she was until he cajoled her into a mock debate. *What sort of tax breaks are you planning for small businesses?* (She didn't know. The tax code confused her.) *If you are a proponent of public school, why did you send your daughter to*

Bellport Academy? (Because her parents paid half the tuition.) *The local museum you proposed is on a Native American burial site. How do you plan to handle that?* (How was she supposed to know what was underground?)

Thank goodness for Nathan. Wealthy, wonky, quirky Nathan, the classmate Melissa never expected to reconnect with. They'd met twice more for coffee to help her prepare. It was at these coffees, which often lingered for more than three or four hours, that she realized the value of having a partner. Someone by her side, cheering for her, not thinking about how the relationship might benefit him. It was the first time in a long time she admitted to herself she missed being married for more than lightbulb changing. There was always an awkward dance when the check arrived. She'd reach for it. "A campaign expense," she would joke, but Nathan would wave her off and pull out a black credit card made of indestructible steel.

He always seemed to have a reason why he needed to be in Connecticut. Visiting his mother, a meeting with a pharmaceutical company in Hartford, a country house a broker insisted he see in Litchfield County. And these obligations always coincided with the moments she reached out for counsel. She knew he had a crush on her. Crush, with its juvenile inflection, was the right word. She asked how he remembered so much about her from high school, down to her favorite song—"Dancing Nancies" by Dave Matthews—though she already knew his answer. Nathan readily confessed to being "obsessed" with her in high school. It baffled Melissa that she hadn't noticed prolonged stares or attempts at interaction. She must have been so busy looking up, at who was more popular, successful, social, athletic, that she managed not to look around.

Nathan was bright, kind, and interesting. He didn't look at his phone when they were together, or name-drop, or talk incessantly about himself. These were admirable qualities in a man, but they weren't the sort that made her heart leap. She was forty-three, had finally figured out what hairstyle was flattering on her, and was in the best shape of her life. Well, maybe not cardiovascularly— the stairs at home knocked the breath out of her. Nathan was short, shorter than she was even in flats. And he had small pimples on his neck that turned red when he was deep in thought, maybe a residual from his psoriasis days. And he was fastidious about cleanliness, using Purell before eating and after shaking hands (though not hers, she noticed). He was perfect friend material. And with his massive bank account and wise counsel, he was a particularly useful ally to have now. Though she did like his smile. And he made her laugh. She'd chuckled and maybe even burst out with a guttural "ha" before spending time with Nathan, but a belly laugh? Not until Nathan did impressions of Kim Konner dangling her bra at the reunion and Giffords mispronouncing his last name when he asked for money had she felt her belly seize from laughter.

Jordan's bar mitzvah, though. That was a totally different scenario. Music. Dancing. Introductions. She didn't know if Nathan had expectations.

"Missy? Are you in there?" Her sister was outside.

Melissa blinked hard.

"Yes. I'm here." *I am here*, she thought. *I am in this dressing room, getting something to wear to my nephew's bar mitzvah that I'm going to with a new man, who's really an old acquaintance whom I hardly remember, and tomorrow I'm debating the town mayor, who has served for two decades, even though I have no political experience beyond the PTA. Yes, I am here. Because it's too late to be anywhere else.*

"Coming out," she said, and quickly shimmied into the dress. It swam on her.

"Mom, come out," Cameron wailed. "I've been waiting for you to see my dress forever."

Melissa opened the door and found her sister and daughter standing sentry outside the dressing room, an agitated saleswoman next to them. The poor woman looked spent, an armful of discarded dresses draped in the crook of her elbow.

"Missy, holy hell. Do you eat anymore?" Karen was goggle-eyed as she looked Melissa up and down. "You're going to get osteoporosis if you don't eat. Bruce's sister has it. She has a hunchback and has to get all her clothes tailored to accommodate it. And, you could enter"—she lowered her voice—"early menopause."

"Do you have this in a size zero?" Melissa asked the saleswoman kindly, ignoring Karen's tirade. "Cam, let me see you." Her daughter was wearing a navy sheath with a satin detail at the hem. It was too matronly for a girl of seventeen and screamed *prosecutor on cable TV.*

"Actually, I love what my daughter's wearing. I'd love to try that in a size . . . my size," Melissa said. "And, Cam, we'll go to Valerie to look for you." Valerie was an overpriced boutique in Bellport that Cam coveted. Melissa didn't understand the hype. The clothing looked the same as what she found at Nordstrom Rack or the Saks outlet. But Melissa could remember these same arguments with her own mother, who didn't notice the subtle stitching on a pair of designer jeans or the deliberate placement of a label on the outside of the garment that made all the difference.

Cam's eyes lit up.

"Awesome. If I'm done here, I'm going to meet up with Hannah. She's in the food court."

"Bye, honey," Karen said, giving her niece a kiss on the forehead and handing her twenty bucks. "My treat. Go have fun." Karen had always been a superb aunt to Cam. It made tolerating her less desirable qualities easier.

"So," Karen said, grabbing Melissa's arm. "Now that she's gone, who is this date you're bringing to the B—the bar mitzvah? I am dying to meet him."

Melissa felt her stomach twist. She had been dreading this.

"His name is Nathan. He's short. Kind of balding. And has very clean hands."

Melissa kicked herself. Had her mouth lost the connection to her brain the way her laptop lost Wi-Fi?

"Wow. I can see what the wait was all about," Karen teased. "Kidding, of course. I can't wait to meet him. Tell me more. What's his last name?"

"Romonofsky." Melissa uttered it like she had a speech impediment, gently twisting the R into a W. It didn't help.

"Excuse me?" Karen's jaw hit her chest. "You are bringing *the* Nathan Romonofsky. As in the billionaire who gave our school twenty-five million dollars? Nathan Romonofsky, the guy who invented the artificial heart valve app or whatever?"

"It was a defibrillator app, but yes. That's my date." Melissa threw her hands up in a *What do I know?* gesture. But she did know. She knew a lot about Nathan. Their talks had meandered well beyond her campaign. She knew he majored in biochemistry at UConn. That he worked at a drugstore throughout college to support himself and that he saw an industry ripe for disruption. She knew he was an only child and had mild dyslexia. She even knew the source of his OCD when it came to cleanliness, a story that nearly made her tell him about her threesome.

"I was lonely," he said to her one evening when they were the last two customers at Harvest, a charming bistro with a great wine list. She had teased him for re-Purelling in between courses when he volunteered an explanation.

"In my thirties, I was very lonely. I had made all this money and the only women who were interested in me were obvious gold diggers. This is before I had gotten my skin under control, so you can imagine. I decided to try one of those high-end escort services. In some ways, it felt far more straightforward than a real date. I did it once, and only once, after a lot of research about discretion and safety. It lasted all of an hour because I was so uncomfortable, after which I sent this lovely NYU graduate student in romance languages on her way. All we did was kiss. A week later, I received an email from the service that she tested positive for herpes, and I should have myself checked out. I'm fine, but after that, I got a little obsessive about hygiene."

"That's quite a story," Melissa said. She signaled the waitress for more wine. *The whole bottle*, she attempted to mime.

"I've never told that to anybody," Nathan said. "Except my doctor, who I made test me three times. I find you're easy to talk to, Melissa. Maybe because you knew me before. There's something very earnest about you and it brings that side out in me. But let's move on from STDs, shall we? I want chocolate cake and you need to eat more."

Looking at her sister now, she imagined telling judgmental Karen that story and laughed out loud.

"Is he funding your campaign? Bruce told me you had a billboard by the McDonald's near the playground."

"Nathan is a campaign advisor. Do you remember him from school?"

"Sorta. I gotta call Bruce. We need to up the flower budget, stat. And I need to move your table. You can't sit with Aunt Lucille if you're with Nathan. I'll put you with the Coopermans. He's a big shot at Goldman Sachs. Wait, wait, you'll sit with the Rothsteins. Mark Rothstein is the top cardiac surgeon at Mount Sinai."

"Karen, don't worry. We can sit anywhere. Nathan is really a normal guy." Minus the Purell. And the fact that he donated a massive amount of money to his alma mater because some kids there used to bully him. A regular joe.

"Jeez, Mel. Some of us care about things like this. Jordan's party is a formal affair. It's a big deal. I know you did that whole casual BBQ for Cam's but that's not the vibe we're going for. I gotta get home and call the party planner. She's gonna freak when I tell her we have to rearrange the tables."

Melissa was about to protest but was relieved to cut the shopping trip short. She had a debate to prepare for and a sister to get away from.

"Melissa, Pissa." Karen studied her with a fierce look in her eyes, using the childhood nickname Melissa despised. "First you lose like a million pounds. Now you have a superrich boyfriend. What's next?"

"Um, I'm running for mayor, so hopefully that," Melissa said, but her sister was already jabbing at her phone.

TURNOUT FOR THE debate was stronger than Melissa could have imagined. Every seat in the town's public high school

gym was filled—there had to be at least two hundred chairs—
and then at least an additional hundred people were standing
against the wall or crammed into the bleacher seating. This was
good and bad. The crowd meant her candidacy had a real
chance. There was no way this many people would pile into a
smelly gym on a Monday evening when football was on unless
they were curious about what she had to say. The bad part was
if she was nervous about debating Bill Thompson before, now
she was downright terrified. If she'd eaten anything at all that
day, she'd be running to the bathroom to bring it up.

"Looks like the ads worked," Nathan said, coming up behind
her. Without being asked, he'd placed a bottle of water on her
designated lectern. These were instincts that Josh never had; the
ability to anticipate her needs was intoxicating.

"A little too well," she said, smoothing her black dress for the
hundredth time.

The bar mitzvah was in two weeks and the election was the
week after that. And she'd promised her friends she'd join them
out west to help Suki. Her time with Nathan was coming to an
end and it made her sad. If she won, she could certainly ping him
for advice. But he'd already mentioned that he was planning on
a long business trip in late December—there was a pharmaceutical company based in Paris looking to partner with him. Paris
around the holidays didn't sound so bad. She'd almost made a
joke about joining before curbing herself. Nathan had never actually asked her out. He hadn't confessed to anything more than a
lingering high school crush. And Melissa did worry his affections
were for the earlier version of herself, the predivorce, pre-
threesome, pre-Cam optimist with far more energy.

"Thompson's here," Nathan said.

She looked over to where Mayor Thompson had a crowd gathering around him, mostly men she imagined were golf buddies, and a few women who clearly enjoyed it when he looked at them for a beat too long. Bill was a flirt, even in his old age. Hell, he'd flirted with Melissa when they ran into each other at the gas station a month earlier, asking her to come over to his side instead of running against him. He said they could discuss it over drinks. The nerve.

"You've got this," Nathan said, patting her on the shoulder. He clearly sensed her mounting apprehension. They'd rehearsed a bunch over Zoom this week. Nathan was a natural coach and a natural debater. He had lived life on the defensive and it made him quick with a retort.

"You should have done debate when you were at Bellport," she said. "You probably could have actually gotten our school some trophies." The trophy case in the school lobby was surprisingly spare, given the resources of the parent body. Bellport was a community where a tutor offering services on how to get the most out of your other tutors would make a killing.

"I never would have had the confidence to speak in public back then. I barely do now. You heard my speech at the reunion. It was like three lines and my knees were buckling. But I'm happy to watch you dazzle tonight."

Josh had once been happy to be the man behind the scenes. When she made her campaign speeches for student government, he'd listen to her practice for hours while he played *Super Mario* with the volume down. He'd keep an eye on the crowd when she delivered the real thing so he could tell her which parts were best received. But over time, Josh hadn't wanted to recede into the background. He didn't want to be the wallpaper on which her painting hung, the hidden battery charging her sparkle.

"Time to start, Mrs. Levin-Levine." One of the clerks from Town Hall gestured for her to take her place at the podium. Another was tapping the microphones to quiet the crowd. Her eyes swept the room once more and she startled to spot Josh and Kelly in the back row, with Cameron to Josh's left. She met Josh's gaze and he gave her a little wave. They were civil to each other. She had divorced with class; not everyone could say that. She waved back and saw him nudge Cameron, who looked up from her phone to flash her a thumbs-up. They looked at each other smiling, the three original Levines, and it was like they were a unit again. Until Josh put his arm around Kelly and the moment was over.

And then it was go time. The first question was upon her.

"Tell me, Candidate Levin-Levine, you've said a lot about helping small businesses stay afloat by offering them tax breaks and other incentives to keep their doors open. But our big-box retailers attract customers as well as make up a substantial portion of the tax base. How can you help small businesses without hurting the town? Your thoughts?"

This was an easy one that she had practiced with Nathan, and yet she deviated from the script spontaneously.

"First off, if I'm going to be mayor of this town, I need to simplify my name. Enough with this Levin-Levine. If I win, you can address your concerns to Mayor Levin."

The minute the words were out of her mouth, she wondered why she hadn't karate-chopped the hyphen when her divorce was final. The crowd laughed at her announcement. Someone yelled, "Let's go!"

"Let's go where?" she called out, and the room fell silent. "Just kidding. I know all the hip lingo from my amazing daughter, Cameron." More laughs from the peanut gallery. She saw Nathan beaming at her from the front row and transitioned into her rehearsed answer to the original question. She was smooth and confident and hit all the key points.

"A response, Mayor Thompson?"

She looked at her opponent, who was standing with his hands in his pockets, the casual attitude of a man waiting in line for bagels on a Sunday morning.

"While Melissa may have tremendous experience on the PTA, I don't think she has what it takes to run this town." Melissa ground her teeth. Where did he get off using her first name, especially after she'd just gone and shortened her last name? And how was that an answer to the question?

The moderator, Britney Bassen, was a local news anchor who lived in Bellport. She wrinkled her ski jump nose and Melissa waited for her to prod Thompson. Instead, she flipped her hair and moved on to the next question.

"Recycling rates are shamefully low in Bellport. Mayor Thompson, how do you account for that and what do you plan to do to increase them?"

All right, Melissa thought, her jaw relaxing. Ms. Perky Tits morning-news-show-host had fired off a real question at Bill.

"Well, Britney, you raise a great point. I wonder why residents in Bellport, like my opponent here, aren't more concerned about the environment. If Melissa had experience beyond the PTA, it would be interesting to hear her ideas."

"Let's turn to her now. Ms. Levine, I mean Ms. Levin, what

do you suggest to get Bellport residents more focused on the environment?"

Oh, hell no. Melissa made a fist and pounded it on the podium.

"First, I'd like to point out that Mayor Thompson hasn't answered either of your questions." There was a chorus of "Yeahs" and "That's rights" from the crowd. Melissa felt emboldened. She looked over to Bill's lectern. His hands had come out of his pockets, but he didn't look remotely rattled. He had the same shit-eating grin she imagined he wore at the golf club after glad-handing the other big shots and overtipping the caddy.

"Second, I am militant about recycling. My daughter is president of the Environmental Club at Bellport Academy. We don't let even a paper receipt from ShopRite end up in the same bin as the plastic bags. Not that we would use plastic bags. We bring our own canvas totes to the grocery store."

"Mayor Thompson, a real response this time?" Britney looked out for blood and Melissa was sorry she had written her off as a glorified weather girl.

"Certainly." He prattled on about dolphins and methane gas and somewhere between losing half the room and talking in circles, Bill managed to save face.

"All right, next topic. Mayor Thompson, I'd love your thoughts on BLM. It's certainly been a topic of—"

"Britney, I'm so glad you asked. Preserving our parks and natural wonders is very important to me. We are lucky to have a beautiful beach here in Bellport and several terrific public greens."

The sound of people whispering to one another and shifting in their seats was audible. Nathan and Melissa locked eyes and shared an invisible thread of smug satisfaction.

"I'm sorry to interrupt you, Mayor Thompson, but I was actually referring to Black Lives Matter. Not the Bureau of Land Management."

"Oh, I, um, well, of course. But, Britney, I'd like to move on to something else, perhaps of even greater importance to this town."

Without waiting for permission, Thompson continued, leaning toward the audience so that he was practically kissing the microphone.

"Morality." He said the word with the authority of a preacher.

"Morality?" Britney repeated. "I'll allow it."

"Everyone in Bellport knows me as a family man. My wife, Betsy, is here in the front row. We've been married forty years. Hey, honey." Since when did Bill Thompson have a Southern drawl? Melissa was certain he was from Queens. He blew a kiss to an elegant lady dressed in a silk blouse and dark slacks, wearing pearls and her hair in a French twist like a first lady. "All four of my boys went to this very high school. Go, Badgers." Some hoots and hollers followed. Boy, this was a fickle crowd. The BLM gaffe was already yesterday's news.

"I'm a family man. I believe in family values. And I don't believe that my opponent shares those values with me."

Melissa snuck a glance at Nathan, whose attention was rapt on Mayor Thompson. She didn't know what the hell Bill was getting at, but if he thought being married to the same woman for four decades was enough to keep his job, he had another think coming.

"Anyway, Britney. You may know Ms. Levin is divorced. Now I have nothing against divorce. Not everyone can be as lucky as me and Betsy. But what you probably don't know is that she was involved, fairly recently, I might add, in a tawdry threesome. A 'throuple,' I think it might be called in some circles. This . . . arrangement . . . is what led to the failure of her marriage."

Melissa felt her knees giving out to the tune of gasps throughout gym. Her face was on fire. Cameron was in this room. Her impressionable, fragile, only-tolerated-her-mother-on-a-goodday daughter.

She glanced at the back of the room to the seats that were occupied by Josh, Kelly, and Cam moments earlier. All she caught were their backs leaving through the emergency exit.

The mike screeched suddenly and Melissa looked up to see Joan Fisher next to Britney. Joan was a mother with whom she'd sparred on the PTA about nearly everything, from whether the senior prom should have three or four security guards to deciding if leaf raking should count as community service. Melissa usually won the arguments. Now she cringed in anticipation. Joan looked pissed.

"I don't see how Ms. Levin's personal life is relevant to whether she'll be a good mayor," Joan said. "This is insulting to listen to." With that, Joan turned on her heel and returned to her seat.

"I agree. You're hardly squeaky clean, Bill," came the gravelly voice of an old woman in a wheelchair parked in the center aisle. Somebody Melissa didn't recognize brought her a wireless microphone. "My daughter works as a waitress at that fancyschmancy golf club of yours and she has seen a thing or two."

"And you admitted to padding your bills at scotch night," came a man's voice, younger and full of gusto. Melissa recognized the speaker, Brian Dennigan. He was a lawyer and a single father with a daughter at Bellport. Just last year Melissa saved

Brian's ass when he forgot to sign up for parent-teacher conferences. She'd gotten his daughter's schedule from the registrar and showed him how to use Schedulicity.

"Mayor Thompson, you promised to work on an affordable housing plan for Bellport five years ago and you've done nothing. Teachers are getting priced out of this town." Melissa looked up to see Mrs. Kaplan, her calculus teacher from a million years ago, who was now teaching Cameron. Melissa knew she loved cinnamon scones and would often leave one on the desk in her classroom.

Melissa caught Nathan's eye. He was smiling, probably the most natural smile she'd ever seen on him. Whether he judged her for "throupling," she didn't know. What she did know was that Nathan, more than anyone, loved a comeback-kid story.

"I'd like to add something," came a familiar voice. Melissa found the speaker in the audience. "I am Ms. Levin's personal accountant, Kenny Alpert. Reasonable rates, available for household and business use. This audience should know that Mel— Ms. Levin—has the squeakiest-clean personal finances I've ever seen. She won't deduct for gas if she so much as ran into the drugstore to pick up something on the way to work."

I Add 4 U, coming through 4 me. Melissa felt their relationship, or whatever it had been, served a higher purpose after all.

"This is getting out of hand," Bill said, putting up his hands as if to physically tamp down any more outbursts against him. "And this debate was meant to end twenty minutes ago. We ought to respect the custodial staff waiting to clean up."

"They are just fine," Melissa said. "I ordered in dinner for everyone who was helping out and said that I would stay to help reset the room."

"It's true, she did," called out a uniformed maintenance worker resting his hand on the end of a broom. Melissa didn't even remember what triggered her impulse to stop at Szechuan Garden en route to the debate. It had been torture inhaling the heavenly smell on the ride over. If she did well, she planned to treat herself to some veggie dumplings and a chopstick pinch of chicken and broccoli. Had she done well? Thompson was suffering from foot-in-mouth disease and the community was speaking up in her defense, but her daughter had fled the building.

"Candidate Levin has helped a lot of people, clearly," Britney said, breaking her code of impartiality.

Melissa beamed, for one blissful second forgetting the public flogging and Cam's disgust. For a beat she was just the doer, the person who had touched many lives in Bellport, whose good deeds were boomeranging back at her.

"Levin, Levin, Levin." A chant was rising, rippling through the crowd like the wave. She threw a spirited fist in the air, like a real politician. She wondered if it would be overkill to shake the hands of those seated in the front row.

She felt in her bones that she was going to win, but she feared she'd already lost too much to make it worth it. Being a woman was zero sum. Get something, give something. If there was anything the experiment with The Mostly Likely Girls proved, it was that.

TWITTER THREAD

WORKERBEE: It's time to end @sukihammer tyranny and treat workers right. Boycott @makeapp today. #hammertime #cancelmakeapp #makeOVER

LISAZELL: #HammerTime for @sukihammer. Toxic work environments will not be tolerated. #boycott

@DOGLOVERINPHILLY: RESPONDING TO @LISAZELL. @MakeApp products are tested on an endangered species of pelican. #truth #animalrights #hammertime @PETA Look into it!!

PETA RESPONDING TO @DOGLOVERINPHILLY. We are investigating all claims against @makeapp and will be posting a response on our website very soon. Animal abuse will not be tolerated. #hammertime

@FAIRTRADENYC #hammertime

@MILLENIALISA #hammertime

@ATREEGROWSINBROOKLINE #hammertime

20

— ❖ —

Suki

MY LAPTOP WAS burning my thighs but I couldn't change positions, paralyzed by the vitriol. I heard Tara shuffling around in the kitchen and knew I ought to go out and greet her. My disappearance the first night when she mentioned Ricky Di-Mateo wasn't the most hospitable thing I've ever done, especially after she'd dropped everything to come see me and cooked me the most delicious meal I'd had in ages.

I spent the next day holed up in one of the studies at Elon's house, behind the privacy afforded by thick, wooden sliding doors, talking to my lawyers and crisis management team. Tara told me not to feel bad, that she hadn't come here to be entertained. She said she was busy creating recipes for TIK's grand opening, making videos in each of Elon's three kitchens. She wouldn't let on that anything was askew until opening night, when she'd call Maya and feign a stomach flu. If there was one thing Maya wouldn't chance on such a momentous night, it was a contagious stomach bug.

I thought a lot about Ricky that first night and the predicament Tara was in. It was a relief to think of someone other than myself for a beat. I could help her. I'd helped her find comfort in her identity during high school in ways I wasn't sure she fully understood. I didn't do it for the recognition, so it didn't matter. Same with helping Priya. And Melissa, when she needed help with legal fees during her divorce proceedings. When I help my friends, it's not because I want them to be indebted to me. I help because I'm a good person despite the terrible things being said about me online.

This country loves a scandal, a scapegoat. Men and women aren't so different in that we aspire to having it all, but deep down we hate anyone actually doing it because it makes us feel bad about ourselves. But there is a special class of schadenfreude reserved for a woman when her world falls apart. That's a spectacle, a train wreck you can't look away from, a traffic accident made for rubbernecking. It's Ripley's Believe It or Not!, step right up, come see the monster in her cage.

And so I'm no longer Suki Hammer, the have-it-all, do-it-all, humanitarian, entrepreneur, icon. I'm a woman with venom running through her veins and a stone in place of a heart. I'm a goddamn meme. I'm a hashtag. The media somehow uncovered footage of me dancing with Melissa in the middle school talent show to "Hammer Time" at the tender age of twelve and now it is a YouTube video with over a million views. It's like I'd written my own roast when I was a naive seventh grader.

I never should have agreed to the *Vogue* cover story with its bald-faced lie of a headline: SUKI HAMMER EXPLAINS HOW TO

HAVE IT ALL. I pictured the framed cover mounted in my office, towering over the sleek white leather chair that looked incredible tucked under my glass desk but was a bitch to sit on. The headline stared at me every day, the words taunting me. HAVE IT ALL.

All of what? All the aggravation of being a female CEO? All the shame in having a husband who I know is thinking about other women during sex, back when we had it? All the stress of juggling a career, a family, a social life, and a public persona? All the responsibility of being a mixed-race celebrity, needing to calibrate exactly how white and Japanese I act and look? All the guilt every time I miss a school play? All the regret when I over-indulge in fattening foods and wine before a photo shoot? All the bitterness at looking at my male counterparts and knowing they aren't facing the same trade-offs? All the weight of the world on my shoulders at any given minute of the day, even when I'm horizontal and sleeping thanks to a double Ambien?

Yeah, I could tell a story about having it all, and I could call on my good friend Priya to chime in with anecdotes of her own. Except it would be a very different list than what Anna Wintour had in mind when she approached me about the article. Instead, I accepted because I was flattered. My mother, a former model, ingested *Vogue*s like oxygen. She never reached the level of success to grace the pages of the most coveted fashion magazine. My mother was in JCPenney catalogs and once in a *Real Simple* spread on dressing for office to cocktails. She had more success in Asia but was considered too short and too a lot of other things to make it in her new home. So when Anna called me and asked me in her stiff British clip to pose for the cover of the April issue three years ago, I said yes before she'd even finished. Not too suave, which was unusual for me. By that point in my career, I

284 • ELYSSA FRIEDLAND

had mastered the art of playing it cool even when my insides were on fire. Like the day the head of the New York Stock Exchange asked me to ring the opening bell. And the day then-President Bush asked me to speak at the White House about female entrepreneurship.

But when Anna called, and I imagined her on the other end of the line with a tweed blazer elegantly slung over her avian shoulders and her eyes hidden behind those oversize sunglasses, I had a fangirl moment. I imagined I was my mother, years earlier, getting the call to walk a major runway show.

My mom had stopped chasing youth and beauty by this point. Her relaxed standards were a gradual undoing. Now she wore loose jogging outfits and didn't mask her grays, though she was still naturally pretty. In a town where the pale ladies leaned into the sun for decades, she aged better than most but lacked the energy to maximize her assets on a daily basis. I had a feeling my *Vogue* cover would reinvigorate her. She always told me beauty equaled power, but that I should be smart enough to invest in the kind of beauty that can't fade. Like makeup. Which can be replenished easily when it expires.

I ended up building a business that preyed on striving and insecurity. MakeApp made money by promising to help regular women achieve the same look as celebrities, only those celebrities are airbrushed and photoshopped until the only thing genuine remaining is their fingerprint. But I did more than that. MakeApp has a 4.9 rating in the App Store. Users love experimenting with new looks, assuming new identities that can be washed away at the end of the day. And I gave a stage to women of color, showcasing their beauty and making products and tutorials available for faces that didn't look like the twins from *Sweet Valley High*.

And so she was the first phone call I made after I hung up with *Vogue*.

"Will you get to pick the clothes?"

"I don't think so."

"Make sure they don't put you in strapless. It's not flattering on you."

"I know."

"Also, avoid wearing orange. It doesn't photograph well with our skin tone."

"Yes, I remember you told me."

"Never let them take a straight-on shot. Always at an angle."

"Angle. Check."

"I'm proud of you, Suki-chan."

We never discussed what I would say in the interview. What message I wanted to share with readers about being a woman in business. It seemed to go without saying I would deliver whatever platitudes were called for. Which was true. When the features editor was on the terrace of my apartment overlooking the bay, and we were sipping green juice smoothies that I prepared myself (having sent all our staff to the country house for the day so Graham and I didn't appear spoiled), I told the editor (a mid-forties gay man in incredible shape wearing tight pants that showed a few inches of bronzed ankles) that the key to managing a busy life hinged on three factors.

I hadn't even rehearsed the list in advance. Because I was making it all up, and nobody would actually be able to put my advice into practice, I rattled off a list that would sell magazines and sell MakeApp. Number One: a belief in myself. Number Two: a strong support system. Number Three: coffee. I don't even drink coffee. I drink tea, but I'd been told by my publicity team to downplay that because I don't want to come across as too Asian, lest MakeApp turn into an ethnic cosmetics brand.

My interviewer, Tristan, was so overly sycophantic that I felt a rectal exam was in order to extract his nose from my ass. Graham was entirely taken with him, because Tristan was so clearly taken with Graham. My interviewer couldn't take his eyes off my husband during the portion of the questions where Graham and I sat together, holding hands on our living room couch, something we've never done before because we don't like to hold hands and we're not royalty or politicians. Nevertheless, we sat that way for nearly an hour, my nail scratching the outside of his palm repeatedly and Graham's hand slicked with moisture. At the time of the interview we hadn't had sex in over a year.

"What would you say to a female entrepreneur at the start of her career?" Tristan leaned in close to me. I could see the outline of his color contact lenses. He was on the couch opposite us, and while he shortened the distance between me and him, his gaze never left my handsome husband. I cleared my throat and cocked my head to the side, as if I were giving the matter deep contemplation. I took the spare moment to think about my honest answer: *Never let down your guard. Be twice as tough as a man. Don't say "sorry," it will be interpreted as weakness. Walk the tightrope between sexy and salacious. Have only one kid, or none.*

"That's a great question, Tristan," I finally said. I paused to smile and recross my legs. "I would tell a young woman starting out that the world is ripe and ready for women to advance. That she should ignore the voices in her head making her doubt if she can have it all. She can have it all while having a ball."

"I love that," Tristan said, handwriting feverishly in a small notebook. Our entire conversation was being taped but apparently this rose to the level of being recorded twice.

"Me too, honey." Graham grazed his lips on my cheek, but lightly enough so as not to mess up my makeup. He'd done that always, even when we were madly in love at the start of our courtship. "I don't want to be the guy responsible for ruining Suki Hammer's perfect visage just because I'm desperate for a kiss." He'd said something to that effect when we were out for dinner with friends—back when we'd had a normal social life and our calendar wasn't micromanaged and carved into twenty-minute segments. I'd eaten it up, told him he could mess up my lipstick any day. The truth was that I'd kill him if he gave me so much as a smudge now.

The kids were brought in soon after. They were tiny things back then. We had finalized the adoption only a year earlier, the most gorgeous boy and girl twins I had ever laid eyes on. They were adorable in the photo shoot. When I changed into an Oscar de la Renta ball gown, they both crawled underneath and poked their heads out just when the camera clicked. It was the picture that made the cover. Graham was in the background, making himself a drink at our mahogany-and-vintage-glass bar, but when Tristan wrote the caption, he said Graham was playing bartender so he could fix his beloved wife a cocktail.

"I know you don't want too much focus on the children," Tristan said, after I had put them both in their rooms and down for naps. I hadn't put my own children down for naptime in at least six months and in truth I wasn't even sure if they still took pacifiers.

"Yes." I nodded, back in my sleeveless silk blouse and tailored slacks. So far I had showcased the casual mom/wife look (jeans and a sweater for making smoothies), a ballgown representative of what I wore when Graham and I went out on the charity circuit, and now a work outfit by Tom Ford that I'd pulled from my own closet.

"Just a little then. I won't push too hard. But your adoption story. It's so inspirational. It showcases just how magnanimous you are. And Graham, of course." Tristan used that moment to look my husband up and down again. Graham was loving the attention. I couldn't remember the last time I told my husband he was handsome. I thought it all the time, but without a trace of desire. I looked at him the same way I admired a beautiful painting in a museum. I had no more desire to touch Graham than I did to take the *Mona Lisa* off the wall and bring it home with me. That said, if the *Mona Lisa* in question—i.e., Graham— would wink at me every now and then, I might reconsider.

"I would just like to hear a little bit of what made you and Graham decide to adopt. You've spoken a lot about helping underprivileged children and I know your foundation is very active in rural Japan. Can you speak more about that?"

I'd lied through my teeth the entire interview, but this was different. Offering up vague aspirational statements about the value of hard work and self-confidence and following one's passion was different than lying about my own kids. And, yet, here I was, ready to do it, albeit with more hesitation. Graham had returned to the couch with a martini for himself. The bastard hadn't even asked me if I wanted one and my throat was parched from the buildup of lies.

"Well, as you can imagine, having great success can be eye-opening in many ways. As MakeApp grew, so did my visibility on the world stage. And it expanded my travel horizons. I had the chance to visit many villages all over Asia, including where my mother is from, and something just changed in that moment. For Graham, too. It just felt wrong to try for a child when there were so many in need already in the world, struggling to survive."

I got teary telling this to Tristan, a detail he made much of in the article. Apparently, it showed my humanity and the effectiveness of MakeApp's waterproof mascara. In fact, I was crying because the story of how we came to adopt Lucas and Francesca was a bald-faced lie, manufactured by the head of Visionary, MakeApp's PR firm. They do a great job for the company, but I couldn't fire them, anyway, even if they sucked. They know too much.

This is how it happened. How the story of my becoming a mother turned into a human-interest story instead of a sob story.

I had miscarried for the fifth time the morning before my first meeting with Louisa Paulson, the CEO of Visionary. This time I wasn't that far along, just six weeks and three days. With conception feeling more like a science project than a romantic gambit, I was very attuned to exactly how many days each fetus was with me. I could have charted it. I sometimes did, on Excel. That morning, the blood in the toilet and the thickish clot that passed told me everything I needed to know. I watched my hopes of becoming a biological parent sinking in a circular motion to the bottom of the toilet. This was it. Graham and I decided that if the fifth time didn't work, we would adopt. It was neither of our first choice. Graham is half-Chilean, half-Icelandic. I have a Japanese mother and a father from the Midwest, with cornfield looks. We were mystified and thrilled to see how our genes would combine. And we wanted to have what so many had—the ability to make love/have sex/fuck/whatever you want to call it—and make a human. But the disappointment was taking its toll on both of us, and the clock was ticking. I was thirty-six, already categorized as a geriatric pregnancy on the doctor's forms. Adoption was our next step. It was something we both agreed on, rare even in those days.

"Graham, she's gone," I called out in the direction of his study. We always referred to our lost babies as girls. There's a deeper commentary there, obviously. When there was no answer after a few more attempts, I remembered that he had left early for a meeting in Los Angeles and wouldn't be back until the next morning. I flushed the toilet, got dressed, and went to meet Louisa, whom I was interviewing to do public relations for my company, the only thing I seemed able to successfully grow.

"Your eyes are red. What's wrong?" Louisa was dressed in a power suit and four-inch stilettos. She had left two husbands in her wake and wore both the engagement rings they had given her. I found that online while researching her. I found myself looking between the brilliant oval on her right hand and the glass-like emerald on her left, imagining them as souvenirs, like her marriages were trips to Europe and not legal, binding commitments.

"I just had—" *a crappy night's sleep, an irritating phone call with my mother, a supplier bail on me.* These were all viable answers I could have given. Instead, I opted for the truth, my nonviable fetus. "A miscarriage this morning."

Louisa insisted we get hammered. She rightly pointed out that the very small positive I could hang on to in the face of heartbreaking loss was that I could continue to drink. Two bottles of Gavi di Gavi later, we were chain-smoking cigarettes in the parking lot of Liholiho Yacht Club like high schoolers. I thought about Tara then. How fun it had been to smoke cigarettes with her. I hadn't had one in probably fifteen years.

"You know what you could do?" Louisa lowered her voice conspiratorially. "You could really spin this thing. No one needs to know you and Graham can't have a baby naturally. You adopt and we make it a splashy, humanitarian story. You're going to adopt anyway. Might as well make it into a nice sound bite that could inspire others to do the same."

It made sense to me and so I agreed, drunk and buzzed from the nicotine, to use my barren womb for the greater good. Perhaps I would inspire more women to adopt. Louisa had a way of making fiction feel more real than the truth, and she created a narrative that I could regurgitate easily. I was sanguine coming home from lunch, armed with a new PR agent who felt more like a friend than a hired gun, and a story to dovetail with my adoption journey.

But what came after was anything but easy. Louisa was a whiz at her job. Instead of giving exclusives to magazines and morning shows about my adoption story, she let it slip in the right circles that Graham and I had chosen adoption over having our own children because we couldn't imagine doing it any other way. Graham was amenable and didn't have much trouble keeping up the charade. It was like my overnight stays at the hospital following D&Cs were just business trips and the time I nearly bled out during Thanksgiving dinner at his parents' house was due to nicking myself while slicing potatoes. To be fair, he was asked about our children about one one-hundredth of the times I was asked, so he had little occasion to opine on adoption.

For me, it was excruciating. It's one thing to lie about makeup products being 100 percent organic (there really is wiggle room). It's not the same as fudging the EBITDA in a board meeting (again, wiggle room). Lying about my twins was a lie in triplicate. I wasn't just lying for myself, but them, too, and I had no right to do that. And sure, it was nice to inspire more women to adopt. But what about being an empathetic role model to all those women who are struggling to conceive and carry to term? I don't think my holier-than-thou act does them any good.

I had to get Tristan out of my house so I did what I needed to do. I told the story Louisa crafted for me in bare-bones form until he was satisfied. The issue of *Vogue* bearing my face was one of their bestselling issues that year.

The article was in the past. I made peace with it. What wasn't in the past, what was very much on my mind, what was keeping me up at night, was my book deal.

Only Louisa and my literary agent knew about it. I hadn't told Graham. I hadn't told my mother. I hadn't told any of my friends or coworkers, or the Bellport girls. Maybe I knew something would go wrong. Maybe I was just afraid of breaking the contract, which stated that I had to keep the deal quiet until the official announcement from the publisher. Maybe I just felt sick about more lies. My memoir, *Have It All While Having a Ball*, was set to be published in a year. I received a million-dollar advance for it. A ghostwriter had been hired. All I had to do was tell my story. Except what was my story now? A meteoric rise? An epic downfall? Business icon or robber baron? I pitied this ghostwriter, an MFA graduate in her twenties tasked with transcribing my life in page-turning fashion. Everything happened so quickly for me once MakeApp took off, my own memories were layered like tissue paper in my brain. And there were things I simply didn't want to talk about, and I knew it was on this young, wet-behind-the-ears writer to extract as much as she could from me.

The photo shoot for the cover was scheduled for a month from now. Six different ball gowns were hanging in my walk-in closet, their structures preserved by stiff paper and their exteriors protected by smooth garment bags especially created for dresses with full skirts. The plan was for me to reenact ringing the opening bell at the stock exchange in one of these dresses, my family in the foreground with me, and in the background a lineup of glamorous models dressed in starched aesthetician coats and holding MakeApp products. The book title would appear to be written with lipstick. It was gorgeous—I had seen a computer mock-up.

I agreed to do the book because I needed the money. Nobody would ever have believed it if they didn't see my personal and corporate bank accounts, the staggering length of MakeApp's liability column. In fact, when I pushed my agent to negotiate as hard as he could against the publisher, he made several comments about my being a shark and a fox and a tiger. All animals, that last one feeling like an ethnic slur. He didn't know that I wasn't simply greedy, but that an extra hundred thousand dollars would go a long way to paying the lawyers, my own and MakeApp's. In the end he struck a very favorable deal. I gave myself pep talks about manufacturing sound bites and sharing vignettes meant to paint myself as both an everyday woman and a superhero. My life had been co-opted ages ago; this memoir would simply create a written record of the ways in which the person that was Suki Hammer had been sold off for parts.

But would I even have the chance now?

I toggled away from Twitter and back to my email, staring at the unread message from my agent, Michael McManus.

IMPORTANT—READ NOW.

I thought about everything else I could do instead of opening the email. The most obvious was to call my children. Francesca and Lucas both cried when I kissed them goodbye and walked out the front door trailing a rolling suitcase last week. They were used to me traveling for work extensively, and rarely did they seem distraught about it, and so I realized they were able to sense something bad was afoot. So far I had only texted with them through their iPads. Yes, they have their own electronic devices. Feel free to add that to the list of things I'm judged for. I knew the minute I would see their faces in the rectangle of FaceTime, or hear their high-pitched voices, I would break down. And so I stuck to text, peppering the exchanges with silly emojis to delight them.

I could also call my mother. She was blunt to a fault—from the time I was in kindergarten, she would say that because I inherited my father's wider build and crooked smile, I would never be a model. In her mind this wasn't a bad thing. She wanted me to have an enduring career. Bluntness was what I needed, though without opening the email from Michael, I'd be giving her only an outdated version of current events. Besides, she didn't understand cancel culture. In her day, photographers grabbed asses, editors spoke unapologetically about ethnic physical traits, and models just did what they were told, working all hours of the night without daring to push back. People got away with things. Bad things. She would hardly comprehend her baby girl getting canceled for being tough.

What else was left that could be done before opening the email that would confirm my worst suspicions? I could give myself a manicure. Work out in Elon's gym. Check on Tara. Get drunk again.

No, I thought. Man up. No, woman up. Open the damn email. And so I did.

Suki,

I've been trying to reach you for the past week and haven't been able to track you down at home or at work. I hope everything is okay. I mean, I know it's not, but I hope you're hanging in there. Listen, this isn't easy to tell you, and I hate to have to do it over email, but I can't delay any further. Magellan is seeking to null and void your book contract. They have already retained an attorney. They are claiming that in light of recent events, the intent of your memoir—to empower and inspire women—is no longer achievable. They cited the hostile work environment at MakeApp as evidence. Suki, I know. It sucks. I'm sorry. I'm not sure how you want me to proceed. I realize that returning the advance is the least of your concerns and that your primary injury is reputational. While the book deal hasn't been

publicly announced, it's hard to imagine this won't
make the papers, given the social media campaign
against you. Please call me.

Yours,
MM

The message said exactly what I knew it would, and yet it
stung worse and stressed me more than I'd expected.

The shame of a canceled book contract wasn't the worst thing
in the world to go public, but who knew what the papers would
do with the story? I had no faith in the splashy magazines and
the gossip columns. The picture they ran of Graham out with a
"mysterious" blonde after he'd "moved out" of our home was false
on two levels. He hadn't moved anywhere—his lawyers were
advising him to go nowhere lest he lose his rights to our family
home and lose advantage in a custody battle. The bag he was
photographed with was a gym bag and the moving truck outside
our home was actually parked four houses down and was trans-
porting a Steinway to a new neighbor. The hot blonde sharing
martinis with Graham at the Four Seasons downtown was none
other than my sister-in-law, Jacqueline. I'd miss Jacqui the most
after the divorce. She was single, and a corporate lawyer—the
papers had gotten it right that she was an attorney—but she
wasn't advising Graham on strategy, she was telling him to get
his shit together and realize what a gem he had at home. She had
texted me right after their drinks to relay the conversation.

I didn't want Graham to stay. Our marriage had been love-
less for a long time, and his fealty during the shit show that was
now my life was literally the opposite of a knight. Besides, he

was shacking up with a woman he worked with. Cristina! She was a beauty from Malaysia certified in massage and Reiki. The guy definitely had a type.

I texted Michael. My agent had to be sweating buckets. He was entitled to 15 percent of my advance. I knew he'd been looking at getting a boat with his partner.

"I will call my lawyer today," I wrote back, and vowed to actually do it. I didn't want to write the book anymore. I was sick of the lies and it was clear there wasn't much appetite for the Suki Hammer story anyway. But I didn't want to give back the advance.

My phone dinged and I thought it was going to be Michael. But it was a group text with Priya, Tara, Melissa, and me on it.

We landed! Melissa had sent a picture of her and Priya at the airport, holding coffee cups and dragging luggage with fraying ribbons tied to the handles, both of them dressed in the female version of Tony Soprano sweatsuits. Melissa looked skeletal, Priya exhausted.

What a foursome we made.

Melissa told us what happened during the debate, linking to an article from the local paper. Cameron hadn't slept at home since. Priya shared that Dev was having an affair with his mother, that she'd caught them in the act of inappropriate babying while Dev pretended to be sick. Through the walls, I had heard Tara cry softly a few times, clearly shook that Ricky was back to haunt her.

Our gang was going to be back together for the first time in four years. I've never needed a support system more, but looking at the picture of my friends at the airport, their literal baggage weightless compared to their emotional load, I wondered what we could do for one another at this point.

21

·÷·

Melissa

SHE CHECKED HER cell phone for the twentieth time since the plane from JFK touched down in California, and there was still no message from Cameron. There were nine missed calls from her mother and three from her father, undoubtedly made at her mother's behest. There was one other missed call on her log. Nathan. She wanted to talk to him, but first she needed to resolve things with her daughter.

"Put the phone away, Mel," Tara said. "I'm going to make dinner for all of us. Cam will come around. She just needs time." The Most Likely Girls, plus Suki, were hanging in the kitchen of Elon Musk's house. It was their first time all together since the ski vacation four years earlier, and there was an awkwardness threading them together, or maybe keeping them apart. Melissa felt self-conscious of her every move and word, something she'd never felt before in front of the girls.

"I can't."

THE MOST LIKELY CLUB • 299

She grasped the phone tighter. If she squeezed it any more, it would melt. Which might not be a bad thing. What good news did the phone ever bring? If she never saw another Facebook post from a Bellport mom bragging about her rose garden, it couldn't come soon enough. If the phone wasn't necessary to track Cameron's whereabouts, she'd throw it into the Long Island Sound.

Somebody was tugging at her hand. Suki.

"Give me the phone, Mel. Take an hour off. I'm being skewered on Twitter and canceled on Reddit and ridiculed on Page Six, and I put my phone in a lockbox until tomorrow morning." Suki was remarkably strong, and before Melissa could fight back, her phone was in Suki's hand. She quickly tossed it to Priya, who passed it to Tara, who put it in her back pocket. Melissa would get it back when Tara was distracted at the stove.

"You're going to get carpal tunnel from that thing," Priya said. "Holding it for that long is really bad for your metacarpophalangeal joint."

"Not my concern right now. My problem is that my daughter thinks I sacrificed her happy family life for a threesome. For the record, she's got it all wrong. I wanted to keep Josh happy and our family intact. That's why I did what I did."

"Okay, but you can see from Cam's perspective how it's hard to buy into you having sex with a woman to preserve the family," Priya said. "But she'll come around. You just need a chance to explain things to her. What the hell is wrong with this coffeemaker?" She pounded the front of a metal canister built into the kitchen cabinetry.

"Um, Priya, I need to return the house in proper condition," Suki said.

"Why didn't you tell us about this when it happened?" Tara asked. "I thought Josh just up and left you for Kelly."

"Does it make a difference? You think I'm to blame?" Melissa was surprised at Tara pointing fingers. She would have expected the most understanding from her. "He *did* leave me. And Cam. We had an understanding that Kelly was there to spice up our marriage, not destroy it."

"This is silly to be arguing over," Suki said. "You didn't tell us about what happened because you didn't want to. That's your prerogative. We're your friends and we're here to support you no matter what you choose to share with us."

"Of course you would say that," Priya said, and they all whipped around to face her. She had given up on the coffee-maker and was chugging a Diet Coke. "What? I'm just saying that you had a lot of problems going on in your marriage and your business and you told us everything was hunky-dory. That you couldn't attend the reunion because you were too busy being fabulous."

"Priya? Really? You're going to come after me?" Suki stood up and put her hands on her hips. Melissa didn't understand the look that passed between them.

"You're right, I'm sorry. I shouldn't have said that." Priya was looking at Suki with pleading eyes now. "We're all entitled to our privacy."

"What the hell is going on? What are you two not saying?" Melissa asked, looking between them. For the first moment since the debate debacle, her focus was not on herself, and it felt like the world rolling off Atlas's shoulders.

"Let's just say Priya shouldn't be throwing shade my way," Suki said. "She owes a lot to me. A LOT."

"Can we please not all be so cryptic? I spilled my guts to you all when the Ricky thing happened. I let you all feel my tits after the surgery. What does Priya owe you for?"

All eyes turned to Suki.

"It doesn't matter," Suki said firmly. "It was a long time ago."

"Tell them," Priya said. She was opening another can of soda.

Melissa looked back at Suki, who was staring at Priya.

"Go on," Priya said. "Do it."

When Suki was done, Melissa nearly collapsed from shock. Priya? Miss Perfect who wouldn't even drink or stay out past curfew, sleeping with a teacher? This revelation made her three-some seem about as scandalous as stealing a hot lunch.

"Wow. I literally have never been this shocked," she finally said. "Was it consensual? Like, did Mr. Walter take advantage of you?"

"I mean, I guess technically yes, given that I was a student and he was my teacher. But we were in love. Now that I'm a mother, obviously I see things differently. I would lose my mind if Asha or Bela got involved with a teacher. All I can say is that the whole thing wrecked me, not that I could ever let on that anything was wrong."

"How did you know about this? I remember Mr. Walter being gone all of a sudden but none of us knew why," Tara asked Suki. "And how did you convince Giffords it was you and not to do anything about it?"

"Honestly, I got lucky. Everyone was buzzing about Mr. Walter being gone. I honestly thought he was shtupping another teacher or something. And then the day after it happened, I realized I left my Discman in the locker room and my mom drove me to school early so I could get it before someone snatched it.

302 • ELYSSA FRIEDLAND

I walked in and found our sweet Priya sobbing in one of the shower stalls, holding the rag that Mr. Walter used to wipe down the lab tables. I guess you could call it my spidey sense, but I figured it out pretty quickly."

"And then," Priya interrupted, clearly wanting to get the story out more quickly, "Suki went to see Giffords. She knew he was fascinated by the Yakuza because of some total dumbass comment he'd once made to her. She managed to convince him that Sakura had ties to the Yakuza, even though that's crazy, and that if he did anything about the surveillance footage, including embarrassing her parents by mentioning it to them, Suki's mom would turn the gangsters on him."

"This is insane," Melissa said, shaking her head.

"Not as crazy as me thinking you were having an affair with Dev," Priya said with a laugh. She threw her head back and her hair fell from its ponytail.

"You thought what?" Melissa froze. Had she heard that correctly?

Priya took a handful of M&M's that were in a crystal bowl on a coffee table and tossed a few in her mouth.

"I saw these texts on Dev's phone that seemed suggestive. Taken out of context, it seemed like maybe he and this person were having an affair. The contact was saved in his phone as M. You guys have always gotten along so well, I thought maybe M was for Melissa. You."

"Oh, so I'm just some lonely, pathetic divorcée so desperate for a man that I would screw my friend's husband? That is a really horrible thing to think of me, even for a second."

"Calm down, Mel," Tara said. "We all think crazy thoughts sometimes."

"No. I have never thought that any of you were cheating, backstabbing whores."

"I didn't say you're a lonely whore," Priya objected. "I'm sorry you're interpreting it that way. Dev doesn't know any other Ms. It was just a thought I had for a second. M turned out to be his mother! The joke's on me. My husband is hiding a relationship with a seventy-five-year-old woman."

"That's not a real problem," Melissa said. "Suki has a real problem with Graham and her company. Tara has a real problem with the opening of TIK and Ricky's involvement. You have a real problem and you don't even know it."

"Calm down," Tara said. "Take a deep breath. We're all fired up."

Melissa wouldn't be told to calm down. Priya needed to get off her high horse once and for all. If Melissa had to push her off it, so be it.

"I do?" Priya asked. Her voice cracked like a child's.

"I need my phone," Melissa said. "Give me my damn phone back."

Tara knew better than to object.

Melissa pulled up her text messages with Cam. The last ten were one-directional. After scrolling up for a minute, she found what she was looking for.

"Here's your problem." She handed the phone to Priya, who stared down in disbelief. Melissa could see her hand start to shake. She was looking at pictures and videos of Asha that Cameron had found and sent to her—far more provocative than the original bikini pic. In these, Asha was practically naked, gyrating on TikTok in a lace bra and panties. "I'm kind of surprised you're not more vigilant, given what you got up to in high school with Mr. Walter."

"Oh my God," Priya said, and threw the phone back at Melissa. "Why didn't you show me these earlier?"

Melissa was about to fight back, to go on the defensive. But she lost her will.

"I don't know," she said, her earlier anger just a shadow of itself.

"What's wrong with us? Why are we fighting?" Tara said. "We need to eat. Melissa, you really need to eat. And Priya, you need to stop with the caffeine. I know what happened at the hospital benefit. Dev texted me and Mel to make sure we kept a close eye on you this weekend. Apparently, Vid counted his pills and—?"

"Dev texted you about that? You've got to be kidding me. I'm not the one who needs looking after. Let me read you the last four texts I've gotten from him: **Where do we keep the laundry detergent? What day does Bela have band practice? Can you send me the vet's phone number? Is Vid allowed to sleep at Hunter's house?** I swear Dev is everywhere I turn when he wants to have sex, but he's Houdini when I need him for something."

"At least he wants to have sex with you," Suki said.

"I guess," Priya said. "I mean we're not ripping each other's clothes off but it's a solid once a—" As she was speaking, an alarm on her phone interrupted.

"What is that?" Melissa asked. The pinging was growing louder.

"It's an alarm I set to remind the kids to walk Wiggles."

Suki grabbed the phone from Priya's hands. There was an awful lot of phone confiscation going on.

"No. You will not remind your children to walk your dog. You will not"—Suki paused, reading through Priya's texts—"edit

Asha's history paper on the French Revolution. You will not"—
another pause—"do a Zoom tomorrow about Bela's sweet sixteen, which is nine months away. You will not remind Dev
which foods give Vid hives, or tell Asha where the extra school
supplies are kept, or explain to Bela how to work the washing
machine because she stained the shirt she wants to wear to a
party. You are not their slave. They have brains and hands and
there's Google, for heaven's sake. Let Dev step up. He is just as
much their parent as you are, Pri. Do you have security cameras
in your house?"

Priya nodded feebly.

"Good. We will watch them. If we see Jeet so much as drop
off a casserole while you're here, Dev is finished. You got it?"
Suki handed the phone back to Priya. "Now power that thing off
and let's get drunk."

"What am I going to do about Asha?" Priya said feebly. "I
thought she was my easy one."

"Nothing tonight," Melissa said. "The thing about problems
is that they will be there tomorrow."

"Amen," Tara said. "I hope everyone is hungry. I'm making
Chilean sea bass with teriyaki glaze on a bed of mashed potatoes and cumin-roasted carrots. And for dessert we're having
mug brownies. I want to hate everything served at TIK, but
these are actually amazing. And Melissa, if you don't lick your
plate clean, I will force-feed you myself."

Melissa blanched. She wished she were a lighting director
and could move the spotlight elsewhere. She pulled the sides of
her cardigan closed.

"Buttoning your sweater isn't fooling anyone. You're a

skeleton," Suki said. "We are too old to be worrying about being size zeroes. And you have Cam to think about."

Cam. Melissa didn't tell her friends about the fake superlative, the one saying Cam was most likely to be a contestant on *The Biggest Loser.* Nor did she tell them about the graffiti in the bathroom, even though they were together the day she found it. The only person she told was Nathan, who she knew could relate to high school cruelty. Her girlfriends were walled off from one another, the days of Truth or Dare, Ouija boarding, and trading secrets buried in the past.

"I promise I'll eat." Whenever she and Nathan were together, he pushed fattening foods toward her. The last time he came to Connecticut he brought a cookie platter from Zabar's for her campaign staff, knowing the staff consisted of only her and a part-time Hannah.

"Dev just filled the dishwasher with laundry detergent," Priya said. She was watching the home surveillance app on her phone. When she reached for another soda, Melissa, Suki, and Tara charged for her at once. "Fine. Fine. No more pills. Or massive amounts of caffeine. But I'm just saying I'll never get everything done."

"There's no such thing as getting everything done," Melissa said, surprising herself. She prayed at the altar of checklists. But it was an absolute truth that every time she crossed one item off her list, she added two more. "Women our age are on a treadmill that never turns off. Oh, and it doesn't burn calories, either."

"Facts," Tara added. "It's what the kids say."

Melissa's cell phone dinged in her hand. She jumped, hoping finally it was Cam. But it was her sister. She skimmed the text and then read it aloud.

Hope you're hanging in there . . . Letting
you know we canceled Jordan's bar
mitzvah. You were right. He's not
sleeping and the cantor said he threw
up during his last practice session.
Thank you for caring. XO.

Melissa felt relief on her nephew's behalf. And she was thrilled to avoid a party where at least half the guests would know about her tryst. But something in the text had given her a sinking feeling.

Nathan. Without the bar mitzvah, they had no set plans to see each other again.

"You look sad," Tara said. "Isn't this good news?"

"It's—yes. It is good news. And definitely the right decision. It's just—" Should she tell the girls she might have developed feelings for Nathan? Her life was such a mess right now, it was hard to tell what was real. There was a very large part of her that expected to wake up in a cold sweat at any moment, smack her alarm clock, and get on with her actual life.

The doorbell rang.

"I hope that's pizza," Melissa said. "Not that I don't want your food, Tara, but now that I've committed to eating, I can't wait another second."

"I'll go check who it is," Suki said. A moment later, she called out, "Um, Mel, it's for you."

"Uh-huh. Does it have toppings?"

"No, for real. Get up."

Melissa made her way to the front door, expecting some kind of practical joke to be waiting on the other side.

Instead she faced a giant bouquet of pink azaleas.

"Who would send these to me?" She racked her brain. Josh? He knew where she was. It was part of their civil divorce code— they never went anywhere without telling the other. Karen? She also knew Melissa's whereabouts and was now sitting on a huge credit with the florist.

"Me," came a voice behind the bouquet. The flowers dropped down about ten inches and Melissa gasped.

"Nathan! How did you—oh my goodness—this is crazy."

"I went to space with Elon last year. You can really get to know a guy in eight minutes, I'm telling you."

She took the flowers from his hands and hugged him. Even barefoot, she was taller than him. But who cared? Who honestly gave a shit? He flew across the country to hand-deliver her fa- vorite flowers to her. If that didn't equal at least four inches, she didn't know what did.

"Can I come in?" Nathan looked past Melissa and gave a small wave. She turned around. Priya, Tara, and Suki were stand- ing in a cluster, staring at Nathan as though they were her par- ents greeting her prom date.

"Of course," the four of them said in unison.

"I HAVEN'T EATEN such a delicious meal in I can't remem- ber how long," Nathan said, patting his belly.

"Told you," Melissa said. She was giddy sitting around the table with her friends and Nathan after so many years of being the one without a partner. "Way better than anything at the fancy-schmancy New York City restaurants."

"There's still dessert coming," Tara said, popping up to grab spoons for the mug cakes.

"I have to head out," Nathan said. "I have an early-morning meeting tomorrow in the city. Can I take mine to go? I promise to mail the mug back to Elon."

"You came all this way to deliver flowers to Melissa and you can't even spend the night?" Priya asked, shaking her head in disbelief.

"I did. And it was so great to see all of you again," Nathan said. He rose and kissed Melissa on the cheek. "I'll text you when I land."

I'll text you when I land. Were there any sweeter six words?

She walked him to the door.

"I hope it's okay I surprised you like this," he said. "After the debate, I knew your priority was going to be Cameron. And I didn't want to force a conversation about us on you over the phone while you were distracted. I'd like to know, though, where things stand. I guess, to throw it back to our origins, I'm asking if you like me or if you like-like me?"

Melissa laughed.

"I like-like you, Nathan. If we were in class, I would write it on a note and pass it to you when the teacher's back is turned. But since we're not in class, I'll do this."

She leaned forward and pressed her lips to Nathan's. Gently they both opened their mouths and let their tongues find each other. The kiss was wonderful, the next step in discovering each other. The Melissa and Nathan of today, not 1997.

"That was even better than I imagined it would be. And trust me, I imagined it a lot," Nathan said. "One more thing, before I go. I'm sure you've been wondering how Thompson knew about your—you know. It was Paula, from the coffee shop. It turns out she's Kelly's aunt. They are very close, and Kelly confided in her when she first got involved with you and Josh."

"That was ages ago."

"I don't know what made her tell Thompson about it, but let's just say my IT guys know it was her. You did something to piss her off, I guess."

"The stupid PTA. I dinged Paula from catering a school event. One of Kelly's friends is on the PTA board with me—I guess she blabbed. I may have said her food tasted like garbage. And maybe something about seeing a mouse there once." She buried her face in her hands, embarrassed but also so grateful to be done with the Machiavellian PTA politics.

"Don't worry about it. I just figured you'd want to know. I have to get going now." Nathan pecked her cheek and walked to a waiting town car.

When he was gone, the four of them dug into their mug cakes, each friend taking turns complimenting Nathan until there was nothing left to praise but the color of his socks. Melissa couldn't stop marveling at the unexpectedness of beginning a new romance. She planned for so much in her life, and yet this had come without a to-do list or a step-by-step plan.

"I'm not tired," Suki said after the last bit of chocolate was scraped from a mug. "I should be exhausted and yet I have more energy than I've had in weeks. Priya, you didn't put any of Vid's pills in my drink, did you?"

"Too soon," Priya said, but she laughed. "What should we do? I'm not tired, either."

"How about we strategize about fixing Suki's reputation and MakeApp?" Melissa suggested. She wasn't ready to abdicate to-do lists and plans just because one spontaneous thing had worked out for her.

"This feels like when Tara liked Mitch Donner and we stayed up all night trying to figure out how to get him to ask her out," Priya said. "By the way, why didn't he come to the reunion?"

"Jail," Melissa said. "Securities fraud. Not very sexy, I know."

"But he did ask me out!" Tara chimed in. "Which means we have a track record for success."

"You guys are all hired," Suki said. "I may have no more money to pay you, but theoretically, you're now all my top employees. I think this calls for pj's and popcorn, though. Reconvene in ten minutes?"

Soon after, the four of them were splayed on couches in their loungewear, spewing ideas. "Go on the attack," Tara suggested. "Make a list of tough male bosses and show the double standard."

"Have an anonymous complaint box at the office for employees," Melissa said.

"Give out free food," Priya added. "It works at the hospital."

Melissa felt her stomach tingling. She loved their collaboration, the déjà vu so potent they might as well have been crammed in a dressing room together at The Limited, trying on jeans.

The ideas continued to pile up and Melissa took notes on her phone. Leadership training for all female executives, an increased employee discount on MakeApp products, an open letter from Suki to all employees, a five-star trip for the top salespeople, a health care plan with kick-ass daycare, severing Graham's balls. The last one didn't "make the cut," but it got a good laugh.

"You guys are amazing," Suki said. "You've had better ideas than half of my crisis team. I'm seriously grateful that you guys care so much."

Melissa's phone beeped. Nathan was texting a photo from midair. He was above the Rocky Mountains already, which meant they'd been talking for at least two hours.

"I know this isn't exactly a girls' trip like last time," Melissa said. "But I'm really happy we're all together."

22

–:–

Suki

ONE WEEK LATER

THE LAST TIME I was in New York City was a year and a half earlier. Graham and I attended the Tony Awards, walking the red carpet hand in hand and mugging for the flashing cameras, when in fact we weren't even speaking to each other. I was asked to present the award for best costume design. MakeApp had a partnership with several of the Broadway theaters, doing limited-edition collaborations with shows in an effort to get a younger generation excited about theater. I think we sold about three *Phantom of the Opera* eye shadows, but the *Dear Evan Hansen* lipsticks sold out in five hours.

Graham was in a huff because I had scheduled two days of meetings while we were in New York. I guess he had some vision of us having long meals together at the city's great restaurants and going shopping. I was already fairly certain that he was having an affair (I was right), so it didn't seem necessary to leave the days free for us to sightsee like honeymooners. Graham didn't seem to have a problem demanding that I be an attentive wife while he screwed someone else. Call me crazy, but when I started to see the suspicious signs of his affair, I felt a bit off the hook when it came to my wifely duties.

This trip to New York City was entirely different. I was here without Graham—our divorce process was going to be a doozy (*nota bene, working ladies . . . always have a prenup*), but it was at least under way. Instead of having a team of stylists corseting my waist, shellacking my face with enough foundation to trick the high-def cameras, and gluing itchy extensions to my scalp, I was in jeans, a hooded sweatshirt topped with a gigantic winter puffer, and sunglasses, lurking in the shadows on a gritty street on the Lower East Side, praying nobody would notice me.

It was opening night of TIK.

The night everyone was arguing at Elon's house, the pit in my stomach grew uncomfortably large at the discord among my closest friends. Priya was mad at Melissa for not telling her about the pictures of Asha sooner. Melissa was angry that Priya could have thought for even a second that she would sleep with Dev. Tara was sick about that sleaze Ricky DiMateo reappearing in her life, and Melissa was the laughingstock of Bellport, or so she was convinced. I couldn't solve everyone's problems; I could barely manage my own. But I could do something to help Tara, the one member of our foursome who was always honest with us. I should have tried years earlier.

Convincing Tara to work the TIK grand opening had not been easy. I repeated "just trust me," over and over again until finally I wore her down. I couldn't reveal my plan to her in advance. Even I was skeptical. I confirmed with Eva Sugar's people that morning that she would show, but with the Hollywood set, you couldn't count on anything for certain. Which is why I'd swallowed three Imodium already today. Eva was currently the highest-paid actress in Hollywood. She cut her teeth on quality indies, made a few pleasant rom-coms—that's when I snagged her for the MakeApp ambassadorship—and was now shooting the fifth in a superhero franchise. If Eva cut her hair short, the next day the salons were booked. If she dressed androgynously for a premiere, every woman would borrow her husband's blazer. She was that powerful, the Kim Konner of the world stage, admired, envied, and vulnerable to betrayal.

There was a hot pink carpet running all the way down the block with a black musical note motif design. At least a dozen paparazzi stood at attention with giant cameras pressed to their faces. Melissa, Priya, and Tara were inside the restaurant, as was Cameron, who forgave Melissa the embarrassment of what happened at the debate fairly quickly when she was offered a meet and greet with Addison Rae (a stalwart MakeApp brand ambassador) and a seat at one of the best tables at TIK on opening night. Bela and Asha were not there, however. Asha was under house arrest after a deep dive into her social media accounts revealed that she revealed . . . a lot. And Bela wasn't allowed to come because it turned out Priya had been right to be surprised Vid noticed a single pill missing from his medication. Bela had sold a dozen of his pills to finance a skateboard purchase Priya and Dev had rejected.

Prancing down the pink carpet were throngs of young girls in outrageous platform sneakers and guys who looked like the offspring of the nineties boy bands. A large crowd of onlookers stood behind a rope screaming "Charli!" "Addison!" And "Bella!" These were starlets who got fame overnight because of viral videos and sexy dance moves, not from the trifecta of blood, sweat, and tears that were the mud of MakeApp's building blocks. I wasn't jealous of them. Let them have their fifteen minutes. Hopefully it would work out better for them than me.

Maya, the proprietor, was outside doing interviews. She was dressed in a sequin bodysuit and cat ears, a look that should be reserved for Beyoncé, and Beyoncé alone. Yet the paps were eating her up. I felt a little bad about what I had planned. I didn't want to take away from Maya's big night or the success of the restaurant. I told myself that the extra publicity would be a good thing. To use a food analogy, you can't make an omelet without breaking some eggs. Hopefully the eggs I was about to break would lead to some spectacular omelets for everyone involved— Tara, Maya, Eva—everyone but Ricky.

There was still no sign of Eva, and I noticed Ricky and his publicist and manager arriving, jumping out of a black Escalade. Ricky looked carefree and ebullient, dressed in his typical look: an untucked denim shirt and black leather pants with a wallet chain. He was head-cheffing the opening in name only. He vaguely consulted on the menu—his signature ceviche was a passed item—but he was there mainly for photo opportunities in the kitchen and with guests. But if things went according to plan, Ricky would never step foot inside TIK. And Tara would never come face-to-face with him.

But where the hell was Eva?

Ricky was inching closer to the entrance of the restaurant, though he was stopping every few feet to pose for a picture and feed the reporters the sound bites they needed. Still, the carpet was only about a hundred feet long and he was at least halfway down it. I checked my phone for the hundredth time and texted my assistants to see what they'd heard from Eva's people. I was about to write something like **DO YOU KNOW WHERE THE FUCK SHE IS?** but given the mounting culture war against me and the fact that I'm lucky that Aimee and Ramie are still in my employ, I toned it down to, **Has anyone heard from Eva?**

Ramie responded that Eva's car was about to turn onto the block. I was about to stick my phone back into my purse when I remembered to respond, **Thank you**. It's the little things, right? I wish. MakeApp employees don't only want their pleases and thank-yous, they want work-from-home Fridays and crazy salary bumps. If my company lived to fight another day, I'd consider both demands. I was already working overtime to implement many of my friends' suggestions.

Ricky was about ten feet from TIK's front door now. I saw Maya walking to greet him, her arms open for an embrace. He did a funny shuffle thing down the carpet that I assumed was some asinine TikTok move. It was now or never. Tara was upstairs, dripping sweat into the frying pans, apparently muttering, *Why did I agree to this?* over and over. I told Priya and Melissa to keep her calm. To give her alcohol but not too much. In a few minutes she'd be the only chef around and there were a lot of mouths to feed.

"Eva Sugar! Eva Sugar!"

I heard the chants and relaxed for the first time all day. Sure enough, my girl was walking the pink carpet in a stunning leather dress and sky-high stilettos. I recognized her look immediately—she was wearing the MakeApp x Eva Wild Winter palette, down to the gingerbread spice eye shadow. The pumpkin spice lipstick we created for her fall collection sold more tubes than Starbucks sold lattes.

I caught her eye briefly—her people knew what I was wearing and that she should look out for me. She flashed me a thumbs-up, all the assurance I needed.

Maya's jaw dropped when she saw Eva on her pink carpet. Sure, she had packed the restaurant with other famous people, but they were mainly social media stars. Eva was a genuine legend. It didn't take long for Maya to realize the opportunity at her fingertips. She pounced (the cat ears matched her reflexes) and quickly had Eva in one hand and Ricky in the other. She smushed them together for a series of photos—first with her in the middle and then just the two of them. The cameras flashed wildly. The rumor mill was already in motion. Was Ricky dating Eva? Was his marriage on the rocks?

I watched with pleasure as Ricky tried to maintain composure. Eva told me they hadn't seen each other since the night he assaulted her. That was eleven years ago. She was eating at Ricardo, already a starlet but nowhere near the megacelebrity she was today. He, being the proper chef-entrepreneur, spent most of the evening charming her table. When he asked her if she wanted to see the wine cellar, she felt bad saying no. When they were alone in the dark, cavernous space—which Eva remembers being freezing—he groped her and pulled her skirt above her waist. "I knew you wanted to be alone with me," he said. She shook him off but not before he pulled so hard on her panties that they snapped back and left a mark.

She didn't come forward when the other women did because she had just landed a huge movie role in a Disney film. Eva worried they would take the part away. Nobody wants to think about the woman playing Rapunzel in the modern adaptation having her panties yanked in a dank basement. And who knows what Ricky would have made up about her? The only reason I know about their encounter is because Eva was in my office and a commercial for one of Ricky's shows came on the TV in my office. I said, "I hate that guy," with enough disgust that Eva could tell I knew his true nature. She confided in me and swore me to secrecy. I regretted not pushing her then, especially because it could have helped Tara. But I was treading gingerly around Eva, worried about dismantling a lucrative contract. I know, selfish. I doubt I could have swayed her anyway. To this day, she doesn't want to come forward publicly. But that's not what she plans to tell Ricky tonight.

I watched as his face turned from bronze, to white, to green. She had clearly told him she wanted to speak to him alone. He had no choice but to follow her. They stood just around the corner from TIK, away from the cameras but within my sight line. I wished I could see his face, but when his body started contorting and his arms waved wildly, I was satisfied the mission was a success.

She headed back toward the pink carpet, toward the flash of bulbs and shouts from the reporters. I knew she didn't plan to stay for opening night. Eva was in postproduction and needed rest. I also knew she didn't want to think about that night with Ricky a second longer than she needed to. She flashed me the smile that earned her the big bucks and I knew it had worked. I exhaled a breath that could have knocked down a building. My entire body felt like it was going to float away.

I watched Ricky punch something into his phone and a minute later his Escalade rounded the corner. He climbed in, calls of "Where you going, chef?" at his back.

Maya was beside herself. I could see from the way her face

320 • ELYSSA FRIEDLAND

was crumpling that she didn't know what hit her. I risked getting noticed in order to walk toward her and whispered in her ear: "You have an incredibly talented chef upstairs. You don't need Ricky. Tonight is going to be amazing."

I didn't wait around to see if she was mollified. I texted an update to my friends in the kitchen and sped off to Tara's apartment, where I would be waiting for them at night's end. As I went to put my phone away, a FaceTime came through from my twins. I'd never been so happy to see their angelic faces.

"Hi, loves. Tell Mommy everything."

"THAT WAS TRULY incredible," Priya said. She was stretched on Tara's couch with Bernie curled in a ball on her stomach. "It's funny how much I like other people's pets more than my own." Her T-shirt said: I DANCED MY SOCKS OFF AT MELISSA'S BAT MITZVAH. We were all wearing them. Melissa had unearthed a box of them recently while searching through the attic. I'll never forget that night. It was my first time playing spin the bottle and I had to kiss Melissa's cousin from Great Neck, who sent me love letters for a month afterward.

"Agree. Tonight was amazing," Melissa said. She was eating pink and black Gummy Worms from a Chinese takeout container covered in the TIK logo, the evening's party favor. She was starting to look like her former self again, with the addition of a glow I knew came from one thing alone, and it wasn't sold by MakeApp. Still, she was oddly subdued, given our triumph. She was saying all the typical Melissa things, but missing the spunk.

"I know. Suki, I can't thank you enough. Whatever Eva Sugar

said to Ricky, it worked. Maya said he never made it through the front door."

I smiled and waved her off. She hadn't asked me how I'd made this happen, which was just as well. I didn't want to share any more of Eva's private life than I needed to.

"Why didn't Rachel come?" I asked Tara. "I would think she'd be all excited about TIK."

"About that. We broke up. She wanted a more serious commitment. She talked about starting a family together. I knew Rachel wasn't The One, whatever that means. But no matter who I end up with, if I settle down at all, I don't want kids. I want to work in a restaurant until three a.m. and be totally consumed with work. I don't want the responsibility. I don't have the urge. Does that make me a freak?" Tara looked at us, three mothers, so earnestly it broke my heart.

"It makes you honest. Children are a lot of fucking work." I never regretted starting a family. Even with my marriage imploding, I was glad. But I knew plenty of women without children who led fulfilling lives. And I was proud to see my friend figure out for herself what she wanted.

"Thanks, Sukes."

"You okay?" I asked Melissa. She had been gnawing on the same rope of gummy for a while. "I heard Nathan was hilarious in the Charli booth, trying to learn a dance. What he lacks in rhythm he makes up for in—"

"Money?" Priya offered. We all chuckled, though Melissa less so. Now I was worried. She was normally totally game for a good ribbing about Nathan's wealth.

"Mel, what's going on? You're Bellport's new mayor. You have a devoted man in your life. What is bothering you?" I persisted.

She looked up with a solemn expression and all the air in the room evaporated.

"I felt something this morning in the shower. A lump."

"Oh, man. But you've been getting mammograms, right?" Tara asked. "When was your last one? Actually now I'm trying to remember when my last one was."

I reflexively palmed my chest. I couldn't remember the last time I saw my doctor, either. Obviously, I had a lot going on, but I couldn't even remember thinking about it.

"We always all go at the same time, right?" Tara said. "We go when—"

"When I tell you guys to go," Priya said. She was biting her lower lip like a contrite child.

That was exactly right. Priya took care of their tits. And their skin. When she went for her yearly mammogram and mole check, she would send them a picture, reminding them to make their appointments. It was as good as a calendar alert. Had been.

"Things were crazy with the kids and work. I had to cancel my mammogram and I guess I never rescheduled it. Which then affected you guys. Melissa, I'm so sorry."

"It's okay. I finally got a man and a job I'm excited about. I needed something bad to happen for balance."

I wanted to say that I agreed with her. You can't have it all. Instead, I said, "Nonsense. You'll get checked out and you'll be fine, Melissa." With that reminder of all the different ways my friends and I took care of one another, I texted my assistants and asked them, politely, to schedule a mammogram for me.

23

—◦—

SIX MONTHS LATER

"AND SO, AS I look out at your eager faces, your fingers twitching to toss those caps in the air, I want to say a few parting words. Who you are today does not define who you will be in the future. Your time at Bellport Academy has well prepared you for the road ahead. You have an excellent education that will serve you in anything you choose to do. Try to hold on to your happy memories, the times you laughed the hardest and felt the best about yourselves, and let go of the tougher times. You are just starting on your life journey. Let the past buoy you, not drag you down. And while the SATs are behind you, don't put down that number two pencil just yet. You may be tempted to write your life plan in pen, but use pencil. Give yourself the freedom to erase and make changes. I wish you all the best of luck, and remember that Bellport Academy will always be here for you. When the re-union chair comes knocking on your door, think twice before saying you're too busy to attend. If you've been as lucky as I have been, you've made lifelong friends here. Mine are here sitting in the fourth row. Now, it's diploma time. Congratulations!"

Principal Giffords joined Melissa at the podium and gave her a warm pat on the back.

"Mayor Levin, class of 1997, I don't think we could have asked for a more inspirational speaker. And how especially meaningful that your daughter, Cameron, is in today's graduating class."

Melissa looked into the sea of blue caps and gowns and found her daughter, who looked rather displeased to have been singled out. And here Melissa had resisted every urge to call out Cameron during her speech, only to be thwarted by the principal.

Melissa dismounted from the stage and took her seat next to Nathan, who slipped an arm around her.

"Amazing job," he whispered.

"It helps that I didn't have an opponent talking about my threesome," she whispered back. Nathan squeezed her shoulder.

"Thanks for the shoutout," Priya said. She was seated to Melissa's left. Next to Priya sat Suki and Tara. Melissa was throwing a graduation party for Cameron after the ceremony and had included her friends in the Paperless Post, mostly aspirationally. One by one, their replies trickled in. They all planned to attend graduation to hear Melissa's alumni address and to celebrate Cameron at the party.

Melissa winked at them.

The graduates of the class of 2023 were called up to receive their diplomas. Cameron's best friend, Hannah, stumbled up the steps and smacked her knee on the stage. A sweet boy named Tucker took his diploma as someone from the crowd yelled, "Way to go, Fucker!" Helena Siegel accepted her degree to a chorus of boos, for which Melissa felt no remorse. With the help of the IT department at Nathan's office, Helena was identified as the sole content creator of @BellportBlabber. Melissa let it be known who the perpetrator was, again calling on the computer guys to create a new account called @BellportBeKind, where daily affirmations and compliments were given out. All the seniors were given access to the handle; any rude or hurtful posts led to an immediate revocation of privileges. To this day, nobody knew Melissa was behind it. She held her breath as her daughter's name was called and watched with pride as Cameron made it safely across without incident. Melissa looked over at Josh, Kelly, and Madison, who was seated on Josh's lap and holding a homemade CONGRATS, CAM sign. Their girl was headed to Lehigh in the fall. Close enough that Melissa could visit by car; far enough that she wasn't tempted to do so every weekend.

When Giffords was finally through the Zs, the graduates rose in tandem and tossed their hats in the air. As the caps soared to the sky, Melissa imagined the hopes of each of these kids taking flight. She tried not to think about what it meant when they all came crashing back to the grass a moment later. It was time to dash home and make sure the caterers were on their game.

THE HOUSE SMELLED like waffles, eggs, and gasoline when she walked through the front door. Melissa rushed to the kitchen and found three members of the catering staff bent over her stove.

"There was a small fire," one of them said. "Nothing to worry about. We have it all under control."

"I know how to use the fire extinguisher," she offered. After Cam's mishap with the brownies, Melissa watched a YouTube tutorial on how to operate it. Inspired, she also learned how to change a flat tire and plunge a toilet. Ironically, now that she was armed with these skills, she was no longer single. But that didn't mean self-reliance was any less valuable. Besides, at five foot six with a frame slighter than her own and an aversion to dirt, Nathan was hardly the type to sully his hands with a greasy jack.

"It's all set, Ms. Levin. We will be ready for your guests shortly," a man in a denim button-down tucked into white pants said, extending a platter of bite-size frittatas to her. She selected one with crispy edges and extra cheddar and popped it into her mouth. It was delicious and possibly worth a small kitchen fire.

This particular cater-waiter was gorgeous, definitely an actor or a model moonlighting as a server. Melissa's initial confusing of Nathan for a server had turned into a joke between them. After she had a needle biopsy in her breast, which thankfully was benign, Nathan came to the hospital holding a silver tray with smoked salmon roses resting on mini potato pancakes.

"Holy shit, they're not there."

Melissa heard Cameron's voice coming through the front door.

"Let me see that. Gimme." That was Hannah speaking. The girls were right on time to help with setup. Melissa still needed to change her dress, fix her makeup, and make sure the tables in the backyard were properly arranged.

"I promise you. I looked four times. They're not there," Cameron said. "Mom, you are not going to believe this." She came into the kitchen with Hannah at her side, both looking regal with their royal blue robes flapping. "There are no superlatives in the yearbook. We voted on them and everything and they aren't here."

"What? How can that be?" Melissa took the book from her daughter and quickly leafed through it to confirm.

"People are going to be pissed. Zoey Tanner has been lobbying for Most Likely to Be Famous since like freaking eighth grade when she got a walk-on role in that Netflix show about the vampire," Hannah said, helping herself to some crudité.

"I know, right?" Cam said. "And she wasn't even good in it."

"I'm sure there's a good reason why it's not there," Melissa said. "Can you girls please make sure the outside setup looks all right? I think the DJ wanted to know if you had any requests."

The girls scurried to the backyard, debating whether Lil Nas X or The Kid Laroi should be the first dance song, as Nathan came into the kitchen.

"Can I help with anything?" He was dressed in a smart blazer and khakis, but true to what he told her at their first coffee, he wore a T-shirt in lieu of a button-down. "Any trays need passing?"

"Very funny. Just keep an eye out for my parents. My mother is concerned the caterer is not giving me top-shelf nova and might try to take a sample for lab testing."

Nathan saluted her and was off. She turned back to the sink wall and opened the cabinet holding the water glasses. As she did so, the knob popped off. It was no longer her problem. She had sold her house to a young couple just last week and was moving out in a month. She would be splitting her time between a new house she and Nathan purchased across town and Nathan's apartment in Manhattan.

The swinging door pushed open and Nathan was back.

"Hey, your mother says it's freezing in the house. Where is the thermostat?"

Melissa felt something inside her brain click.

"Nathan, do you happen to know something about the year-book no longer having superlatives?"

"I may have told Giffords that the next payment on my pledge was contingent on getting rid of the superlatives. Mel, your mother is very upset about the temperature. I think if I can't fix it, she's going to hate me."

"On the wall in the den. Give the lever a jiggle. It gets stuck."

Nathan offered a second salute and retreated. She shook her head in disbelief. She had told Nathan just last week how worried she was about Cam's superlative—getting one, not getting one, feeling disappointed—not to mention her own experience.

"Hi, there," came a chirpy voice. "We brought champagne. Even I'm going to have some today."

Melissa looked at Josh, Kelly, and Madison, standing in what would soon be her former kitchen, which used to be her and Josh's kitchen, and was now crowded with a half-dozen caterers and the gigantic mass of Kelly's pregnant belly. That turned out to be the source of Josh's worried expression the night of the reunion. Kelly and Josh had just learned about the baby and Josh was busy calculating how he would afford it all.

"Thank you. You didn't have to bring anything," she said, taking the bottle from Kelly. "How are you feeling?"

"Big as a house," Kelly said, patting her stomach. *Whose house?* a more bitter Melissa might have once thought. *Your sprawling McMansion or my humble abode?* Today she was just grateful not to be the pregnant one.

"Melissa, you spoke beautifully today," Josh said, leaning in to kiss her on the cheek. For the first time in what felt like forever, she felt absolutely nothing. Certainly there was no longing for her ex, but she didn't even want him to want her. It was a feeling she had never been entirely certain of until she experienced its absence.

"Thank you. Go outside with everyone. The guests are arriving and we need to make sure Cam's friends don't get plastered and puke on the lawn." She waved them off.

"You look pretty, Auntie Mel," Madison said. "I like your dress."

"I like yours, too," Melissa said. "I wish it came in my size."

The three of them left the kitchen and Melissa was alone again with the caterers, but only for a second.

"Smells amazing in here," Tara said, entering with Suki and Priya, the three of them giggling.

"What's so funny?"

"Just your sister asking Nathan to see pictures of his apartment and pretending it's because she has a background in interior design," Priya said.

"She did have a very decorated locker at school. If I remember correctly, her mirror was hot pink and lit up," Suki said. "I used to jimmy her lock to check my makeup."

Melissa buried her face in her hands.

"Don't worry. Nathan is handling both Karen and your mother like a pro." Tara surveyed the trays of hors d'oeuvres approvingly. "I would have done this for you, Mel. I am, as you know, a very fancy private chef nowadays."

"That is true," Suki said. "I brought her in to prepare a meal for the C-suite and now she's too busy to fit me on her calendar."

It had been three months since Tara relocated out west. She had volunteered to cater a dinner for Suki and her most fabulous friends, which led to jobs working in the most exclusive homes in Northern California. Three of her clients were practically begging to back her in a restaurant.

She still made the occasional video for TIK and a collaboration with the restaurant and MakeApp was under consideration.

"I will always make time for you, Suki," Tara said.

"I'm planning an entire chapter of my book on this topic," Suki added. "It's called, 'If People Don't Like You, Feed Them.' My editor loves it."

"How is the book going?" Melissa asked. Suki's book contract was salvaged after many months of tough negotiations. She convinced her publisher that an honest memoir would sell. Her business had recovered because no matter what people thought of Suki, they couldn't resist her fabulous products. Even her personal reputation was mostly mended, thanks to appearances on several major talk shows with sympathetic—and female— interviewers. A new book title had yet to be agreed upon, but on Suki's computer it was provisionally titled *Having It All Is a Crock of Shit*. She routinely shared drafts with Melissa, Tara, and Priya.

"It's going. Telling the truth is a lot easier than lying, and I love including the anecdotes you guys have given me. Speaking of which, Priya, another chapter is called 'This Is Bullshit.' It's about how absurd it is in two-working-parent households that the mother still has to do all the grunt work."

"I love it," Priya said. "So Dev went for it, by the way. Giving me one day a week to focus on my needs and what I want while he does the bulk of the housework. I've been spending more one-on-one time with each of the kids. The Asha debacle showed me how out of the loop I was, even though I was technically right there. And I created a mentorship program at the hospital pairing senior doctors with residents, role models that look like their mentees, who can identify with each other. There is a shit ton of impostor syndrome that needs eradicating. I've been using my extra day mostly for that while Dev attempts laundry."

"How is it going?" Melissa asked. She was beaming. The family day off had been her idea.

"I still feel like I'm one toe stub away from a nervous breakdown, but I suppose I just have to give it time. In the meantime, Thursday is officially renamed Pri-day."

"Speak of the devil," Suki said as Dev joined them in the kitchen.

"Hi, ladies," he said. "Terrific speech, Melissa. Priya, sorry to bother you but Asha just called and she can't find her—"

Priya put a finger to her husband's lip.

"Uh-uh. Do not finish that sentence," she warned.

"But she needs this and Vid said his loafers aren't—" Dev mumbled, and then looked around. "Uh, I think I'm going to call Asha back and figure out her problem without you," Dev said. Priya smiled and kissed him tenderly.

Dev left the kitchen and the girls whooped in unison.

"That was fucking awesome," Suki said.

"Hallelujah!" Melissa added.

"Cheers to that," Tara said, uncorking the champagne on the counter.

The four of them watched the smoke rise and disintegrate.

"Cheers to us! The Most Likely Girls," Suki said. "I'm a late joiner but I'm happy to be here now."

"Can we drop the 'Girls,' please?" Melissa said. "My OB says I'm a hop, skip, and a jump away from menopause."

"How about 'The Most Likely Club'?" Priya suggested.

"I think that was a book," Tara said. "No, wait, that's *The Joy Luck Club*. The Most Likely Club has a nice ring to it."

"Agree," Suki said.

"Club it is. Can I be president?" Melissa asked. When they gaped at her, she quickly added, "I'm kidding!"

"Most likely to what, though?" Priya asked. "What are we most likely to do again?"

"Most likely to get drunk?" Tara suggested, taking a swig from the bottle.

"Most likely to get canceled?" Suki suggested.

"Most likely to be friends for—" Melissa started to say when Cam burst in.

"Mom! Some kids were smoking and one of the butts landed on a stack of napkins. There's a fire, come now."

"I got it! Most likely to put out fires . . . while lighting the world on fire," Melissa said. She took the bottle from Tara's hands, downed a sip, and headed toward the flames.

Acknowledgments

—:—

My high school superlative was *Most Likely to Forget Someone in the Acknowledgments*. Just kidding. There are so many incredible people who helped make *The Most Likely Club* possible that I will not be one of those buffoons who forgets to thank their spouse or costar at the Oscars.

First and foremost, my editor, Kerry Donovan. We now have four books under our belt together, and our partnership continues to grow stronger. You are an amazing editor who always manages to elevate my work, make just the right suggestions, and have the patience to hash out ideas with me whenever I need. Also at Berkley, thank you to editor in chief Claire Zion, who brought me into the Berkley family and has championed my work since *The Intermission*. Danielle Keir and Tina Joell, under the guidance of the fabulous Craig Burke, work tirelessly to bring attention to my work, and I'm so grateful that they don't hate me every time I email them with "Did you pitch so-and-so yet?" Jeanne-Marie Hudson and Fareeda Bullert are expert marketers, and their enthusiasm for this book was palpable from day one. The talented Lila Selle created countless book jackets until we landed on our magnificent selection. Production editor Lindsey Tulloch ensured this book was produced on time and in tip-top shape.

Thank you to Stefanie Lieberman, my fearless agent, who keeps me sane the best she can and is an indefatigable advocate for me. She is both agent and friend, and that's quite special. Ann-Marie Nieves is my awesome publicist, who is funny, creative, and devoted to the work.

To my writer tribe, I love our shared bond, our frequent texts, and our commitment to always show up for one another. Catherine McKenzie, Lauren Smith Brody, Leigh Abramson, Pam Jenoff, Fiona Davis, Andrea Katz (writer by association), Lisa Barr, Rochelle Weinstein, Jamie Brenner, Brenda Janowitz, Amy Poeppel, Allison Winn Scotch, and Courtney Marzilli (another writer by association) . . . you guys are my people, and I love you.

I was very lucky to have editorial and research assistance from one of my former Yale students, the multitalented Alaina Anderson. Not only is she a brilliant writer, but she is also currently performing in the national tour of *Dear Evan Hansen*. Yes, some people are just that exceptional.

A special shout-out to a very cool chick, Pippa Millstone. She was my Gen Z voice, my TikTok explainer, my teenage lingo specialist, and much more. You are a star, Pippa, and I can't wait to see how high you soar. Your mom, Jennifer, is also pretty awesome. She was a helpful early reader and kept my spirits up with daily affirmations.

Bookstagrammers. I wish I could name you all, but there are just too many. The enthusiasm you've shown for my work and the time you took to write reviews and to share beautiful pictures have helped grow my readership immensely. I am deeply indebted to you.

I have a large, loving family of Folks and Friedlands who cheer me on and listen to me whine ad nauseam. Writing can be isolating at times, but your constant affection assures I never feel alone. Thank you to my supportive in-laws, Marilyn and Larry Friedland, and my devoted parents, Rochelle and Jerry Folk. My whip-smart mom can find a typo in a haystack, so please blame her for any errors in the book. Her email is RJF@ . . . kidding! My children, Charlie, Lila, and Sam, are the worthiest distraction. Kids: I love your smiles, your stories, and your zest for life. I hope you continue to find meaning in words, to stay as close as you are, and to remember that a book is an iPad without a plug. Finally, my husband, William. It's a wild ride at times. Us creative types have *a lot* of feelings. You're the yin to my yang, and I'm sure glad that you are by my side.

As always, I want to thank my readers. In a dizzying world pulling us in a million different directions, you still choose to plant your nose in a book. Thank you for planting it in mine.

The Most Likely Club

ELYSSA FRIEDLAND

The Most Likely (Book) Club Discussion Questions

1. If you had a high school superlative, do you remember what it was? Or what do you think it would have been?

2. How have your dreams and goals evolved since you were a teenager?

3. Which one of the four women in *The Most Likely Club* did you identify with the most, and why? Who did you relate to the least? Did any of the characters remind you of friends in your own life?

4. The women all struggle with the idea of "having it all." What does *having it all* mean to you? The entrepreneur Randi Zuckerberg wrote a book called *Pick Three: You Can Have It All (Just Not Every Day)* where she encourages women to pick three things to focus on each day among work, sleep, family, fitness, and friends. What would be your top three (not limited to the above choices)?

5. Priya and Melissa, two of the mothers in the group, try to prevent their children from making the same mistakes and avoiding the same lows they experienced in high school, but it's not easy. Why do you think it's so hard to help your children avoid some of the pitfalls you experienced in your own life?

6. Can you name one way that each of the four women has changed since high school? In what ways have they stayed the same?

7. Suki faces unique difficulties as a female CEO. What do you think is at the root of why powerful women face a double standard in our society when they act like strong leaders?

8. The primary issue in Priya and Dev's marriage is division of labor, a common issue between many couples, particularly in households with two working parents. Dev promises to change and contribute more. Do you think he will hold up his end of the bargain? Explain why or why not.

9. Melissa's weight is a continuing source of concern to her, even as the culture around her has made strides toward embracing body positivity. Why do you think she is hung up on wanting to be thin? Should she have worried more about how her behavior could affect her daughter?

10. Nathan is brutally honest with Melissa about why he gave the donation to Bellport. Have you ever made a choice in your life that was clearly influenced by something that happened to you in high school?

11. Do you think high school superlatives are a good idea? Do you think students should choose their own superlatives?

12. What do you wish you could tell your teenage self today? How would your adult advice have sounded to you back when you were in high school?

13. Discuss the friendship between the four women. How does their bond help them through difficult times? Do you agree with the saying "Make new friends, but keep the old. One is silver and the other is gold"?

Don't miss Elyssa Friedland's

The Floating Feldmans

Available now! Keep reading for a preview.

IT STARTED WITH a shriek. Then a series of gasps. Finally, from somewhere deep in the room, came a chorus of "Fight, fight, fight!" The chant quickly grew in volume, and suddenly it seemed like everyone was shouting for blood.

"Ladies and gentlemen, may I *please* have your attention!" Julian Masterino attempted to calm the chaos for a third time, but he was no match for the angry rabble. From his perch on the bandstand, they looked like a swarm of flies, circling and buzzing in a cacophonous roar. Normally Julian's uniform, a fitted white sailor's jumper and his ever-present megaphone, was enough to will a hush over a rambunctious crowd. But tonight, in a black tuxedo, he blended in with everyone else on the ship. To make matters worse, the volume lever on his megaphone was broken. Meanwhile, babies wailed in high chairs, the elderly guests whined from motorized scooters, and the able-bodied adults dashed about in their formal wear vying for a better look at the crime scene. The leader of the barbershop quartet, the evening's opening act, gazed desperately at Julian from under his bowler hat and plucked a few helpless chords in C on his banjo. Julian gave him the universal symbol for "not now," a quick slash to the neck, and he quieted down.

The paramedic team skidded onto the dance floor, propelled into the scrum of people by the weight of equipment they probably wouldn't need. To Julian's practiced eye, the two gentlemen who had, moments earlier, been throwing punches at each other were not the sort of people for whom violence was a preferred method of conflict resolution. They were amateurs at best—and the injuries they had sustained were undoubtedly more to their psyches than physical. Still, the older guy was on the ground, blood running from his nose. It was time to clear the room.

But how could it be done? Julian was a seasoned pro, but even he had never tried a last-minute relocation of three thousand hungry diners. Short of an iceberg, he'd never envisioned a scenario that would require such a thing. And now, faced with a ship full of guests determined to ignore his instructions, there weren't a lot of good options left. Julian could think of only one surefire way to regain command of his people. Throwing caution to the wind, he reached for his megaphone and pressed firmly on the talk button.

"Attention, all guests aboard the *Ocean Queen*. The main buffet and all-night ice cream bar on the Starboard Deck will be closed until further notice."

A shocked hush immediately dropped over the crowd, and Julian smiled to himself.

"That's not fair," complained an anguished mother of three. "My kids are still hungry!"

Hungry? On average, passengers aboard the *Ocean Queen* consumed six thousand calories per day, sitting down to no less than five full meals. The midmorning "snack" consisted of pastries, a full salad bar, and a taco station. Afternoon tea was the least dainty meal Julian had ever laid eyes on. Instead of finger sandwiches and bite-size lemon tarts, the kitchen staff put out twelve-foot loaves of streusel from which the guests could hack off as much as they liked. And, as far as Julian could tell, they liked a lot of streusel.

"This is an all-inclusive ship," barked a burly fellow who stood to the left of the bandstand. He had accessorized his tuxedo with a bolo tie and cowboy hat and was already working his way through a plate piled high with meat. "And we all know you save the best food for the formal night!"

Julian was prepared to promise an impromptu chocolate fountain and make-your-own-sushi opportunity, if only everyone would exit in an orderly fashion. But before he could position his megaphone, an attractive older woman stood up and addressed the crowd. She had been crouching on the floor, tending to the more senior of the two bloodied combatants—the sad-faced man who was now cradling his knee. Julian couldn't help but admire the way the woman presented herself: She wore a beautiful blue satin gown that stretched forgivingly across her wide hips and her hair was swept into a precise chignon.

"What is wrong with you people?" she shouted, her voice impressive and thunderous. "From the minute you woke up this morning, you've been stuffing your faces, pushing and shoving in the buffet lines like you've never seen a croissant before. Get a grip on yourselves. My husband was just punched in the face by my son-in-law, who has apparently hated our family for the past twenty years."

"That's not true," said the other erstwhile combatant in a breathy voice as he was lifted onto a stretcher by the paramedics. This second, younger man was obviously the bitter son-in-law. "It's just . . . you guys . . . acting juvenile . . . and I . . ."

"You do not need to defend yourself!" belted a younger woman in a pink dress who stood beside the man's stretcher. She stared daggers at the ballsy lady in the blue satin and said, "Mitch has *nothing* to apologize for, *Mother.*"

Holy hell. A dueling mother-daughter ensemble was certainly not needed on the night that was meant to be the crescendo of the trip, the black-tie party known as An Enchanted Evening, which would set the tone for how generous the guests would be when parceling out gratuities. And if they weren't opening their wallets widely, Julian would be hearing about it from everyone on the staff, from the lifeguards down to the porters, the whole crew blaming him for not keeping the guests happy.

"Everyone, listen to the cruise director, and get off of this deck *now*," yelled the mother. Then the daughter chimed in: "You will be fed. You will have your formal night. You will be 'enchanted,' for heaven's sake. Just let the doctors attend to my husband in peace."

"Mom? Elise? What the hell is going on?" asked a middle-aged man as he pushed through the crowd. The newcomer had graying hair tied in a bun, and, as Julian couldn't help noticing, his outfit did not conform to the night's dress code requirement. He was tugging on the hand of a human Barbie doll teetering along in four-inch heels. Julian blinked twice. This overly made-up girl wearing a dress that could have doubled as an Ace bandage was none other than the amazing yogini he'd met in Ashtanga class earlier that day.

A picture was forming in Julian's mind. This was the Feldman family. He vaguely remembered chatting with them at the around-the-world dinner the night before, and he'd seen the daughter—her name was Elise—just hours earlier in the coffee shop. They were all on board to celebrate a big birthday. If memory served him correctly, they were vacationing together in honor of the matriarch in blue.

Julian hated to see things like this happen on one of his trips, and not just because it meant reduced gratuities and filing extra paperwork with the corporate office. It truly broke his heart when a family with grand plans to bond and share quality time was reduced to blows and name-calling. This wasn't the first time it had happened. And it wouldn't be the last. Maybe it was the fact that passengers on cruise vacations were sequestered from the outside world—and that submerged feelings were bound to surface whenever people volunteered to isolate themselves. Or maybe it was the consistent low-level nausea they experienced at sea that activated bad behavior. Julian had one theory, originally espoused by the ship's previous captain, that involved those motion sickness patches everyone stuck behind their ears: He posited that they actually worked like hearing aids, amplifying all the irritations that normally went unnoticed.

Julian's assistant, Lindsay, approached him from behind and whispered something in his ear. He smiled, knowing the immediate crisis had been solved.

"Attention, all passengers," Julian said, clearing his throat for emphasis and raising his megaphone once again. "A free drink will be provided to all guests who relocate to the Mariposa Ballroom on the Discovery Deck."

It was like shouting "fire" in a crowded room. The adults grabbed their children by the wrists, gave their elder counterparts a firm push at the back of their wheelchairs, and set out dutifully to secure their complimentary cocktail. The *Ocean Queen* was an all-inclusive ship when it came to food and most onboard activities, but alcohol was strictly pay-to-play.

Once the room was cleared of everyone except himself, the Feldmans, and a few overzealous paramedics, it was terribly quiet.

"Is there anything I can do?" Julian asked. He approached the family cautiously, stationing himself directly in between the two stretchers. His role in these situations could vary greatly. He could be anything from therapist to ice pack bearer, arbitrator, or bouncer. Sometimes all he needed was to present a voucher for a complimentary land excursion, and the entire family was able to put aside their squabbling in deference to the freebie.

It was hard to read the Feldmans, though. The older woman was tough. He could tell from her rant. The daughter, Elise, was just as voluble but far less confident—she fell a little more on the hysterical side of the spectrum. The rest of the family? Julian couldn't make heads or tails of the dynamic there.

"We're sorry for the trouble," the elder Mrs. Feldman said to Julian, looking mortified as she tended to her husband's busted nose.

"You and Dad started it," Elise snapped.

"Let's not worry about blame now," Julian said. "I just want to make sure everyone is feeling well enough to enjoy the remainder of the trip." *And that I don't need to throw anyone in the brig,* he thought to himself.

The teenage girl bent over Mitch on stretcher #2, and Julian was relieved to see signs of life in her vacant face.

"Sweetie," Mitch said, rolling with great effort onto his side to access the wallet in his pocket. "Take a few twenties and go with your brother to the arcade."

The girl started combing through a wad of bills.

"No! No money!" Elise roared, grabbing the wallet away from her. "We have *no* money to spare. Zero. And honestly, Rachel, your father probably dislocated his shoulder and is clearly in agony. Your grandfather is also in serious pain. How can you be so selfish?"

Man-Bun stepped forward gallantly.

"Rachel, here's two hundred. Take Darius and go." The blonde on stilts looked at him like he was Jesus and Mother Teresa rolled into one.

"Take it, Rachel," the grandfather said firmly from stretcher #1. "You kids need to clear out of here."

"Over my dead body!" said Elise. "No one wants your drug money, Freddy!"

Drug money? Julian stared at Freddy, imagining bags of cocaine hidden all over the ship. He felt a prickle of nervous sweat beginning to form at his hairline and debated asking one of the paramedics to take his blood pressure. But no, he needed to stay in command.

Who was this family? The *Ocean Queen* regularly attracted a motley crew, but its passengers' foibles were, for the most part, the extremely visible kind. Like with the BDSMers—everyone basically knew who they were, especially Housekeeping, who had to step over the gags and harnesses on the cabin floor every morning. The Feldmans, on the other hand, were outfitted like schoolteachers chaperoning the prom. All except Freddy, but that didn't make him any less of an enigma. He had an aging Jimmy Buffett sort of vibe; he looked far more like a goofy beer snob with a trophy girlfriend than a drug dealer.

"Let's not get excited again," Julian said, slipping into the therapist role. "Why don't we let the paramedics finish their job, and then I'm sure you can all calmly discuss everything in a more intimate setting. I'd be happy to offer you one of our private dining rooms—we can set up a cheese plate and a few bottles of good burgundy, absolutely free of charge." Julian couldn't have these crazy people airing their (potentially criminal) dirty laundry all over the *Ocean Queen*. He'd get crushed on TripAdvisor.

"I think it's probably best if you just leave us alone now," said Freddy's too-young girlfriend. As the words left the girl's pillow lips, Elise's face contorted in rage.

"And I think that *you* don't get to have an opinion," Elise shouted at the younger woman. "You aren't even a member of this family!"

Julian could tell that, for Mrs. Feldman, this exchange was the last straw. She stepped in between Freddy and Elise, who were obviously about to go a few rounds themselves, and said, "Everyone: *Cut it out*. This is my birthday celebration. We will all get along for the next twenty-four hours or else."

Mrs. Feldman hadn't actually raised her voice during this little speech, but the intensity of feeling behind her words was clear. A seam in her blue gown had ripped from the sheer force of her heaving bosom.

Julian took a sudden step back. Shouting, blood, threats, raised fists. It wasn't what he'd call a successful night aboard ship. And he'd done all he could to simmer things down. If free food and alcohol couldn't help the Feldman clan, they were perhaps beyond repair. He quietly slipped out of the room and headed toward his own cabin on the staff floor, which was below sea level, leaving the warring family members on deck to berate each other until sunrise.

Boat life was a matter of simple rinse and repeat. Eat, argue, bingo. Eat, argue, show. Eat, argue, excursion. And then eat some more. If he didn't see the Feldmans at breakfast the next morning—if the feud was enough to overtake their appetites—he'd know they were in real trouble.

Photo by Lucia Engstrom

Elyssa Friedland is the acclaimed author of *Last Summer at the Golden Hotel*, *The Floating Feldmans*, *The Intermission*, and *Love and Miss Communication*. Elyssa is a graduate of Yale University and Columbia Law School and currently teaches novel writing at Yale. She lives with her husband and three children in New York City, the best place on earth.

CONNECT ONLINE

ElyssaFriedland.com

⊡ ElyssaFriedland

f AuthorElyssaFriedland

🐦 ElyssaFriedland

Ready to find
your next great read?

Let us help.

Visit prh.com/nextread

Penguin
Random
House